EXILES OF TITAN

EXILES OF TITAN

The Martian PHASE

by

DAVID CHRISTMAS

YOUCAXTON PUBLICATIONS
OXFORD & SHREWSBURY

ISBN 978-1-911175-72-8
Printed and bound in Great Britain.
Published by YouCaxton Publications 2017

YouCaxton Publications
enquiries@youcaxton.co.uk

For Amanda, Kate and Matthew

Chapter 1

DEIRA FLICKED THE visor of her helmet down and activated her night-vision facility.

The closing of the warehouse door had left the two agents in darkness so profound it was almost tangible – even their latest tech struggling to render the surrounding barrels and crates into the familiar ghostly green. A sweet, sickly smell permeated the place. It could have been something rotting in one of the containers but Deira had smelled something similar from decomposing corpses.

She took a moment to configure her head-up display (HUD) as a white schematic on her visor. It showed their current position in the warehouse and a suggested route to the room they wanted at the top of some stairs about fifty metres away. All very straightforward as long as they could avoid the detritus that was scattered over the floor like some form of trap for the unwary. She glanced at Adam and tapped her visor. He replied with a thumbs-up and they began to pick their way slowly towards the distant staircase. They were utterly silent and virtually invisible, their black uniforms and sculpted body armour merging seamlessly into the surrounding darkness.

They were only part-way to their destination when they heard a sound from above followed by a light coming on in an upstairs room. They froze, hardly daring to breathe, their helmets automatically discontinuing night-vision. Shadows moved behind the glass panel of the door to the room and two voices could be heard, clearly arguing. The voices became louder as the argument spun rapidly out of control and there was movement elsewhere in the warehouse as others began to take an interest in what was going down. The agents looked at each other in dismay. This was exactly what they didn't need. Should they abort the mission?

Suddenly, a gunshot rang out, closely followed by the sound of running feet. More lights came on upstairs and a crowd began to gather, converging on the sound of the gunshot. Deira watched with mixed emotions. Whatever they might have been considering was now irrelevant – the decision had been made for them. A mission abort was just not possible.

The only thing in the agents' favour now was that nobody was looking at the warehouse floor where they were in plain view. Adam signalled Deira to head towards the nearest cover, a pile of crates a few metres to their right, and they edged slowly forward, trying not to make any sudden movements that might attract the attention of the crowd above. They were making good progress when, suddenly, a man appeared from behind the crates and almost walked into them.

For the briefest of moments they all stood looking at each other, the man's mouth dropping open in surprise. Then they all moved at once. The two agents drew their staves and flicked them to combat mode, the baton-sized weapons extending to two metres and extruding wicked-looking half-metre blades at either end. The man simply drew a gun and fired.

The bullet glanced across Adam's left arm and bounced off his body armour. The man fumbled with his gun – but before he could get off a second shot Adam's blade flashed out and neatly sliced his throat open from ear to ear. He collapsed to the floor, blood spurting through his fingers as he clutched helplessly at the wound, and his eyes slowly glazed over. Unfortunately, the damage was done. The agents' cover was blown. At the sound of the gunshot all eyes swivelled in their direction – to be followed by shouts and pointed fingers. Then the crowd that had gathered outside the room upstairs was charging down the stairs. Most of the men already had weapons but those that didn't grabbed whatever came to hand. Many of them had guns and weren't reluctant to use them.

'Force fields!' Adam pressed a stud on his wrist and looked anxiously at Deira. He needn't have worried – she'd anticipated this. Her force field was already on, outlining her in a pale blue aura.

'Copy that. Force field on.'

When the firing started, the bullets rebounded harmlessly off the force fields but the combined impact, with associated transfer of momentum, was still considerable and forced the agents down on one knee into "brace position". Simultaneously, their helmets went into audio-safe mode, screening out the noise and enabling agent-to-agent communication via tight beam.

'You okay?' Adam said.

'No problem. We've got a load of incoming crap, though.'

The shooting stopped as the shooters realised they were having no effect and risked hitting their own men. The pack cautiously circled the agents, eying the blades on their staves and yelling taunts and curses. Most carried knives, mainly long and heavily serrated, and a number wielded antique-looking but still sharp swords. One man, a giant who appeared to be a leader of sorts, hefted an enormous cudgel. Deira shot Adam a worried look. This was a real threat. Their force fields could repel anything with high kinetic energy, such as bullets, but were vulnerable to a low kinetic energy knife-thrust. Even their graphene body armour could be penetrated if there was enough strength behind the thrust – a fact unfortunately well-known to the criminal underworld.

Adam moved away slightly to give them both more space. Back-to-back fighting might be what the tri-vids pedalled in this situation but it would seriously hamper the effective use of a weapon like a staff.

'Do whatever's necessary,' he said. 'Don't worry about the mess.'

'Don't worry – I won't.'

Deira gulped as the crowd round them grew by the second. The agents were faced with a veritable army of misfits, all armed to the teeth and baying for blood. She wouldn't normally baulk at a fight – in fact she rather enjoyed combat. She'd been a black belt in Karate while she was still at GCHQ and had received advanced training in the use of the Bo, or staff, on her recruitment to the Bureau. She was confident about dealing with half-a-dozen assailants or even slightly more – no problem – but this was something else again. She roughly estimated the number facing them to be about forty. Say twenty each. That was far too many.

The men charged. Deira knew that the trick was to keep them at a distance and pick them off as they came within range, a strategy for which the staff was ideally suited. Her opportunity to test this came almost immediately. One man, slightly ahead of the rest and obviously fancying his chances, came at her with an overhead sword swipe aimed at her head. She parried automatically with one end of her staff, whirled on the spot, and neatly sliced open his carotid artery with the blade on the other end. He clutched his neck and dropped to his knees, blood spurting in a high arc onto the concrete, where it lay in a widening pool. For a moment he stared disbelievingly at the sight, then his eyes darkened and, with a gurgling sigh, he fell forward onto his face. One down. Deira moved on in anticipation of the next but it was clear nobody was going to try something like that again. Instead they all attacked at once. Now she really had her work cut out.

Adam had already dispatched two of his attackers when he came up against the man with the cudgel. The giant stepped close, inside the arc of Adam's staff, and brought his cudgel down with such force that it would have crushed Adam's head had it connected. Luckily, it didn't. Adam leaped backwards just in time and the cudgel smashed into the concrete of the floor, sending shards flying in all directions. The giant roared in anger and hefted his weapon for another try but the slight pause was all Adam needed. He stepped back another pace, altered his grip on his staff, and thrust upwards, using it like a pike. It penetrated the man's groin and continued up into his abdomen, severing his femoral artery and slicing open his guts. It was a particularly cruel way to die and the man roared and writhed in agony for some time before he finally lay still. His death caused a momentary pause in the action as the rest of the throng gazed at the agents' knives with more respect. It didn't last long.

The ensuing mass attack left both agents fighting for their lives. They used every combat move they knew, and even made up a few, but the number of their assailants was simply overwhelming and they knew they were going to lose. Deira was breathing heavily and trying not to slip in the growing pool of blood and gore that surrounded her. She skewered another assailant who'd chanced his luck by getting too close, and ventured a swift glance in Adam's direction. A flash of orange caught her attention deep in the shadows some distance behind him – a flash of orange that resolved itself into something completely unexpected.

'Unknown coming in fast at four o'clock,' she shouted. 'Force field evident and suggestion of body armour.'

'Copy that,' Adam acknowledged, though he was facing the wrong way to see the new arrival. 'Another agent?'

'Could be – but his force field's orange!'

Deira tried to keep an eye on the newcomer but couldn't risk taking her attention away from the fight. Her assailants were pressing in on all sides and had learned from their earlier mistakes, darting in here and there but largely keeping out of range of her blades. Their intention was obvious – to tire her out and wait for her focus to fail. One mistake was all they needed. Then it would all be over. She rapidly forgot about the newcomer and tried to formulate a new strategy. Unfortunately, nothing came to her.

She continued her thrusts and parries, successfully keeping the mob at bay and occasionally managing to slice one of her opponents who made the mistake of getting too close. However, she was working hard to achieve very little and she knew she couldn't keep it up forever – the numbers were simply too great. Then – quite suddenly – they weren't.

It was then she remembered the newcomer. This had to be something to do with him. She looked round, catching the flash of orange again, and couldn't believe what she was seeing. The guy was moving so fast he seemed to be everywhere at once, his staff almost invisible such was the rate he was spinning it. He was like a force of nature scything through the army of misfits as if they were stalks of corn. Some tried to escape but were cut down ruthlessly with the rest. Finally, only four remained and the agent, if that was what he was, abruptly stopped and signalled to Deira that she and Adam should deal with these four. Then he gave a smart salute, turned back the way he'd come, and vanished into the darkness behind a stack of crates.

Deira and Adam finished off the remaining bad guys and stood panting in the sudden silence, sweat rolling down their faces and blood trickling from their blades. They turned off their force fields and returned their staves to standard mode, holstering the now baton-sized weapons.

'What the hell was that?' Deira said.

'Search me. I've never seen anyone move so fast in my life.'

'Nor me. At least he was on our side!'

'So it would appear – but that raises more questions.' Adam holstered his staff. 'Okay, we'll park this for now and move on. We need to get the data wafer.'

'Copy that.' Deira checked her HUD again. She pointed up the nearby stairs. 'Up there – room on the left where the light came on.'

'Yeah. Hope the damned thing's still there.'

'Only one way to find out.'

They moved slowly up the stairs, alert for any sign of an ambush. Nothing stirred. All was quiet. Perhaps they really had finished off all the opposition. The light was still on in the room and a body lay near the door, a neat bullet-hole in its forehead. A large safe stood in the right-hand corner and, despite the recent action, its door remained securely locked. This was what they were looking for, and the fact it was locked presented no problem to Adam – he set his staff in laser mode and casually removed the entire safe door with a single swipe. He rummaged through a collection of papers and wads of currency until he found what he was looking for – a single data wafer that was carefully stored inside a small box. He interrogated it with his wrist console and nodded.

'It checks out – Q-ship schematics and security protocols. We're good to go.'

They carefully retraced their steps back to the warehouse floor and started back towards the distant door, taking a circuitous route to avoid the pile of blood, gore and bodies that was their legacy to this place.

'Better take no chances,' Adam said. 'Activate force field again.'

'Copy that. Force field activated.'

They'd no sooner activated their force fields when Deira noticed a movement in the shadows behind a stack of packing cases they were passing. Then a small object came arcing through the air towards them.

'Grenade!' she shouted automatically. 'Incoming eight o'clock!'

Both agents dropped to brace position as the explosion ripped through the warehouse. Their force fields protected them from flying shrapnel but the shockwave threw them back several metres and left them stunned. By the time they'd recovered sufficiently to stand, a fire had started and rapidly taken hold, blocking their way to the warehouse door. They scanned for alternative routes of escape but hadn't gone more than a few metres before some drums of industrial solvent exploded. A further wave of intense heat passed over them and they were enveloped by a cloud of acrid fumes from the vaporising solvents. They doubled over in pain and vomited on the floor.

'Oh crap!'

Deira felt terrible. Every breath sent an agonising pain lancing through her chest and her eyes were so swollen and pouring tears that she could hardly see – not that she'd have been able to see much though the thick smoke anyway. She could feel the heat of the flames over to her right and instinctively angled left, hoping she could get to the exit that way. She wondered where Adam was and tried raising him on the comm, but there was no response. The electronics were probably damaged – either by the explosion or the subsequent wave of heat – so she was on her own. She gulped and started moving towards the left again. Then she felt a hand on hers.

'This way! Take my hand!'

'Adam!'

She grabbed his hand and felt him pull her firmly towards the right – towards the heat. She baulked slightly, but her faith in him was absolute. She followed his lead, and together they moved steadily through the roiling clouds of noxious fumes. At one point she stopped, uncertain, because it seemed they were heading straight into the roaring conflagration, but the pull on her hand was insistent and she followed once more.

It was the longest few minutes of Deira's life. She felt like she'd been struggling through heat, smoke and toxic fumes for ever and was never going to escape this place. Then she felt a sudden cool breeze on her face. What could that be but the doorway? She squinted through the murk and there, a few metres ahead, she could just make out the warehouse door, still jammed open as they'd left it. Such was her eagerness to get outside, she didn't notice her guide's hand release her, and she staggered the last few steps on her own. She almost fell through the door opening, slipping in the mud of the alley and almost losing her footing. Then she was taking long rasping breaths of the cool night air and turning her face to the falling rain as if it were a long-lost friend.

She bent double, coughing and gasping, and it was a few minutes before she was properly able to focus again. Adam was leaning against the wall a few metres away trying to get his breath. If anything, he was suffering more than she was, but when he saw her he stumbled over, still wheezing, and grabbed her arm.

'We need to get away from here,' he whispered hoarsely. 'The whole warehouse is going up.'

They staggered along the filthy alley, stopping once to gaze back when the warehouse roof collapsed with a mighty crash. The sound of fire-vehicle sirens split the night and they picked up speed, needing to be away before the fire crews arrived. Finally, they reached their parked Fast Transport Vehicle (FTV) and collapsed inside. Adam confirmed ID by iris scan and fingerprint, gave the autopilot the coordinates of the local Bureau Office, and they fastened their seat belts. The little car shot off into the night.

Deira relaxed at last. Her chest still hurt but her adrenaline levels were up and her intense green eyes blazed with excitement.

'Way to go!' she said. 'One thing about this job – it's never boring!' She gazed at Adam, who was also wired, though still wheezing badly. 'Thanks for the guiding hand, by the way – I wouldn't have got out of there on my own.'

Adam looked surprised. 'What guiding hand? I couldn't find you. It was all I could do to get out myself.'

Chapter 2

CHAYKA GAZED OUT of the shuttle window while the little craft powered out of Earth's gravity-well towards the waiting Q-ship. It was a far cry from the chemical rockets of twenty years ago with their bone-rattling, stomach-churning, high-G lift offs. Because of the QUAVER-powered gravity generators the ride was a comfortable one-G all the way and even atmospheric turbulence was almost imperceptible now that the new inertial dampeners had come on line. Chayka allowed himself a small smile of satisfaction. None of this would have been possible without his discovery of sub-quantal physics.

He glanced at his companion sitting in the seat in front of him. Nicolau Dominguez was Portuguese and had been his colleague and friend ever since their early days at the Moscow Institute. He had an extraordinary talent in the field of experimental sub-quantal physics and Chayka knew that the sub-quantal revolution could not have occurred without him.

Nicolau was watching the azure blue of the upper atmosphere fade into the blackness of space, his short legs curled beneath him and his large, bulbous head pressed against the window. He was an achondroplastic dwarf, a figure of ridicule to some but to those who knew him a towering intellect, a phenomenon equal to Chayka himself. He was also one of the very few people Chayka truly respected.

As if he were aware that Chayka was watching him, Nicolau turned and grinned.

'An awesome sight, eh Sergei?'

Chayka permitted no-one else to use that name. He had determined he would have no more use for it shortly after he moved to Cambridge. He was deliberately cultivating an image – a persona – Professor Chayka, the Father of sub-quantal physics and, by extension, the saviour of the world.

'Indeed Nicolau,' he said, 'though I'd have happily done without it if I could have remained in Cambridge. It would have been far more comfortable working in familiar surroundings with the original team. How do you feel about relocating to Titan?'

'I relish the prospect. It will provide us with the ideal conditions for our life-generation experiments and may be the catalyst for so much more. Even your past accomplishments may be eclipsed out there, Sergei.'

'Hmmm.' Chayka was less than convinced but had to admit there were distinct possibilities. It was not the transfer itself that rankled with him but the manner in which it had happened. For many years he'd been able to dictate his own terms when it came to his work, and it had been a huge shock when the enquiry had published its report and the Bureau Director had virtually ordered him to take his team to Titan. Perhaps Nicolau was right and he ought to embrace the opportunity offered.

He turned back to the window to watch the shuttle make its final approach to the waiting Q-ship. The ship itself was vast, an ovoid bulk eight-hundred metres long and five-hundred wide. It hung in the void like some huge egg, the sunlight reflected off its burnished panels giving it the appearance of a gargantuan Christmas-tree bauble.

This was the first time Chayka had seen a Q-ship. Powered by the now ubiquitous Quantum Vacuum Energy Reactors, colloquially known as QUAVERs, that had transformed

Earth's energy future almost overnight, this particular ship was also the first to boast the recently developed space hook that allowed it to drag itself through the very fabric of space. The speed gain over previous generations of space craft was impressive. Their current trip to Titan was scheduled to take only fourteen days – and that included a short stopover on Mars. Even the older generation of Q-ships would have taken over three months.

He was continuing to muse on the wide-ranging applications that had been spawned by his discoveries when his thoughts were interrupted by the pilot's voice informing them that they would shortly be docking. Chayka was one of only four passengers on the small craft, the others being Nicolau and two scientists on their way to take up appointments on Mars. He had no idea what to expect during the docking manoeuvre and he watched with considerable interest as the shuttle simply flew into a vast hangar in the Q-ship and settled down on its deck. It was much more like a landing than a docking.

The huge hangar doors were closed and the hangar pressurised. Then the shuttle passengers were allowed to disembark. Chayka walked down the short flight of steps and stood for a moment, staring round at the vast cavern that was the hangar. His emotional repertoire didn't extend to a sense of awe but he was nevertheless impressed by the size of the space and the realisation that this was only one component of the colossus that was the Q-ship. He felt a faint vibration coming through the floor. This and a soft background hum was the only evidence of the eight QUAVERs that powered everything from the ship's engines, to the gravity generators, to the microwave ovens in the kitchen.

The passengers were given a brief orientation tour of the ship before being taken to their cabins. Chayka was a little disappointed by the size of his cabin but at least it had a work desk and terminal so it would probably suffice. He unpacked his bags and had just finished ordering his things as he liked them when there was a rap at the door. It was Nicolau, staring up at him expectantly.

'I wondered if we should join the rest of the team in the lounge, Sergei,' he said. 'The ship's due to depart soon and, since this is the maiden voyage of this new type of Q-ship, the Captain's throwing a small reception. I know you don't like such things but you will be expected.'

Chayka sighed and stroked his goatee beard absently. He was fully aware of his social limitations. He wasn't a people person by any stretch of the imagination – and frankly he didn't give a damn. However, he'd learned a little about the science of heading up a team over the years and knew that he had to jump through a few hoops to get the best out of the people working for him, even if he resented it.

'You're correct of course, Nicolau,' he said, picking up his jacket. 'Let us do our duty.'

Together, they walked briskly down to the lounge where the reception was already underway. Chayka politely declined the offer of a drink from a smartly-dressed crewman on the way in. He still remembered the distant days of his childhood in Vladivostok. His father, a lowly labourer, had been woefully unequipped to provide for his large family even before Sergei came along as child number six. The fact that this latest addition proved to be a mathematical prodigy – a cuckoo in the family nest – sent his father completely over the top. Increasingly, he found solace in cheap vodka and, following protracted drinking sessions, he would vent his pent-up frustration and anger on both his long-suffering wife and young Sergei.

The beatings had etched themselves into the very fibre of Sergei's being and left him with a lifelong aversion to alcohol. Not only did he recognise it for the neurological poison it was, he also feared possible loss of control – like his father had lost control – and for Chayka, self-control was everything.

Nicolau had no such concerns and helped himself to the proffered glass, grinning broadly.

Chayka gazed round the room at the small assembly. In addition to the Captain and Executive Officer, who were presiding over the gathering, there were the two scientists going to Mars, a security team going, like himself, to Titan, and the other members of his team. A small but select group. He made his way over to the Captain and introduced himself.

The Captain and XO were almost obsequious and Chayka found it mildly embarrassing even though he was used to being lauded and feted. He did his best in this most trying environment, working hard at the small talk and smiling courteously at the Captain's jokes. It was the worst form of torture he knew of, yet he endured it for the sake of his image. Finally, after what seemed an eternity but was probably no more than a few minutes, he felt able to make his excuses and join his team. They were standing in a group by the large forward view-panel and had been watching his performance. They shuffled round to make space for him.

'Welcome Professor!'

That was Simon Chandler, the only one of Chayka's original team, with the exception of Nicolau, to make it through the psychological tests that were mandatory for anyone heading into space. Simon was a thirty-year-old British Mathematician who had worked in Chayka's team at Cambridge ever since he'd completed his doctorate four years ago. He was undoubtedly clever, having already three seminal papers on sub-quantal mechanics to his credit, but at six foot three and all muscle he didn't look like anyone's idea of a mathematician. Unusually for a theoretician of his calibre he was also a keen sportsman.

Chayka nodded to Simon and gratefully accepted the lemonade he'd procured for him. At least someone knew his preferences. He gazed round the rest of the team. Dominguez was obviously well known to him but the other three, while being familiar from the interviews, were still effectively strangers. He sipped his lemonade while he considered what to say but Simon pre-empted him.

'We've all been getting acquainted, Professor,' he said, with what Chayka felt was slightly forced bonhomie. 'I know you were involved with the appointments but perhaps I can re-introduce our new colleagues? First we have the lovely Dr Tirzah Blumstein.'

Tirzah glared at Simon and appeared to be about to protest but instead simply smiled and shook Chayka's hand. For once, Chayka understood the nuances and determined to speak to Simon about it later. Yes, Dr Blumstein was physically striking, her dark brown hair framing an oval face with flawless skin and features in perfect proportion, but the mention of her looks was inappropriate, demeaning and unnecessary. She was an Israeli Biophysicist and came with glowing references. That was all that was important to him.

'Dr Walther Altmeyer,' said Simon, apparently enjoying himself.

Chayka looked up at the man-mountain towering over him, his head almost touching the ceiling. He had to be six foot eight at least and probably three hundred pounds. Yes, he remembered him clearly enough, lumbering into the interview room and amazing everybody with his breadth of knowledge. Altmeyer smiled at Chayka and muttered something in his guttural version of English. He was German, and beneath his caveman looks was a brilliant engineer who'd recently been working in Grenoble on the construction of the second generation of transmission terminals that were used by Bureau agents. Chayka nodded and moved on to the final team member.

'Dr Philippe Fournier,' said Simon.

The slightly-built Frenchman bowed slightly as Chayka took his hand and welcomed him to the team. He was the sub-quantal biochemist of the group and was going to be pivotal to the two major experiments Chayka had planned. He seemed quiet, reserved even, and Chayka thought he would be perfect for the job he had in mind.

'And so we are complete,' Simon said, and Chayka suddenly realised he was drunk. The slight flush, the dilated pupils – he should have noticed before. The man could easily make a fool of himself. He looked round the group again and now saw what he'd previously missed – the others were well aware of the problem. There was a distinct air of discomfort, everyone trying to appear at ease while casting wary glances at Simon. Drs Fournier and Blumstein seemed particularly uncomfortable and were shooting each other worried looks. There was clearly something going on here – undercurrents – and Chayka had never been good with undercurrents.

'I'm delighted to meet the three of you again,' Chayka said, 'and I'm sure we'll work extremely effectively together. This promises to be a most exciting opportunity for all of us.'

'I think…' Simon began, but Chayka didn't intend to let him say what he thought for the time being.

'I'm indebted to Dr Chandler for the introductions,' he interrupted, 'and for keeping you amused prior to my arrival. However, I think it will soon be departure time and I'm sure you'll all wish to witness the event. Shall we go to the rear view-screen?'

He moved off and the others followed him, relief evident on their faces. Simon remained where he was, glaring after them. He pointedly drained his glass and got another before joining them at the view-screen with the rest of the passengers. A few more minutes ticked by then the XO's voice came over the comm.

'Ladies and gentlemen we'll be departing very shortly. You won't notice any apparent acceleration because of our new inertial dampeners – the only clue to our speed will be the rate at which Earth appears to shrink. For those not already in place, this can be witnessed from the rear view-screen.'

A hush descended on the room and expectations mounted. There was a slight change in the tone of the QUAVER-powered engines when the space hook was initiated and then it was as if Earth had been suddenly yanked away on a piece of elastic, so rapidly did it recede. There was a loud cheer and everyone began talking at once. All but Chayka, who took one last look round and slipped out, making for the relative peace of his cabin. He'd had quite enough of the subtleties of human relationships for one night.

Back in the lounge, Tirzah pulled Philippe to one side.

'Do you think he noticed?' she asked urgently.

'I think he noticed *something* but I'm not convinced he's equipped to interpret it.' Phillipe smiled. 'I wouldn't worry about the professor, Tir. It's that big lunk of a mathematician we need to watch. It's obvious he wants you – and it's equally obvious he doesn't like me.'

Tirzah glanced at Simon. He was pretending to ignore them, chatting rather too animatedly with one of the Mars scientists. However, every so often he'd look in their direction and glower. She could see what Philippe meant, but even so…

'I guess we should be subtle about it and take care not to push it in his face,' Philippe said. 'We've still got to work with the guy after all, even if he is – what do they say in English – a prize prick?'

Tirzah laughed, but having had her attention drawn to Simon's obvious jealousy she was letting her imagination take over.

Philippe looked uncertainly at her. 'You're sure you wouldn't rather be with him? You must have mentally undressed him several times over the last few minutes.'

Tirzah dragged her attention back to the frowning Frenchman and gave him one of her most radiant smiles.

'Philippe! How could you think such a thing? Wait until this reception's over and I'll show you who I'd rather be with.'

Philippe's frown faded, to be replaced by an uncertain smile. Tirzah briefly let her hand touch his and took pleasure in the effect it had on him – then she surreptitiously let her eyes stray back to Simon for one last look.

On the other side of the room, Security Chief Julio Cabello stood nursing his drink and watching the little human dramas play themselves out. He was so used to people-watching that he had to keep reminding himself he wasn't actually Chief of Security yet – that title would only become operational when he and his team reached Titan. Now he was just plain Julio, and somehow he'd have to find a way to keep occupied during the next couple of weeks.

He gazed out of the forward view-screen at the inky blackness, trying to imagine what Titan would be like. He knew the basics from the briefing he'd received on Earth and the extensive file on his wrist terminal: gravity similar to the moon but with a thick atmosphere, predominantly nitrogen; huge hydrocarbon reserves concentrated in the great northern seas; tendency for stormy weather in the summer season. But that didn't really tell you what the place would be like.

What he was mainly concerned about was whether he and his team would have much to do when they got there. The reason the Bureau felt they needed a security team was related to the presence of huge hydrocarbon seas. These amounted to hundreds of times more natural gas, oil and other hydrocarbons than in all the known reserves on Earth, and therefore represented one of the greatest natural resources in the solar system. Each one of Earth's political blocs wanted access to this resource and had either already set up a Base near the northern shorelines or were in the process of doing so. The Bureau felt this represented a relatively high risk of conflict that warranted a security presence. Julio wasn't so sure but was very willing to take the offered perks that came with the posting.

He turned away from the view-screen and idly watched his men. They stood in a huddle and nursed their drinks, looking out of place and awkward. He was sure they'd soon be off now that the ship was underway and there was an excuse to leave and he was proved right within a few minutes. One-by-one, they deposited their glasses on a tray and hurried out, presumably intending to continue with a rather more relaxed drinking session in the ship's bar.

Once they'd gone there were very few people remaining. The scientists from Mars left soon after the security men. Then the good-looking woman scientist and her male friend slipped silently out of the room, their fingers intertwined and meaningful looks passing between them. They were watched by the tall, inebriated scientist, who was continuing to drink himself stupid. He acquired himself yet another drink then wandered across the room to where his two colleagues, the giant and the dwarf, were engaged in a quiet conversation. He pushed his way in and was soon loudly expounding on some technical principle and it wasn't long before the other two, clearly embarrassed, were glancing at the door and looking for an opportunity to escape. Eventually, the dwarf could obviously take it no longer and looked pointedly at the time. He nudged his huge colleague who feigned surprise and, amidst many apologies and waves, they took their leave.

Julio watched as Simon, slightly bleary-eyed, looked round the room, presumably searching for his next social victim. He decided it would not be him. Declining to make eye contact, he carefully put his glass down and left, initially intending to join his men in the bar, but subsequently deciding to return to his cabin. The guys should be able to let their hair down sometimes without the inhibiting presence of the boss. He'd content himself with a thorough review of the Titan file instead.

In the early hours of the following morning a call came through on Philippe Fournier's comm. He rolled over in bed and picked up the little instrument, wondering who could possibly want to talk at this hour. He sat bolt upright when he saw the identification tab – it was Professor Chayka. He accepted the call, audio only.

'Good morning, Professor,' he said, 'Philippe Fournier here. How can I help you?' He glanced sideways at Tirzah who was pulling herself up the bed and looking questioningly at him. He shrugged and waited for the response.

'Ah, Dr Fournier,' came the familiar voice. 'I wonder if you would be free to attend my cabin for a few minutes? I'd like to discuss something with you – but not over an open comm.'

'Of course, sir.' Philippe tried to push Tirzah's arm away as it strayed round his waist. 'I'll be there in five minutes.'

'Thank you.' Chayka terminated the connection.

Philippe stared at Tirzah. 'What do you think that could be about?'

'Who knows?' Tirzah stretched languidly. 'Whatever it is can wait for a little more than five minutes, surely?'

The hand round his waist moved under the duvet and her other arm encircled his chest trying to pull him back down. Philippe was tempted.

'That's the professor!' he said, though without much enthusiasm.

'So what? It's one-thirty in the morning for God's sake. He doesn't own your soul.'

The hand under the duvet found what it was seeking and Philippe turned and began to lie down again. Then his curiosity got the better of him. What could Professor Chayka want with him at this time of night? Whatever it was, it would surely be to his advantage not to keep him waiting. He struggled up and sat on the side of the bed. Tirzah pouted as she lay on her side looking up at him.

'Really?'

'It must be important,' he said. 'I've should go.'

He stood up, pulled on some slacks, a t-shirt and some loafers and ran his fingers through his long wavy hair a couple of times.

'See you later,' he said over his shoulder on the way out. 'That's if you're still here.'

'I'll still be here,' Tirzah shouted at the closed door. 'It's my cabin!'

Philippe hurried along the short length of corridor between Tirzah's cabin and the professor's and knocked on the door. Chayka opened it part-way and, after a swift glance in each direction, beckoned him in and indicated he should sit in one of the two work chairs. Chayka took the other chair and sat staring at Philippe in silence. The silence was unnerving and Philippe began to wonder why he'd been summoned here tonight. Did Chayka know of his relationship with Tirzah – and if so, did he disapprove?

Suddenly, Chayka seemed to come to a decision. 'Dr Fournier, I find myself in a somewhat difficult situation. I hope I can rely upon your discretion?'

'Of course, Professor. Always.' Philippe was both relieved and intrigued.

'Hmmm.' Chayka stroked his beard and paused again. 'Have you heard about my research into so-called "mass PHASEing"?'

Now it was Philippe's turn to pause while he organised his thoughts. Chayka waited politely.

'Normal photonic transmission is limited to people with the gamma mutation,' Phillipe said. 'That's a very small proportion of the population. There's been talk that you've been looking into extending things to the general population – the mass PHASEing you mentioned – but the difficulties appear to be insuperable.' He stopped, unsure what to say next and Chayka stepped in.

'Yes, what you say is correct. However, I've reviewed my early work and I now think it could be successful.'

'But that's marvellous! That'd be another historic milestone. Is it going to be one of our work strands while we're on Titan?'

'That's where my problem arises. This posting has only received Bureau approval for the life-generation experiments – indeed, it was primarily organised to facilitate those experiments. The Bureau has specifically banned the mass PHASEing work for the immediate future.'

'But why? That makes no sense. It would bring so many benefits. What could've possessed them to ban it?'

A tinge of red appeared on Chayka's cheeks. 'I suspect it has something to do with their desire to retain the technology for their own use – specifically, transportation of their agents.' He fixed Philippe with a defiant look and went silent again as if debating with himself whether or not he should continue. Philippe waited patiently and Chayka finally got to the point, becoming animated for the first time.

'I will not comply with their stupid diktat. I will continue my research in secret – at least in the first instance. I don't want to tell the rest of the team in case it goes nowhere, but if I'm successful in developing a theoretical framework I'll need their help in the necessary experimental testing.'

'Ahhh.' Philippe finally understood where this was going. Chayka continued.

'My work to date suggests that true mass PHASEing will never be possible because there will still be genetic constraints on the process – but it may be achievable for the majority of individuals. I need to know if I have access to such individuals and for that I will need fully analysed DNA samples.'

He looked expectantly at Philippe, who was feeling distinctly ill.

'You want me to obtain DNA samples from the team without their knowledge?'

Philippe knew this was not only a violation of protocol on every level, it was also illegal. If caught, he would probably get a custodial charge.

Chayka was watching him.

'The samples would only be a screening tool. If nobody in the team has the necessary DNA markers there'd be little point in carrying on because there'd be no suitable test subject. I'd only continue if one or more of our colleagues had the necessary markers, and then, at the testing stage, I'd inform the team of my progress and ask for voluntary DNA samples. They'd never know what you'd done so there'd be no risk to you.'

Philippe pondered this, going over the scenario in his mind. It would be fine – providing he wasn't caught. The benefit to him was a fast-track to the professor's esteem. He made his decision.

'I'll do it, Professor.'

'Excellent!' Chayka seemed to have expected nothing less. He went to a cabinet and brought out two small plastic containers. 'These will get you started. They're DNA samples from Dr Dominguez and myself. The rest you'll have to obtain using your own initiative. Thank you for your help. Please keep me informed of your progress.' He went to the door and held it open. Philippe was dismissed.

Philippe began to have second thoughts the moment he left Chayka's cabin. Had he really just agreed to steal his colleagues' DNA for a secret project? This wasn't him at all. Then he looked at the two plastic containers in his hand and realised that this could be something truly revolutionary. Lost in thought, he walked straight past Tirzah's cabin and continued on to his own.

Chapter 3

THE FTV PARKED up in the vehicle compound of the Marseilles Bureau Office and Deira and Adam stepped out. The trip back from the warehouse hadn't taken long – their ride wasn't called a Fast Transport Vehicle for nothing – and the effects of the smoke and chemical fumes were still very obvious. Both agents had a persistent rasping cough and Adam couldn't shake off a nasty wheeze. Deira felt a couple of days sick leave would be good at this point, with Adam having a day or two more, but she knew that was a triumph of hope over experience – the Bureau didn't have a reputation for being soft on its agents. Sure enough, following a peremptory examination by the in-house medics, they were pronounced operationally fit.

'Now there's a surprise!' Adam said.

Deira laughed. 'If you wanted feather-bedding you should have joined Interpol.'

'Or GCHQ perhaps?'

'Touché!'

'Come on – we'd better get our reports filed before we fall asleep on our feet.'

Deira made a face. The paperwork! The bit all agents hated. The Bureau demanded contemporaneous reporting – all reports written and filed immediately after completion of the mission, while memories remained fresh. Fair enough, except that was precisely the time when the adrenaline surge from the mission was dissipating rapidly leaving a profound weariness. It wasn't unknown for agents to fall asleep halfway through their report.

Thankfully, that didn't happen on this occasion though, after half-an-hour completing the relevant forms and filing their reports, they both felt utterly drained. They headed for their rooms to get some sleep for what was left of the night and it was turned 03.00 by the time Deira finally hit the sack. She was out almost as soon as her head touched the pillow.

She was roused from a deep sleep by the persistent beeping of the "call" signal on her wrist console. She groaned and looked at the time – just past seven o'clock. She'd been expecting a bit of latitude to sleep in late this morning but it obviously wasn't to be. Grumpily, she accepted the call and stared at the virtual screen. It was a recorded message ordering her to report to the Bureau Director of Operations at Brussels HQ – at 09.00 today. She rubbed her eyes and stared again, with disbelief. No, she hadn't misread it – it really did say "Director of Operations". Fully awake now, she climbed out of bed. Then she began to worry. Why would the DO, of all people, want to see her? She had to be well below his radar and if she'd really screwed up something it'd be Adam who'd give her any bad news. It didn't make sense.

Anxiously, she showered, dressed and had a quick coffee. Usually, she'd have a decent breakfast too, but her appetite had suddenly vanished as she contemplated the worst-case scenario of a future outside the Bureau. She packed a small bag and hastened down to the local PHASE terminal, keen to get to Brussels in good time and well aware that there was sometimes a queue of agents waiting for transfer. This morning she was lucky – the terminal was empty except for the PHASE technician, who seemed pleased to finally have a customer. Deira had a brief chat with him then stepped into the chamber and lay on the couch, clutching her staff tightly.

She hated this waiting bit. She still remembered her first day at the Academy, one of six new recruits sitting in the small lecture theatre, excited and a little anxious at the prospect of joining the Bureau. The senior tutor had explained that they were there because they were special – one-in-ten-million special to be exact. They all possessed the extremely rare gamma mutation which enabled them to undergo a process called PHotonic Algorithm-Sequestered Engram transmission – colloquially called PHASEing. This meant they could be transmitted to a trouble spot in almost no time at all, making them extremely valuable assets.

Their first reaction had been to be immensely proud to be one-in-ten-million special people -then they found out what PHASEing was all about and the doubts crept in. The established Special Agents reassured them you got used to it and they were right, you did – it was just better not to think too much about what was actually happening as you went through the process.

The techie spent a little time adjusting his controls before glancing briefly in her direction.

'Good to go?' he asked through the chamber comm.

'Fire when ready,' Deira replied automatically.

'Transmitting now. Tight Beam, Agent.'

The chamber powered up, the low hum always making Deira feel slightly nauseated. Her fingertips tingled as her staff uploaded and stored a sub-quantal copy of her memories through nanodetectors in her skin. In spite of its name, memory loss had been a troublesome side-effect of

PHASEing just a few short years ago and this backup was still a Bureau requirement even though the problem had apparently been resolved with the introduction of the new generation PHASE chambers. Deira tensed up, anticipating the next stage of the process – then everything went black as the electronic neural inhibitor came on and her neural activity ceased.

The hum changed to a high pitched whine and the transmission process began. Deira's body was ripped apart into its component atoms and analysed at the sub-quantal level. The data gathered was then used to generate a stream of so-called "information-rich photons" which were processed into a highly coherent, densely packed laser. Finally, this was fired out of the chamber down a fibre-optic cable to a receiving station, where the process was reversed.

At light speed, Deira covered the distance from Marseilles to Brussels in a matter of milliseconds, materialising in a PHASE chamber that was, to all intents and purposes, identical to the one she'd just left. The chamber discontinued the neural inhibitor and she regained consciousness. She climbed off the couch, thanked the local techie for his attention, and made her way out of the PHASE terminal and up the stairs.

At the top of the stairs a door opened into the main concourse of Bureau HQ – a hugely impressive, brightly-lit atrium, filled with noise and bustle. This was the first time Deira had been here and, coming as she was from the relative calm of the PHASE terminal, she was briefly disorientated by the sudden sensory overload. She took a few moments for her body to adjust and gazed round, trying to get her bearings. Over by the far wall was a pair of receptionists, so she weaved her way across the crowded floor and waited until one of them turned to her.

'Special Agent Deira MacMahon.' She flashed her ID. 'I've an appointment with the DO at 09.00. Can you point me in the right direction.'

'Sure.' The woman touched her terminal screen and a map of the building was transferred to Deira's wrist console. 'Take the elevator to the top floor and you'll find the DO's secretary immediately to your right. You can't miss her – the entire floor's given over to the DO and his staff.'

'Thanks very much.' Deira turned away and glanced at her wrist console. Her destination was highlighted in red on the schematic of the building and she could see it would take only a few minutes to get there. It was now – she checked the time – 07.45. That left over an hour before her appointment. She sighed. She had a tendency to arrive too early for appointments but she'd really overdone herself today. This could get really tedious.

She wandered round the entrance hall for a while, enjoying the buzz of activity and taking in the various items of artwork. When she became bored with that she bought a coffee and read the day's news on her wrist console. Finally, after what seemed like the longest hour in her life, she presented herself at the Director's office. The DO's Personal Assistant checked her in and ushered her politely into an adjoining waiting area – and there was Adam.

'Okay, so what the hell do you think this is all about?' she said, sitting next to him.

'And a big hello to you too,' he said, smiling. 'Yes, I feel quite well today. Wheeze and cough have gone. Thanks for asking.'

Deira coloured. 'Sorry, I'm just anxious. I thought I might be in trouble.'

'I'm pretty sure you're not. I've no more idea than you what this is all about. We'll just have to wait and see, won't we?'

So they waited, and when the large clock on the wall with the irritating tick showed 09.15 Deira began to fidget. She crossed her legs one way, then the other, and finally got up and began pacing round the room. She noticed the look of amusement on Adam's face and could feel herself blushing again.

'I'm sorry. I pace. When I get anxious, I pace. I've always paced. I...'

She shut up as the door to the office opened and the Director himself appeared. Thomas Cheatham, Operations Director of the European Bureau of Investigation, was a big man in every way. Six foot six tall and all of 280 pounds he exuded charisma and seemed to dominate the small waiting area. He was 56 years old and the product of a traditional British upper class education – Eton and Cambridge – followed by a lifetime of administrative posts in increasingly sensitive areas. As befitted his current role, he was a power dresser. His suit was jet black with faint pinstripes and, by the way it hung on his ample frame, it suggested many hours in the company of his tailor. His hair was salt and pepper, pure white over the ears, and cut in a style that was slightly too long to be fashionable but which suited his image perfectly. He smiled at the two agents, displaying a set of perfect white teeth. Adam came rapidly to his feet and Deira, realising she was gaping inanely, closed her mouth.

'Special Agent MacMahon and Supervisory Special Agent Clarke?' He boomed. 'Apologies for the long wait. Come in please.'

He held the door open, and Deira squeezed past him into his office. She had to admit, it was pretty impressive. Positioned overlooking La Grande-Place, it benefited from the afternoon sunlight, which gave what could easily have been a bleak mausoleum of a room a magical lift as the rays bounced round the richly panelled walls. Three of the walls were hung with copies (at least she assumed they were copies) of late renaissance masterpieces while the fourth, behind the huge mahogany desk on the far side of the room, contained row upon row of framed certificates representing the Director's significant achievements.

Deira waited for Adam to join her and they stood rather awkwardly while the Director made his way to his desk and sat down, the springs in his chair groaning in protest.

'Please be seated, both of you. I don't bite.' He indicated the two chairs in front of the desk and they both sat. There was a pause while he gazed intently at his desk console, then he looked up and smiled again.

'I'll come straight to the point. The reports you filed last night referred to an unknown agent who helped you out during your fight in the warehouse. Could either of you add anything to your descriptions of this agent?'

Deira experienced a great desire to pace again. They'd only filed those reports a few hours ago yet the DO already had them in front of him. She knew all reports were initially scanned by software looking for specific words or phrases – so-called "red flags" – and they must have hit the jackpot. Perhaps they'd stumbled on something they weren't supposed to see. She looked to Adam for support. He was sitting ramrod-straight and staring directly ahead, eyes unfocused.

'There's nothing we didn't detail in our reports, sir.' He said. 'Are we in trouble?'

'Heavens no SSA Clarke – far from it. The thing is, the words "unknown agent" set a few alarms off – and the incident occurred at the same time as reports of a strange character on Mars. We think that's too much of a coincidence.'

That was totally unexpected. Deira had no idea the Bureau had a presence on Mars. Indeed, she could see no reason why it should have since Mars Base was a tightly-run, highly controlled community where the likelihood of significant criminality was negligible.

'What's the Bureau doing on Mars, sir?' The words were out of her mouth before she could stop them and Adam glared at her. 'Sorry, sir.'

The Director didn't seem at all put out.

'Not a problem, SA MacMahon. In fact, that's why you're both here.' He leaned back in his chair. 'Perhaps you could tell me how you think an unknown individual came to be on Mars.'

'It doesn't make sense, sir. The only way on or off Mars is by ship, so everybody should be accounted for on a ship's manifest. There shouldn't be any unknowns.'

'Yet all names on manifests have been accounted for and there's still an unidentified person present. No obvious mode of entry.'

He activated the comm on his desk. 'Pat, would you be so kind as to bring us three coffees please?' He glanced up. 'Any preference as to black, white, sugar, and so on?'

Deira felt she'd just fallen down a rabbit-hole. The whole idea of taking coffee with the DO was simply surreal. She waited for Adam to reply but nothing was forthcoming and she realised he was having even more trouble with this than she was. He'd always been deferential to the point of being obsequious. She spoke up for both of them.

'We both take it black, sir, and no sugar. Thank you.'

'Jolly good. Did you get that Pat? Okay. Now, where was I? Ah yes, unidentified person, no obvious mode of entry. Thoughts?'

Now that the topic had turned away from coffee back to business again Adam was suddenly able to speak again.

'Could some private individual or corporation have produced a Q-ship?' He frowned and muttered an answer to his own question. 'No, that wouldn't work – they'd still have to pass through normal Mars Base entry protocols.'

'Correct.' The Director said 'Even if someone had developed such a ship, and we have no evidence to support that, it still wouldn't get them into Mars Base undetected.'

The door opened and Cheatham's secretary brought in the coffee, quickly passed the mugs around and slipped out again. Cheatham took a sip of his and shot a glance at Deira.

'Do you have any thoughts on the matter, SA MacMahon?'

Deira couldn't see where this was going at all and tried to follow the logic. There seemed to be two hard facts – one, you couldn't get to Mars without being on a passenger manifest and two, this interview had only come about because they'd mentioned an unknown agent in their reports. Put them together and… was it possible?

'An agent could get in, sir,' she ventured, 'but there'd have to be a PHASE terminal on Mars.'

'That's impossible!' Adam blurted out. 'Beam power, diffusion, and attenuation wouldn't allow it and…' he trailed off when he saw the Director's face. Deira could see she'd nailed it.

'So there *is* some new PHASE technology,' she said triumphantly.

The Director nodded. 'Very good Agent MacMahon. Yes, there is a new technique for photonic transmission over interplanetary distances. It was developed by Professor Chayka's team.'

Deira frowned. 'But surely it'd be obvious if the terminal had been used?'

'Theoretically, yes.' The Director looked uncomfortable. 'In practice – well, it's confusing. The terminal's fully operational but hasn't been commissioned yet. There's none of the usual evidence of use but the technician's discovered a record of a small, and highly unusual, quantum fluctuation from a few days ago. We haven't a clue what it means.'

He paused to take a gulp of coffee. 'Luckily, it doesn't seem to be anything that would prejudice the human testing programme – which is where you two come in.'

Adam went deathly white. 'You want us to go to Mars by PHASE, sir?'

His voice was low and controlled – an apparent absence of emotion. Deira knew differently because she recognised that voice. It was the one he used when he was trying to conceal how scared he was. His hands were balled tightly in his lap and he was staring blankly ahead again.

The Director had been examining his virtual screen. Now he punched something into his desk console and drained the rest of his coffee.

'Yes, SSA Clarke, that's the plan. We need you on Mars quickly and the only ship capable of doing the trip in the timescale we require is the one currently on its way to Titan. That ship won't be available for at least another four or five weeks and we can't wait that long. If we use the new transmitter we not only get you where you need to be quickly but test the technology at the same time – very efficient.'

Deira had passed through the panic phase and now felt numb. She was only just beginning to get used to PHASEing between sites in Europe and still wasn't entirely comfortable with the process. Now she was going to be transmitted millions of miles through space as one of the first test subjects of a new technology. This had definitely not been on the agenda when she'd signed up. She looked across at Adam and saw he still had his scared-shitless-but-not-admitting-to-it face on. The Director didn't appear to notice and continued.

'I've just sent the mission brief to your personal consoles. You will track down the stranger and discover who he is, how he got to Mars and the reason for his presence there. If he's an agent, we also need to know who he works for and whether or not he has any connection with your mystery agent from the warehouse.

'This would usually be a mission for one agent, and I was planning to send you, SSI Clarke. However, it's been suggested to me that SA MacMahon's prior experience in IT and cryptology may be of benefit in this case so I'm sending you both. Do you have any questions?'

Deira glanced over at Adam but could see he was still deep in thought.

'Just a couple, sir,' she said. 'Do you think it's possible

the unknown agent on Mars is the same one who helped us in the warehouse? If so, it'd seem his motives are benign.'

'We're almost certain they're two different individuals. At the very time you were receiving help in the warehouse from your unknown friend we had a report that our man on Mars was sitting in the Bar chatting to the barman.'

'That's very interesting. Do you have a picture of him?'

'Unfortunately not. The reports we've had have been vague at best and nobody's thought to get a picture. I'm afraid you'll have to start from scratch.'

Okay. Thank you, sir.' Deira was trying very hard to maintain an air of quiet confidence when she was actually in inner turmoil. 'When would you like us to get started?'

'The sooner the better.' The Director smiled and rummaged in one of his desk drawers. 'Have yourselves a decent night's sleep tonight and report to the new transmission terminal in the CERN Bureau facility tomorrow. You'll also need these.' He passed across a couple of plastic badges. 'New security passes – you're now officially level 8. If you have any more questions your contact is Dr Swanson in the Science Directorate.'

He got up and showed them to the door.

'Good luck with your mission, agents. I'm very confident in the new transmission technology and, just think, you'll be making history. I look forward immensely to reading your reports.'

He gave one last smile and closed the door. Deira turned to Adam.

'Have you got it into your brain what we've just signed up for? We're going to PHASE all the way to Mars! Hell, until today I didn't even know you *could* PHASE without a fibre-optic cable.'

'We do it here sometimes,' Adam said vaguely, looking decidedly unhappy, 'and the Americans use it all the time because of the long distances they have to cover and the lack of suitable cables. I've no idea how it can be done over such large distances but I guess it must be okay if the Director says it is.'

'Well I don't know about you but I need a stiff drink,' Deira said.

'Sounds like a plan.'

§

The next morning, Deira met up with Adam for breakfast. She'd had a pretty crappy night, much of it awake or dreaming of Martian agents, and now all she could think of was the projected mega-PHASE. From the dark shadows under his eyes it was plain that Adam had had the same problem. Neither of them could manage anything to eat but had a swift coffee before taking a regular PHASE to the Bureau office at CERN. They wandered round for a while trying to navigate the colossal facility and finally, after a good deal of flashing their new security passes, managed to find the new interplanetary PHASE terminal.

The interior didn't look that different from a standard PHASE terminal, which was good news for Deira, whose adrenaline levels were already pretty high. There was a whole load of extra equipment that the local technician was calibrating, but that wasn't her prime focus. The PHASE chamber itself was what she was interested in, and that looked identical to those she was already familiar with. It helped.

'What's bugging me is how they get the aim right,' she said. 'I know there's plenty more to worry about but that kind of just goes round and round.'

'I can help with that if you want,' Adam said. 'I had a little chat with Dr Swanson last night and got the lowdown on the tech we're going to be using.'

'Don't know whether I really want to know or not.' Deira thought for a moment. 'Yeah, okay. How do they do it?'

'Well, each of the new PHASE terminals emits a beacon at a specific frequency. Let's take Mars as an example. The Mars terminal emits a pulse that the terminal on Earth picks up. Because the pulse travels at light speed, that only tells us where Mars was about four minutes ago. Knowing that, we then use something called the Solar Algorithm to determine where Mars will be in the time it takes us to transmit over there. That's called the "destination locus". Am I making sense so far?'

Deira felt distinctly nauseated. 'You mean they transmit us to where Mars *will be* in *about* four minutes' time using knowledge of where it *was, about* four minutes ago? And you expect me to feel reassured by that?'

Adam laughed. 'Do you want the rest or shall we leave it at that?'

'Definitely leave it at that! If the rest's anywhere near as bad I really don't want to know.'

They wandered over to the luggage bay and deposited their bags in the hopper for regular quantum transmission then sat waiting for the technician to complete his fine-tuning. Once he was happy with the set-up he came over, smiling broadly.

'Hi guys!' The man was wound up as tight as a spring and his face was deeply flushed. 'I'm Carl. I don't know about you but I can't believe we're about to do the first ever human interplanetary PHASE. It's historic! How are you both feeling?'

The last thing on Deira's mind was making history. She was so totally absorbed with the thought that she was about to be fired into interplanetary space that the techie almost got more than he was expecting from his innocent question. Thankfully, Adam took over before Deira could explode. He made all the right noises and smoothed the situation over quite nicely.

'Which one of you is going first for PHASE One?' Carl asked.

'PHASE One?' Adam raised an eyebrow.

'Yeah – didn't you know? We're PHASEing you to the moon first – a nice short one-and-a-half second transmission to get warmed up. Once we're sure you're both okay, we'll get you straight on to Mars.'

'You make it sound like we might *not* be okay?' Deira said, feeling her stomach lurch again.

Carl laughed. 'Sorry – I didn't mean it that way. This new tech's fantastic and all the animal tests went perfectly. The moon PHASE is just to satisfy the bureaucrats. You know what they're like – risk assessments and all that.'

Deira nodded uncertainly and looked at Adam, who seemed to be taking things very much in his stride. This was what Adam did. He might have been shit-scared last night but once he'd processed the data and internalised it he just got on with things. That's what made him so good to have round.

'That's great, Carl,' he said. 'I think I'm first.'

Deira wasn't inclined to argue, being content to delay her own departure for as long as possible. She watched, fascinated, as Adam casually finished his coffee and made his way to the PHASE chamber. He seemed completely at ease – calmness personified – and then he spoiled the effect completely by turning and giving a sickly smile. Deira assumed it was meant to be encouragement, for which of them she wasn't sure, but she wished he hadn't bothered because it hadn't been particularly helpful.

The procedure itself was just like a regular PHASE except that Carl took more time checking and calibrating once again. Finally, he turned from his instruments to where Adam was lying in the cubicle.

'Destination locus confirmed, Agent. Ready to transmit?'

'Fire when ready,' Adam said. The chamber powered up and entered its pre-transmission phase.

'Tight Beam, Agent.' Carl initiated transmit and the low hum changed to the usual high pitched whine. Deira had never seen inside a chamber while a transmission was occurring and she didn't really want to – her imagination provided quite sufficient details. She kept telling herself she'd been through this many times. It would feel no different – just take longer. The thought didn't help much.

'Transmission complete,' Carl called over to Deira. 'Your colleague's on the moon in one piece. When I get the go-ahead from my opposite number out there I'll get you on your way. You can get into the chamber now, if you like, while it's cycling.'

Deira was nothing like ready to go but was functioning on automatic pilot. She entered the chamber and made herself as comfortable as possible on the couch. This was definitely not her idea of the perfect day.

Carl's voice came over the comm. 'Everything's on the green, Agent. Destination locus has been re-confirmed and I'm ready to transmit on your signal.'

Deira knew she couldn't delay this any longer. Adam had already completed his PHASE so the equipment obviously worked just fine. She needed to get a grip.

'Fire when ready,' she said.

The chamber powered up, the neural inhibitor came on, and Deira knew no more. Her body disintegrated and all that was left was the information that made her the unique individual she was. This was encoded in the compressed photon beam and a few seconds later an intense white laser shot out of the terminal building.

Deira MacMahon flew to the moon as a beam of light.

Chapter 4

CHAYKA SAT ALONE with a mug of hot chocolate and gazed through the forward view-screen of the passenger lounge. His thoughts were far away, in the bleak, mind-numbing days and the black, marrow-freezing nights of his native Siberia. This late night contemplation had become a habit since he'd discovered that the inky blackness of space evoked memories of his childhood – memories he'd have preferred to have buried for good but which bubbled up from his subconscious in a never-ending stream. He thought of it as a form of therapy, a means of confronting the past and moving beyond it. In the main it was about being in control – and not being controlled by the traumas of the past.

Round him all was silent except for the distant and ever-present thrum of the QUAVER drive. It was a good time to sit and reminisce, to confront inner demons and put his life in order – because order was essential.

He reluctantly dragged himself away from his recollections and concentrated on the view-screen. Mars appeared as an orange-red disk that took up a good quarter of the field of view. The ship would reach the planet tomorrow – no, later on today Chayka reminded himself, checking the time – and it would stop over for two nights before launching into the second part of the fourteen day journey.

The facility on Mars was the oldest in the solar system with the single exception of Moon Base. It had begun life as a research station in the days when the journey time from Earth was several months and visits by ships were few. The resident scientists had been a hardy bunch by necessity, carefully selected to cope with the psychological rigours of an isolated dome existence. The competition for a posting was fierce because the payback was significant – an enhancement in professional reputation on return to Earth and a huge bonus payment. Chayka knew he would have relished the role. He was just twenty years too late.

The stuttering start in space exploration had been changed almost overnight by the myriad applications that followed Chayka's discoveries in sub-quantal physics. The QUAVER-powered Q-ships had made routine travel to the nearer planets a real possibility for the first time and Chayka had read accounts of those heady days when almost anything seemed possible. Everybody had wanted to witness the wonders of space for themselves and the demand was enough to stimulate the emergence of a new breed of space entrepreneurs. With money and enthusiasm, the original Mars Base had grown beyond all recognition and the facility now boasted, among other things, a mall of shops, two restaurants, and a very well-known bar.

Then there was the Skydome. Fully five kilometres in diameter, it enclosed a virgin piece of Mars landscape, maintained at Martian gravity but provided with an Earth-normal atmosphere. The intention had been to assess experimental terraforming techniques within this enclosed space prior to general implementation, but time had moved on and the dome had rapidly assumed iconic status. It was hugely popular with both visitors and those on long-term contracts at the Base and all attempts at co-opting it for its original purpose had long since been abandoned.

Chayka could happily have dispensed with the short stopover on Mars. However, the ship had to call there anyway in order to drop off the two scientists and the Bureau psychologists felt that a break would be good for the members of his team, who were all very keen to set foot on the fabled Red Planet. He wondered once again how such a dismal place could be so evocative for so many of his fellow human beings. No matter how he tried he simply couldn't understand the attraction. His attention drifted back to the blackness and he shivered as his private demons rose up once more.

He forced himself to move on from the memories of the taunts and beatings to thoughts to happier times – to the presentation of the Nobel Prize and the adulation that followed. The icing on the cake had been the offer of the Lucasian Professorship of Mathematics at Cambridge University, one of the most prestigious in the world, having been previously occupied by such luminaries as Stephen Hawking and Isaac Newton himself. Chayka had accepted with alacrity and, in the years that followed, had worked happily within the confines of the university. Indeed, he would probably still have been there but for the sequence of events that would change his life forever.

Chayka's reverie was abruptly interrupted by the door to the passenger lounge crashing open. He turned irritably to see who had disturbed him and was confronted by one of the crew. The man was considerably worse for wear after a heavy drinking session and had clearly taken a wrong turn. He cast bleary eyes round the room trying to work out where he was before turning and crashing back though the door without so much as an apology. The effects of alcohol couldn't have been more vividly illustrated.

Chayka tried to resume his contemplation but the interruption had broken the mood and left him feeling restless and unsettled. He made himself another hot chocolate in the small kitchenette and stretched his legs, sipping the hot beverage while he wandered round the lounge. Then, he seated himself by the view-screen again, activated his wrist console, and settled down to work. Two hours passed before he finally rubbed his eyes, turned off his wrist console, and made his way to his cabin.

§

Later that morning Chayka awoke at his accustomed time, ship's time 06.30, and made his way to the refectory for a sparse breakfast of muesli and black coffee. He was fastidious about what he ate, refusing to subject his body to the toxic input enjoyed by most of his colleagues and maintaining a strict vegetarian diet with no external stimulants – except coffee, which was his one indulgence.

Philippe Fournier was the only other person having breakfast at this relatively early hour and was studying his wrist console intently, occasionally taking a bite of croissant or a sip of espresso. He was so engrossed in his work he failed to notice Chayka when the professor collected his breakfast and settled himself at his usual table in the far corner of the room. However, when Chayka activated his wrist console the slight noise must have penetrated his concentration. He glanced up and, seeing the professor, left the remains of his breakfast and walked over to his table. Chayka glowered at him – he'd made it quite plain to the whole team on the first day that he ate his meals alone and would not tolerate company. Philippe appeared to have forgotten this.

'Good morning, Professor.' Phillipe smiled as he pulled out a chair and began to sit down. 'May I join you? I badly need to talk to you about the results of the task you gave me.'

'No!' Chayka's hand came down hard, startling Phillipe and spilling coffee over the table-top.

He was appalled by this breech of protocol. He could see that Philippe was distracted but, even so, this lapse was unforgivable.

Philippe stopped in the act of sitting, his smile disappearing as it suddenly dawned on him what he'd done. He backed off, wondering if he could retrieve the situation.

'My apologies, Professor. Maybe after the briefing?'

Chayka was unforgiving. He'd had his breakfast disturbed and felt intensely irritated. 'Perhaps it has escaped you, Dr Fournier, but we are due to land on Mars today. There'll be no briefing. The Bureau made it clear that this break is for you and your colleagues to have some rest time on Mars and they insisted there should be no discussion of work-related issues until the journey to Titan has resumed. Your results will have to wait.'

He turned deliberately back to his breakfast, leaving Philippe to beat a hasty retreat. Chayka watched him scurry away and frowned. This episode was out of character for Fournier. Perhaps he should hear what the man had to say. He pondered for a moment and was about to call him back when he realised it was too late. Philippe had gone.

He returned his attention to breakfast and put the issue of Fournier out of his mind.

§

Philippe hurried along to his cabin, mortified by his gaffe with the professor. He closed the door and sank into a chair, head in his hands and thoughts in tumult. Since Chayka had asked him to collect and analyse the team's DNA things had become – complicated. Getting samples had proved to be more difficult than he'd imagined since it required a subtlety of action and deviousness of character he found most distasteful. To add to his discomfort, he'd put his developing relationship with Tirzah on hold. He couldn't condone sleeping with her on the one hand and stealing her DNA on the other.

When he finally had a full set of samples he'd begun his analyses – and then his problems really started. Nicolau was achondroplastic, and the mutation on the FGFR3 gene that caused the condition was well known. There was no evidence of it in the sample that Chayka had provided. That meant Chayka had made a mistake – and Chayka hated making mistakes. Philippe had pondered on the problem for a while before deciding it would be best if the professor didn't find out. Instead, he would obtain a sample from Nicolau in the same way he'd got the others – by underhanded subterfuge. It hadn't been easy, but he'd finally got what he needed.

Then he wished he hadn't.

He got up and paced round the cabin, thinking furiously. Events were spiralling out of control and he had to do something. He sat down and opened his wrist console, spending several minutes poring over the data he knew he shouldn't have – and certainly shouldn't have boasted to Simon about. That had been a big mistake, and due entirely to his need to get back at the mathematician for all the jibes he'd had to endure since arriving on board the ship. He recalled the look on Simon's face when he'd seen the file. Murderous would be a good description – and with justification.

He reviewed his actions over the past few days and was distressed at how low he'd fallen in his own eyes. He'd read somewhere that once you'd carried out one illegal act it became easier to perform others but he'd never thought it would one day apply to him. He gave a wry smile. If he survived this he could be heading for a future as a career criminal.

That last thought made him pause. Had he actually begun to think his life might be in danger? Was that a realistic assessment of the situation or just a product of his overwrought imagination? Was he having a breakdown? He gazed at himself in the mirror – at the white face, shaking hands, and nervous tic. He really could be losing it.

He grabbed a bottle of Armagnac from his bedside locker and took two large gulps straight from the bottle. The fiery liquid made him gasp but seemed to do the trick and within a few minutes he looked more his normal self – slightly wide-eyed, perhaps, but definitely passable. Perhaps it was just a panic attack. He flopped back in the chair and was about to fix himself some coffee when the Captain's voice came over the comm.

'Ladies and Gentlemen, we're now in final Mars approach and for those who are interested the forward view-screen in the lounge will provide quite a spectacular sight as we go into orbit. Once we've achieved orbital insertion, shuttles will leave for the surface within the hour. Passengers should report to the hangar with their baggage by 08.00.'

Philippe hadn't appreciated they were so close to landing. He swiftly packed his bags and tried to control the anxiety which had become his constant companion over the past couple of days. He was shortly to meet with the other members of the team for the ride down to the surface and he mustn't appear upset. At 07.50 he left his cabin and made for the hangar deck. He passed Walther Altmeyer's room on the way and had a sudden thought. He tapped on the door and, as he'd hoped, there was no response. Walther would have departed for the hangar deck some time ago. He looked up and down the corridor – clear both ways, thank goodness – then rummaged in one of his bags for an item he'd recently acquired to help him with his DNA acquisition. He pulled the small device out of the bag, placed it on the door, and in a few seconds had obtained Walther's door code. Within another thirty seconds he was inside the room.

A few minutes later he emerged and closed the door behind him before hurrying down to the ship's hangar. The waiting area was buzzing with the chatter of the assembled passengers and he could hear Tirzah holding forth on how spectacular the final approach to Mars had been, the planet going from a disk to an orb in virtually no time at all. She spotted Philippe and fell silent, shooting him a hostile look. Needless to say, this caused everyone to stare in his direction – just at the time he was trying to maintain a low profile.

'Philippe! Our mathematical biochemist. How nice of you to join us! We were just wondering if you were going to make it in time for the transfer.' That was Simon Chandler doing his usual thing. 'You *are* alright aren't you – you look a little off-colour.'

'Thanks Simon,' Philippe said. 'I'm fine, and I wouldn't miss the trip down to Mars for the world – any world actually!'

There was a ripple of polite laughter at this sad attempt at humour but he saw that Tirzah wasn't laughing. He badly wanted to explain to her why he'd been so distant for the last couple of days but to do that he'd need her alone for a while. Perhaps there'd be a chance when they were on the surface. He lugged his bags up to the group and wondered what to say to defuse the palpably hostile atmosphere. Luckily, he was saved the effort by the boarding announcement. Everyone hustled on board one of the little shuttles and scrabbled about trying to store their luggage and find a suitable seat. Phillipe didn't want to sit next to Tirzah, Simon or Dominguez and managed to get next to Walther. The big man was soon doing his best to be companionable.

'So Philippe,' he said, smiling, 'I trust you will be joining us tonight at The Bar on the Mall? It is supposed to be quite famous.'

Philippe's heart sank. There was no way to escape this ordeal. It was well known that he liked his drink and to back out would be suspicious in the extreme. He smiled at Walther and nodded.

'Wild horses couldn't keep me away Walther.'

There was a pause while both men considered what he'd just said. Philippe had been learning colloquial English in preparation for this posting and thought he'd got the appropriate phrase for the occasion. Walther, however, still struggled with basic English, and this talk of horses had clearly confused him. In turn, Walther's lack of understanding made Philippe doubt himself. It would have been amusing if both participants had recognised their individual roles. In the event it was simply difficult.

'I would very much like to join you all,' Philippe clarified. 'It should be a most enjoyable evening.'

'Ahh. Yes indeed.' Walther grinned from ear to ear.

Both men fell silent.

Thanks to the inertial dampeners the flight down to the surface was as uneventful as the flight into Earth orbit. The passengers were processed efficiently through the necessary formalities, provided with a Mars Base information file for their wrist consoles, and taken to their rooms in the habitat zone.

Philippe closed his door with relief and flopped wearily onto the bed, glad to be away from the others. He closed his eyes and massaged his temples, trying to persuade a nagging headache to leave him alone. It was very tempting to remain like that and pretend his current tribulations were all a bad dream – very tempting but not realistic. He sighed and stirred himself. Time to get down to work.

To avoid interruption, he took what he needed to the library and spent several hours completing his self-imposed tasks. He'd only been back in his room a few minutes, and feeling badly in need of a shower, when there was a knock at the door. It was Tirzah. She barged in without waiting for an invitation and stood accusingly, hands on her hips.

'I know what you're doing.'

That was the thing about Tirzah – you got it straight from the hip. No social niceties.

'Tir I...'

'Don't try to deny it – you don't lie well enough. I know you've been stealing DNA.'

Philippe stared at her, completely at a loss what to say. It was bad enough that he'd got into this in the first place but now it appeared he'd been nowhere near as clever as he'd imagined. If Tirzah knew, how many others did?

'I presume it's to do with the mass PHASEing project?' Tirzah was getting into her stride now. 'You're a fool to let the professor play you like this. It was that night in my room wasn't it? He asked you to do it then?'

'Tir, there's more to it than that.'

'I'm sure – and it's eating you up from the inside. Share it with me. Let me help. I…'

'I can't!' The pain in Phillipe's head flared up again. He felt trapped. There was nothing he'd rather do than share his problem with Tirzah but he was scared of the consequences.

Tirzah looked disgusted and walked to the door.

'You're pathetic! If you change your mind and want someone to talk to I'm still here for you. For God's sake, Philippe – man up!'

She left, leaving Philippe clenching and unclenching his fists, his thoughts in turmoil. He was about to run after her when there was another knock and his spirits rose. She must have changed her mind. He opened the door in anticipation.

'Tir I…'

Nicolau Dominguez stood there, smiling broadly. He was the last person Philippe expected to see. He was also the last person he wanted to see.

'My friend Philippe,' Nicolau said, 'I think we have a little unfinished business. May I come in?'

Philippe badly wanted to shut the door in the dwarf's face. 'Please.' He held the door open.

Nicolau gave a little nod of appreciation and came in. Philippe knew he was in no fit state to be having this meeting – he was an emotional wreck. He waited for the dwarf to start, expecting a difficult few minutes. Instead, everything seemed to go quite well, and when Nicolau finally departed it was on a positive note and following a firm handshake. Philippe watched him disappear round the bend in the corridor and wondered whether he'd done the right thing. Perhaps the long-promised shower would help.

The shower did, indeed, seem to be helpful, clearing his head and bringing the meeting with Nicolau into greater perspective. He knew he badly needed to talk with Chayka but the professor had made it perfectly clear he wouldn't discuss work until they were back on the ship. He was stymied.

He checked the time and realised he was already late for the team gathering in the bar so he slipped on a jacket and hurried along to the Mall. He paused outside the door, wondering if this was a good idea. He was in no mood to socialise tonight and, with the exception of Walther, he couldn't think of anyone who might want to socialise with him. What the hell was this evening about anyway? Team-building? Team-mending would be more appropriate – and they'd need more than glue to mend this particular team. Reinforced concrete sprang to mind.

He knew he could debate with himself all night but he had little choice but to put in an appearance and the sooner he got it over with the better. He pushed open the door and scanned the room. It was really very impressive. The bar was designed in the shape of a massive cave, presumably intended to play to atavistic feelings of security. There was even a holographic tableau in one corner of the room consisting of a sabre-tooth tiger being kept at bay by a large fire. Philippe thought this was particularly apt given that the team's own friendly caveman, in the shape of Walther, was standing at the far end of the bar in conversation with Nicolau – not so very far from the tiger.

The men from the Titan security team were grouped halfway along the bar and were clearly enjoying themselves. Their boss, Julio Cabello, was sitting at a table with Chayka, who sipped on an elderflower presse. Philippe wondered how those two had got together. Cabello was manfully attempting to make conversation with the professor and occasionally did manage to elicit a monosyllabic response. Chayka was his usual impassive self and Phillipe guessed he was probably bored and irritated in equal degree. He'd almost certainly leave when he'd finished his drink, Cabello or no Cabello.

Tirzah was leaning on the bar next to Simon and saw Philippe come in. He gave a half-smile and started towards her but she deliberately turned away and said something to Simon, who smiled unpleasantly. Phillipe stopped, unsure what to do. After his experience on the shuttle he didn't fancy trying to carry out a conversation with Walther all evening. And Nicolau? He shuddered at the thought. He got himself a Remy Martin and wondered again what the hell he was doing here. This had been a really bad idea.

Tirzah struggled down to breakfast the next day feeling bleary-eyed and fuzzy. She had dark smudges under her eyes that no amount of make-up could conceal and she expected some snide comments from the other members of the team. However, when she saw the rest of them she knew she was home free. With the single exception of Nicolau, who looked none the worse for his excesses the previous evening and was tucking into breakfast with gusto, they looked no better than she did.

Simon looked glum and was idly playing with his breakfast cereal. He, too, had a set of dark smudges under his eyes and he looked exhausted, but he roused himself enough to glare at Tirzah.

'What?' she said.

'Nothing important.'

He looked back down and continued half-heartedly picking at his breakfast. There was obviously something wrong but Tirzah couldn't think what it might be and she was in no mood to indulge him further by making an issue of it. She picked up her own breakfast and sat down, glancing at Walther, who was drinking black coffee and popping aspirins.

'Bad one Walther?'

Walther was a strange colour, somewhere between white and khaki, and was trying hard not to look at Nicolau, who was shovelling bacon into his mouth.

'Ach! Ich habe einen schlechten kater.'

'Sorry Walther – I don't speak German.'

Walther stared vacantly at her for a moment as if he didn't know who she was. With what appeared to be a great effort, he pulled himself together.

'My apologies. I am overhung by alcohol.'

Tirzah smiled. She liked Walther – even if he did look like he'd walked straight out of a prehistoric tri-vid. He was gentle, polite, and self-effacing and did his best with his limited English. She wished some of the other members of the team were as pleasant. Simon was undoubtedly handsome, and her thoughts kept wandering to what he might be like in bed, but he was self-opinionated and boorish. He'd suffice for a short-term liaison but that was all.

Now Philippe was a different matter – courteous, good-looking and good in bed. She thought back to the previous evening. She hadn't been expecting him after her behaviour in the bar but somehow that made it all the better when it happened. He'd still been edgy and irritable – definitely holding back on something – and she'd tried to get him to open up to her. He wouldn't budge, insisting it was in her best interests not to know, but she wondered if he'd relent on that in the cold light of day. She glanced round and only now saw he wasn't there.

'Has anyone seen Philippe?'

Simon glared at her again. 'Probably still in his room. He wasn't exactly the life and soul of the party last night but I think he got what he was after later on – wouldn't you say?'

Tirzah suddenly realised what his problem was. He must have seen Philippe go into her room. She turned away and tried to change the subject.

'What about a visit to the Skydome today? It's supposed to be a "must see". We could stop off at Philippe's room on the way and see if he wants to go too.'

There was no enthusiasm whatsoever for this suggestion, responses ranging from lukewarm at best to frankly hostile. Tirzah just lost it.

'What the hell's the matter with you all? This is the most talked-about attraction in the solar system and you lot are seriously thinking of giving it a miss? Well if you don't want to go that's fine, but I'm going – and if Philippe's in his room I'm sure he will too.'

As Tirzah had hoped, the mention of Phillipe was a game-changer – at least as far as Simon was concerned. He immediately changed his mind and said he was up for a visit. The other two were still doubtful until Walther's good nature got the better of him. He agreed he'd like to see the Skydome while he had the opportunity, and struggled to his feet. After this, Nicolau seemed to feel he had no option but to fall in line. Tirzah looked round the sad little company with an unaccustomed feeling of triumph and set off for Philippe's room. Simon followed closely, unwilling to let her out of his sight, and Nicolau hung back to keep Walther company as the big man slouched slowly along.

Once back in the residential area, Tirzah knocked gently on Philippe's door. There was no answer. She was about to knock louder when Simon pushed her out of the way and pummelled on it aggressively, shouting for Philippe to open up. Still nothing.

'Okay, that's it. Let's go.'

Simon began to move off and Walther and Nicolau followed. Tirzah was appalled and stood her ground.

'Suppose he's ill or something? I know you guys don't like Philippe but I'm not leaving here until I get this door open.'

She put in a call to the Residence Warden and requested that Phillipe's door be opened. Simon grumbled while they waited and made no attempt to conceal his dislike of the Frenchman.

'I don't know why you bother with him,' he said to Tirzah. 'The man's obviously unstable.'

'You don't know what he's been going through.'

'Well why don't you enlighten me?'

Tirzah glared. There was no way she was going to tell Simon about the DNA theft. Luckily, she was spared any further debate by the arrival of the warden with the room code. The room was empty – and it was clear Philippe hadn't slept there at all the previous night. So where was he?

Tirzah was really worried. Phillipe's performance in bed the previous evening had been lacklustre in the extreme – certainly not the Phillipe she knew. She'd tried to get him to stay but he'd refused, saying he had things to do, and as he'd slouched out he'd looked thoroughly depressed. Now she was left wondering what these "things" might be that he had to do in the early hours of the morning. The possible answers weren't encouraging.

She called him over the comm but there was no reply, just an automated response. Then she looked at the others, wondering how far she could push them. Not very far, judging from the expressions on their faces. She didn't think she had a hope in hell of persuading them to carry out a search and, to be fair, she wouldn't know where to start herself. Then there was the outside chance that Philippe might simply have found some other company last night and was sleeping late – and how pathetic would she look then?

'Well, screw this!' said Simon. 'If you want to go to the Skydome, fine – let's go. Philippe's a big boy. He can look after himself.'

Tirzah knew she'd run out of allies. Nicolau and Walther were already shuffling in the direction of the Mall while Simon stared belligerently at her, daring her to come up with some other ploy to find Philippe. With a sigh, she gave up and followed Walther and Nicolau. Simon took up the rear, a little smile playing over his lips.

The Mall was a large open space at the junction of several habitation zone corridors. Over the years, it had become a kind of central commercial district for the Base, and contained numerous retail outlets as well as the bar in which they'd spent the previous evening. It was also the centre of a web of corridors that linked the various Base facilities and, as they emerged from the Residence corridor, they could see the route to the Skydome almost diametrically opposite.

It didn't take them long to pass down the entry corridor to the Skydome and enter the dome proper. It was a fascinating piece of architecture because it was absolutely transparent. As they closed the door behind them it was difficult to see where the enclosed red desert ended and the "real" landscape outside began. Then, when the entrance door disappeared behind a rock, the illusion of walking across Mars was complete.

Tirzah was entranced. The sky was deep red, fading to violet near the horizon, and the distant sun was pale and insipid, just over half its size when seen from Earth. It did its best to cast some light and heat on the desolate landscape outside the dome and created an effect something like a cloudy day on Earth – a very cold cloudy day, because the surface temperature was in the region of minus 30C. Tirzah checked the internal ambient temperature on her wrist console – it was steady at the usual 22C.

She saw that the twin moons, Phobos and Deimos, were both high in the sky at the same time – a comparative rarity – and she could just make out the orbiting Q-ship as a bright point moving rapidly across the sky on the far horizon. This really was amazing. The word that sprang to mind was "spiritual"– and it appeared the rest of the group felt as she did because they'd begun to talk in whispers and were proceeding slowly and almost reverentially. The mood was further enhanced when they came to an area of rocky extrusions – massive blocks and towering columns. The impression was of being in a vast alien cathedral.

Tirzah wondered along some way ahead of the rest of the group, enjoying the feeling of isolation amidst the stark beauty, and awestruck by the towering rocks. She'd just rounded one particular rocky outcrop and was about to call back to the rest of the team when she looked up. She stopped and stared, eyes wide and mouth gaping.

'Oh my God!'

Her stomach lurched violently and she fell to her knees, vomiting on the sand. The others moved quickly to her side, concern showing in their faces – then they saw it too. At the highest point of the rock, a man was hanging. A noose was round his neck, his face was blue-black and bloated, and his swollen tongue protruded through grey lips.

It was Philippe Fournier – and he was quite obviously dead.

They stared in horror and Walther finally lost his ongoing battle to keep his stomach contents where they belonged. Simon was as shocked as the rest but had the sense to call Security and Security Chief Monroe arrived in a little over three minutes. He immediately took charge, gently easing the scientists away from the scene of death and placing an urgent call to the senior Pathologist, Dr Barinson.

'Cut him down! Please cut him down!'

Tirzah was almost hysterical and kept trying to get back to the rock from which Philippe's body hung. Simon put his arm round her, trying to offer some comfort, but she pulled away and stared again at the body.

'We'll get him down when we can, Miss,' Monroe said, 'but we need our Pathologist to give us the okay. Why don't you all return to your rooms for now? I'll catch up with you later and make sure your professor's informed.'

They shambled slowly away, passing Barinson on his way in with his team. The Pathologist conducted a rapid initial scan of the scene then had the body taken down for a more detailed examination. His team took photographs and samples while he satisfied himself they'd obtained what information they could. Finally, he gave permission for the body to be removed to the mortuary and turned to Monroe.

'Pending a formal post-mortem, this seems to be a classic case of asphyxiation by hanging. The marks round the neck and the swelling of the facial structures are consistent with strangulation by the rope that was found in situ. Obviously, there'll have to be an inquest, but I'm ninety-nine percent sure this was suicide.'

'Thanks, Doc.' Monroe put in a call to the Base coroner and after a brief discussion turned back to Barinson. 'How quickly can you get the post-mortem done, Doc? If you can do it today, and my lads get the necessary statements from the deceased's colleagues, the coroner says he can schedule the inquest for tomorrow. The thing is, these guys are on a high profile Bureau mission to Titan and if there are genuinely no inconsistencies I'd like to get things processed quickly so they can be on their way.'

'Well that's most irregular.' Barinson frowned and tutted to himself. 'However, I suppose if it's cleared with the coroner...'

'Thanks Doc.' Monroe got on the comm to his sergeant. 'Joe? Monroe here. Listen, it looks like we've got a suicide here – one of those scientists who arrived yesterday on that Q-ship. We're aiming for a quick-fire inquest so I need you and the lads to get over to the habitation zone and get statements from his colleagues. Oh, and while you're at it, you'd better get some from the security guys who are going on to Titan – they might have noticed something. Okay? Thanks.' He looked at Barinson. 'You'd better get a move on doc – don't want to keep the coroner waiting do we?'

Despite everybody's best intentions, it took two days to get the post-mortem performed, the interviews done, and the inquest held. According to the coroner, this was a record – both on Mars and Earth – and he appeared inordinately pleased with himself when he pronounced the verdict of suicide. Following the verdict, the Captain of the Q-ship lost no time getting re-embarkation underway and the traumatised passengers were soon back in their cabins preparing for the long journey ahead.

Ckayka felt intensely uncomfortable. There must have been something terrible playing on Fournier's mind for him to have taken his own life and he'd had the opportunity of talking to him about it. There were very few times when Chayka doubted himself but on this occasion he was forced to consider his actions – and he didn't come out of it very well. Not very well at all.

He shook himself from his introspection. This was not being very productive. He needed to arrange a replacement for Fournier as quickly as possible. He frowned. This really was going to be extremely tiresome. Dr Fournier had been integral to his plans and now everything would have to be put on hold. He put in a call to the Bureau and formally made his request.

The Bureau acknowledged the problem but said they couldn't get a replacement to him any time soon. They promised to make an appointment within the next three weeks. However, the only Q-ship capable of reaching Titan in a reasonable time was the one Chayka was on – and that wasn't due back for another four to six weeks. Then there was the necessary break for the crew. The best-case scenario was that a new biochemist might make it to Titan in round three months. Chayka was appalled.

While he was making his call, the ship leaped forward on the next step of its voyage, Mars receding rapidly in the rear view-screen as the space hook took hold. This time there was no announcement and no party in the lounge. Nobody felt like celebrating. In fact, nobody wanted to see Mars again for some considerable time – if ever.

Chayka fixed himself some hot chocolate and settled down to think. He knew his chances of achieving a positive result with mass PHASEing had died with Dr Fournier. He could still work on the equations but without the DNA samples he couldn't make further progress. He now had to decide whether there was any way the team could move forward on the life-generation project in the absence of a sub-quantal biochemist. He knew his lack of empathy was considered by many to be a severe character flaw but it had the decided benefit of enabling him to continue functioning even after an event that had shaken his colleagues to the core. He smiled to himself. That was why he was so successful.

Chapter 5

Deira opened her eyes, awareness returning slowly. Coming round from a PHASE was more like coming round from general anaesthesia than from normal sleep. There was that strange feeling of no elapsed time between loss of consciousness and waking up. There was also a sense of deep unease, as if the body somehow remembered being torn apart and reassembled and was coming to terms with an entirely new set of atoms. Nobody had ever found a physical reason for this, and it had eventually been labelled "psychological". Most agents felt it had a deeper explanation and had coined a phrase to describe it – "the cells remember".

She sat up and swung her legs over the side of the couch before tentatively standing up. She felt pretty good considering she'd just PHASEd three hundred and eighty-five-thousand kilometres through vacuum. Her balance was unimpaired and there was no evidence of nausea, photophobia or cramps, the tell-tale signs of a bad PHASE. Everything was on the green. She was so engrossed in self-analysis she was startled when the door to the chamber snapped open and Adam put his head in, a big smile on his face.

'You coming out of there? We need to get on to PHASE Two of this little jaunt.'

Deira grinned and left the chamber. 'Can't say I'm so keen myself but I guess that wasn't too bad.'

In truth, it had been like any other PHASE. The new tech had performed right on the button and she felt far more confident about the next transmission. Adam was also more upbeat. His shit-scared look and sickly smile were gone and he seemed his usual confident self again.

The two agents had a few minutes wait while the local technician – Adam said his name was Paulo – conferred with Carl back on Earth. There was a good deal of checking of readouts and comparison of data but Paulo finally confirmed that PHASE One had been a huge success. Now they could move on to PHASE Two.

Deira had never been one to avoid a challenge. To be absolutely honest, a sit down with a few drinks would have been her own preference at this point but she could see that Adam had got the bit between his teeth and was eager to get going again. Paulo returned to his bank of equipment and Adam was about to enter the PHASE chamber when his wrist console indicated an incoming call. It was the Director of Operations again.

'Ah, SSA Clarke. Sorry to interrupt your schedule but I'm afraid your mission's just become a bit more complicated. If you and SA MacMahon will take a seat I'll explain.'

'Yes sir. One second please while I let the techie know.'

Adam walked across to Paulo, who'd been looking enquiringly at him, and explained that they'd have to put things on hold for a minute because the Director was on the line. The techie was clearly impressed that they were having direct calls from the DO and placed his equipment into stand-by before discretely taking himself out of earshot. Adam returned to Deira and put his wrist console into conference mode, only to find that the Director had gone away to take an urgent call on another line. They sat quietly, wondering what this was all about, and finally the DO's face reappeared on Adam's virtual screen.

'Sorry about that,' he said. 'Something that couldn't wait.' He looked at Deira. 'Bit of background first, I think. SA MacMahon, you've recently graduated from the Academy. What did they tell you about Professor Sergei Chayka?'

'Just what's in the public domain, sir. Child prodigy, born in Vladivosktok and later sent to an academy in Moscow. Developed sub-quantal physics at the age of nineteen and produced the theory for the Quantum Vacuum Energy Reactor two years later. Won a Nobel Prize at twenty-three and took up the Lucasion Professorship at Cambridge at twenty-five. Basically, he's been almost single-handedly responsible for the world we live in – QUAVERS, Q-ships, PHASEing – the lot.'

'A very nice potted bio. The man is certainly amazing. Unfortunately, we've recently upset him by transferring him and his team off-world.'

'I heard that on the news a few days ago,' Deira said. 'Something about an explosion at Cambridge?'

'Yes, his team were performing experiments on the sub-quantal generation of life when oxygen leaked into the test atmosphere and caused the explosion. It was very destructive but, thankfully, nobody was killed. Since we were funding the work, our first thought was to have it discontinued. However, we were informed it could easily link-up with parallel work on artificial intelligence, with potentially massive benefits, so we decided on a different approach. Titan, the sixth moon of Saturn, has no oxygen in its atmosphere, making it a safe environment for this type of work. As we've recently established a research base there, it seemed a logical place to transfer this particular project to. The Q-ship, with the team on board, left five days ago.'

'How long will it take the ship to reach Titan?' Adam asked.

'About fourteen days for this particular Q-ship. It's a new design and we only have one at the moment. Two more have been commissioned but they're in the shipyard partially complete.' The Director looked momentarily lost. 'Now where was I?'

'You'd sent a Q-ship off to Titan with Professor Chayka's team on board,' Deira said.

'Ah yes. Well, I'm sure you know that anyone intending to go into space must undergo strict psychological testing – and there's a fifty percent failure rate. Luckily, Professor Chayka passed the tests but half his team didn't. We were able to find replacements quite quickly but the professor wasn't amused. His relationship with the Bureau's about as strained as it possibly could be right now.

'Anyway, as I said, the team boarded the Q-ship five days ago. We arranged a short stopover on Mars for them, to break the journey and allow for some sightseeing, but things went catastrophically wrong. One of the new team members, a Frenchman by the name of Fournier, hanged himself in the Skydome. Did it a couple of days ago, actually, but the Mars Base coroner's only just released the inquest details – which is a damned nuisance because the Q-ship's already set off for Titan again.'

Adam frowned. 'That doesn't make sense, sir. Severe depression with suicidal tendencies would surely have been detected by the psychological tests.'

'Exactly!'

'So, there are three possibilities. First, the psychological tests might be flawed – and that would be a disaster for our ongoing space programme. Second, something could have happened soon after Fournier boarded the ship to cause a catastrophic deterioration in his mental health. Third, it wasn't suicide.'

'Very good, SSA Clarke. So, I need you to investigate Fournier's death in a little more detail. If you're convinced it was suicide with no contributing factors then we have a huge problem. The tests will probably have to be re-designed from the bottom up and space travel put on hold for all new applicants for an unspecified time. If there were contributing factors that caused a critical deterioration then I need to know what those factors were. Finally, if you are convinced it wasn't suicide you have a different sort of investigation on your hands.'

Adam looked thoughtful. 'Do you think it could have anything to do with the stranger we're looking for?'

'That's the question of course. It's impossible to say at this point. I'm sending you the post-mortem results and the inquest findings, together with the investigation carried out by the local security team. See what you make of them and do a bit of snooping of your own. You'll need to make contact with the Chief of Security before you begin – his name's Monroe and he has a pretty good reputation. I'm sending you his file too. Everything clear?'

'Absolutely clear, sir.'

'Any questions?'

Adam glanced at Deira and she shook her head. It all seemed straightforward.

'No sir. We're happy with the brief.'

'Splendid. Best of luck.' The transmission ended.

'Okay,' Deira said. 'That's different.'

'Things just keep getting better, don't they? Come on! We need to get to Mars.'

At a nod from Adam, Paulo brought his equipment back on line and Adam lay down in the chamber. Deira waited while the now-familiar process run its course, apprehension beginning to gnaw at her again. This time there was a considerable delay before a small beep sounded from Paulo's instruments. He checked them thoroughly and turned to Deira.

'Agent Clarke confirmed at destination. Are you good to go, Agent MacMahon?'

'Sure thing.'

Deira tried to push the anxiety away. The Director had been right about the new PHASE tech, it really was just like the stuff she was familiar with on Earth. No problem. Except – for her – there was. She thought she'd overcome her fear of this transfer but the long wait to have Adam's arrival confirmed had brought it home to her what she was about to do. She'd be a disembodied stream of photons flying through open space for over four minutes! Her stomach seemed to do a little cartwheel and all her carefully-cultivated bravado disappeared. She entered the chamber and lay tensed up, waiting for the hum to end. Then – nothingness.

Four minutes and thirteen seconds later she regained consciousness and opened her eyes. A wave of nausea and photophobia swept over her and she closed her eyes tight again. This had to be a bad PHASE.

Deira had never experienced a bad PHASE though she'd been told about them by more experienced agents. Since the newer PHASE terminals had come on line they'd become less common but agents still had to learn how to deal with them. She went carefully through the recommended series of muscle relaxation techniques, tensing and relaxing each muscle group in turn before moving on to the next. Then she tried opening her eyes again. Things had certainly improved. Her vision remained blurred but the light didn't hurt any more. Furthermore, she no longer felt like she needed a bucket to puke in. Her muscles were still very painful, as if she'd just finished a session of bare-back riding on a bucking bronco, and her head ached a little, but she thought she could cope with a few aches and pains.

Her vision gradually cleared and the room came into focus, revealing what looked like a teenage girl watching her apprehensively. The girl was slim and pretty, her long blond hair tied into a ponytail that further accentuated her youthful appearance. This had to be the local techie, though she didn't look old enough to be out on her own never mind operating a multi-million-Euro PHASE terminal.

'Hi! Welcome to Mars Agent MacMahon.' The Irish accent was very evident. 'I'm Amelie and I'll be working with you to get your post-PHASE tests done. Before that though – are you alright? You took a while to come round and you look a bit groggy.'

'Hello Amelie. Please call me Deira. Yeah, I do feel pretty rough.' In fact her headache had suddenly taken a turn for the worse.

Amelie frowned. 'Can you be more specific? Any cramps or other obvious physical problems?'

'Nausea and photophobia when I first came round but they've gone now. My muscles ache like hell and I feel completely, I don't know, "deflated" would probably be the best word. Like a post-adrenaline rush, but ten times worse. It's probably nothing.'

'Actually, it could be quite important.' Amelie rapidly made notes on her wrist console. 'PHASEing over spatial distances involves the use of an advanced form of compression technology. The "you" that arrives at your destination doesn't contain all the information that would have originally been "you" at the transmission end – it's the job of the new equipment to sample the information at the one end and fill in the blanks at the other. Bit like the process for digitising music but much more sophisticated. Anyway, the feeling you're talking about could very well relate to the filling in process. I think you agents have a phrase for how you feel after a normal PHASE…'

'The cells remember. Yes, there's normally a strange feeling, but it's nothing like this.'

'Well we'll be doing a whole series of post-PHASE tests later so we'll see if anything turns up. We're very much into unchartered waters here – we've never had a human to describe how they're feeling before. What's it like to be first, or perhaps I should say second?'

Deira harrumphed. She'd had misgivings about these long-distance PHASES from the start but had been lulled into a false sense of security after the moon trip. Granted, she was still in one piece and she certainly felt like the same Deira who'd left the moon a few minutes ago. It was just that her head hurt and she felt so tired – she could hardly keep her eyes open. And what was all that about sampling, compression and filling in? Nobody had mentioned that before.

Suddenly, Amelie's comment about her being the second transferee reminded her she wasn't here on her own. She looked round for Adam and was surprised to find he wasn't there. Perhaps he felt bad too and had gone to lie down.

'How's Adam?'

'Seemed fine when he arrived. I thought he'd hang around and wait for you but he was out of the terminal as fast as he could go. Said he was going for a stiff drink. Is he always so grumpy or is he just having a bad day?'

Deira couldn't believe what she was hearing. Adam would *always* wait for her – and he certainly wouldn't go to a bar while she was part-way through an interplanetary PHASE. In fact, she'd never known him go to a bar *at all* on his own – she usually had to push him into having a drink. And he was almost never grumpy. Something was very wrong and she knew she ought to check it out – she just didn't feel capable. Her head felt like it was going to explode soon if she didn't lie down somewhere.

'That's not the Adam I know. I'll look into it later. At the moment, though, I really am feeling pretty dreadful – my head's killing me and I can hardly stay awake. I think I need to lie down in a dark room for a while.'

Amelie was kind and efficient. She showed Deira to her assigned room and left her a couple of aspirins before closing the door gently.

Deira popped the aspirins, slipped her boots off and climbed into bed fully clothed. Without bidding, her eyes closed and she fell asleep. It wasn't a very restful sleep and she tossed and turned fitfully for some time before waking with a start. She sat up, sweating profusely. This wasn't good – she had psychological tests scheduled for the next day and failing them was unthinkable. It was still only 12.00 so she made herself a drink of warm milk, changed into her bed clothes, and settled down to read for a while. That seemed to do the trick and when her eyelids drooped again she fell into a prolonged, deep sleep that was uninterrupted. When she finally came round it was well into the next morning, almost twenty-four hours later. She'd never slept so long in her life. It was almost as if her body had performed a hard reset.

Thankfully, the headache and tiredness of the previous day had completely vanished and she felt fresh and ready to go – though she was ravenously hungry and sticky with sweat. That was soon sorted by a thorough clean-up in the small bathroom and a mighty breakfast in the refectory. Then she felt ready for anything Amelie could throw at her.

When she presented herself at the PHASE terminal for the mandatory set of post-PHASE tests there was still no sign of Adam, but Amelie insisted they continue with Deira's tests and she'd chase him up later. Standard post-PHASE tests were pretty basic and took very little time. These tests were of a different order entirely. First, a local medic carried out a full physical exam and took samples of blood, skin, hair and urine. When he'd finished, Amelie supervised the comprehensive psychological tests. Finally, there was a total body quantum scan.

It was late afternoon by the time they were finished and, though most results were available and satisfactory, some wouldn't be available until the next day. Amelie apologised to Deira, explaining that she couldn't officially sign her off until those results had been received and checked. Deira didn't actually care. Her main concern was Adam and what he was up to. According to her wrist console he was in the bar again – unless, of course, he'd never left! She flashed up a schematic of the Base design on her virtual screen and soon found her way to The Mall. There was the bar she wanted, directly in front of her, and there was Adam just emerging – Adam like she'd never seen him before.

She was sure he was still wearing the clothes he'd PHASEd in and he couldn't have washed either because, when she got nearer, she smelled stale sweat and booze. She took in with alarm the stubble and black rims to his reddened eyes. Had he slept? He staggered slightly as he drew level with her and she reached out to offer support. The response was immediate and aggressive. He angrily swatted the hand away and glared at her.

'Fuck off bitch. When I want some of that I'll ask for it.'

Deira involuntarily took a step back in alarm. 'Adam – it's me – Deira.'

He leered horribly, making her recoil further. 'Deira is it? Don't think I know you darlin' Want to play?'

She flinched and put in a call to Amelie.

'Amelie? Yes, it's Deira. Listen, I've found Adam and there's something horribly wrong. He's drunk and doesn't seem to recognise me.'

'Deira, stay with him. I've got him tagged on my console and I'm putting in an urgent call to security. I won't be able to tell if it's a PHASE problem until I can get some tests done but the first priority is to get him to a place of safety and sober him up.'

'Okay.' Deira watched with disgust as Adam turned to one side and urinated on a nearby shop front. 'Try to get security to hurry will you?'

'They're on their way. The security office is just down the corridor off The Mall so they should be with you in a few minutes.'

Even as Amelie was speaking Deira heard the sound of running feet and two burly security men emerged on to the Mall. She waved to attract their attention and pointed at

Adam who was in the process of zipping himself up. They acknowledged her and walked smartly over to Adam, taking an arm each and trying to attach a set of handcuffs. This was not a good plan. Whatever had happened to Adam's mind, his body responded to this perceived attack by slipping effortlessly into well-rehearsed combat moves. He appeared to collapse, his weight loosening the holds of the security men. Then, as he fell to a squatting position one leg shot out and round, sweeping both men off their feet and leaving them floundering on the floor. He gave a deep-throated growl and turned on Deira, his face contorted with rage.

'Fucking bitch – this is your fault.'

His body tensed and she knew she'd got three of four seconds max before he went for her. The security men were still picking themselves up so there was no point looking there for help. She had no option but to pre-empt him.

'Okay Adam, this is for you own good.'

In one fluid movement she whipped out her staff, extended it to maximum length and swept his feet out from under him. Then, while he lay on the floor, she brought one end of the staff down in a sharp blow to his temple. He gave a low groan and sank back unconscious. It was all over in seconds.

The security men climbed to their feet and stared with interest at the staff. She guessed it was probably the first time either of them had seen an agent in action and it was clear they were impressed, even if also slightly embarrassed by their own efforts. Between them they gathered Adam up and carried him to the security office where they lay him down in a cell. Deira considered staying until he was awake but the thought of confronting that awful lewd personality again was too much.

She wandered slowly away, feeling guilty for not being more supportive but horrified by the monster Adam appeared to have become. Without being consciously aware of it she retraced her steps to the PHASE terminal and found Amelie finishing up for the day. The techie took one look at her and stopped what she was doing.

'You okay? How's Adam?'

'He's completely out of it.' Deira explained what she'd had to do. 'It was awful, Amelie. He was so totally not Adam.'

'God, I'm really sorry, but if he's that different I think the chances of him recovering quickly are very slim. If I were you, I'd hope for the best, but expect the worst.'

This thought had been flitting round the edge of Deira's awareness but she'd been trying to ignore it. Now she was forced to confront it. She knew the score. There were no cases on record of self-limiting psychological problems after a PHASE – they were all permanent. Although Adam's situation as the first interplanetary transferee was unique, there was no reason to suppose things would be any different for him. So, she needed to sort herself out. Yes, she'd lost her supervisor and yes, it was hard, but she was left with no alternative but to go it alone on the mission. And there was the question, right there. Was she capable of it?

She was confident in her physical abilities – but psychologically? That was the nub of it. Adam had recently told her she was as ready to run a mission as she'd ever be. However, even if he'd given her control he'd have still been there providing support and, she admitted, keeping her wilder side contained. Without him, she was going to have to grow up as an agent pretty damned fast. She turned to Amelie.

'Fancy a drink?'

She was trying not to show the feeling of loss and abject terror that had come over her but could tell she wasn't succeeding.

'Could kill for one. Come on, we'll get ourselves a little bottled therapy.'

Amelie took Deira's arm and steered her back to the Mall and into the same bar that Adam had recently left. They perched on a couple of stools and had a brief chat with the barman, and it wasn't long before Deira found herself loosening up and even beginning to enjoy Amelie's company. They were laughing at a story Amelie had just recounted when there were raised voices a little way across the room and a big guy with a tattoo on his arm suddenly went berserk. He lashed out at one of his drinking companions, flattening his nose and causing him to reel back against the wall. The assaulted man put a hand to his face and stared in disbelief when it came away covered in blood. He looked stunned for a moment then gave a low growl and threw himself at his attacker, landing a nasty blow to the man's left kidney. Pandemonium ensued, and it took the barman, a security man and a couple of other drinkers to calm things down and eject the troublemaker. It was a while before things returned to normal. Unfortunately for Deira, the episode destroyed the mood and all her worries came flooding back.

Amelie saw the sudden change and tried to deflect the dark thoughts. 'So where does the name "Deira" come from?' she said. 'It's not one I've heard before.'

Deira winced. 'It's not one you're likely to hear again, either! My father's interested in English medieval history, particularly the fifth and sixth centuries. There were two Anglian kingdoms in northern England at that time, Deira and Bernicia, and he thought they'd make great names. And yes, before you ask I do have a younger sister – and her name's Bernicia.'

Amelie laughed. 'You don't sound very happy with it.'

'Actually, I don't mind it that much. I'd quite like to have a short form – my sister's called Bernie and at school I was always called…'

She was interrupted by a sharp nudge in the ribs from Amelie who'd been gazing idly round the bar and had noticed a tall, muscular man who seemed to be taking more than a passing interest in them. Deira finished her drink and tried to get the attention of the barman while she sneaked a quick look. He was certainly a big guy and had a kind of easy physicality that spoke of athletic ability. And Amelie was right – he was watching them.

The two women continued to chat while taking every opportunity to glance in the guy's direction. He, in turn, continued surreptitiously watching them, turning now and again to say a few words to the man sitting next to him. This mutual observation continued for a few more minutes before he gave up on the game. With one last glance in their direction, he downed the remainder of his drink, bade goodbye to his drinking buddy, and wandered off. The two girls were left slightly baffled by the incident and Amelie joked that it didn't do much for a girl's self-confidence when a guy took himself off like that without so much as an introduction. Deira was left feeling uneasy but not knowing why.

The evening wore on and the strange man was soon forgotten. Deira was very aware that she'd just recovered from a bad PHASE, so kept her alcohol intake down, changing to soft drinks after three tequilas. Amelie had considerably more, and was leaning heavily on Deira when they finally emerged from the bar some time later.

Deira stared round The Mall, fascinated by its collection of outlets and, as her gaze fell upon the hardware store just across from them, she saw him again – the tall man from the bar. When he saw her his face briefly lit up, as if in expectation, but this was rapidly replaced by a look of disappointment when he saw her supporting Amelie. He momentarily locked eyes with her then gave a resigned shrug and turned away down another corridor. Deira nudged Amelie.

'That was him again.'

'What? Who?'

'The guy from the bar. The one that kept looking at us. I think he might have waited here for us to come out.'

Amelie frowned. 'We do get some strange customers around here at times. How about we shack up together tonight just in case?'

There was no way Deira was worried about being attacked by a pervert. She almost wished he'd try it. However, the techie clearly felt uneasy and Deira wasn't going to leave her on her own and potentially exposed. They stumbled back to Deira's room and Deira made Amelie comfortable in bed. She fell asleep almost immediately and was soon snoring gently.

Deira made up a bed on the floor for herself but sleep just wouldn't come. She kept seeing Adam in his dishevelled state, swearing and about to take a swing at her. It was almost like he'd been possessed, like in the old horror movies. In fact the more she thought about it the more that seemed to describe the situation perfectly. She didn't believe in possession but she was Irish and came from a staunchly catholic family. There were many things she'd picked up as a child and later rejected, and most of them had found a permanent home in her subconscious. Even now she felt herself trying to rationalise the concept of possession. Surely it had to have come from somewhere – have some basis in reality that had been warped beyond recognition?

She shuddered and deliberately pushed such dark thoughts away, concentrating instead on the strange man in the bar. Amelie's comment about getting some strange characters about couldn't really have meant what she'd first assumed. All incomers to Mars were carefully screened for a criminal history or abnormal personality profile so the chance of finding any sort of major deviant was close to zero. That meant the strange man had to have taken an interest in her for some other reason. What could that be?

She lay, pondering the problem, and began to feel strange. She knew it wasn't the alcohol because she'd kept her intake well below her tolerance level, but it did feel a little like intoxication. First, there was a sensation of falling, then nausea, and then dissociation. Then it became really weird. Without conscious effort, her brain began to test answers to the question she'd just asked herself about the strange man. It switched from one line of reasoning to another so fast she couldn't keep up, reminding her of a supercomputer. Throughout all this she seemed to be observing from the side-lines – actually watching the workings of her own brain. It simply didn't seem possible and it brought back all her worries about being affected by the PHASE.

As quickly as they'd started, the super-brain computations stopped and she felt normal again. No residual symptoms. She was left with the primary solution regarding the man in the bar – 97.6% certain he was the unknown agent she was looking for. In retrospect it was so obvious and it was probably the reason she'd felt uneasy about him in the bar.

She activated her wrist console and accessed the security office files containing the details of everyone officially on Mars. Next, she tried to remember what the guy looked like – and made her next startling discovery. Her memory of faces had always been above average but in this case it was nothing less than remarkable. When she concentrated on the stranger she found it was almost like he was back in the room with her. She didn't think she'd taken that much notice of him, either in the bar or outside in the Mall, but her inner vision rendered him perfectly, down to the ridges and furrows on his face. Was this what an eidetic memory was like? And was it a one-off or permanent? She'd need to talk to Amelie the next day about these mental aberrations. That's if she was still in a fit state to talk.

She input all the characteristics she could "see" into an identikit application and, after a little tweaking, there was the man from the bar staring out of the screen. Excitedly, she used facial recognition software to cross-reference the picture with the records from the security files – and came up with nothing. Officially, this man didn't exist on Mars. He had to be the one she was looking for.

She silently cursed. She'd been so close to completing part of the mission and she hadn't been sharp enough. But if the man was the unknown agent, why had he been interested in her? Did he know who and what she was? If so, how had he got to find out so soon after her arrival on Mars – she hadn't exactly advertised her presence until earlier in the evening when she'd used her staff. If he did know who she was, why did he seem so comfortable in her presence? She would have expected him to avoid her at all costs. The questions went on and on and her brain just refused to give it up and get some rest even though, on this occasion, there were too few facts to be able to reach a logical conclusion.

When it had first happened, Deira had been intrigued by her new super-charged brain, but this continuous circular thinking was exhausting and not a little scary. She was stuck in a never-ending cycle, wanting to make it stop and not knowing how. To make matters worse, her head had begun to throb again, like it had after the PHASE.

Half-an-hour later it was still going strong and she was desperate for some relief. She tried various distractions but nothing seemed to deflect her brain from its endless cycling. Round and round it went, following the same circuitous route and getting precisely nowhere. She was about to put in an emergency call to the medics when, as she later described it, it was as if an off switch had been pushed. She just had time to fall into bed on the floor – then the computations stopped and she fell into a deep, dreamless sleep.

Chapter 6

It was a subdued team that gathered in the "work room" on the Q-ship the day after it departed Mars. When he'd found they were going to be in space for two weeks, Chayka had insisted on having a room on board for regular group briefings and ad hoc link-ups. He hadn't felt that the use of personal cabins for this purpose was appropriate and, somewhat reluctantly, the bureaucrats had agreed.

The work room wasn't attractive. It was a simple four metre square space with a narrow workbench down the left side and a large plastic table and six matching chairs towards the far right corner. For Chayka's purposes it was more than adequate and that morning he sat at the head of the table ready to chair the morning briefing. He found it interesting that, although they had only had three such briefings since boarding the ship, the others had already adopted their own regular positions round the table. He gave a thin smile as the recognised the inherent territoriality in this – something that was deeply embedded in the genome.

On that particular morning one small piece of territory, the chair usually occupied by Philippe Fournier, went conspicuously unclaimed.

Chayka began in his usual way, going round the table for updates, insights, etc. There was no enthusiasm and talk drifted aimlessly back to the results of the inquiry following the explosion. Chayka was fascinated watching the team dynamics. Nobody mentioned Phillipe Fournier

– by unconscious agreement the subject seemed to be off limits. It was Nicolau Dominguez who broke ranks first.

'For God's sake! Can we just move on? This is all old stuff. Okay, like everyone, I'm sorry for Philippe's death but let's face it, if he was that unstable it was going to happen sooner or later anyway. Better sooner – before the team's bonded too closely.'

Tirzah erupted with fury. 'Who says we haven't bonded you miserable, thoughtless, excuse for a man? Philippe was a brilliant colleague and a lovely man and I, for one, will miss him dreadfully. Bastard!'

Nicolau turned almost puce and leaped to his feet but Chayka placed a hand on his shoulder and eased him back into his seat.

'Steady, Dr. Dominguez.'

'I'm perfectly steady, thank you, but this *woman...*' he almost spat the last word out.

'I understand, but you need to calm down. Dr Blumstein, shouting insults isn't going to improve our situation.'

'But he said...' Tirzah began.

'I recognise the provocation.' Chayka acknowledged, keeping a firm grip on Nicolau's shoulder. 'However, arguing among ourselves won't bring Dr Fournier back and will be extremely destructive to our ambitions as a team.'

He gazed round the table and felt himself adrift on a sea of emotions. Walther was as upset as Tirzah and was clearly struggling to keep his tears at bay. Simon was un-characteristically silent. Tirzah and Nicolau sat and glared at each other. Chayka was way outside his comfort zone and knew it. He cast his mind back to similar situations and how others, better trained than he, had handled them.

'The psychologists would say we're suffering from a delayed grief response,' he said. 'We're all grieving for Dr Fournier, but we're bottling up our grief – keeping our thoughts and feelings to ourselves. It's inevitable that such repression will lead to what we've just witnessed – disagreement and rancour. We need to express ourselves more openly.' He inwardly grimaced to think he'd actually vocalised such psychobabble but managed to keep his face impassive. 'Would anyone like to say something to get us started?'

'I can't believe you just said that shit,' Nicolau said, looking first contemptuous then disgusted. He folded his arms and turned sullenly away, determined not to take part in this exercise.

When nobody volunteered anything, Chayka opted to go round the table. Simon was first, and Chayka initially thought he was going to react like Nicolau. He looked discomfited and was reluctant to engage. However, following a meaningful glare from Tirzah, he made a token effort. All the words were right but they sounded flat and insincere. In truth, he couldn't get emotionally exercised by Phillipe's death even though he knew it would have repercussions on the team's ability to perform. Tirzah was next round the table and, through a torrent of tears, was gushing in her praise for Philippe, talking at length about his many accomplishments even though she'd only known him for a few days. Finally, it was Walther's turn. Like Tirzah, the big man was now openly weeping and, unlikely though it was with his limited English, he produced a remarkably eloquent eulogy.

Chayka studied the responses of his team members with interest. On a purely theoretical level it was fascinating. He'd anticipated an emotional reaction, and Walther and

Tirzah had responded exactly as he'd expected, appearing to find the exercise cathartic. However, he was surprised at the reactions of Nicolau and Simon. Not only did they appear not to care about Fournier's death, they seemed frankly hostile about him. Was there something here he'd failed to pick up on? He waited a few more minutes for Tirzah to dry her eyes then called the meeting back to order.

'Perhaps we can now discuss Dr Fournier's work.' he said. 'On the morning before his death, he approached me while I was having breakfast. He said he wanted to discuss something he'd been working on that was giving him cause for concern. Unfortunately, and to my great regret, I declined to enter into a conversation with him at that time. Do any of you know what might have affected him so much that he was prepared to take his own life? Did he talk about what he was doing? I'm assuming his wrist console has been impounded on Mars and I've no idea whether we'll get access to it later or not.'

'I know exactly what he was up to,' Tirzah said, still sniffling. 'Philippe thought you wanted to continue with the mass PHASEing project, Professor.' Tears welled up again, and she gulped and dabbed at her face. 'He and I were pretty good friends before he started this work...' Simon snorted and Tirzah glowered at him. '... but he soon became obsessed with it. He didn't think I knew what he was up to, but I did. He was running DNA screens to provide baselines for any future practical trials.'

This was badly received round the table. Not only was this a clear breach of professional etiquette, it was also illegal. An individual's DNA was his or her property, and consent was required for samples to be taken. Nicolau was particularly offended, saying he had many times had to refuse requests from colleagues for samples of his DNA for research purposes and he objected to such samples being acquired surreptitiously. Walther supported this stance, while Simon looked uncomfortable but remained silent. Chayka was horrified that this was out in the open. Dr Blumstein had obviously found out during one of her liaisons with Fournier, but what about the others? It would be a disaster if he were implicated.

'I don't know where Dr Fournier got the idea I required DNA samples,' Chayka lied. 'The results of his analysis will obviously have to be destroyed.'

This appeared to satisfy Nicolau and Walther but Simon looked flushed and angry.

'You're not going to continue the work on mass PHASEing?' he said. 'I got the impression you were planning to carry on, regardless of what the Bureau said. Of course, we should definitely wipe the DNA data if you've changed you mind but if you still mean to continue with the research we'll need that data sometime so destroying it makes no sense.'

'It's a point of principle Dr Chandler,' Chayka said, trying to distance himself from the whole affair. 'Unlawfully-obtained DNA cannot be used for research purposes. I'll continue the theoretical work in my own time. If I'm successful, each individual will be free to decide whether or not to participate in the subsequent trials. Does this sound reasonable?'

Everyone nodded, though Simon continued to radiate hostility.

'Good!' Chayka was relieved to have successfully navigated this little crisis. 'Now, while this has been very interesting, I find it hard to believe Dr Fournier would have taken his own life simply because he was illegally obtaining DNA. Does anyone know anything else that might have affected him?'

Nobody did. Even Tirzah doubted this would have been sufficient in itself. She remembered Phillipe's response when she'd accused him of stealing DNA. He was surprised and upset that she'd found out but there was something else – something he didn't feel able to share with her. She stared at Chayka, a thoughtful expression on her face.

'If there's nothing more to say,' Chayka said, 'I think I'll call a halt to this meeting. Emotions are running high this morning and it might be better to wait another twenty-four hours before we begin serious discussions once more.'

He stood and left the room, keen to reach the relative calm of his cabin. Tirzah pointedly ignored Dominguez and leaned over to Simon.

'What the hell was that all about? You were positively hostile.'

'The Prof's playing a game,' he said, face colouring and voice rising. 'I know he had no intention of being deflected from his mass PHASEing project and I suspect he and Philippe were working on it together.'

'I'm sure you're right. I know for a fact the Prof instigated the whole DNA thing. He seemed pretty uncomfortable during the meeting, didn't he?'

'Damned right he did. But did you know Phillipe had a complete set of equations for mass PHASEing? He showed them to me just before we got to Mars – rubbed my face in them, actually.'

'What?' Tirzah was staggered. 'I'd no idea. Where could he have got them?'

'Well he couldn't have compiled them himself so he must have got them from the Prof. But why wasn't I involved?'

Tirzah shrugged. She was as baffled as Simon.

Simon puffed himself up. 'I think our esteemed leader isn't so fucking esteemed!' he shouted.

The other three were stunned by this outburst. Walter got up to leave and Nicolau followed, looking back over his shoulder with distaste.

'You two needn't look so offended, either,' Simon shouted at their retreating backs. 'Nicolau, I'm sure you know exactly what happened to that goddamned experiment that got us sent out here – you're the experimental wizard, after all. Walther, you must have discussed the problem with your predecessor when you had your pre-mission briefing yet you never mentioned anything. And Tirzah, you were pretty damn close to Philippe, both professionally and socially. You admit you knew about the DNA samples he was taking but you didn't tell anybody. Can it really be that you don't know anything else? Perhaps a little pillow-talk on Mars the night he died? Yes, I saw him going into your room.'

He paused for breath, red-faced and panting, then stormed from the room. Tirzah was appalled and ran after him. Walther and Nicolau looked stunned, staring after the mathematician in disbelief. It was Nicolau who broke the silence.

'So, fellow conspirator Walther, shall we adjourn to my cabin and continue our plotting?'

It took Walther a moment to appreciate the nuances of this but when he realised Nicolau wasn't being serious he smiled.

'Why don't you come to mine, Nicolau – I've a very old bottle of Cognac that I've been meaning to open when the time was right. This isn't exactly what I had in mind but I think it's as good a time as any to enjoy it.'

'Truly an invitation too good to turn down – even if it's far too early in the day for such an indulgence. Lead on my friend and let us sample your wares.'

The two unlikely friends made their way to Walther's room. Meanwhile Tirzah caught up with Simon as he was about to enter his cabin.

'That was totally unfair!' she said, coming up behind him. 'Whether or not I slept with Philippe is none of your damned business. You were completely out of order back there. What's wrong with you?'

'Nothing that a decent night out on Earth wouldn't put right.' He spun round and glared at her. 'It was brought home to me the other night on Mars that we're going to be stuck in a succession of tin cans and habitat domes for the next six months. No fresh air, nowhere to go. Then there was you and Philippe on Mars – you did sort of flaunt it.'

'I did nothing of the sort! I admit I'd had a few drinks and was a bit flirty but it was two-thirty in the morning, for God's sake! I had no idea you were wandering round, so how could I flaunt it? I thought you were fitted up for the night. If I'd known you weren't I might well have come knocking on your door. As to being stuck in a "tin can", I thought you were okay with that. You knew what to expect, and the psych tests obviously suggested you'd be fine.'

'Actually, they were equivocal.'

'What the hell does that mean?'

'It means exactly that. The tests were set with a pass mark – and I hit it. Not above it and not below it – right on the button! They couldn't decide what to do with me. They could hardly say I'd failed, but my score wasn't exactly a glowing testimonial. Eventually, they gave me a choice and I, like the fool I am, chose to go to Titan because I knew that if Chayka was there that's where the action would be. Now, I'm beginning to wish I hadn't.

'This team is done for, Tirzah. We've lost Philippe and, whatever I might have felt about him on a personal level, he was pretty essential to the project. Then there's the professor – what's he up to? The problem is, everything here's so – in your face. There's no getting away from it.'

Tirzah suddenly understood – Simon was feeling claustrophobic. But if he'd managed to slip through the psych screening tests perhaps Philippe had too. She took Simon's hand and gently encouraged him into his room. Once inside, with the door firmly locked, she took his other hand, looked up at him and gave him her most radiant smile.

'I understand what you're feeling,' she lied. 'I feel the same to an extent – and I do like you, Simon. If I'd known you were free on Mars I'd have definitely come to your room.'

He looked hungrily at her.

She gently stroked his face then placed one hand behind his neck and pulled his head down towards her. She kissed him full on the lips and he responded urgently, his mouth and tongue joining hers. His left hand snaked behind her, pulling her pelvis to his, and his right hand squeezed her left breast. She gave a little moan and they staggered together to the bed in the corner, undressing each other on the way.

Tirzah smiled to herself as they finally fell naked into bed. She didn't care whether her partners were male or female as long as she fancied them – and Simon was very fanciable! Now that Philippe was gone he'd provide many hours of physical release from the interminable sub-quantal science that would otherwise occupy every waking moment.

Unlike Simon, Tirzah had passed her psych tests with flying colours – and it showed.

Over in Walther Altmeyer's cabin, Walther opened the promised bottle of Cognac and poured two generous glasses. He handed one to Nicolau, who rolled the spirit appreciatively round the glass and looked thoughtful.

'What do you make of Simon's accusations?' Nicolau said.

Walther took a long pull of the brandy and let it wash round his mouth before swallowing and giving a satisfied sigh. He was very distant and appeared reluctant to enter into this discussion.

'I only know what was disclosed at the hearing. What about you?'

'The same.' Nicolau put down his Cognac and began to wander round the cabin. 'Simon's been a good colleague for some years now and I don't understand why he's suddenly so belligerent. I suppose he's upset by Phillipe's death – we all are – but I don't see that as an adequate excuse for his outburst.'

He watched Walther take another long swig of brandy and continued round the room, picking up an award that Walther had been given at CERN and examining it with interest. He carefully placed it back where it belonged and his gaze passed over Walther's bed. He squinted as his sharp eyes saw something, then he pushed his hand down the side of the bed and pulled out a small object. It was a pad, a very old type of hand-held computer, somewhat battered but probably still usable. He held it out to Walther.

'You'll have missed this before long, Walther – I'm glad I spotted it. I haven't seen one of these little things for many years. It must almost be an antique.'

Walther put his Cognac down and took the proffered pad, turning it over in his hands and frowning. He turned it on, trying to find an owner's name, but the thing was password-protected and he couldn't get past the login screen.

'This isn't mine and I've no idea where it came from.' He handed it back to Nicolau. 'Can you get into it?'

Nicolau gave it a go, but he couldn't get past the password-protection page either. Walther took it back and put it on his bedside locker.

'I have no patience with this,' he said, picking up his glass again. 'I'll hand it to the ship's authorities later and see if they can identify its owner. Now, I suggest we forget antiques, forget Simon Chandler, forget Phillipe Fournier, and simply enjoy our drinks.'

The two men spent the next couple of hours chatting amiably. When Nicolau finally took his leave, his intention was to return to his cabin to do some work, but he changed his mind as he was about to let himself in and continued along the corridor to the next cabin but one. Smiling in anticipation of the reaction to what he was about to propose, he rang the bell.

Simon Chandler opened the door. Tirzah had left only a few minutes before and he was in the process of making himself presentable again. He was feeling more relaxed than he had for days and the last thing he wanted at this precise time was a further confrontation with Nicolau. Surprisingly, however, the dwarf was smiling.

'Simon,' he said, 'we need to clear the air between us. I think both of us said things we didn't mean at the briefing – I certainly did – and I'd like us to be good colleagues again. Can I come in?'

Although he was pleasantly surprised, Simon really wasn't interested in having this conversation at this particular time. However, he was enough of a realist to recognise that their strained relationship needed sorting out if they were to work effectively again – and it was, after all, Nicolau holding out the olive branch. He sighed and, reluctantly, invited him in.

Following the traumatic briefing, Chayka hurried straight back to his cabin to immerse himself in work – to escape from the rampant emotions that had been let loose. He usually found it easy to slip into the relaxed mind-set that allowed him to visualise the sub-quantal world but today he found himself distracted. His team was in disarray and, despite his half-heated attempt at group psychology, he knew he didn't have the skills to heal the rifts. He made himself a strong black coffee and sipped at the bitter liquid, pondering the events that had led to this moment.

The ability to transmit solid objects as beams of coherent, information-rich, photons had been around for some years but was limited to non-living items only. Attempts to apply the technique to experimental animals had, without exception, failed – the test animal turning up dead or mindless when re-materialised. It was only with the advent of Chayka's discoveries in sub-quantal physics that the reason for this became less opaque. Consciousness appeared to operate at the sub-quantal level and to successfully transmit a living organism required analysis and encoding at this level. Even then, only the occasional individual was able to withstand the process with little or no physical or psychological damage, and it was soon discovered that this ability was linked to a particular genetic mutation – the gamma mutation.

Predictably, the Bureau recognised the opportunity this presented. A person with such a mutation, if physically and mentally fit and properly trained, would make a perfect agent – able to be "transmitted" to a trouble spot within minutes. Because the number of individuals with the anomalous mutation was small, the number suitable for training as an agent was tiny. Agents were, therefore, members of an elite group.

Chayka had no problem with elite groups as long as he was included – and in this case he wasn't. Consequently, he'd made it a goal for his team to find a method of overcoming the restriction on photonic transfer to make it available to everyone – the mass PHASEing project. They'd been making steady progress when Dr Chandler had made an entirely separate discovery – nothing less than a sub-quantal method for the generation of life itself. The mathematics were persuasive and the team had diverted from the photonic transmission project and set up a chamber with a primordial hydrocarbon atmosphere in which to test the hypothesis.

All went well with the first few experiments and they finally reached the critical testing phase – the application of a sub-quantal pulse. It was during this test that the explosion had occurred – the explosion that had changed Chayka's life. The subsequent inquiry had supported the Bureau Director, agreeing with him that the responsibility for the research should be transferred from the university to the Bureau. The work would then be relocated to Titan – and would become classified.

Chayka had been appalled. Relocation to Titan hadn't concerned him – one place of work was similar to another as far as he was concerned. But being *classified* – that meant he wouldn't be able to publish, and *that* meant he wouldn't receive the continuing attention from the scientific community he'd begun to think of as his right. His work on mass photonic transmission would also have to stop because the Bureau refused to authorise it.

Initially he'd opposed the suggestion of moving to Titan, but it soon became clear that the Director was going to have his way. He had no option but to acquiesce. To make matters worse, the team he'd built up at Cambridge had to be split up because a number of the team members failed their psychological tests. He'd been forced to recruit from a number of pre-tested individuals, resulting in Walther, Tirzah and Philippe joining the team. Perhaps the project had been doomed from the start. It had certainly not begun well.

He drained the remainder of the coffee and felt himself relaxing. He had to get back to work – and he might yet be able to salvage something from this ongoing disaster.

Chapter 7

DESPITE HER HYPERACTIVE brain the previous night and a mere four hours sleep on the floor, Deira woke the next day feeling good. Better, in fact, than she'd felt for a long time. Amelie had already gone so she showered, dressed, and had a quick breakfast before contemplating the day ahead. Lots of things to do – but first there was the issue of Adam. She really didn't want to confront him again in his current state and it was easy to justify staying away because it was unlikely she'd be able to do any good. But this was Adam. She knew she'd never be able to live with herself if she left him languishing alone in his cell when there was an outside chance she could help. Determinedly, she set off for Security.

She could tell Adam was no better as she got closer to the security office because his shouts and curses echoed down the corridor and were almost audible on The Mall. Her determination wavered and she paused uncertainly. There were more shouts and some particularly unpleasant screams and she winced and turned to leave. She just couldn't do it. She asked herself what Adam would do if their positions were reversed, and she knew damned well what the answer was. He'd stick with her through anything. Reluctantly, she turned back and continued towards the terrible noise.

She checked in with the guy at the front desk and flashed her ID. He was one of the two security men who'd helped carry Adam from the Mall the previous day and he waved her through immediately.

'We all know who you are, Agent MacMahon. Go straight on down. I guess you can tell he's no better?'

'Yes. Thanks.'

The noises from the cell block were almost deafening now, prompting a strong desire to cut and run. However, a combination of guilt and pride kept her walking mechanically down the stairs and she was soon being greeted by the two guards who'd been posted to keep an eye on Adam. They looked understandably exhausted. The older of the two pointed at Adam in his cell.

'He's been like that all night – ever since he came round. Any chance you can do anything?'

'I doubt it but I'll do my best.'

Deira knew there was very little chance of her being able to accomplish anything – from what she'd seen of Adam in The Mall yesterday he was too far gone. However, the whole point of her being here was to make the attempt. She cautiously approached his cell, preparing herself for whatever verbal onslaught might be forthcoming. It didn't come. In fact, as she got closer to him his ravings quietened.

She glanced back at the security men and saw they'd noticed it too – he was definitely calming down. By the time she reached the bars of his cell he was completely silent. It was the first time he'd been quiet since he'd woken up in the security cell and it should have been encouraging. In fact, it was unnerving. His face had become motionless, almost mask-like, and his unblinking eyes, completely devoid of emotion, appeared to be focused on a point somewhere in the near distance. She smiled uncertainly.

'Hello, Adam. How are you feeling?'

She cringed as she realised how inept this sounded. She'd have to up her game considerably if she were to stand a chance of getting through to him. Adam continued to look straight through her, his soul-less gaze and unexpected silence almost as disturbing as his previous ranting. He'd been drooling, leaving a white residue running from the corners of his mouth down his chin, and it was obvious he'd soiled his trousers. Deira stared at him with horror. She pictured Adam as she'd known him, the laughing ever-so-proper friend and colleague. She simply couldn't square that image with the human wreck standing less than a metre in front of her. She turned away, thinking there was no way she could go on with this – then shivered as she felt a sudden chill.

The chill passed quickly enough but was followed by an intense wave of vertigo and nausea. Her vision clouded, and she was reminded of the previous evening when her brain had become hyperactive. So what the hell was happening now? She stumbled, and would have fallen if one of the guards hadn't caught her. The other guard brought a chair and sat her down.

Adam remained motionless, no suggestion of a lucid personality within his mannequin-like exterior. He was like an empty slate. Then his eyes flickered and, for a brief moment, Deira was convinced she saw something of the old Adam. He was gone again soon enough but it was enough to give her renewed hope.

'I know you're still there, Adam. I can see it. Please talk to me. I'm lost without you. Tell me what I should do.'

At last the eyes moved. They remained blank and uncomprehending but the movement itself, though slow, was purposeful – and it was in her direction. She gazed into those bleak wells of despair, searching for the Adam she knew so well and willing him to come back to her – demanding he come back to her.

She felt herself changing, dissociating, the guards and prison cell fading to a shadowy pseudo-reality that existed at the periphery of her vision in shades of grey. Meanwhile, Adam stood in a halo of light amidst darkness so profound it was almost palpable. He had become the centre of her world – the focus of her being. As she continued to concentrate on him some muscle tone returned to his doll's-head face and a small frown creased his forehead. His mouth opened and closed. It was aimless, like a fish out of water, but it was something nevertheless. Deira held her breath, sensing his internal struggle and watching as his lips began to form definite shapes. Finally, he managed a single word.

'Deira.'

'What?' Deira released her breath in a gasp, hardly believing what she'd heard. He recognised her! 'Yes Adam. Yes, I'm here. What...'

She stopped when she saw he was trying to say something else.

'Deira...they're everywhere...everywhere...I...fucking bitch whore.' The expletives came out in a rasping growl.

'No Adam, don't let it take you again. Come back to me. You can do this.'

The darkness round Adam lightened slightly and Deira willed him on. She was more confident now, realising that her own mental changes had somehow punched a comm line through to wherever Adam was languishing in the labyrinthine caves of his own mind. Perhaps she could lead him back from wherever he'd become lost.

Adam shook himself like a wet dog trying to dry off and his face contorted in anguish as he wrestled with his internal demons.

'Deira… complete mission… you can do it… find out… what's going on. Can't fight them. They're everywhere. I…'

That was all he could manage. His face contorted with rage again and the curses began once more.

It was as if a spell had been broken. One instant Deira was concentrating furiously in her pseudo-reality and the next she was plunged back to the here-and-now. She slumped like a rag doll, briefly exhausted, and would have slipped out of the chair if the security men hadn't grabbed her and held her in place. She sat limply, breathing slowly and laboriously, but recovery came swiftly and within a couple of minutes her strength had returned. The security men stared at her in amazement – they'd witnessed Adam's response and heard his few lucid words.

Deira was overcome with a mixture of elation and anxiety: elation that Adam was still there – wherever "there" was – bringing hope that he might recover; anxiety that her own mental changes hadn't yet run their course and could be leading her to a similar fate to Adam. The brain thing, whatever it was, was changing – mutating – and the question was what would it change to next?

Now that it was over and the beast had returned to abuse Adam's body once more, she was keen to get out of the place. She thanked the security guards and hurried up the stairs and out of the building, breathing a sigh of guilty relief when she could no longer hear the animal sounds and swearing coming from the cell block. She badly wanted a drink but knew that alcohol would only dull her brain and she needed to be able to concentrate. Instead, she returned to her room for a strong coffee – and it wasn't until she was halfway through the bitter drink that she was fully able to move on.

What to do now? Adam had said something about "them" being everywhere. She shuddered. The dark thoughts of the previous night came back to her as well as memories of stories her mother used to tell her and of horror tri-vids she'd seen as a teenager. It was crazy. This was reality and such things didn't exist except as part of Adam's tortured subconscious. Did they? She moved swiftly on. Dwelling on this wouldn't help. She was already worried enough about the changes she was experiencing without factoring in invisible demons as well. She should stick with what she knew and stop indulging in childish fantasies.

Her normal pragmatism quickly began to reassert itself. In his moment of lucidity Adam had told her to complete the mission, and the mere fact he thought she was up to it was enough for a new-found confidence to bubble up from somewhere deep within herself. She could do this – but first she'd have to get herself back on active duty again. She placed a call to Amelie.

'All the results are back and you're good to go.' Amelie said, consulting her notes. 'There are a couple of interesting findings.'

'Interesting good, or interesting bad?'

'Too early to say but – hey – you're still you. First, you've lost a significant amount of non-coding DNA; second, there are quite major changes on your most recent brain scan. We think the two are linked.'

Deira knew damned well there were changes going on in her head – she just wasn't sure whether this new information was positive or not. She mentally reviewed what she knew about non-coding DNA. There had been huge strides recently in understanding the function of the 98% or so of the human genome that had no obvious functional significance – so-called "junk DNA". However, to her knowledge there was still a sizeable portion whose function could not be accounted for.

'So what does that mean?' she said. 'Where's this non-coding stuff gone?'

'It's possible there's been an exchange – non-coding DNA has become coding DNA – and the new coding DNA's responsible for the changes in your brain scan. Have you noticed anything different?'

'Have I? My brain's doing all sorts of weird things.'

Deira described her memory improvement and the way her brain had seemed to go into overdrive before finally shutting down. Then she talked about the episode with Adam.

'It's all a bit scary, if I'm honest. I'm worried I'll turn out like Adam one of these days.'

'Don't forget Adam was changed from the minute he came out of the PHASE chamber. Your changes are happening more slowly and seem to be completely different. I don't think you should be too concerned.'

'Easy for you to say – it's not your brain!'

Amelie laughed but looked uncomfortable.

'What's up?' said Deira. 'I can see there's something.'

'About Adam.'

'What about him?'

'The medics are transferring him to the infirmary. He'll be sedated so we can get some tests done – the physical ones, in any case – and then we might have a better idea of what's happened to him. Unfortunately, I don't think he's going to be of much help to you anytime soon.'

Deira had already come to terms with this, unpalatable though it may be. After the episode in security she had renewed hopes that Adam might recover. However, she knew this wasn't going to be a quick process and had resolved to do what he wanted and continue the mission on her own. It would be hard but there was no alternative – and at least she had Amelie's support.

'I've already reached that conclusion. Adam wants me to complete the mission on my own and that's what I intend to do – starting right now.'

They had a brief chat then Deira closed the connection and sat thinking. Most of the sightings of the unknown agent, including her own, had been in the bar, so it made sense to hang out there again in the hope he'd re-appear. She resolved to return there later in the day and, until then, would familiarise herself with the Fournier file.

Security Chief Hector Monroe wasn't happy. That damned noise! His entire staff were exhausted by it, their nerves frayed beyond endurance, and he'd already had a couple of call-ins claiming sickness. Something was going to have to change soon. This was simply intolerable.

'Obviously no better,' he said, gazing at Adam as he raged in his cell. The detail sergeant shook his head.

'We thought there'd been a breakthrough a few minutes ago. That Bureau agent's been to see him and things got a bit weird for a while.'

'Weird? In what way?'

'Well, the prisoner shut up, for one thing. He seemed

to be watching Agent MacMahon as she went over to him – and then he actually spoke.'

'What – lucidly?'

'Only briefly, but yes. Then he went back to his usual shouting again. There was something strange about the agent too. She seemed to go into a kind of trance or something – wasn't with us, if you know what I mean.'

Monroe was suddenly interested. The agent in the cell had been badly damaged by his recent PHASE from the moon. Now the other agent was doing strange things. Was she heading the same way as her colleague?

'Did you notice anything else or was it just this trance thing?'

'It was mainly the trance. She did shiver at one point – and she almost collapsed when it was all over – but she recovered very quickly. She seemed fine when she left.'

'Hmmm.' Monroe's ruddy face creased in a frown and he stroked his bald head absently. He'd have to give some thought to this but the priority was to get the agent in the cell some medical treatment. 'Okay. Contact the infirmary and get the medics to transfer the prisoner to the infirmary. He's their problem, not mine, and I'll be damned if I'll have my operation blighted by this thing.'

Without waiting for the sergeant to reply, he turned and strode swiftly up the stairs and back to his office. He could still hear the noise from the cells even with the door closed but at least it was muted. He sighed and sat at his desk. What the sergeant had said about MacMahon going into some sort of trance had him worried. First a scientist committed suicide, then an agent had a catastrophic accident. The last thing he needed was something happening to

MacMahon as well. He determined to keep an eye on her for a while – a simple tail would be sufficient. He'd also ask around a bit and see if anybody had noticed anything strange about her. If he remembered correctly, agents had tests done after a PHASE, so a visit to the PHASE technician would be a good place to start. He glanced at the time. Okay, he'd make a start with that a little later. Right now he had to do some admin that should have been finished days ago.

Sometime later there was a knock on Monroe's door and the young man from the front desk hurried in and came to attention.

'Sir, Agent MacMahon's at the front desk – wonders if you'd see her.'

Monroe looked up. So, Agent MacMahon was here. It was to be expected that she'd show up sometime and it was to her credit that it was earlier rather than later.

'Tell her I'll be out shortly.'

'Yes sir.'

Monroe sat thinking for a minute. Meeting MacMahon face-to-face would provide the perfect opportunity to assess her and decide for himself whether she had any obvious ongoing issues. Of course, it also worked the other way round – she'd almost certainly be assessing him too. He stood and smoothed out his uniform before walking smartly out to the front desk.

He wasn't exactly sure what he'd been expecting but Agent MacMahon wasn't it. For a start, she wasn't wearing her uniform. Monroe had met plenty of agents over the years and they'd always worn that black, skin-tight body armour and helmet that lent them an aura of confidence and authority. There was none of that here. Instead, there was simply an attractive young woman dressed in a dark-blue top and black slacks. She was probably about five-eight tall, six inches shorter than his own six-two. Her hair was red-brown and cut short above the ears and Monroe guessed that was probably deliberate – easier to cope with when she wore her helmet. Her most striking attributes were undoubtedly her eyes. They were the most intense emerald green Monroe had ever seen and he had to force himself not to stare. He extended an arm and shook her hand.

'Security Chief Monroe. How can I be of help, Agent?'

She flinched slightly at his handshake and he wondered briefly if he'd overdone the firm grip. He didn't think so. She was much more reticent than he'd imagined and when she spoke her voice wavered a little.

'Good Morning Chief. I'm Deira MacMahon. Thanks for seeing me. The Bureau's asked me to review the events round Dr Fournier's apparent suicide. Do you have anywhere we can talk in private? I'll try not to take up too much of your time.'

Monroe raised an eyebrow and beckoned her to follow him. The fact she'd said "apparent suicide" wasn't lost on him and he wondered where this was heading. The girl certainly came across as pleasant enough – not as overbearing as many of her agent colleagues – and he relaxed a little as he led her back to his office. They sat – him upright and proper behind his desk and her perched nervously on the edge of the seat across from him. He gazed expectantly at her, but she seemed to be having some trouble getting started, as if her confidence had deserted her. She gave him the impression of a schoolgirl up before the headmaster. Not at all what he was expecting. Finally, she got her act together.

'I thought I ought to introduce myself,' she said. 'I'm well aware I'm working on your turf and I don't want to cause any upset.'

'Well thanks for that. It's good to meet you too, Agent.'

Monroe saw a brief look of dismay pass over her face and silently castigated himself for not being more welcoming. It was simply the way he was with people he didn't know, and he was well aware that his lowland Scottish accent didn't help – making him sound brusque even though it wasn't intended. The lass appeared to be having some problems – not surprising given what had happened to her partner – and he definitely wasn't helping. Nevertheless, she wasn't functioning as he would have expected.

'I understand you have Dr Fournier's wrist console,' she said. 'I suspect something on it might have been missed – a ghost file or something – and I wondered if I might take a look at it. Would that be alright?'

There it was again – that undue deference that was entirely out of character for an agent. Was it simply a reaction to the loss of her partner or something more? Monroe suddenly decided he didn't care – he'd take her as she was and be grateful she wasn't some bumptious Bureau upstart. He smiled.

'Agent, you're entitled to anything you want – but thanks for asking. The wrist console's in our evidence room so I can get it for you now, if you like.' He paused. 'You've got doubts about the verdict?'

'Yeah, a few, but they don't amount to anything at the moment. If I could look at that wrist console it might help.'

'No problem. Follow me.'

Monroe led her to the basement where a reinforced steel door sat alone in the middle of a wall. He input the security code and the huge door swung open revealing heavily-laden shelves that completely covered the walls. The shelves held items collected from cases over many years, all carefully stacked and coded, and Monroe didn't hesitate. He went directly to the far end of a shelf and lifted down a wrist console.

'Do you want to examine it here or take it out?'

He watched her with interest. She seemed surprised at that, as if she hadn't given any thought to actually being able to take the wrist console away.

'It'd be great if I could take it out. I shouldn't need it long and I'll keep it in the safe in my room when I'm not using it.'

'In that case, I just need you to sign for it.' He activated his wrist console and watched while she electronically signed for it. 'There you go then – all yours. Anything else I can be helping you with?' He closed the steel door again and they started back up the stairs.

'Not at the moment, thanks. You've been very kind. If I need anything else…'

'Feel free to ask. Now if that's all…'

'Oh. Sure. Thanks again Chief'

'You're very welcome.'

Monroe watched as she turned and left, feeling guilty that he hadn't been very forthcoming with her. It was just his way, but people often judged him badly for it. For her part, she'd come over as a pleasant lass who was, perhaps, slightly out of her depth. He was surprised she'd been given this assignment if she was normally so lacking in confidence. In fact, he thought she certainly wouldn't have been. He decided to continue watching her – and perhaps have a chat with the PHASE technician to see if she could throw some light on Agent MacMahon's behaviour.

By mid-afternoon Monroe had got the beginnings of a file on Agent MacMahon. Although he wasn't privy to her Bureau file, he'd managed to find out she'd only been out of the Academy for six months and the agent damaged by the PHASE was her supervisor. That, alone, would account for much of her apparent lack of confidence. He'd also discovered that she'd previously been employed by GCHQ and had experience in cryptology, which was presumably why she was so interested in Fournier's wrist console. So far, so ordinary.

His interview with the PHASE technician hadn't been very useful. She was a cheerful Irish girl but had refused point-blank to answer his questions about MacMahon's condition, saying that was privileged information. The senior medic he'd spoken to was no better, except the word he used was "confidential". Monroe hated those two words. How many investigations had foundered on evidence being retained because it was "privileged" or "confidential"? However, it hadn't all been negative. Sometimes, what wasn't said could be as instructive as what was. Neither technician nor medic had been prepared to confirm that there were no ongoing medical issues with the agent – indeed, their uneasy looks when he mentioned the episode in the cell block spoke volumes. Something was obviously not right. He just wasn't sure how important it was.

When he'd finished with the medic he'd had word that MacMahon had been to see Dr Barinson, the taciturn Swedish Pathologist who'd presided over the post-mortem. He arrived at the Doctor's office not long after she'd left to find him still very upset. As far as he could tell MacMahon had, in Barinson's eyes, impugned his professional reputation. She'd wanted to know how much experience he had in cases of death by hanging and had asked some pretty detailed questions about his findings at the post-mortem.

Barinson said he'd told her in no uncertain terms that he was very experienced with hangings and had even presided over one in the Skydome a few years previously. He'd thought that would be enough for her but, instead, she seemed surprised and wanted to question him further. He admitted he'd had enough by that time. He felt she'd been rude and objectionable and had ejected her from his office without further ado. Monroe smiled as he remembered Barinson's haughty arrogance and pseudo-hurt pride. He couldn't square the phrase "rude and objectionable" with the young woman he'd seen earlier – but they were certainly words he'd sometimes used when discussing Barinson. Interestingly, the Pathologist hadn't seen any obvious signs of aberrant behaviour. He said she was a typical agent.

Following his interview with Barinson, Monroe had returned to his office and found a message from the tail he'd placed on MacMahon. When she'd left Barinson, she'd visited the Skydome and climbed to the site of Fournier's death. Then she'd just sat there on top of the rock gazing at her wrist console and occasionally closing her eyes, as if deep in contemplation. It was quite some time later when she'd finally started back down the rock face, and whether from tiredness or inattention she missed a foothold and fell some distance to the ground. Her tail had initially been a little concerned and thought he might have to show himself and offer help. However, she hadn't appeared to be badly injured and had hurried back to her room. She hadn't been seen since.

So where did that leave him? Had he really learned anything? He was still concerned that there was something going on with her psychologically. She hadn't come over as very confident when she'd visited him earlier and his talks with the PHASE technician and the medics had reinforced the feeling of something being a little "off". On the other hand, her actual behaviour was completely rational and coincided with what he would have done in her shoes. She'd interviewed the doctor involved with the death and visited the scene of death. He was just a little concerned about what she might have been up to in her room for the past hour or two – although she might simply have been examining Fournier's wrist console.

At that moment, a call came through from the front desk. Agent MacMahon had left a message asking him to meet her at 16.00 at the site of Philippe Fournier's death. He checked the time -15.50 – and hurried out of his office towards the Skydome.

As he approached the scene of death he noticed a long ladder placed against the rock face and Agent MacMahon at the top, studying the ground apprehensively. He suddenly had a bad feeling about this and shouted up to her.

'What did you want to talk to me about, Agent?'

'Tell you soon – I'll be down in a minute.'

"I think it'd be better if you came down now.'

'I want to show you something first'.

'There's no need to. Come down and we'll discuss it.'

There was no response to this and Monroe suddenly noticed she'd set up a rope and noose similar to the one

Fournier had used. He immediately got a very bad feeling –
too late, the agent slipped the noose over her neck, stepped
off the ladder, and kicked it to the ground. She dangled in
the air scrabbling at the noose.

Monroe cursed under his breath and ran to the ladder.
He positioned the ladder against the rock face and began
climbing – fast. He reached Deira and yanked her feet back
onto the ladder, trying to determine how much damage
she'd done herself. Then he realised that she seemed fine.
She looked gratefully at him and gave a thin smile.

'Thanks Chief.'

'You stupid girl. What were you thinking?'

'I was thinking that I hoped you'd be quick with that
ladder.'

Chapter 8

DEIRA WAS PLEASED at the effectiveness of her little demonstration but could see that Monroe was struggling to maintain a professional demeanour. She knew she owed him an explanation.

'I'm sorry about that,' she said. 'I was pretty certain of my findings but not so certain that I thought I could convince you without a demonstration. You can see I haven't come to any permanent harm from "hanging myself" up there. Yes, it was uncomfortable, but I could probably have hung there all day and still been able to breathe – and so would Philippe Fournier.'

'But how?' Monroe had gone from angry to confused.

'Surprisingly simple really. The pressure on the windpipe needed to cause strangulation is well documented. Pressure is force per unit area and the force, during a hanging, is the victim's body weight. We're currently in the Skydome, so that force is significantly reduced because of the lower gravity. That point was brought home to me earlier today when I fell off this rock. I should have broken something but was just winded.'

'Yes, but hanging is still possible under Mars gravity,' Monroe objected. 'I know Barinson told you we had one a few years ago.'

Deira nodded. 'I agree, but don't forget the second part of the equation. Pressure is force *per unit area*. The area of contact of the rope on the windpipe is crucial in this environment – and that depends on the thickness of the rope. The thicker the rope, the greater the area of contact and the lower the pressure exerted. I looked back at the previous hanging in the Skydome and found that a metallic cable was used. It had a small diameter, therefore a small area of contact. Small area of contact equals high pressure. Very effective if you want to top yourself.'

'But in Fournier's case...' Monroe started to say.

'The rope was too thick. He might have been able to hang himself with it in Earth gravity, but not here in the Skydome.'

She looked at him triumphantly.

'Philippe Fournier didn't commit suicide. He was murdered.'

Deira watched Monroe as he assimilated the new evidence. She thought he looked faintly amused but wasn't expecting him to suddenly burst out laughing.

'It's priceless,' he said, his eyes twinkling. 'I'd love to see the look on Barinson's face when he finds out!'

Deira gave an unsure smile. 'So you're not mad at me?'

'Mad at you? Of course I'm mad at you. You worried the hell out of me up there. But you've given us our first murder for twenty years. Twenty years! Can you imagine how exciting that is when you normally spend your life hauling in drunks and rescuing the odd cat?' His enthusiasm suddenly died and he ran his hand over his head in a gesture Deira would get used to over the next few days. 'A bloody murder – and I've let most of the suspects go! I'll never live it down.'

Deira tried to cheer him up again. 'I'm sure we'll do okay. For a start, the evidence still points to the rope being the murder weapon. But strangling Fournier with something that thick and then hauling the body up that rock face wouldn't be easy. Seems to me we're looking for somebody big and strong.'

'I agree, and I think we've already got two people who fit that description.' Monroe was consulting his wrist console. 'Dr Chandler's a keen sportsman with a pretty impressive physique and Dr Altmeyer was actually a champion body-builder some years back.' He suddenly looked serious. 'What about you Agent? Are you alright?'

Deira was taken by surprise at the abruptness of the question. What was he getting at?

'I'm fine thanks. I'll admit that I wasn't quite myself when we met earlier but as of now – yeah, I'm good. Why do you ask?'

'There was a little episode in the cell block this morning. You couldn't shed some light on that could you?'

So that was it. The guards had obviously told him about her fugue and the brief lucidity it had brought about in Adam. Now he was fishing – trying to discover whether she'd suffered from the PHASE too. She couldn't actually blame him.

'You're asking whether I've noticed any changes in myself after the PHASE?'

'I suppose I am. You've got to admit, that trance you went into isn't normal.'

Deira nodded. 'You're right, and I'd be thinking the same thing in your shoes. Yes, I have had a few strange episodes following the PHASE but, if anything, they seem to be enhancements.'

She went on to describe the super-brain episode and the fugue in the cell block. She also mentioned the development of an eidetic memory and Monroe, for once, looked impressed.

'What I wouldn't give for that,' he muttered. 'My memory seems to get worse every year.' He leaned back in his chair and smiled. 'Thanks for being so honest. So – what are your plans now, what with your comrade in the infirmary and all?'

Deira knew exactly what she was going to do next. 'I thought I'd visit the bar again this evening. The unknown agent seems to turn up there quite regularly and...'

'Unknown agent? You got something else you'd like to tell me?'

Deira suddenly realised she hadn't told Monroe about the second part of her mission. It hadn't been deliberate, it had simply got lost in the amateur dramatics of her Skydome demonstration. The guy certainly deserved to know. After all, this was his patch. She apologised for the omission and showed him the identikit picture she'd put together of her suspect. She admitted she didn't know if he was an agent but had a strong suspicion he was.

'Well if you've a strong suspicion I'd go with that. I've a feeling your intuition's a particularly powerful tool, Agent. Probably worth a handful of decent leads.'

Deira was beginning to find the excessive formality tiresome, particularly now that she was going to be working more closely with Monroe.

'Please call me Deira, Chief.'

'Only if you call me Hector.'

She hadn't anticipated that. Although she liked Monroe now that he'd loosened up, he still reminded her of a parade ground sergeant-major and was also old enough to be her father.

'I'm not sure I can do that. You're far and away my senior.'

'Well that's the deal – take it or leave it.'

Monroe sat back and gazed challengingly at her, a small smile on his face. Deira paused for a moment, unsure how to respond, then took herself in hand. She was an agent, for God's sake – she should start behaving like one. Monroe had hinted at it earlier.

'Okay, Hector it is. Deal.'

'Excellent! So, Deira – you're planning a trip to the bar later? What say we bring that visit forward a little and take a look at the output from their security cameras?' He stood and smoothed his uniform – another little affectation – before heading to the door and turning back. 'You coming?'

Deira nodded and followed him out of the office, silently berating herself for not having thought of the security cameras. If nothing else they'd lend objective support to the statements made by the scientists, and there was always the possibility they might provide further clues.

'I hadn't thought about cameras,' she admitted, then had a thought. 'What about CCTV in the Skydome? Surely you'd be able to see directly what happened to Fournier?'

Monroe smacked his head with his hand. 'Oh, of course! Why didn't we think about those?' He gave Deira a quizzical look and she realised how patronising she'd just been.

'You've already looked at them,' she said, feeling stupid.

'No, because there aren't any to look at. This is Mars Base, Deira. Everyone coming here is psychologically screened. Crime's almost non-existent except for the occasional fight in the bar. It's also a closed environment – claustrophobic enough without the thought that everything you do is being watched. We get by.'

Deira felt stupid all over again. 'Sorry Hector,' she said. 'This is all new to me. It'll take me some time to get used to things.'

'Don't worry yourself, lass. Let's just see what we can find from the cameras we do have available. Look, there's the Bar across the way there – and that's Sam the barman just opening up.'

Sam was a friendly young man in his mid-twenties and it transpired he'd been on duty the evening before the murder. When Monroe explained what they wanted he said he was pretty sure nothing unusual had happened that evening. However, he was very happy to provide the code for the security footage and it wasn't long before Deira and Monroe were huddled together in a small back room watching the recording.

Monroe fast-forwarded until the passengers from the Q-ship came in. First were the men of the new Titan security team, clearly determined to have a good time. They ordered drinks and two of them began a game of pool in an adjoining room while the rest clustered round the bar, chatting and laughing.

The scientists came in a little later and presented a very different picture. Deira recognised Drs Chandler and Blumstein from their files. They entered together and looked to be in the middle of a heated conversation which they continued at the bar. They were followed by Drs Dominguez and Altmeyer, who found a couple of stools at the far end of the bar – as far away as they could get from Chandler and Blumstein.

The last to come in was a tall, thin man sporting a goatee beard. Deira had no need of a file to identify him because he was very well-known indeed. It was Professor Chayka. He looked ill at ease in this unfamiliar environment and found a table to himself, away from the rest of the throng.

There was no sign of Phillipe Fournier so Monroe fast-forwarded again. One of the security men, a swarthy Hispanic of moderate height, who Monroe said was Security Chief Cabello, left his colleagues and went across to Professor Chayka's table. Chayka appeared mildly irritated but shook hands with Cabello and offered him a seat. The two men sat quietly, Chayka gazing into the near distance and providing abrupt and short-lived responses to Cabello's attempt at conversation. There was no meaningful interaction at all and Deira wondered why Cabello had bothered to make the effort.

At last, Fournier arrived. He looked decidedly apprehensive and made no attempt to engage with any of his colleagues. He bought a drink, wondered around a bit, watched the security men at their game of pool for a while, and finally found a table on his own. Not long afterwards, Chayka and Cabello left and a drinking match started. This seemed to go on for most of the evening so Monroe fast-forwarded to its conclusion. Surprisingly, Dr Dominguez comprehensively out-drank everyone yet still managed to look pretty good. Dr Altmeyer, on the other hand, was in a terrible state. Deira made a note in her wrist console.

Drs Chandler and Blumstein took no interest in the drinking contest and soon went their separate ways. Chandler picked up a young blonde woman, a hydroponicist according to his statement, and Blumstein latched on to a buxom brunette – supposedly a biochemist.

Fournier spent the whole evening on his own looking anxious and depressed. He took an occasional sip from his glass but he looked like a man who'd have preferred to be anywhere but where he was. It was 22.10 when the unexpected happened. A tall man, dressed all in black, strode over to his table and sat down without waiting for an invitation. Deira did a double take.

'I've seen that man!' she said. Monroe stopped the playback. 'That's the guy who was watching me the other night. My unknown agent.'

Monroe started the recording again and they continued watching. Fournier and the unknown man sat hunched over the small table, talking quietly and occasionally glancing surreptitiously round the room. At one point, Fournier became agitated and stood as if to leave, but the strange man said something and put a hand on his arm, pointedly looking over at the bar. Whatever he'd said clearly had the desired effect because Fournier cast a scared glance in the direction of the drinking contest and abruptly sat down again.

There was a brief silence while Fournier drained his drink and seemed to be trying to get himself together again. The stranger sat watching him, concern evident on his face. He gave him a few minutes and then whispered something to him. Phillipe looked up, obviously startled, and whispered something back. From his body language it was apparent that he was uncomfortable with the subject of their discussion but at one point the stranger showed him something on his wrist console and he seemed to relax a little. So it continued. After a further twenty minutes it appeared that some decision had been made because the stranger shook hands with Fournier, pushed his chair back and sauntered over to the exit. He paused for a moment to glance back at Fournier then opened the door and left.

Fournier went to the bar and bought another drink which he took back to his table. Then he sat and scanned the room, tapping his fingers nervously on the table and occasionally checking the time. Fifteen minutes later he stood and tried to emulate the stranger's easy-going saunter to the exit. His attempt was woeful in the extreme and his obvious awkwardness simply served to draw attention to him. Over at the bar, Simon Chandler watched his behaviour with interest while he chatted to his pick-up.

Soon after Fournier left, Dominguez excused himself and disappeared in the direction of the Men's Room. He didn't return for a good twenty-five minutes.

Monroe fast-forwarded again but Fournier didn't return and nothing else of any interest occurred for the rest of the evening. It was 1.00 am when Chandler left, his prize holding his hand and trotting along beside him. Tirzah Blumstein was next to leave with the brunette, and finally Walther Altmeyer managed to get himself upright and stumbled out, partly supported by Dominguez, as far as that was possible given the disparity in their heights.

Monroe stopped the playback. Deira wanted to know what the tall man had been doing before he'd approached Fournier and, with a little cross-referencing of the output from different cameras, she found the answer – he'd been standing at the bar chatting to Sam. He'd also been watching everybody in the room and had taken a particular interest in Fournier. When he walked over to Fournier's table there was a brief period when his face was clearly visible – and his jacket parted slightly to reveal what looked like a shoulder holster complete with staff. Now Deira knew she was on the right track. The guy was certainly an agent.

Monroe called Sam and asked him what he knew about the tall man. He was just another punter as far as Sam was concerned. He'd been coming into the bar regularly during the week prior to the murder. He generally got on well with the other regulars, never drank excessively and rarely stayed after 23.00. The only information Sam got out of him during their chats was that he was waiting for a friend to arrive on the Q-ship that was stopping over on its way to Titan.

Sam said that on the evening of the murder the tall guy turned up early and was having his usual drink when the scientists came in. He seemed particularly interested when Fournier arrived but initially made no attempt to join him. Sam thought that was unusual.

'I asked him whether the Frenchman was his friend and he said yes, but he wanted to surprise him. I don't know what happened next because I got distracted by some customers and next time I looked he'd gone over to the Frenchie's table. I didn't take much notice after that.'

'What about the two pick-ups?' Monroe said. 'We're told one's a biochemist and one's a hydroponicist.'

'Well the biochemist is truly a biochemist, but hydroponicist? You've got to be kidding! That's Rosalie – always here, looking for a mark. Doesn't come cheap either.'

Monroe consulted his wrist console. 'According to Chandler's statement, he was with her all night.'

'Well if he was he's the first I've ever heard of! It's a matter of cash-flow for Rosalie – she doesn't hang about. He probably had an hour – two at most.'

'Hmmm.' Monroe made an entry in his console. 'Any idea where I can find Rosalie?'

'She'll almost certainly be here soon.'

'That's very helpful,' Monroe turned to Deira. 'Unless my colleague here wants to ask you anything else I think we're done.' Deira shook her head. 'Okay, that's it. Thanks.'

'Well, that's opened up a can of worms.' Deira said as soon as Sam had gone.

The recordings had created more questions than answers. First, there was the tall stranger who'd spoken to Fournier. Deira was convinced he was an agent and if he didn't belong to the Bureau he was almost certainly American. He and Fournier had left the bar within minutes of each other, the agent with practiced nonchalance and Fournier with obvious agitation. Deira thought they'd probably agreed to a private meeting outside the bar – and that meant the agent might have been the last person to see Fournier alive.

Next, there was Chandler, who'd been taking a considerable interest in the meeting between Fournier and the tall guy. In his initial interview he'd said that at some unspecified time in the evening he'd suddenly noticed Fournier had gone but the cameras clearly showed him watch Fournier leave. Deira suspected his alibi wouldn't check out either. Put those facts together with his physicality and he was definitely a suspect.

Finally, there was Altmeyer. In spite of his previous body-building experience, which had made him a clear suspect in Deira's mind, he'd consumed a considerable amount of alcohol in the drinking contest and looked pretty rough by the end of the evening. She just couldn't square his physical state with the ability to commit murder.

Monroe had been making further entries in his console. He turned to Deira and put into words what she'd just been thinking.

'We seem to have three possible suspects, the two scientists you mentioned earlier and the large man who talked to Fournier. We can't do anything about the unknown guy unless we can find him. I've serious doubts about Altmeyer – I don't think he was any state to do anything but fall into bed. As for Chandler, we need to see if his alibi pans out. That means talking to Rosalie – so I guess I'll be keeping you company here for a while.'

'Always happy for some company over a drink, Hector.'

They wandered back to the main bar and made themselves comfortable on a couple of stools with a beer and a tequila. Monroe opened a picture of Rosalie on his wrist console and they watched with interest as the regulars began to drift in.

They didn't have long to wait. Within twenty minutes Rosalie strolled in and made for what was clearly her favourite perch at the bar, two stools along from Deira. Deira glanced questioningly at Monroe and he nodded, indicating that he'd take this. He got up and moved to the stool on Rosalie's right. Deira moved to her left. Rosalie turned towards Monroe and flashed him a radiant smile – to be replaced by a scowl when he presented his ID. She started to get up to leave but Deira put a hand firmly on her shoulder, keeping her gently but insistently in place.

'Don't worry lass, you're not in any trouble,' Monroe said. 'This is my colleague, Special Agent MacMahon. We just want to ask you some questions about one of your clients from a few nights ago.'

Rosalie looked from one to the other. 'Buy me a drink and I'll think about it.'

Deira smiled. 'We'll do better than that. The Chief here will buy you a drink to get you started. If you give us the information we need, I'll provide you with top-ups until either you make a hit or the guy I'm waiting for turns up. Deal?'

'Deal!' Rosalie looked unduly pleased with herself.

'Okay. Your round Chief.'

Monroe's main aim was to verify, or otherwise, Chandler's alibi for the night in question. It turned out just as Sam had suggested – Rosalie had spent no more than an hour-and-a-half with him, leaving his room at about 02.30. She remembered him being angry about something and unduly rough with her. She pulled the sleeve of her top up and seemed to take some pride in showing off a couple of new bruises on her arm. Monroe made sympathetic tutting noises but was clearly uninterested. He asked whether Chandler had said anything that might indicate why he was so angry?

'He did say something about his work. He's a scientist of some kind and he'd been trying to work out some equaz . . . equasio . . . '

'Equations?' Deira said.

'Yes those! He was mad that one of the other scientists had beaten him to it and he couldn't understand how.'

'Think hard,' Monroe said. 'Did he mention a name? This bit's really important.'

She shook her head. 'No name – but he did mention a Frenchman.'

Yes! Deira did a mental high five. There must have been considerable friction between Fournier and Chandler – but was it motive enough for murder? Monroe asked a few more questions but Rosalie couldn't help any further. He glanced at the time, thanked her, and stood up ready to leave.

'I'd better be off,' he said. 'Our friend Rosalie here's been most helpful but I've got to get home. I'll get a search started for our agent friend tomorrow. As of now, I'm treating him as our prime suspect. I'll also contact Julio Cabello on board the Q-ship and see if he can get some sort of investigation started on board.'

'Sounds good, Hector. Catch up with you tomorrow.'

It turned out to be a very long evening and Deira had nothing tangible to show for it, the stranger electing to stay away. Aware that she was effectively on duty and performing a stakeout, she kept her drinking under control and by 23.00 she was bored silly. As Sam had said the stranger usually left by this time, she thought it pointless remaining. However, she covered her bases by leaving Sam with the code for her console so he could contact her directly if the tall agent came in again. Then she made for her room and what she considered to be a well-earned rest.

The following day she rose early and called the infirmary for an update on Adam. One of the interns took her call and confirmed that the test results that were back didn't look particularly hopeful – Adam's genome was irreparably damaged and his brain scan was abnormal. They had other tests planned and the intern agreed to let her know if there were any changes in Adam's condition.

Deira's mood was still fluctuating. After the low yesterday when she'd first met Monroe, she'd swung the other way and felt quite euphoric when she'd completed her re-enactment. Then she'd come down to earth again, feeling like her normal self while she subsequently chatted to Monroe and watched the security tapes. Now she felt alone and apprehensive, worried about Adam and unsure of herself. This had to stop. Adam's condition wasn't going to change anytime soon and she simply had to get used to functioning on her own. She thought the important thing was to keep busy – and that meant getting to grips with Fournier's wrist console.

On the face of it, the wrist console was unremarkable, its contents being the usual mixture of files that would be expected for a scientist of Fournier's specialty and seniority. Deira could see why it had been discounted as being unimportant but her gut told her something different. She set to with a will, employing all her formidable IT skills to tease out what she strongly suspected was there.

Several hours later she finally found what she was after – and even then she almost missed them. There were several, barely apparent, ghost files – files that had been deleted with such skill that only someone with Deira's background would have had any chance of finding them. Eagerly she chased down the date stamps and found the deletions had taken place round the time of Fournier's death. Unfortunately, that was all she could get. There was no way she could recover the files and she'd had it for today in any case – couldn't think straight any more. Wearily she turned off the wrist console and put in a call to Monroe.

'There was definitely something important on that wrist console,' she said. 'Could be a motive for murder but we won't know unless we can find out what it was. I'd guess there'd be a copy somewhere. Fournier was a scientist and a trained computer-user and you'd expect him to make some sort of backup of his data, especially if it was as important as it looks to be.'

'Where would such a copy be? What would you do in Fournier's place?'

'Good question. I'd probably opt for a two-pronged solution – a backup in the datasphere in the form of a cloud file and another one on a data wafer. The cloud file would be virtually impossible to find unless you knew its location but if there's a wafer round somewhere...'

'I'll get a search started straight away. We'll back-track Fournier's movements and search all the locations he may have frequented in his last forty-eight hours. I was about to speak to Julio Cabello on the Q-ship – perhaps he could conduct a similar search at his end.' He paused and looked down at something on his desk. 'By the way, I had a thought about the rope.'

'What about it?'

'I was wondering whether there'd been any recent purchases of rope of that gauge – so I enquired at the hardware store on the Mall.'

'Good thought. What did they say?'

'That a certain Dr Altmeyer bought a rope just like it. Fifty metres of the stuff – and we know that five metres was used in the murder. Now, if Dr Altmeyer happens to have a forty-five metre length of rope and can't account for the rest I'd say that definitely makes him prime suspect, don't you?'

'But what about his physical state the night of the murder?'

'Could just be a damned good actor with an eye for an alibi. "Sorry Chief, I was so drunk I can't remember anything, but my good friend Nicolau swears he put me to bed and that's where I woke next morning." You can just hear it can't you? Anyway, I'm going to ask Julio to search his cabin and interrogate him again.' He paused and appeared a little embarrassed. 'Can I ask a favour?'

Having spent all day with her eyes glued to a virtual screen hunting for ghost files, Deira wasn't feeling up to doing favours, but she liked Monroe even if she still found him slightly scary.

'Sure thing, name it.'

'I've heard Sam won't be working this evening so we won't be getting any heads-up if our suspect turns up at the bar. I wondered if you'd be able to do a stakeout of the place again? I wouldn't normally ask but...'

'You don't need an excuse, Hector, a bar stakeout is just what I need in any case. Give me half-an-hour to grab some food and I'll get down there.'

'Thanks, I owe you one. See you tomorrow?'

'Will do. See you Hector.'

She terminated the call and smiled. If this was doing a favour, bring it on.

Chapter 9

S OL OPENED HIS eyes – then immediately closed them again. The light was awful – intense and painful – it burned his eyes and left a yellow afterglow.

He was lying on something soft, a couch by the feel of it, but he couldn't remember where the couch might be or why he was lying on it in the first place. He swung his legs over the side and sat up. Bad idea – a wave of nausea washed over him and his gut protested. He gagged and leaned forward to puke violently on the floor – then wished he hadn't because all the muscles in his body seemed to go into spasm at once. He groaned. He felt like shit – and then some. He tried to concentrate, battling a pain that was spreading through his head like a bushfire. The only thing that came to mind was that this must be a bad PHASE.

He latched on to that thought. This was progress. He remembered he was an agent and he'd just PHASEd from somewhere. Therefore the couch must be in a PHASE cubicle. Unfortunately he couldn't remember anything else. It was a complete blank – no knowledge of source, terminus, or mission parameters. He changed tack and concentrated on personal memories instead – parents, family, favourite tri-vid – that sort of thing. Absolutely everything appeared to have gone. He tried not to panic, forcing himself to concentrate on the things he did know instead of those he didn't. He knew his name – but apart from that all he could remember was that he was an agent.

Although not part of the recommended protocol for a bad PHASE, concentrating on his memory loss appeared to be therapeutic. The nausea rapidly resolved and the head pain faded, leaving a dull, residual ache. Since things appeared to be on the up he took a chance and opened his eyes again – very slowly. This time, the light was bearable and he wasn't surprised when it slowly resolved into a rather antiquated-looking PHASE chamber.

There was no PHASE technician to be seen. This was highly unusual because he or she should have been operating the transmission machinery and by now would have noticed that Sol was having trouble. Sol took some comfort from the fact that he seemed to know about the nuts and bolts of PHASEing.

Suddenly, a deep male voice spoke inside his head.

'Sol, I have a problem. I've lost some memories – memories my diagnostics confirm were uploaded and present at the time of transmission. From the changes in your neurochemistry I deduce you may be having similar problems.'

'What? Who?'

'Sol, you must shake yourself out of this. You know me.'

Sol looked round frantically, unwilling to believe this was coming from within his own head. This was crazy. There was nobody else there. Ignoring the voice and carefully avoiding the mess on the floor, he climbed off the PHASE couch and stood up. He was expecting further problems but none materialised. He still had a dull ache over his right temple but the rest of the physical side-effects of the PHASE had pretty much dissipated. Psychologically? Well, what do you call someone who hears voices? As if on cue, the voice came again in his head.

'Sol, think about the phrase "bonding sessions". How you agreed to have the communication node implanted and the nannites injected. Concentrate.'

Whatever it was, the voice was certainly determined. Actually, the words "node" and "nannites" did seem vaguely familiar, though the phrase "bonding sessions" had no resonance at all. He concentrated, trying to hook the memories that he felt were still there in his sub-conscious. Absolutely nothing happened. So, was the voice a post-PHASE psychological construct or was it real, the problem being his memory loss. On balance, since many of the words the voice used were familiar, he felt it had to be real. However, he was well aware that if that was not the case and he started talking to it he could initiate a self-perpetuating psychosis.

He was still trying to decide how to proceed when the door to the PHASE chamber opened and a face peered in. The face belonged to a young man in his mid-twenties, probably third or fourth generation West African by the look of his relatively European features. Clean shaven. Short, curly black hair. The rest of the man followed his face into the chamber and he stared apprehensively at Sol – and the mess on the floor.

'Who are you?'

Sol realised this had to be the local PHASE technician – he'd been expecting him much sooner than this. He followed the techie's gaze to the pile on the floor then looked sheepishly up. 'Sol Smith,' he said. 'Sorry about the mess.'

There was a pause while the techie thought things through. The fact that Sol was physically present in the PHASE chamber made him his problem, whether he liked it or not. Sol knew that and said nothing, partly to give the man some thinking space but mainly because he couldn't think of anything useful to say. The techie finally seemed to get himself together.

'I'm Amadi Okafor – resident PHASE technician. Now, Agent Smith...'

'Just Sol please.'

'Sol then.' A pause. 'Sol – like the sun?'

'Sol short for "Solomon". Can't stand the name, myself. Called after a famous great-great-grandfather, I'm told. And as for "Smith"! What the hell do you do with a name like Smith? So, just Sol please.'

'Sol it is then.' Amadi seemed more relaxed. 'Where did you come from, Sol? I had an unauthorised transmission alarm a few minutes ago but my instruments fail to show a point of origin. That's not supposed to be possible.'

'Sorry, can't help you. Not that I don't want to. It's just that my memory's fried – almost completely. I don't want to resort to last restore point because I don't know what I'd be left with.'

Amadi nodded sympathetically. All memory caches stored after a designated restore point would be lost if that restore point was utilised so he could understand Sol's reluctance to use the facility.

'Could you at least tell me where I am, buddy?' Sol said. 'And what do I call you – Ami, Am?'

'Amadi will do fine.' Amadi frowned. 'So you don't know where you are or where you've come from? That's a serious problem as I'm sure you know. You're on Titan – Euro-Base.'

Something fell into place in the back of Sol's mind. A memory. A memory of a massive nuclear explosion on Titan some years ago that had resulted in it being quarantined. No ships were allowed within two million miles – and certainly no PHASE chambers.

'Titan?' he ventured. 'Like moon-of-Saturn Titan? But that's off limits.'

'Interesting response – but as you can see Titan certainly isn't off limits. I wonder where you got that idea from. Memory loss after a PHASE is one thing but I've never heard of false memories being implanted.'

Now Sol was really confused. Not only had he lost almost all his memories, but the ones he still had seemed to be wrong. He needed a few minutes alone to try and get his thoughts together.

'So we've a bit of a mystery, haven't we? By the way, any chance of using the bathroom?'

'Oh sure,' Amadi pointed in the direction of the exit. 'It's just outside the PHASE terminal, round the corner.'

Sol grinned his thanks and took himself off to do what nature required. He stood a while in the relative privacy of the bathroom taking in his reflection in the mirror. At least he still remembered what he looked like, even though his current appearance left a lot to be desired. A lot less, actually – he looked like shit. His square face was covered with stubble and he had dark circles round both eyes. His red-brown, closely cropped hair was greasy and he had an ugly bruise over his left cheek. He splashed some water on his face and rubbed his hair in a half-hearted attempt at making himself look at least partially presentable. Unfortunately his efforts only had the effect of making him look even wilder than before. With a final disgusted look in the mirror, he turned to leave.

'You look positively bedraggled. Do you still not remember me?' The voice was in his head again.

'For God's sake leave me alone!' Sol clutched his head as if he was trying to squeeze out the entity that seemed to have taken up abode in his skull. 'You're not really there.'

'I assure you I *am* really here. I'm not part of your subconscious and you're not going mad. Keep working on it Sol. You must sort this out if I'm to be of any use to you.'

'Go to hell!'

Sol ran out of the bathroom and skidded round the corner into the main body of the terminal. Amadi looked up in alarm from where he was preparing a battery of post-PHASE tests and Sol rapidly came to a halt. The last thing he wanted to do at this point was to alienate the techie – he might need him later.

He tried smoothing his hair again and did his best to smile but the look on Amadi's face suggested this wasn't particularly reassuring. He removed the smile and sat in the chair the techie had carefully placed opposite his own.

'A few basic tests if you're up to it.' Amadi said.

Sol sat. He was pretty sure these were going to be a little more than the standard post-PHASE tests and in this he was not mistaken. After an hour he managed to persuade Amadi he'd had enough for one day and the techie asked a junior administrator to show him to some quarters that had been hastily arranged. Sol gratefully closed the door behind him and took a hot shower – then he collapsed on the bed and was asleep almost immediately.

He woke well over ten hours later feeling a whole lot better but hungry as hell. He shaved and showered then looked for his uniform. It wasn't there, but some sort of general purpose coverall had been left in exchange, so he guessed the uniform had been taken for much-needed laundering while he slept. Thank God they hadn't touched his PWC, which was lying where he'd left it on a chair near the bed. He lost no time donning the coverall and slipping the PWC into its holster on his belt. Okay, next up was food.

He hunted round for a Base schematic or a network terminal that might give him some clue to the direction of the refectory but there was nothing obvious. In the end, he decided to follow his nose. It had always served him well when it came to locating food and he could see no reason why it should fail him now. He left his room and turned left, sniffing the air as he went, and it wasn't long before he picked up the unmistakable aromas of bacon and coffee. Sure enough, round the next bend he came upon the refectory. He made a beeline for the counter and was soon contentedly munching his way through a full English breakfast and slurping a large black coffee. Satisfied, he leaned back in his chair and gave a sigh of contentment.

'I hope you feel better now. We badly need to confer.'

'Shit! Not here. Not now.'

Sol shot out of his seat and rushed back to his room, holding his head as if that would shut the voice up. Then, with the door closed and locked, he settled down to have a conversation with himself.

'Okay, you've got my attention. Just who the hell are you?'

'Oh dear, you really do have a problem don't you?'

The voice sounded uncertain, as if it hadn't anticipated this set of circumstances. It gave Sol some comfort to know he wasn't the only one having a bad day. For some reason he kept thinking of vegetables. He'd caught sight of some chef's helpers preparing lunch in the refectory and he couldn't get them out of his mind. Vegetables – and not just any sort of vegetables but green vegetables – like cabbage and broccoli and…

'Chard?' he said hesitantly.

The name seemed to act as a catalyst, causing a tsunami of memories to wash through him. He physically reeled from the mental onslaught – memories re-establishing themselves, neural networks opening up, and neurochemicals flooding dormant synapses. He took long, deep breaths while everything settled. He knew now who his invisible friend was.

'Hey, buddy,' he said. 'I've got you. We need to confer.'

'Hello Sol,' Chard said. 'I was beginning to think I was going to have to perform neurochemicolysis on you. Do you remember who I am now?'

'Sure do, and it wasn't the phrase "bonding sessions" that did it for me – it was the sight of vegetables in the refectory.'

'I could take offence but the important thing is that you're back. Have all your memories returned?'

'Not by a long shot.' Sol swiftly ran through the usual protocol to check on memory status. 'It's weird. I remember you and our bonding sessions now but there's a whole shed-load of stuff relating to our mission that's still missing – and the memories of my personal life are all gone. It sure doesn't compute as simple transmission loss. In fact, putting it all together I get only one answer.'

'Sabotage. That would explain my own problems too. I have loss of both memory and networking capability, two very different elements of my neural architecture. I cannot begin to imagine how it might have been done. Somebody seems to have taken a great deal of trouble to render us ineffective. Do you have any data that might throw some light on this?'

'Nothing I can prove. I look like shit – like I've been active somewhere. I think it's more than likely I've already attempted or completed whatever mission I was given and I'm now on the run. I'm guessing that, during the escape, I emergency PHASEd with no set terminus and the chamber went into failsafe mode and transmitted us here–here being Titan, by the way. It may well be we're part of a black-ops scenario–our original destination withheld from us to create plausible deniability'

'You remember all this?'

'It's more a hunch than a memory–but it fits the existing facts.'

'We should beware of assumptions. While I'm a great fan of the mental heuristics you call "hunches" they're by no means infallible. You're extrapolating from inadequate data – trying to make sense of things. Seeing patterns where none exist is a very human attribute.'

'I agree–but something tells me this particular hunch isn't that far off the mark.'

'In that case we must take great care while we continue to probe our situation. You say we're on Titan?'

'Yeah, I know that makes no sense. The place is supposed to be radioactive and unfit for exploration–yet here we are with a viable Base and PHASE chamber.'

'This must be reconciled quickly,' Chard had a distinctly human-like sound of concern in his voice. 'We need hard facts urgently.'

'Okay. I'll do a bit of snooping and see what I can come up with. While I do that …' Sol flinched because another set of synapses suddenly flared into life.

'What is it?'

'I just had a memory flash about our point of origin. I'm pretty sure we came from Mars. That must be where I carried out my mission.'

'My networking capability is severely limited at present but I may be able to access the local Base terminal. We need to see if there are any recent news items relating to Mars.'

There was a long pause and Sol could tell something of interest had come up.

'Okay – out with it! Whatever you've found must be pretty damned interesting for you to take this long.'

'Apologies,' Chard said. 'I was backtracking from the main event to complete a coherent story arc. Five days ago, a scientist on his way to Titan was found hanged in the Skydome on Mars. The initial verdict was suicide but this was subsequently overturned when an investigation by a Bureau agent found further evidence. The man was actually murdered – the first murder on Mars for twenty years.'

'And it happened when I was there. Shit!' Sol tried once more to remember something – anything – about his recent activities. Nothing came. 'So what's happening as of now?'

'The Bureau agent and the Mars security team are searching for a stranger who was seen talking to the deceased man on the evening of the murder. The man's scientific colleagues are on their way to Titan at this moment on board a Q-ship, and the new Titan security team is conducting a parallel investigation on that ship.'

'Buddy, there seem to be a hell of a lot of different folk on their way to Titan. What's so goddamned important about Titan all of a sudden? Did we miss something?'

Chard continued with the whole story – the explosion on Earth resulting in the transfer of Chayka's team to Titan;

the multiple Bases sprouting up round the northern seas of Titan and the subsequent dispatch of the security team; the overturning of the suicide verdict on Mars – and the complete lack of any information pertaining to an explosion on Titan with resulting radiation contamination. Finally, he came back to the stranger on Mars.

'I have accessed the official description of this person. Male, approximately six foot six tall with a square face and short red-brown hair.'

'You mean it's me?'

'It certainly sounds like you.'

'So I'm supposed to have murdered a scientist? Doesn't sound like a mission the Agency would condone – and I'm not sure I could've gone through with it even if they did. Something doesn't feel right here.'

'I agree, but the authorities are almost convinced you committed the murder – and from their point of view your memory loss would seem a bit too convenient.'

'So unless I can retrieve my memories it's going to be assumed I'm guilty – and to make matters worse, a new security team's heading in my direction. I need those memories.'

'I concur. Perhaps you should approach Amadi Okafor again and see whether he can help.'

'Good idea. But we also need an escape plan. Can you find out what the surface conditions are like and whether there's an American Base close by? If there is, we could use it as a route out of here.'

'I'll certainly examine all possibilities. However, don't forget your previous suggestion that we could be part of a black-ops scenario with plausible deniability. If that's true, even the Americans may not want us.'

'Copy that. Unfortunately, it may be all we've got. I'm off to see Ami. Do what you can.'

'Leave it with me and I'll see what I can come up with.'

Chapter 10

J ULIO CABELLO WAS watching an old tri-vid in his cabin
when Monroe's call came through from Mars. He smiled
as Monroe's ruddy face appeared on his virtual screen. They
were old friends.

'Evening Hector,' he said. 'Evening for us, at any rate.'

'Morning Julio.' Monroe grinned. 'Good to see you. Sorry
I missed you on Mars.'

'Indeed.' Cabello wondered where this was going – Hector
wasn't one for social calls. 'It was a shame we didn't have
time to catch up but you obviously had your hands full.
Everything settled down again?'

'Not by a long shot. The Bureau sent a couple of agents
to investigate the suicide – by PHASE!'

'"I didn't think that was possible.'

'I didn't either. It's some sort of new technology – and
obviously has some teething issues because one of the agents
ended up in the infirmary. The other agent's caused quite a
stir though – she's actually got the suicide verdict overturned.
I've got a genuine murder on my hands, Julio. First in twenty
years! I'm sending you a file of our findings to date but I
thought you might appreciate a verbal summary.'

Cabello listened carefully while Monroe detailed recent
events. He'd never been completely comfortable with the
verdict of suicide. Although he hadn't been particularly close
to Fournier, he'd seen him round the ship on a number of
occasions and had noticed the change in him after the first
day on board. He'd seemed preoccupied and anxious but

nowhere near suicidal. Cabello had gone so far as to get his file out but he'd found his Bureau psychological tests suggested he was a particularly stable individual. Those tests had always proved to be remarkably robust, yet they'd been passed over at the inquest as if they were of no consequence.

Monroe completed his briefing. 'I need help, Julio. I pushed through Fournier's inquest quickly because Barinson said everything was cut and dried. Now I'm stuck with a murder case – and I've let almost all the suspects go.'

'Sounds like I need to open an investigation at this end.'

'Could you? How do you think it'd go down with ship's security?'

'There isn't any. This is the ship's maiden voyage. There's only a skeleton crew and very few passengers – no obvious need for a security team. Leave it with me. I'm sure I'll be able to do something.'

'Excellent!'

'I presume you'll be continuing the search for the unknown agent?'

'I will – but I'm not confident we'll find him. By the way, according to Dr Blumstein's statement, Fournier had an old-fashioned pad that seemed to have some sort of sentimental attachment for him. We've found no trace of it and I was wondering…'

'A pad? Dr Altmeyer recently found a pad in his room. I'll get hold of it and see if my IT specialist can find anything interesting on it.'

'That's great, Julio. Thanks for your help.'

'Thanks for giving me something to do. Things were getting pretty dull round here and we've still got several days to go. Talk to you again soon.'

Cabello terminated the call and sat for a moment reviewing his notes. He checked the time wondering if he should brief his men but decided against it when he saw it was already seven thirty in the evening. Body clocks would be starting to wind down by now so tomorrow would be better. What he could do this evening was square things with the Executive Officer.

The XO was more than happy for Cabello to proceed with the investigation. He handed over the pad that Altmeyer had found and even made a room available to use as a temporary security office. Cabello felt energised again. This was more like it – better than sitting round waiting for this interminable voyage to end.

The following morning Cabello was up early, in uniform, and intent on getting his men up to speed. Most of them were bored and drinking more than was good for them, and he felt that a bit of purpose was just what they needed. There was a comm terminal in his new security office so he placed calls to the five members of the team, telling them to meet him there in fifteen minutes. Most of them managed it in less. Cabello looked them over as they filed in and took their seats.

He went down his list, quickly putting names to faces.

Baxter was English and had previously been an IT specialist in the British Army. He'd ended up in security when his fledgling business went belly-up and he needed some cash rapidly. Petrelli was a small intense Italian and had been in security ever since his brother had been killed by the Cosa Nostra. Landau was an ebullient Frenchman who cultivated a small moustache that he kept stroking gently; he didn't seem to know why he'd gone into security. Fingal was a slightly podgy redheaded Englishman who'd left school ten years previously with no qualifications and little in the way of prospects. After drifting from job to job for a while, followed by a long period of unemployment he eventually settled on the security business. Finally, there was the baby of the bunch, nineteen-year-old Josh Hunstan, English again and only out of school a year. Cabello had been friends with his family for years and had been instrumental in persuading him that he could make a good career in security.

All of them had taken the opportunity offered by going to Titan – a higher than normal salary, a lump sum invested for them in a major institution on Earth, and a guaranteed promotion on their return.

The excited chatter faded and ceased under the stern eye of Cabello. When there was complete silence he began his briefing on the changed nature of the events on Mars and what they had been asked to do.

'I need hardly add,' he finished, 'that this is our first major investigation as a team. It'll be a good test. You'll find the Fournier file on your wrist consoles. I'll give you half-an-hour to study it then we'll get down to duty allocation.'

The men got busy reading and Cabello checked his allocation list to make sure he hadn't forgotten anything. He sat and waited, skimming the Fournier file again to pass the time. At the end of the allotted half-hour he called the men back to attention.

'Now,' he said. 'Tasks. Baxter – take a look at the pad Dr Altmeyer found. I want to know its contents in detail. Petrelli – focus on Dr Altmeyer. Review his original statement with him to see if there are any holes in it, then conduct a full search of his room and anywhere else he might spend time. If you can find that rope he bought, see if any of it is missing. Landau, Fingal and Hunstan – you're looking for a data wafer containing backup files from Fournier's wrist console. Full ship search, but start with areas he'd be expected to frequent and work out from there. I'll be interviewing Professor Chayka and the rest of his team. Any questions?'

There were quite a number and Cabello dealt with them comprehensively but efficiently.

'Alright,' he said at last. 'You have your orders. Debrief at 18.00. Dismissed!'

Cabello decided to start his interviews with Professor Chayka. He had to ring the doorbell three times before an irritated professor finally decided his unwanted visitor wasn't going away and opened the door. He squinted from Cabello's face to his name tag, to his uniform, and then back to his face again, clearly uncertain whether he knew him or not.

'Yes? Can I help you?'

'Professor Chayka, I'm Security Chief Cabello of the Titan Security Team. We met the other night in the bar.' Cabello saw sudden recognition in Chayka's eyes and he pressed on. 'I'm sorry to interrupt your work but I need to speak with you regarding Philippe Fournier's death. May I come in?'

Cheyka tsked and tutted a few times in obvious exasperation. He cleared a few books off one of his work chairs – real paper books, Cabello noted with interest – and beckoned him in. The room was an obsessional's delight. It wasn't that there were no possessions visible, it was simply that each one was neatly placed in what looked like a pre-planned position, giving the cabin the feel of a show apartment. Cabello gazed round, fascinated, then sat in the work chair Chayka indicated.

'Yes, I do remember talking to you – sorry for not recognising you in uniform. How can I help? There's nothing I can add to my previous statement.'

Cabello reached into his tunic pocket and took out a notebook and pencil. He was gratified by the look of surprise on Chayka's face. That was exactly why he employed such an old-fashioned device – to create surprise and distraction. Indeed, the sight of him scribbling in his notebook appeared to have an unduly disconcerting effect on most interviewees.

'I understand Dr Fournier's death was a terrible shock,' he said. 'Unfortunately, I have to inform you that the suicide verdict has been overturned. We now know Dr Fournier was murdered.'

He waited for a response from Chayka but none was forthcoming. The news didn't even seem to register on his long, narrow, face. What on Earth was the matter with the man? Okay, he had a reputation for being un-shockable but this was taking things a bit far. Cabello pretended to make a note in his book while he waited for the professor to say something. He didn't – he just sat and stared into the middle distance, apparently unfocused. After a full minute of this Cabello felt he had no option but to continue even though he wasn't convinced the professor was actually taking in what he was saying.

"I've agreed to conduct one half of the murder investigation on board this ship while Chief Monroe carries out the other half on Mars.' Still no reaction from Chayka. 'This will mean searching all cabins, including yours Professor. I hope I can rely upon your cooperation in this matter.'

This seemed to be the trigger that brought Chayka back from wherever he'd been. He visibly started and his face creased into a frown.

'Search? Search my cabin? Search it for what? I object most strongly to this invasion of my privacy Chief…'

He stared at Cabello's name tag and Cabello thought he was probably wondering how to pronounce it.

'It's "Cabayo"'.

'Yes, yes, I can read! Chief, this is my workspace as well as my cabin. I cannot have security men wandering all over it, turning things upside down. I refuse access. If you persist I shall have no option but to take it to the Captain.'

A reaction at last. Cabello smiled pleasantly. 'Of course, that's your right. However, you should know that I've been given full authority in this case. My apologies for any inconvenience but the search will go ahead as planned. My men will cause as little disruption as possible.'

Chayka was fighting to maintain his cool and Cabello thought now was the time to get into the interview proper

'We'll get started with the search later today,' he said. 'At the moment, however, I need to talk to you and your team in light of the new information. Perhaps you could start me off. Can you tell me your whereabouts on the night of Dr Fournier's death?'

Chayka was visibly angry but doing his best to regain some equanimity.

'As you're well aware, Chief Cabello, I was in the bar until 20.30 talking to you. We left together and went our separate ways, I to my room, where I read until round 23.30. I went to bed at approximately midnight…' He glared at Cabello. '…and the answer to your next question is no, nobody can corroborate that because I was entirely alone at the time. If you're really stupid enough to consider me a suspect, I suggest you ask yourself what possible motive I could have for murdering one of my most valuable team members. Furthermore, I cannot imagine anybody on board this ship wanting to cause harm to Dr Fournier. It seems to me far more likely that the culprit is still on Mars.'

'That's possible of course. How well do you know the individual members of your team, Professor?'

'Dr Dominguez and I have been friends and colleagues for many years. Dr Chandler has been a valuable member of my team for the past four years and I know him reasonably well. I must confess to not knowing the other three – two now of course. They were all hired at relatively short notice when my original team members failed their psychological tests.'

'So you'd be prepared to give a character reference for Drs Dominguez and Chandler if required?'

'Of course I…'

'But not the other two?'

'I… no I suppose not – but I don't think either of them would be capable of murder.'

'I never suggested it. I take it from your comments you don't think I should be concerned about either of them? I mean, Dr Altmeyer's a big man. If he were to accidentally hit someone he…'

'No, no, no,' Chayka interrupted. 'Dr Altmeyer has always appeared to be a very gentle man.'

'For what – five days? You've only known him for that time, haven't you? You've already said you wouldn't be prepared to give him a character reference yet now you seem to be suggesting otherwise. Which is it to be Professor?'

Chayka closed his eyes, stroked his beard and said nothing. Cabello waited. No response. Finally, he realised that this was Chayka's reaction to a situation where he wasn't in control. It was almost catatonia, except he was pretty sure the professor knew exactly what he was doing. Sighing, he got to his feet and let himself out – taking one last glance at the still immobile professor.

On his way to his next interview, he checked in at the security office to see how Baxter was doing with the pad and found the IT man very frustrated. Baxter waved the pad in disgust and handed it to Cabello.

'Chief, I've spent a heck of a lot of time on this and all I've managed to do is get past the first password-protected screen. The rest's heavily encrypted – almost like military grade. It definitely belonged to Fournier, but not Philippe – the name on the first screen is Armand Fournier, his father. I did some checking on the guy and found he was a fairly well-known conspiracy theorist in his time – that is when he wasn't locked up in a Parisian mental hospital. I was surprised young Fournier was allowed into space with that sort of family history but I found there's no proven genetic component – and Philippe passed all the psychological tests with flying colours.'

Cabello stared at the pad. 'So is it relevant? It's difficult to see any link but it's strange it was pushed behind Altmayer's bed – and why should it be encrypted? Can it be connected it to the datasphere?'

Baxter shook his head. 'Not a chance. That part of its hardware's been removed – some time ago, I'd say.'

'Hmm. That's a shame because the agent Hector Monroe's working with on Mars has a background in cryptology – she may have been able to decrypt it. What about you, Baxter? Could you do it?'

'I'll carry on working on it but I don't think I'll get any further.'

'Keep trying for now. You could also try contacting Agent MacMahon on Mars and see if she can suggest anything that might help. If you need to requisition anything from the Bureau let me know and I'll sanction it.'

'Right you are, Chief. Leave it with me and I'll do my best.'

Cabello carefully transcribed the notes he'd made from his discussion with Chayka then prepared to interview Dr Chandler. The man had some explaining to do from what Chief Monroe had told him, and it would be interesting to see how he handled it. He found Chandler in his cabin and, unlike Chayka, the mathematician recognised him.

'To what do I owe this pleasure, Chief Cabello? Can I assume this is to be a more formal meeting than we've had up to now?' He showed Cabello into the room and indicated an armchair.

'You may indeed, Dr Chandler.' Cabello sat down and took out his notebook. 'I'm following up on the statements you and your colleagues made after the death of Dr Fournier.' He watched Chandler's reaction – perhaps a little frown, but certainly nothing of note. The mathematician sat in the other armchair and appeared relaxed and unconcerned.

'Well, I'm very happy to oblige but I don't know what else to say about poor Philippe. I simply don't understand how he could have passed his psychological tests.'

Cabello said nothing and made a big play of consulting his notebook. Chandler looked nervous and began to fidget and Cabello smiled to himself. Perhaps he did have something to hide. He looked up from his notebook and sighed.

'Doctor, I'm afraid I've some bad news for you. Dr Fournier didn't commit suicide – he was murdered.'

The reaction from Chandler looked genuine, the colour draining from his cheeks and a look of horror coming over his face.

'You can't be serious? Who'd want to kill Philippe?'

'That's exactly what we're trying to determine. Can you tell me where you were the night Dr Fournier was killed?'

'Me? Surely you don't think I had anything to do with it?' Small beads of sweat appeared on Chandler's forehead.

'Dr Chandler, at the moment everybody's a suspect. Would you answer the question please.'

'I've already told the security team on Mars that I left the bar and went to my room. I was there all night.'

'You were on your own?'

'No, I'm sure you're aware that I was in the company of a young lady I met in the bar.'

Cabello gave him a long stare before consulting his notebook again and flicking back a few pages. Having apparently found what he was searching for he looked up at Chandler who was doing his best to appear unruffled.

'In your original interview you stated that you spent the night in the company of this young woman. Is that correct?'

'Yes of course. My colleagues will confirm that.'

'Your colleagues agree that you left the bar with this woman – and that's confirmed by the security cameras. However, what you did subsequently is the issue.'

'Well why don't you talk to the girl I was with? She works in the hydroponics section.' More sweat appeared on his forehead and his right index finger began twitching spasmodically.

'Doctor, I think you know as well as I that she doesn't work in the hydroponics section or any other section – unless you call the sex trade a section. In fact, we have talked to her and she's stated quite categorically that she spent no more than an hour-and-a-half with you that night, leaving a little before 02.30. She also said you were very angry at the time and you made some comments about a French colleague.'

Chandler got up and poured a large scotch. From habit, he offered one to Cabello but the Chief waved his hand in dismissal and waited until he'd settled again. Chandler took a swig and wiped his forehead. He was visibly shaking now.

'I'm sorry. I didn't think it was particularly important when I gave my original statement. I honestly thought Philippe had committed suicide and I didn't particularly want to go over my time with Rosalie in detail. I'm sure you can understand.'

Cabello sighed. 'Alright Doctor – suppose we start again? What happened on the night of Dr Fournier's murder?'

Chandler took another gulp of his drink and tried to get his large frame comfortable in his chair.

'Okay. I left the bar with Rosalie and we went to my room. I admit I was upset and things got a little out of control.'

'That's alright, doctor, I'm not interested in that. What I want to know is what you told Rosalie. I assume there was a degree of professional rivalry between you and Dr Fournier?'

"I was jealous as hell of him.' Chandler drained the rest of his drink and got up to get another. Cabello was impressed. That admission had taken quite a lot of courage under the circumstances and his estimation of the man went up a notch. 'He was a new member of the team,' Chandler continued when he'd refilled his glass. 'I was told by Chayka that he came with a glowing resume and excellent references. I've always assigned that collection of attributes to myself – and I guess I saw him as competition. Then, to make matters worse, he and Tirzah Blumstein hit it off and... well I don't know whether you've noticed but she is kind of gorgeous.'

'So the tension between you was both personal and professional.' Cabello scribbled in his notebook.

'Yes, I think we disliked each other almost immediately.' Chandler leaned forward slightly trying to see what Cabello was writing. The Chief, without appearing to notice, sat back slightly, taking the notebook out of his line of sight. A small smile played round the corner of his mouth.

'Alright. Now Rosalie mentioned some equations. What would their relevance be?'

Chandler downed his drink in one. 'I suppose you know that I'm the mathematician of our team? Well, my stock in trade is equations – it's what I work with every day of my life. One of the projects we'd been working on at Cambridge, when we got side-tracked into the life-generation experiments, was a method of making photonic transmission – PHASEing – available to everybody. We called it "mass PHASEing". I'd personally invested many hours trying to work up a suitable set of equations and had got precisely nowhere. How do you think I felt when

Philippe told me he'd managed to develop just such a set of equations?'

'Angry I would think.'

'Angry doesn't begin to describe it – I was absolutely furious. Then I got thinking and realised how unlikely it was. Philippe was a sub-quantal biochemist not a mathematician. He'd certainly understand sub-quantal equations – but that's a far cry from developing a revolutionary new set. I thought it had to be a wind-up, so I demanded proof.'

'And?'

'He provided me with proof! He showed me a set of equations that accurately described mass PHASEing.'

'It must have been very frustrating.'

'But that's the point. There was no way he could have done it – not on his own, anyway. That had to mean he'd been working with Chayka behind my back.'

'I see. Now can we move on to what happened when Rosalie left?'

'Rosalie left at about 02.20 and I thought I'd go for a walk to clear my head. As I came out of my room Tirzah was waving her biochemist friend goodbye and the first thing that went through my mind was that she might like to come to my room for a drink.' Cabello stopped writing and looked up questioningly. 'Okay, okay. I suppose I was hoping for a bit more than that – but it didn't get past the hoping stage because Philippe suddenly appeared from round the corner. He made a beeline for Tirzah and they disappeared back into her room.'

'That couldn't have helped your mood.'

'Too true.'

'So what did you do next?'

'I just wondered round. Most of it's just a blur – I was so mad. I went back to my room eventually. I suppose it'd be about 03.15 by then. I lay awake for a while and then at some point drifted off to sleep. That's it.'

He looked hopefully at Cabello, who deliberately took some time finishing his notes. He put his notebook away and stared long and hard at Chandler. The man's testimony had the ring of truth about it – in particular the rivalry between an established team member and a new one. Although there was clearly motive enough for murder, and Chandler was a big enough man to be able to pull it off, Cabello surprised himself by believing him. He got up to leave.

'Dr Chandler, it took a little encouragement but I think you've been very honest with me today. However, you have both motive and opportunity – so you'll remain one of our suspects. Thank you for your cooperation.'

Giving the visibly deflated scientist one last piercing stare, he left the room, pausing outside the door while he checked his interview list. Next up was Dr Blumstein.

He found Tirzah in the room the XO had allocated to Chayka's team. She looked startled when he said he'd like to talk to her privately but promptly stopped what she was doing and went with him back to her cabin.

'Dr Blumstein,' Cabello began, 'I gather you knew Dr Fournier better than most of your colleagues.'

Tirzah didn't seem fazed by this at all.

'You've been talking to Simon. He hated Philippe from the moment he first saw him. Yes, I knew him better than the others – and yes, we were having an affair.' She looked challengingly at Cabello, who pulled out his notebook and made a brief entry.

'You saw him in the bar the night before he died?'

'I saw him – but not to talk to. We'd had a falling-out and I was giving him a hard time. He didn't come anywhere near me – just wondered round with a face like thunder. He eventually sat on his own at a table and a bit later in the evening was joined by a big guy I've never seen before. I got a bit distracted at that point but a bit later I noticed they'd both left. That's it.'

'But you saw him again later, didn't you?'

'Simon again! Yes, that's true. We spent about an hour together.'

Cabello referred back to her original statement. 'According to this, you originally stated you spent the entire night in your room.'

'I did. I just didn't specify who I spent it with. From the time I left the bar until about 02.30 I was with Yvonne and then, from the time she left until about 03.45, I was with Philippe. When he left I spent the rest of the night alone.'

'And how did Dr Fournier seem? It seems a little strange that he'd come to your room after you'd ignored him in the bar all evening'

'Yeah, I was pretty horrible to him. I don't know why he came to me – it may be he wasn't intending to until he saw me in the corridor.'

'And what was he like? Did he seem depressed?'

'I wouldn't say he was clinically depressed but he was definitely on a downer. I could tell he was still holding back on something and I tried to get him to tell me what it was but he wouldn't budge. He said it would be dangerous if I knew.'

Cabello's ears pricked up. 'How so?'

'I've no idea. He refused to elaborate on it. Then he changed the subject.'

'To what?'

'To sex – but he wasn't himself even with that. His performance was definitely off.'

Cabello ignored the obvious attempt to throw him off his stride. 'So did you part on good terms?'

'Not particularly. I was grumpy after the bad sex and he was pretty low when he left. I did try to get him to stay but he simply wouldn't. Said he had things to do.'

'At that time in the morning? Didn't he even give you a hint of what they might be?'

'No, he didn't. He just insisted on leaving. Can't say I blame him really – I wasn't being particularly nice. I didn't see him again until…' Tirzah's face clouded over and her eyes filled with tears. She pulled out a tissue and began dabbing at her eyes. 'Is there anything else, Chief?'

Cabello actually felt guilty about what he had to do next. Dr Blumstein clearly hadn't yet recovered from seeing her lover hanging from a rock and it must have been very hard on her to think he'd committed suicide. Now he was going to make things far worse. Unfortunately, he had no alternative – and she would find out the truth from her colleagues in any case.

'Yes, just one thing. I'm very sorry but I have to inform you that Dr Fournier didn't commit suicide as we initially thought.' Tirzah looked confused. 'We now know he was murdered.'

A look of horror passed over her face. 'No! It can't be!'

'I'm afraid there's no doubt about it – and you told me he mentioned something being too dangerous to tell you.'

Tirzah was now openly sobbing. 'Yes, but I don't know what it was. Oh God! What was he doing?'

Cabello frowned but couldn't think of any reason to prolong this. As far as he was concerned, the woman had nothing to do with Fournier's death – although she seemed to be partly blaming herself for it because of her self-perceived failings in being more supportive. He stood and made his way to the door.

'I think that will be all for now, Dr Blumstein. Thank you for your cooperation and I'm sorry for your loss.'

He left Tirzah crying her eyes out in the armchair and stood for a moment outside her door replaying the encounter in his head. Dr Blumstein was clearly a confident, outgoing young woman who was comfortable in her own skin and had been quite open in her responses to his questions. She'd also seemed genuinely upset by Fournier's death, suggesting her feelings towards him had been much more than her flippant replies implied.

Her comments about Fournier's state of mind were interesting because they seemed to bear out Cabello's own observations of a man who was troubled but not suicidal. The other comment about Fournier refusing to confide something in her because of his fears that it might be dangerous to her was the clincher. If they hadn't already known Fournier had been murdered, these two facts would have been highly suggestive. Unfortunately, Dr Blumstein had not made either of them available to the inquest. He sighed. People never seemed to get it. They failed to realise that even the most inconsequential comment could have a huge impact on how things turned out. Ah well – too late to worry about it now. In his view, Blumstein wasn't a suspect. Time to move on to Dr Dominguez.

Cabello's interview with Dominguez was short and very unhelpful. The security tapes showed that the dwarf had remained in the bar until late and had then helped Dr Altmeyer back to his room. According to his previous statement he'd remained in his room all night and he still maintained that this was the case. Cabello didn't prolong things any more than he had with Dr Blumstein as it was clear that Dominguez was physically incapable of committing the murder.

Back in the interim security office Cabello met up with the rest of the team for the 18.00 debrief. Baxter hadn't had any luck with his attempts to access the pad and Deira had confirmed there was nothing she could do at a distance unless a datasphere connection could be established. Landau, Hunstan and Fingal had covered a good portion of the ship in the search for a data wafer but had found nothing. Petrelli had had the most luck with Dr Altmeyer.

There was still nothing of interest in Altmayer's statement because the man couldn't actually remember anything after about 22.00 and awoke the next morning in his bed not knowing how he'd got there. This was supported by the images from the security cameras. However, a search of his room had revealed a length of rope, forty-five metres long, the gauge of which exactly matched that used in the hanging. Petrelli had also come across an old hunting knife that Altmeyer admitted belonged to him and, following a careful check, had found that this was what had been used to cut the rope. Dr Altmeyer admitted to buying the rope but said he had no idea that a length was missing or that his knife had been used to cut it.

Cabello congratulated Petrelli on a good job then summarised the day's work.

'Our progress is limited. We have one suspect, Dr Chandler, who has motive and opportunity but no means as far as we can tell; another suspect, Dr Altmeyer, has the means, in the shape of the rope, but no motive. Unfortunately, he'd appear to have little opportunity if the security tapes are correct. We can't find any evidence of a hidden data wafer and the pad belonging to Dr Fournier, which could be our best piece of evidence, is heavily encrypted and we can't get into it. From Dr Blumstien's comments, we know that Dr Fournier was engaged in something he thought was dangerous, but we have no idea what that might have been. Where does that leave us?'

'Sir,' Baxter said, 'I don't think there's much more we can do. I'd say the most likely suspect is that stranger on Mars.'

'Thank you Mr Baxter. That sums up my own feelings – except we haven't quite completed the search for the data wafer.' He looked round the men. 'Report here at 08.00 tomorrow and we'll see if we can get the search finished quickly. Dismissed.'

Cabello waited while the men filed out then got a coffee and settled down to compose his report. It could be summarised in two words – "no progress". They'd confirmed Altmeyer and Chandler as continuing suspects and found the rope and pad – but that was about it.

He put the final touches to the report and opened a channel to Monroe.

'Hello Hector,' he said when Monroe's ruddy face appeared. 'Well, we've done our best up here but I don't think it'll help much. I'm sending you my report now.'

'Hello Julio. I didn't expect you to solve the case but I thought perhaps something would turn up.' He looked down briefly. 'Okay, got the report.'

'Okay. Despite some circumstantial evidence I'm not convinced our murderer's one of the scientists – I think your stranger is a much more likely prospect. Our main problem is accessing the contents of Fournier's pad. My IT guy has already been in touch with Agent MacMahon and she hasn't been able to help because the blasted thing's completely off-line. If she could give some further thought to it I'd be grateful.'

'I'll ask her. She's only six months out of the Academy and trying very hard to be a proper field agent. It was her supervisor who suffered catastrophic side-effects from the moon-Mars PHASE. Part of her mission is to find our stranger and she's convinced he's a foreign agent, possibly American. I'm with you in thinking he's almost certainly linked to Fournier's death in some way.'

'I get the feeling he could be pivotal to the case. I hope you find him soon.'

'We'll keep working on it.'

The two men exchanged a little general chit-chat before Cabello closed the line. He sat back and mulled over the proceedings. With the exception of completing the search for the data wafer there was precious little he and his team could do now. They needed a break, and he couldn't see one coming any time soon. He closed down his terminal. Perhaps sleeping on it would produce some new ideas, though he strongly doubted it.

Chapter 11

Deira was bored – bored and exasperated. After the excitement of her demonstration and their review of the security camera output from the bar she'd begun to think that she and Monroe were onto something. Unfortunately, Chief Cabello's investigation on the Q-ship hadn't provided any conclusive evidence against either Drs Chandler or Altmeyer and Cabello wasn't convinced either of them had been involved in the murder. That left the unknown agent as their prime suspect – and he'd completely vanished. He'd stopped frequenting the bar and repeated searches had found no sign of him.

The picture from the security cameras had been run through every major database, including those containing the highly classified identities of Bureau agents, and they'd come up with a big fat zero. Of course, if he was an American agent he'd only appear on a classified database to which neither she nor Monroe had access. They'd come up against a brick wall.

There hadn't been much progress with Adam either. The medics had used every test they could think of to determine what his problem was. They knew his DNA had been badly damaged during the PHASE and they'd had to assume this was responsible for the psychological changes that were so distressing. Unfortunately, they had no idea what might constitute a treatment and had tried a number of ad hoc therapeutic interventions based on best guess scenarios. Nothing had worked and it seemed that the next step was to transfer him back to Earth so he could be investigated using state-of-the-art facilities only available there. The senior consultant told Monroe that they'd be filing a report soon – and that report would recommend mothballing the interplanetary PHASE programme for the immediate future. If the Bureau agreed to this, Deira would be stuck on Mars until a Q-ship came her way – and none were scheduled for the next three weeks at least.

Deira's comm suddenly indicated a call from Monroe and his normally ruddy face appeared on her virtual screen almost glowing with excitement.

'We've had a sighting of your agent,' he said. 'A hydroponics engineer caught a glimpse of him in their facility yesterday evening. Apparently it's the second time he'd seen him but didn't have the gumption to come forward until today.'

Deira got to her feet, feeling the adrenaline start to flow. Of course! Hydroponics would be a perfect place to hide. Plenty of cover, relatively small number of workers, warm and comfortable. She knew they'd covered the facility in one of the searches but that wouldn't stop their mystery agent using it as a place to sleep. Perhaps this was the break they needed.

'That's great news!' she said. 'Hector, I'd keep your men away if I were you. They wouldn't have much luck capturing him even if they found him – and they might get hurt.'

'So what do you suggest?' Monroe looked a little deflated.

'I'll stake the place out tonight. If he appears I'll at least have a chance of taking him out.

'Okay, I'll go with that for tonight, but take care – he could be a mean bastard.'

'Will do. Wish me luck.'

Later that evening, Deira put on her Bureau uniform and carefully went through the checklist to ensure she was mission-ready. This was the first time she'd worn the suit since arriving on Mars and it felt strange to be doing this without Adam. She slipped silently into the moist, inky blackness of Hydroponics and immediately knew she was on the right track. There was something about the scent of fertiliser and foliage – it was where she'd hang out if she were in the same position as the unknown agent. She selected a hiding place among some particularly large-leaved plants and settled down to wait.

Time passed. One hour. Two. In spite of her training her muscles began to stiffen up and she yearned to be able to move round a little. She stifled a yawn and was just thinking this was going to be a waste of time when she sensed something. She tensed, and peered through the darkness. There it was – for a fleeting second, a shadow, dark against the foliage. Then it was gone again. Deira remained frozen in place, hardly daring to breathe and trying to get a fix on the man she knew was just a few metres away. Finally, she saw him. He was standing amidst the foliage looking round uncertainly as if he sensed something different but couldn't be sure. He continued to scan the area for some time, and she could have sworn he looked straight at her on one occasion. Obviously not, however, because he eventually seemed satisfied and visibly relaxed. He hunkered down, took something out of his jacket pocket and began to eat.

Deira let out her breath very slowly and shifted her position slightly. It was almost noiseless but the man must have been on high alert because his head shot up. He stared again in her direction – and this time it was clear he'd seen her.

Deira knew she'd only get this one chance to take him while he was still unprepared so she drew her staff and ran at him. The man reacted like a coiled spring, leaping up and drawing his own staff before she was even halfway to him. She gasped. How could he move that fast? Her advantage had disappeared in the blink of an eye. The two agents faced off, moving easily into combat stance and circling slowly, the eyes of each fixed on those of their opponent. It was the man who finally broke the impasse.

'You've got things wrong about me, you know. I'm not your enemy.'

Well that was one thing cleared up – he was definitely American. Deira continued circling. They'd been warned about this in the Academy. Beware opponents who tried to talk to you – pleasantly or otherwise. It was almost always an attempt to ruin your concentration and get you to let your guard down. Well it wasn't going to work. She shifted her staff from one hand to the other and looked for an opening in his defence. Then he did the unexpected – he stopped dead and lowered his staff.

'This is stupid' he said 'I know I'm looking a bit rough but you must see that...'

Deira took the offered opportunity and landed a sharp jab to his left cheek, raising an ugly weal. The man's hand went automatically to his face and he looked surprised. Then he raised his staff and moved in to the attack. It was so fast that Deira was completely unprepared. Nobody could have been prepared.

It was a weird fight. Despite his clear advantage, the man didn't seem to want to capitalise on it. Deira was fighting to the very best of her ability but somehow her opponent was able to anticipate her every move and apply the appropriate counter. He made no offensive moves of his own and was so relaxed he could have been on a Sunday afternoon walk. He didn't even seem to be working up a sweat. It was obvious he was holding back and Deira knew he could overwhelm her in an instant if he really wanted to. What the hell was going on here?

Deira was just beginning to wonder how she was going to extricate herself from this situation when the man made the decision for her. Having been fighting defensively for so long, he executed a series of lightning offensive moves that culminated in her staff being knocked out of her grip and sent flying across the floor. She prepared to defend herself as well as she could without her staff though she knew it was hopeless. She was completely outclassed. The man lowered his staff and smiled.

'Whatever you think I've done, you've got it all wrong,' he said. 'We really need to talk...'

Before he could say any more there was a sudden commotion from a dark area immediately behind him and somebody came hurtling out of the undergrowth screaming like a banshee and waving a staff round like a mad thing. It was Adam. What the hell was he doing here?

Adam launched himself at the American with an animal-like aggression Deira had never seen before. What he lacked in technique he made up for in sheer energy and by rights the American should have been lying on the floor senseless in no time. However, that was to ignore his incredible reflexes, and once again Deira witnessed them used in a manner that was almost unreal. She knew that if the positions had been reversed there was no way she'd have been able to fend off Adam – he was too close and had the advantage of surprise. The American, on the other hand, whirled on the spot and parried the first few swipes of the staff before neatly tripping Adam up and tapping him lightly on the head. It was precisely the move Deira had previously used.

Deira expected Adam to drop silently to the floor. Instead he gave an almighty bellow and clutched his chest. All she could see were the whites of his eyes as he fell to his knees, still roaring. Then he fell forward and lay still. She rushed to him and felt for a pulse. Nothing. Desperately she turned him over and listened for breathing. Again nothing. She commenced CPR, pounding his chest with all her strength and yelling for him to wake up. How long this lasted she couldn't say but she was brought up short when she felt a hand on her shoulder. It was the American and he seemed genuinely sad.

'I think you should stop – he's gone.'

She gave up with Adam and climbed to her feet, lashing out with her fists.

'You killed him! First you killed Fournier and now you've killed Adam. Murderer!'

There was such a mixture of emotions running through her she could hardly think but she still had the sense to flick the emergency call button on her wrist console. The American grabbed her flailing fists and looked at Adam with shock.

'I didn't kill him.' he spoke in a voice so low she could hardly hear him. 'That small tap couldn't have killed him.' It sounded like he was trying to convince himself of the fact.

'He was sick," Deira yelled, pulling her hands away. 'A small tap might have been all that was needed. You're...'

She was interrupted by the sound of running feet and the American started out of his reverie. He glanced hurriedly round before turning back to her.

'Got to go but we'll talk again soon. I'm sorry about your friend–I didn't mean to hurt him' He spun on his heels and ran.

Deira made no attempt to follow. She was all done in and knew she'd never be able to get the better of him. She knelt down and took Adam in her arms while she waited for the cavalry to arrive.

Later, when all the pandemonium had settled down, she sat with a blanket over her shoulders and a cup of hot coffee, replaying the evening's events in her head. She'd been well and truly outmatched and she knew it. Apart from training sessions, she'd never had to face off against another agent, but she'd always felt she'd give a good account of herself if that ever happened. Now she felt completely useless – worse than useless – and Adam was now gone for good.

She kept thinking about the speed at which the American moved. There was something familiar about it–something she'd seen before. Then she remembered – the warehouse. The strange agent with the orange force field had moved in exactly the same way. Come to think of it he'd been a similar size too. He couldn't be the same person because of what the Director had said. So what did that leave? A new breed of American agent? Clones? Her mind began to fly again, just like it had some days ago.

Luckily she was interrupted by the door opening. Monroe hastened in, took one look at her and put an arm round her shoulder in a fatherly way.

'You all right, lass?'

Deira nodded miserably. 'I couldn't stop him, Hector. He was incredibly fast. He's got to be our murderer because he killed Adam.'

'No he didn't. I've just been talking to the medics. Adam was able to throw off his sedation tonight because he went into a hyper-adrenal state. He was manic, and it was just luck that nobody was with him when he left the infirmary because they'd have probably been badly hurt. There'll have to be a formal autopsy, of course, but the attending doctor is absolutely convinced he died of a massive heart attack brought on by the adrenaline flooding his system – a system that was already badly compromised. The knock on the head was purely coincidental.'

Deira remembered the look of shock on the American's face when Adam collapsed and his quiet denial that he was responsible. Could he be innocent? She felt humbled, stupid and angry – and now she began to feel scared as her mind once more threatened to move into overdrive. She looked pleadingly at Monroe.

'You think I could get a sedative? I need my brain switched off for a few hours.'

Monroe called the lead medic who agreed that a period of sedation would be beneficial. He gave Deira a couple of tablets and led her to a bed in the infirmary. She smiled as the sedative took hold and her thoughts began to fade out.

When she woke the next morning she felt like crap. After a quick examination, the medics said she was good to go so she lost no time getting back to her room for a shower and change of clothes. She visited the refectory for breakfast and had three cups of coffee in an attempt to buck herself up but soon realised it was going to take more than caffeine to sort her out today. All she could think of was Adam, still not fully believing he'd gone forever. She badly needed something to distract her.

Almost on cue, her comm beeped and Monroe appeared on her virtual screen.

'Hope you're feeling better today. I thought you'd be interested in a report that's just come through from Titan.'

'Sure. What's it about?'

'Wait and see.'

Her wrist console flashed to indicate receipt of the file and Monroe cut the connection.

The report was from the PHASE techie on Titan, Amadi Okafor, and it related to an unauthorised incoming transmission three days ago. The transmission was probably an emergency PHASE and the transferee was a tall man with partial amnesia who sounded American. From the technical viewpoint the most troubling thing was the complete failure of the instruments to show a transmission locus – this was supposed to be impossible. For Deira, the key word was "American" and she quickly moved to the enclosed picture. There he was – the same guy she'd fought the previous night – complete with a livid bruise on his left cheek.

She put in a call back to Monroe who, from the speed of his answer, was clearly waiting for it.

'Hector, this is impossible. This is the guy I fought last night and it was me that gave him that bruise. But this report says he's been on Titan for three days – and the bruise looks about three days old. How in all hell can he be in two different places, separated by millions of miles, at the same time?'

'I said you'd be interested. I confess, I haven't got a clue what's going on but this guy seems to be at the centre of it all.'

'Well if he's on Titan, that's where I'm going. You're right – he's the key to all this.' Deira stopped when she saw the look on Monroe's face. 'What?' she said.

'You're not going anywhere lass. The medics have been dithering about sending their report on Adam to the Bureau but last night's little affair crystallised things for them. It's literally about to go – and it recommends putting a hold on all interplanetary PHASES until the possible side-effects are clarified.'

'No! They can't do that – it'll completely screw the mission.' Scowling, she activated her wrist console and input her new security codes. 'You say it hasn't gone yet?' she rapidly scanned communications traffic.

'Not yet, but you'll never…'

'Got it!' she interrupted. 'It was in the outgoing buffer and about to go but I've intercepted it.'

'You can't do that. They'll throw you out of the Bureau and possibly into prison. Come to that *I* ought to throw you in prison!'

'Good luck with that. Now, if I make sure it still gets sent but with a slightly different time stamp …' she was working fast now, '… it'll give me time to get to Titan.' She finished and looked at Monroe. 'You didn't hear any of that, did you Hector?'

'Any of what?'

'I owe you one, Chief.'

'Oh get out of here.' Monroe gave a weak smile. 'Go and catch that bastard.' There was a brief pause. 'And take care of yourself.' He cut the connection.

Deira flew round the room throwing her belongings into her bags. She changed back into her uniform and hurried down the corridor to the PHASE terminal where she found Amelie already shutting things down. She looked surprised to see Deira.

'If you're looking to go somewhere I can't help, Deira. The medics tell me I've got to shut up shop until things have been sorted out.'

'You don't have to shut down for another...' She checked the time. '... thirty minutes. The report hasn't gone yet so turn your stuff back on and get started because I want to be PHASEd to Titan before this ban comes into force.'

Amelie looked uncomfortable but turned her equipment back on and began to prepare for transmission.

'Titan? Why Titan?'

'Because that's where my American fugitive is.' Deira shoved her bags unceremoniously into the quantum transmitter. 'I'm guessing he used your equipment for an emergency PHASE when you weren't here.'

'That's impossible. The new equipment can't be operated and used by the same person – it's far too sensitive and the setting of the destination locus needs fine-tuning right up to the point of transmission.'

'Then how did he get to Titan?' Deira mused. 'More to the point how could he have been there while he was still here?'

'You're not making a lot of sense, you know, but I'm getting the message loud and clear. You badly need to be on Titan. You realise this'll be a long trip?'

Deira had only just begun to think of that. The distance involved was pretty terrifying, making the moon to Mars trip pale into insignificance. She watched the minutes and seconds tick by while Amelie worked to get her apparatus set up and ready.

Amelie worked like a mad thing but it still took twenty-six minutes before she finally said she was happy to proceed. Deira hurried into the PHASE chamber and lay on the couch, clutching her staff and trying to think of something not related to disintegration. Amelie's voice came through the comm.

'You okay in there Deira? Ready for transmission on your signal.'

Deira gulped and squeezed her staff even tighter as her nerves began to get the better of her. This was unacceptable – she was on the verge of bottling out altogether. She had to get control.

'Fire when ready.' The phrase tripped out of her mouth before she knew she was going to say it and Amelie responded immediately.

'Okay. Transmission protocol initiated. Tight Beam Deira. You'll be gone on my mark. Three... two... one'

Deira lay still, her hear hammering. Now she was committed – no turning back.

She glanced up when Amelie reached "one" on her countdown and saw a familiar figure loom up behind the young techie. She couldn't believe it – it was the American agent, a lopsided grin on his face.

Desperately she tried to shout a warning but the comm was always turned off immediately prior to transmission and Amelie was concentrating on the destination locus. The last thing Deira saw before the neural blocker hit was the man raising his staff above Amelie's head.

Then all went black.

Chapter 12

S OL SAT CROSS-LEGGED on his bed and concentrated, his only movement an intermittent twitch of his mouth and throat. The memories of his first encounter with Chard had returned – the implantation of the node in his brain through which the AI communicated and the struggle he'd had trying to form his thoughts into coherent words and phrases that it could understand. At the Agency bonding session this had been referred to as "structured thinking" – and he'd found he just couldn't hack it. Then, when he'd virtually given up, he'd suddenly thought about his attempts at ventriloquism when he was younger – and that worked! Now, he was practicing sub-vocalisation – his best attempt at structured thinking.

'We need to get our act together, buddy,' he sub-vocalised. 'It's been three days now and we've made no progress.'

He thought back to his attempts to elicit help from Amadi. The young techie had been delighted when Sol had reappeared to complete his post-PHASE tests but Sol thought he detected some suspicion too. It was, after all, most unusual for agents to be so compliant.

Trying to get anything out of him turned out to be so much wasted effort – the techie was fixated on the tests and was virtually monosyllabic in his responses to Sol's gentle probing. It hadn't been an enlightening experience at all and Sol had soon given up in disgust. Luckily, Chard was several steps ahead of him. Despite his ongoing networking problems he'd been able to log on to the local net and obtain a substantial amount of information about the surface conditions on Titan.

'I had hoped some of your memories would have returned by now,' said Chard. 'Their continued absence creates a big problem for us. The evidence, circumstantial though it might be, is quite damning. You were almost certainly on Mars when the first murder for twenty years took place. In addition, your physical appearance and significant post-PHASE effects suggest an emergency transfer – as if you were attempting to escape.'

'I get it, I get it. If it looks like a rabbit and hops like a rabbit it probably is a rabbit. I know it looks like I'm responsible for the death of that scientist but it still doesn't feel right. Isn't there anything you can do to kind of kick-start my neurones?'

'I've many ways of modifying your physiology and neurochemistry Sol but I'm unable to retrieve lost memories. We agree we're probably victims of sabotage and it would appear that you've suffered transmission damage as well. The situation we find ourselves in is at odds with the memories that remain. We urgently require more data to make sense of things.'

Sol knew Chard was right. What memories they had left suggested Titan was off limits due to radiation contamination – yet Chard's access to the environmental systems confirmed nominal conditions on the surface. No excess radiation. It was impossible to square the circle – and would remain so until more data were forthcoming.

'So what now?' Sol said. 'Ammy might know something about memory retrieval – these techies are often pretty good at sub-quantal physics. If I could get even a few memories back it might help. As to escape, I think we're pretty much agreed that we're going to have to make for the American Base. I could try PHASEing out but I can't see Ammy helping us with that. I suppose I could disable him and go through another emergency transmission but somehow I don't think that'd be a good idea.'

'I concur. Some of your memory loss is undoubtedly due to your previous transmission. Another emergency jump would be foolhardy in the extreme. However, we do need to consider taking action soon – certainly before the new security team arrives.'

'Yeah, once the new square-heads get here we're toast. Could we use the Q-ship as an escape route?'

'The ship won't land – the passengers will be sent down by shuttle. Stowing away on a shuttle's virtually impossible because of the lack of hiding places and, even if we did make it to the ship, we'd still be vulnerable because it will be remaining in orbit for a few days while necessary repairs are carried out. Once our absence is confirmed, the ship's the obvious place to search.'

Sol stood and stretched. He'd gone over these scenarios in his own mind enough times but he tended to use the AI as a convenient sounding board to test his conclusions.

'So we're back to a surface escape. How far is the American Base?'

'Not far – between three and four kilometres. However, such a journey could be hazardous. I've acquired a considerable amount of data about the surface conditions but that's not the same as being out there. We don't know what pitfalls we might encounter. There's also the question of what sort of welcome we'll get if we *do* reach the Americans.'

'Do we have any alternatives?'

'It would appear not. If you do this, you'll have to use one of the specially-designed exosuits which should work well enough for a short trek. The full space suits that are used for more extensive undertakings are kept locked away and any attempt to obtain one would immediately give us away.'

'Okay, so first I'll try Ammy again and put a bit more pressure on him about my memory loss.'

Amadi was hard at work when Sol arrived in the PHASE terminal. Ever since Sol had unexpectedly turned up in his PHASE chamber the techie had been obsessed with finding out what had happened and he clearly wasn't giving up easily. Sol had become used to a big beaming grin from him but today was different. He looked up warily.

'Oh, hello Sol.' He sounded distinctly uneasy as well. 'I still haven't found out what went wrong with your PHASE. It's a real mystery.'

'It'll probably stay that way until I get some memories back.' Sol thought this was the ideal way to get Amadi engaged in memory retrieval. 'What say...' he began.

'You do have a very strange quantum signature,' Amadi interrupted, still engrossed in his instruments.

'Something many of my lady friends tell me!' Sol grinned broadly. He peered over Amadi's shoulder at the graphs the techie had been examining. They meant nothing at all to him but one particular graph caught his eye. It was generally unremarkable – a smooth upward curve and a downward curve with a notch on it. What was remarkable was a tag attached to the notch. It read "Unknown in this space-time continuum." He blinked and wondered what the hell that meant. Then he put it to one side and got onto more important issues.

'Ammy,' he said. 'I still haven't got any memories back. Is there anything at all you can suggest?'

'Well, I could point you in the right direction.' Amadi definitely wasn't his normal self, appearing uneasy and reluctant to engage. He pulled out a data wafer and slipped it into his wrist terminal. A tome entitled "Neurological Effects of Photonic Transmission in the Human." appeared on his virtual screen.

'This is the most complete text available on post-PHASE memory loss. You're welcome to have it.'

Sol looked at the e-book, got Amadi to flick through the four hundred or so pages and inwardly groaned. It might be a complete text to Amadi, but to Sol it was so much gobbledegook. He looked forlornly at Amadi.

'Please tell me you know what's in this.'

'I'm very well acquainted with it – my PhD was on post-PHASE amnesia.'

'So are there any solutions available?'

'Yes and no.'

'Meaning?'

'There are various solutions available for specific types of amnesia but, as far as I know, there's nothing suitable in your case. If I knew how you managed to get here I might be able to find some avenues worth exploring, but it's unlikely I'll have anything within, say, a week.'

That ruled out memory retrieval in the time remaining before the Q-ship arrived. The only option now was a surface escape. Sol switched the book off and put his arm round Amadi's shoulder. It was meant to be a comradely sort of gesture but it clearly made the techie very uncomfortable.

'Ammy,' he said, 'I'm going stir-crazy round the Base with nothing to do. I need a little action and I was considering a short trip outside. Do you know where I might find the exosuits?'

Amadi's suspicious look appeared again – then there was a beeping noise from a small screen that Sol hadn't previously noticed. Amadi glanced down – and whatever he saw seemed to shock him badly. His hands began to shake and sweat stood out on his brow. He looked scared to death.

'Your picture and description have just appeared on the datasphere, Sol.' Chard's voice was urgent. 'That beeping was Amadi's live news feed. The reason he looks so frightened is that he appears to think you're a murderer.'

Amadi did, indeed, look scared out of his wits as he gazed up at Sol. He glanced in the direction of the door but must have realised he had no chance of making a run for it. Sol moved swiftly to reassure him.

'Ammy, whatever they're saying I promise you I'm not a murderer. You're quite safe with me.'

Amadi looked up and was obviously still unsure but with a bit more coaxing he regained some of his usual bounce.

'The picture's only just appeared.' He spoke so softly that Sol could hardly hear him.

'I know Ammy. Don't worry. We'll soon clear this up…'

'The description came over earlier today.'

'That's okay…' Sol stopped as he realised the techie was trying to tell him something. 'What did you do, Amadi?'

'When the description arrived I sent a report to Security Chief Monroe on Mars saying that it sounded like you and that you'd been here for three days. I also sent a picture.' Amadi now looked more embarrassed than scared. 'I'm sorry Sol. I'd been trying to find out who you were, and then this description came through, and it seemed to match, and they didn't say anything about a murder investigation, and...'

'Stop! I get the message. You didn't know you were dumping me in it. You were trying to help me find out who I really am. Okay. It's not all bad – we've got some time before the Q-ship arrives.'

'But you haven't much time before Agent MacMahon gets here. She saw my report and immediately PHASEd for Titan. She's already on her way.'

Sol couldn't believe this. His day had just gone from pleasant to shitty in ten seconds flat.

'When's she due?'

'About...' Amadi consulted his instruments, '... thirty minutes, give or take a couple of minutes. Sol I'm...'

Sol didn't wait round to find out what Amadi was or wasn't. With a disgusted 'Oh fuck!' he charged out of the terminal and along the corridor to his room. He dashed inside, locked the door, and let out a huge groan.

'OH FUCK!'

'I heard all that,' Chard said. 'It appears our worst fears are true and this female agent is on to us. This changes everything. We're out of time. We must leave this Base immediately, before she arrives.'

'Too damned true! Have you got all the data we'll need?'

'Yes, already done. I must say the technology is quite primitive – I wasn't aware the Europeans were so far behind us.'

'That'll help us anyway – we could do with a break. Do you know where they store the exosuits? I never did find out from Ammy. Once we're on the surface you'll have to guide me to the American Base.'

'Concur! The exosuit locker is outside the airlock, a few hundred metres from here. If you exit this room, turn right, proceed for a hundred metres and then turn left you should find the airlock on your left after a further two hundred metres. It'll be clearly signed and the suits will be outside.'

'Copy that.'

Sol charged out of the door and dashed along the corridor, skidding round a corner and almost knocking over a young female tech he'd have taken more interest in under normal circumstances. However, with the circumstances being as they were, the pheromones didn't have time to kick in before he was charging on again. In two minutes he was standing outside the airlock and in another five he'd torn open the door of the locker and put on one of the exosuits.

'I've followed the instructions but how do I know this damned thing's fitted properly? I don't want it leaking or something.'

'The suit's made from intellifabric so it will automatically fit to your size. The thickness of the suit is to maintain warmth, not pressure. The atmospheric pressure of Titan is slightly higher than Earth so you're in no danger of decompressing, as you would be on the moon. You've already found that the helmet fits over your uniform helmet. It contains one mechanism to filter out the low levels of hydrocarbons present in the atmosphere and another to vent expired carbon dioxide. The bulk of Titan's atmosphere is nitrogen. This is fed to your suit with sufficient oxygen from your tanks to make up a reasonably normal air mix.

The good news is that even a moderate leak won't kill you – though you may end up with a headache.'

'That's comforting.' Sol winced as he struggled with the oxygen delivery system, finally getting the last strap tight. 'Well, what do you think? Good to go?'

'You're ready as you're ever likely to be. This isn't a structured mission'

'You don't say.'

He opened the airlock door and stepped inside. Everything appeared to be straightforward. A pictorial representation of the airlock cycle lit up as soon as he closed the inner door and he watched impatiently as the light moved ponderously through the cycle, from "Inner Hatch Locked" to "Oxygen Evacuated" and finally to "Outer Hatch Unlocked". After what seemed an eternity the outer door hissed open and he stepped out onto the surface. He glanced briefly round and, with Chard providing directions, set out for the American Base. The AI had clearly decided to act as tour guide as well because he kept up a running commentary.

'Over to your left is Ligeia Mare, one of the major north polar seas. You need to keep that on your left – but don't get too close to the shoreline because it's a sticky mess of solid hydrocarbons from evaporation of the sea and could prove dangerous. This means you need to take a slightly curved path, moving away from the sea as you go.'

'Whatever you say, buddy. I'm content to be aimed and fired. No risky business. Let's just get there in one piece.'

He loped over the ground at a fair pace feeling strangely at ease in this unfamiliar environment.

'How do you feel?' Chard asked.

'Good. The suit works just fine – though it still seems a bit crude.'

'It's very simple technology but perfectly adequate for short jaunts such as this one.'

'Yeah, I'm even warming up from all this exercise! How're we doing for distance?'

'We've covered about one K. Move slightly to your right now.'

'Copy that.'

Sol veered off right. The looming presence of the sea was visible over to his left and he could make out the dark stain of the "shore" about a hundred metres away. There had been a light breeze when he'd started out but a wind had picked up and was now gusting strongly, making walking difficult. He leaned into the gusts, trying to avoid being blown over in the light gravity.

'What's with the wind?'

'A breeze is a relatively constant feature,' said Chard. 'It's thought to be caused by tidal forces from Saturn on Titan's atmosphere. The wind you're currently experiencing is more common during Titan summer – which is now in case you're interested.'

Sol stopped and frowned, staring at what looked like large, dark amber clouds gathering overhead.

'Looks like we could be in for a storm. Does Titan have storms?'

'Indeed. They're not uncommon – again predominantly during Titan summer. We might expect lashings of methane rain and very high winds. There's also a risk of sea surges, so again I would urge you to stay well clear of the shoreline.'

Sol grunted unhappily and kept moving. He hated getting wet – even when that simply implied a good soaking with water. He didn't even want to contemplate getting caught in a methane storm.

'I hope these cheap Euro-suits are waterproof.'

'I'm not sure they've ever been tested – there's nothing in the Base manual on the subject. I get the impression they're only intended for use in good weather conditions.'

'Now he tells me! Better hope the weather holds out.'

No sooner were the words out than the wind ramped up, gusting ferociously. Then rain began to fall, freezing droplets of liquid methane that lashed across the landscape in wind-blown sheets. Visibility dropped to a few metres and Sol, while grumbling gently to himself, gave silent thanks for Chard and his unerring guidance. Suddenly, he felt wet inside his suit.

'Shit! The suit leaks! God, I hate getting wet!'

'Actually, given the surface temperature, getting wet would be a significant problem – the insulation in the suit would be compromised and you'd freeze to death very quickly. I suggest activating the energy shield in your uniform since it should provide protection from both wind and rain. I'll also turn on the uniform's heater to help dry out your suit. You may smell fumes until the methane has evaporated, but it shouldn't last long.'

'Damn, but I never thought of that. Just do it!'

The shield flared into life round him, effectively shutting out the weather, and as the uniform's heater came on he began to feel warmer. There was some discomfort while the methane already in the fabric of the suit evaporated, but it was bearable and he was soon feeling much better.

'How much further?'

'Another kilometre. Should take us about twenty minutes.'

Sol grimaced 'Fucking bad weather!' he growled unhappily 'All I seem to get on missions is fucking bad weather.'

He paused and grinned. 'Well how about that? Another memory flash!'

Chapter 13

Deira opened her eyes and gazed round at the featureless PHASE chamber. For a moment, she was disorientated – then the enormity of what she'd just done hit her. She'd just PHASEd over 800 million miles through empty space. She was on Titan.

Anxiously, she went through some basic memory tests and was relieved to find that everything appeared to be fine. This was nothing like the moon-Mars PHASE, that was for sure. She confidently climbed off the couch and checked her balance. Again no problems – things were looking good. This had been a monumental PHASE yet she seemed to be absolutely fine. She felt a rosy glow of contentment. Then a memory slipped back into place – the final few seconds in the Mars PHASE chamber – and her self-congratulation was cut short by the resulting adrenaline surge. She flung open the chamber door to find a black techie she took to be Amadi Okafor staring at her in alarm.

'Emergency containment,' she snapped. 'There may be another transmission coming through shortly. I want this chamber on full lock-down.'

Amadi gaped at her. 'Containment?' he said.

'You heard me. Get it done!'

Amadi had to consult his wrist terminal to find the procedure for lock-down, an original design feature of PHASE chambers that had never previously been implemented. Once activated, it would divert the information stored in the incoming photon beam into a superconductor-lined storage chamber – effectively placing the transferee into suspended animation pending later integration. Although the theory was sound and limited animal tests had been successful, nobody knew for certain if it would work in practice. This meant there was a real risk of losing the transferee, something Amadi was well aware of as he worked the protocol. His hands shook and sweat poured off his face. Finally, he sat back and pronounced they were secure. Deira had been pacing up and down impatiently during Amadi's frenetic activity. Now she collapsed with relief into the nearest chair.

'Anything on your instruments?' she said.

'I have a point of origin for a transmission from Mars but nothing's come through. It doesn't make any sense.' Amadi flicked some switches and checked a read-out. 'Who was the other transmission?'

'The American – the one whose picture you sent Chief Monroe. I presume you're Amadi Okafor?'

Amadi nodded but said nothing – he was too busy trying to work out what had happened to the transmission and whether it was his fault that nobody had come through. No transferee had ever been lost in the history of PHASEing and Amadi didn't want to think of the consequences if this turned out to be the first. His career would be done for, that was for certain.

Now that the immediate risk was controlled, Deira could take stock. She reviewed her last memories of Mars. There was Amelie doing her techie bit – and then the American appeared over her shoulder, brandishing something.

'Amelie!'

She turned to Amadi, who was looking more stricken by the minute.

'The guy looked like he was about to attack her,' she said. 'Can you get Mars on line and check that Amelie's okay?'

Amadi stopped his increasingly desperate attempts to locate the transferee and tuned in the requisite sub-quantal frequency for Mars Base. Amelie soon confirmed she was completely uninjured. Apparently she'd been stunned by something but hadn't been out long and had woken in time to see the American transfer out.

'You sure you're okay?' Deira said. 'I tried shouting a warning but it was too late.'

'I'm absolutely fine. Thanks for asking.'

'Okay. I've got to go now. Take care.'

'You too.' Amelie cut the contact.

Amadi had been listening to this and looked confused. 'I don't understand,' he said.

'What? What don't you understand?'

'Well, Amelie saw the American follow you through the MARS PHASE terminal?'

'That's what she just said.'

'Yet he hasn't appeared in our containment chamber and I can find no evidence that I've lost him.'

'So what does that mean?'

'I don't know – but I do know he was here with me just half-an-hour ago. When I told him you were coming he shot out of here as if the Devil himself was on his tail.'

'What! You told him I was coming? You told him I was coming imminently? By PHASE?'

She stopped ranting as the significance of what she'd just heard dawned on her. Now she was confused too.

'He was here half-an-hour ago? But he can't have been – he was on Mars forty minutes ago. What the crap's going on here?'

'I don't know.'

Amadi was trembling from the rapid sequence of events, and Deira wasn't making things any easier. She was pacing up and down and glaring at the techie.

'If he was here half-an-hour ago, he might still be here,' she said. 'Where would he go?'

'I suppose he might be in his room.'

'Unlikely but worth a try. Take me to it! Now!'

Deira marched Amadi smartly out of the terminal and, within a few minutes, they were standing outside Sol's door. Deira told Amadi to stand clear. Then she drew her staff, opened the door and moved swiftly in, passing quickly round the main room and checking out the bathroom. She wasn't surprised to find nobody there and angrily holstered her staff.

'Damn and blast! So where could he be now?'

Amadi crossed to the network terminal and interrogated the system.

'He must have used the terminal because the entire data file's been downloaded. I didn't think he'd be able to do that because he didn't seem to have any wrist console or other computer hardware.'

Deira was confused, frustrated and angry. 'Doesn't seem to me you think of anything much.'

She was rewarded with a look somewhere between guilt and terror from the stressed-out techie, and she forced herself to calm down. Ranting wasn't helpful – exactly the opposite actually. She needed this guy onside.

'Okay,' she said, deliberately modulating her voice, 'let's go back a little. Amadi – may I call you Amadi–what did the American say to you? Was it just generalities or was there anything more specific?'

Amadi seemed to be helped a little by her use of his first name. He closed his eyes, trying to remember Sol's exact words.

'Well, he said he was thinking about a short trip on the surface and wanted to know more about outside clothing,' he said.

'He's considering going outside? Why?' She suddenly had an idea. 'Is there an American Base near here?'

'Yes there is. It's about four kilometres north-east of here.'

"That's it then. He can't escape off planet from this Base but he might be able to from an American Base. I've got to stop him getting there. Where's the airlock?'

'Not far.' Amadi showed Deira the location on the Base schematic and she charged off. When she got there it was clear someone had recently used it because there was an open suit locker and a missing suit but when she tried to open the airlock it refused access. A puffing Amadi finally caught up with her and explained that the lock was recycling to stand-by mode. It was entirely automatic and couldn't be aborted.

'How long does it take?' Deira was pacing again with frustration.

Amadi checked a dial on the airlock and consulted his wrist terminal.

'The whole process takes ten minutes – two minutes left.'

'So we've only missed him by eight minutes. He can't have got far in that time.' She grabbed one of the exosuits and began pulling it on, following the fitting instructions on the wall.

Amadi was appalled. 'But what will you do if you *do* catch him? He's much bigger than you and seems very capable.'

Deira continued pulling the suit on but this comment had hit a nerve. Her last confrontation with the American had been embarrassing to say the least and she had no new strategy for dealing with him if she should get up close and personal again. She could be putting herself in grave danger and yet… for some reason she didn't see him as a threat. If he'd intended her harm he'd had plenty of opportunity on Mars, but instead he seemed to have taken care not to hurt her. For some reason, he also seemed vaguely familiar.

'I haven't the faintest idea,' she admitted. 'I've already come off second-best on one occasion, even if I did give him a bruise for his trouble. But I can't just let him escape.'

She adjusted the last straps on the exosuit and tested the oxygen delivery system. Then she turned to Amadi.

'Look, Amadi, I'm sorry we didn't get off to a very good start. I was angry and confused and had no right to yell at you when you had your own problems to deal with. While I'm outside I need you to do some work for me – liaise with Amelie and see if you can discover what's going on. Whatever it is, it sure as hell isn't normal, so try to think the unthinkable. Can you do that for me?'

'No problem.' Amadi needed to work out what had happened in any case because the Bureau wouldn't let it rest until they had a definitive answer. He was also anxious to get back into Deira's good books.

A low pitched beep sounded from the airlock as it completed its cycle and re-entered stand-by mode. Without waiting to have second thoughts, Deira stepped inside and activated the cycling mechanism. Now she was committed. It seemed to take forever but eventually the atmosphere was changed and the outer door slid open. Deira took a deep breath and steadied her nerves.

She stepped onto the surface.

The airlock door hissed shut and she stood for a moment taking in the flat, boulder-strewn surface. She peered through the pale orange-brown murk that passed for the atmosphere and was stunned by the sight of the huge bulk of Saturn hanging at an impressive angle on the eastern horizon, its rings appearing to impale Titan's surface. She couldn't see any more of the sky because of the orange haze but, undoubtedly, it would have been quite a sight.

Over to the north was the edge of a vast area of what appeared to be liquid that rippled gently in the breeze. Deira activated her wrist terminal map and saw that this was Ligeia Mare, one of the great northern seas of Titan. A dark area spreading out from the shore line for about a hundred metres was labelled simply as "evaporation zone", giving her very little clue as to its nature.

She took a few tentative steps to familiarise herself with the difference in gravity and experimented with various ways of getting along, settling eventually on a sort of slow lope. She headed off towards the "seashore", stopping when she'd gone about a hundred metres and turning to look back at the Base. It sat like some enormous bug on the surface. The three central habitat domes lay close together in a cloverleaf pattern and were connected by a web of corridors that linked sleeping, eating and recreational facilities with support services like laundry, refectory, infirmary, etc. Sprouting radially from this central zone, like spokes on a wheel, were the corridors that served the various research modules. Because much of the research carried out on Titan was inherently risky, these modules were deliberately sited some distance from the habitat zone, which accounted for the length of the connecting corridors. The Base was a standard Bureau research facility, built for functionality not aesthetics. Because it was modular it could be enlarged as required and, when the Q-ship arrived, it would gain two new modules – Chayka's research lab, and Cabello's Security Block, complete with holding cell.

She checked her virtual screen for directions to the American Base. It was shown in red on the screen, a blue line indicating the direction of travel and an estimate of the distance – three point eight kilometres. Now she just had to orient herself. She was currently facing Ligeia Mare which was north of the Base. The American Base was off to the north-east, so that meant turning half-right and proceeding along the seashore.

She loped off, sending pebbles and small rocks skittering over the hard rock. At least the going was easy. All she had to do was get to the American before he reached the other Base. For the tenth time in as many minutes she checked her oxygen supply. She and breathing apparatus had never really hit it off due to a mild claustrophobia and she'd always shied away from sports that required its use. Her current apparatus appeared to be working exactly as intended and she reassured herself once more that she had plenty of oxygen for her intended journey.

The 'MacMahon lope', as she was beginning to think of it, was very effective at covering the ground, and the low gravity was a joy. She experimented with a few jumps and whooped with exhilaration during one particularly big one. However, the next time she tried it she landed awkwardly and ended up rolling head over heels for several metres before finally coming to a stop, her head next to a particularly large rock. She eyed it with concern, admonishing herself for behaving like a child. Playtime had to stop – she had serious work to do.

She stood and brushed herself off then pulled up her virtual screen again and checked her route. She caught a movement out of the corner of her eye and squinted into the gloom, just making out a figure in the distance loping over the ground. The American! He was a good half kilometre ahead of her and further to her right – and making very good progress. Deira doubted she could catch him before he reached the other Base. Whatever – she'd give it a damned good try.

The next few minutes resulted in stalemate, the distance between Deira and the American remaining unchanged. Deira suspected the man hadn't yet realised he was being followed because he'd made no attempt to increase his stride. Unfortunately for her, it made little difference.

She tried increasing her stride length but found this destabilising, almost causing her to fall. She tried increasing her stride rate, only to discover that there was a natural limit to what she could manage due to the thickness of the suit. She glanced again at her virtual screen and noticed that, by changing direction to follow the American, she had moved off the projected route. For some reason, he wasn't taking the most direct route but a more curved path. Why?

She looked over to her left. The sea was not so very far away, and there was that unknown feature her wrist console labelled the "evaporation zone" – a black band extending from the sea out in her direction. There was no explanation of the feature on her console, but the American's route appeared to skirt it, suggesting it might be dangerous in some way. She frowned. If she moved back onto the blue line of her original route she could theoretically cut him off before he reached his destination – but that would take her through this evaporation zone, with unknown consequences. What should she do?

For a moment she remained undecided, but she so desperately wanted to apprehend this man she knew she only had one choice. She turned left towards the seashore in an attempt to head him off. She knew it'd be a damned close-run thing but she thought she might make it if she could keep her speed up. She loped on, and before long noticed the ground underfoot begin to change, from solid rock to something sticky and glutinous, resembling wet tar. The stuff clung to her boots, slowing her down and increasing her risk of falling, and she cursed silently. This had to be the evaporation zone – and she'd almost certainly made a huge mistake.

Her progress slowed to such an extent that she realised her chance of catching the American had all but disappeared. Indeed, there were more immediate problems to hand. Her tenacity had driven her on even as her innate sense of caution had been telling her to stop and go back. Now, she'd reached a critical point – she was finding it hard to move at all.

When she was a child, she'd once been playing on the sands of a bay near her home and had encountered an area of quicksand. By the time she'd realised what it was she was well and truly trapped and up to her knees in it. She still recalled the terror as she felt herself being dragged slowly down, and it was only the swift actions of her father, who had been fossil hunting nearby, that had prevented a tragedy. She was getting that same feeling of terror now.

With an effort, she yanked her right foot out of the gloop, swivelled her pelvis, and placed it back down again a little further forward. That was hard – and slow. There was no way she'd catch the American now. In fact, he was the least of her problems. She had to get out of this crap. She tried turning back the way she'd come in order to get further from the sea, but found she couldn't move. She summoned up all her strength and tried again. It was truly a herculean effort, and she did manage to free one boot – then she was stuck fast, unable to move at all.

She stared at the crap holding her fast, trying in vain to think of a way out. It was going to be highly embarrassing to have to call for help. What could she do? She was still pondering this when she realised a wind had picked up. She hadn't noticed those gusts a few minutes ago – and were those storm clouds building? She watched in alarm as the clouds rapidly built into what looked like giant yellow-brown thunderheads. Did they have electrical storms on Titan? There was certainly something going on. The wind gusted, and she would have had trouble standing upright if she'd not been stuck fast.

She tried to concentrate on her main problem once more, but was distracted by the sudden onset of rain. The sudden fall of liquid methane loosened the gloop a little and, for a moment, she thought this would be the solution to her problem. Unfortunately, what the gunk lost in stickiness it gained in depth, and she was soon standing almost up to her knees in what was rapidly becoming a vast tar pit.

She looked across at the sea. Its surface had begun to roil and heave in the gusting wind and occasionally what looked like a large wave rolled over the inner part of the evaporation zone. Those waves were getting more frequent and coming further inland each time, getting closer to the spot where Deira was stuck. With increasing dread, she realised she was in serious trouble. It was highly unlikely that help would be forthcoming in the face of this storm so whether she got out of this or not was all down to her. However, if she didn't get out she'd probably die out here.

Chapter 14

THE NEXT FEW minutes were the most frightening Deira had ever experienced – worse even than the fire in the warehouse. She'd never missed Adam more. She was completely on her own – stuck in a glutinous tarry mess amidst elements that appeared to be intent on her destruction. The wind roared, driving the rain in horizontal sheets that soaked into the fabric of her exosuit. She shivered with the sudden chill of insulation failure and knew she'd die if she didn't do something very soon.

She forced herself to think logically. In this sort of situation Adam would have said she needed to review her resources. Unfortunately, she couldn't think of any resources she might have. She'd run straight out of the Base with just her uniform and staff. Then she got it. Her uniform. With a renewed sense of purpose she activated her uniform's personal force field. She was banking on two things; firstly that the kinetic energy of the rain would be sufficient for the field to exclude it, and secondly that the field, being a closed system, would extend beneath her feet and partially free her from the cloying tar.

She was correct on both counts. The force field flared on and she abruptly found herself in a dry bubble amidst the roaring chaos. Simultaneously, her feet came partially free of the gloop and she found she could move again. She peered through the murk and rain trying to get her bearings but visibility was close to zero and she was completely disorientated. She couldn't even begin to work out which way she'd come to get into this mess but she had to make a choice – which direction would get her out again.

She mentally tossed a coin and started off in what she hoped was the direction of the American Base. She had a sudden thought and tried the exosuit's powerful searchlight but found it wasn't working. In fact, the raging elements seemed to have rendered most of her tech useless. Her suit's night-vision facility was out of action and, more worryingly, her wrist console with its mapping application had also failed. The only thing to do was to take it slowly, one cautious step at a time. She managed six steps without anything disastrous happening and her confidence began to return. All was not lost. She took another two steps, and could almost hear Adam lending her encouragement.

Suddenly, something touched her shoulder. It was real, it was solid, and it was so unexpected in this alien maelstrom that it shocked her to the core. Pulse racing, she slowly turned, fearful of what she might see. It was a human hand encased in an exosuit glove similar to her own and, when she turned a little further, she could make out the owner of the hand. The American! The last time she'd seen him he'd been way ahead of her. Now he was standing right next to her, beckoning energetically and pointing over his shoulder.

She noticed he, too, had some form of force field round him – a familiar orange one. She could see him trying to say something but she couldn't make out what it was and the comm wasn't working. He gave up and began pulling her insistently and, probably because his orange force field reminded her of the strange agent who'd helped her in the warehouse, she followed him instinctively, holding onto his arm as he turned into the storm.

Heads down and leaning into the wind the two agents struggled on, Deira getting some protection from the bulk of the American walking in front of her. Even with the assistance of the force field, the sticky tar made each step a trial, but the effort gradually became less as they made progress and the ground perceptibly firmed up. After a hundred metres or so, they were walking on solid rock once more. They'd left the evaporation zone. It was a humbling moment for Deira because she realised she'd previously been going in entirely the wrong direction and would have ended up in the sea if the American hadn't come back for her. This was the guy who was the prime suspect in a murder case – and he'd just saved her life of the person who wanted to lock him up.

They struggled on, the American appearing confident despite the almost complete darkness. The wind howled and the rain lashed with cold fury but they remained dry within their respective force fields and they made good progress now they were back on solid ground.

A wall loomed out of the darkness directly in front of them and the American stopped and began searching along it. He moved slowly to the right, feeling as he went, and it wasn't long before he found what he was looking for. An airlock door slid open, and he urged her into the welcoming space beyond. There was a short pause while he found the closing button and then the door slid shut, the resulting silence being almost startling after the rage of the elements. They turned off their force fields and waited for the airlock to cycle. When the inner door finally opened, they removed their helmets.

Deira stared at the man in front of her. He certainly looked like the guy she'd fought on Mars, even down to the bruise on his cheek, but how could he have been on Titan at the same time she'd seen him attack Amelie on Mars? And was he really a killer? When they'd fought on Mars he'd seemed to take care not to hurt her, and when Adam attacked he'd done the bare minimum to render him safe – whatever she'd thought at the time. And now he'd just saved her life. Nothing made sense. The man held out his hand.

'Sol Smith. Just call me Sol.'

Deira automatically took the hand. 'Deira MacMahon. Thanks for the help out there.' The words appeared out of her mouth totally unbidden and she wished she could have bitten them back. She'd been rehearsing what she might say when she finally caught up with this guy and it certainly wasn't this. She needed to be in control.

'You're very welcome.' Sol was having his own problems finding the right words – but for a different reason. He subvocalised Chard.

'She's quite something isn't she?'

Chard responded with his own version of a sigh. 'She does have excellent physical characteristics, and she conforms very much to your personal definition of beauty. However, I'd remind you that she's a very capable agent and still thinks you're a murderer.'

'Yeah, yeah, copy all that.' He still couldn't take his eyes off her.

Deira watched him closely while she removed her exosuit, noting his obvious interest and intrigued by the movement of his throat muscles. Her mother had once hired a ventriloquist for one of her birthday parties and he'd made what looked like exactly the same movements.

'Are you talking to somebody?' she asked.

Sol was mortified. That hadn't been on the agenda at al. Now he was going to have to admit to his inadequacies.

'Well, I suppose it was bound to happen.' Chard sounded far more human than AI. 'If you'd mastered structured thinking you'd have avoided this. You might as well own up to your shortcomings – she's going to find out in the end anyway.'

'Easy for you to say, buddy!' Sol sub-vocalised. He felt himself blushing and wondered when he'd last done that. Sometime in his late teens he suspected. He couldn't even meet her gaze. 'Just chatting to my PWC,' he said, trying to employ a throwaway manner as if it was really of no consequence. 'Never learned the art of structured thinking, I'm afraid.'

The man could have been speaking Chinese for all the sense he was making to Deira.

'PWC? Structured thinking? Is that some sort of American slang or what?'

That really confused Sol. At the very least, he'd thought that admitting his shortcomings with regard to structured thinking would clarify the situation, but it seemed to have made things worse. He didn't know what to say now and felt like a complete fool.

Deira noted his confusion and decided now was the time to take control of the situation.

'Perhaps we should start again – Agent Smith.' Sol made a face – he hated being called that. 'Putting your PWCs on one side for a minute, I need you to understand your situation. You were on Mars and yet there was no record of who you are or where you came from. While you were on Mars a murder took place and you seem to have been the last person to see the murdered man alive. What would you think if you were me?'

'I'd probably think exactly what you're thinking – but I'd also wonder how an agent could stoop to murdering a civilian. I don't think you've any hard evidence to implicate me otherwise we wouldn't be having this chat. So, if all you've got is circumstantial I think you ought to give me the benefit of the doubt. That's what I'd do.'

Deira was impressed by his logic but was determined to stay in control.

'I guess that's the least I can do as one agent to another – but I'll need a full account of your actions as soon as possible.'

'Understood. I promise I'll level with you but what say we start by introducing ourselves to whoever's in charge of this Base. Then it'd be good to get some food and drink – I don't know about you but I could eat a horse, hooves included!'

He'd certainly got a way with words. At the mention of food, Deira's stomach began to growl. She couldn't remember how long it had been since she'd last eaten properly – she'd only had a snack before leaving Mars and had scooted out of Titan Base soon after she'd arrived. A good meal would be very welcome. She realised Agent Smith was also correct regarding the need to report to the Base Commander. She should have thought about that herself.

'I agree,' she said, allowing herself a small smile. 'Introductions to the natives first, then food and drink – and afterwards, we talk.'

'Okay. After you.' He pointed down the corridor.

'No. After you. For one thing, I don't want you behind me at the moment, and for another, well – I haven't the faintest idea which way to go. You'll presumably know the design of this station?'

'Nope. No idea. I didn't even know there was an American Base on Titan until a few days ago – there certainly isn't supposed to be according to what few memories I have left. Don't worry, though, my trusty PWC can direct us. Isn't yours working? I was surprised when you went the wrong way on the surface and ended up in the tar pit.'

They started down the right-hand corridor. Sol was genuinely surprised at the failure of Deira's PWC since it looked undamaged, but Chard confirmed he couldn't contact the resident AI so there was clearly something very wrong.

'There you go again. PWC! What's a PWC when it's at home?'

'You've got one sitting in that holster of yours. PWC – Personal Weaponised Companion.'

Deira glanced at her staff that was sitting unobtrusively, and not particularly companionably, in its holster. There was something very unusual about Sol Smith and it could probably be summed up in that one three letter acronym – PWC.

'We just call it a staff and it doesn't do much advising about anything. Are you telling me your... PWC... communicates with you?'

Sol had never met agents from other blocs so had no idea about their tech, but for a PWC not to have an AI, even a low-level AI, didn't seem likely. On the other hand, Deira's PWC did appear to be pretty basic. He sub-vocalised Chard.

'Are you getting this buddy? How can the Europeans be so far behind us? Is it me or are we missing something here?'

'We're definitely missing something,' Chard said. 'There's no common ground to your communication. You are, as you would say, talking at cross purposes.'

Sol stopped and turned to face Deira. 'I guess we should talk about this as soon as possible but shall we get the niceties over first? My PWC tells me the Chief Administrator's office is just down here on the left. No Base Commander, I'm afraid. Not even a security team. Sorry to ruin your preconceptions.'

Deira said nothing. She was considering what Sol had just said. If there was a two-way communication between staff and agent the implications were staggering. First, the staff would have to have some sort of AI inbuilt and second, the agent would need some sort of communication device implanted somewhere on his person. Both these technologies were years ahead of the Bureau's...

Her musings were interrupted by the sound of running feet and two men and a woman skidded round the nearby corner and almost collided with them. They were clearly not military, or even security, so perhaps Sol was correct – this was a purely civilian enterprise.

The tallest man, whose huge paunch looked like it might burst out of his grey coverall at any moment, carried a large spanner, slightly raised like a weapon. He took up position behind the other two, a man and a woman, both of whom looked like admin types – no sign of a uniform. The man was young, probably early twenties, about five-eight, with a slight physique and sandy hair. The woman looked to be in her early thirties, five three or so with jet black hair that fell to her shoulders. She had an unfortunately sharp and pock-marked face and it was perfectly clear from the way she held herself that she was in charge.

'Who the fuck are you?' She almost spat the words, her harsh voice straight out of the Bronx. 'Explain yourselves! Now!'

Deira's patience, never her strong point, was at the end of its very short tether. She'd had a hell of a day with a succession of crises and her stress levels were only just returning to normal. The last thing she expected or needed was this sort of welcome from some jumped-up administrator with a face like a bomb site. She was about to let rip in return when Sol took over.

'Special Agent Sol Smith.' He offered his hand and the woman shook it somewhat reluctantly. 'Sorry we've caused you a bit of trouble. We were out on the surface when the storm blew up and we just headed for the nearest shelter. We'd sure be grateful if you'd let us stay here until it blows over.'

Deira was impressed. She couldn't possibly have managed such an emollient speech at that moment. And his body language was extraordinary. He somehow contrived to look something like an over-eager-to-please hound dog – so much so that she almost expected his tongue to loll out and for him to start panting. If it was an act it was a very good one, and it certainly seemed to have the desired effect on the sharp-faced woman because she noticeably relaxed and indicated to the large man that he should lower his spanner. She looked round Sol's bulk at Deira.

'And you are?'

Deira took her lead from Sol. She couldn't bring herself to be friendly but did manage to keep her voice neutral.

'Bureau Special Agent Deira MacMahon. I agree with my colleague. Any help you could give us would be very welcome.'

The woman nodded and looked somewhat mollified. 'Okay, we'll see what we can do to get you comfortable. It must be fucking awful outside at the moment. I'm surprised you weren't warned about the storm.'

Sol got in again before Deira could say anything.

'It was all a spur-of-the-moment thing. We didn't think to get a weather forecast. We won't make the same mistake again, believe me.'

The woman finally melted. 'Well, you fucked up big time, but I guess you won't do it again in a hurry. We just need an identity check with Euro-Base and then we'll get you sorted. Follow me!'

She turned on her heels and marched off down the corridor, the smaller man scurrying behind like a pet poodle. The large man fell in behind Sol and Deira, still clutching his spanner and ready to use it if needed. The sharp-faced woman called back over her shoulder.

'By the way, I'm Base Administrator Ferrelli.'

'Nice to meet you, too,' Sol mumbled, wondering where the hell they'd found this witch.

Ferrelli led the way to her office and dismissed her two male companions, sitting herself behind a huge, mock walnut desk which she probably felt lent her a degree of authority, but which actually had the opposite effect, making her look even smaller than she was. Deira and Sol took seats on the opposite side of the desk, and the Administrator activated her terminal. Sol was intrigued. The terminal was almost identical to the one in Euro-Base. Same level of tech – despite being American. So what did that mean?

Ferrelli soon got hold of her opposite number on Euro-Base, a dapper middle-aged man called Dexter, and proceeded to give him a hard time about his identity check procedures. Dexter explained that Sol had been a guest on the station for the past few days but he'd never met him personally. He also knew of Special Agent MacMahon's arrival but hadn't had the opportunity to make her acquaintance. That being so, he couldn't vouch for the identities of the two people with the Administrator.

'Fuck that!' Ferrelli said. 'You must have files on these guys so just send them over.'

This was where it became slightly difficult because there was no file on either of them.

'Excuse me.' Deira activated her wrist console and transferred her security clearance through the datasphere to Dexter's terminal. 'I've just given you authority to access the Bureau database. You'll find me there.'

Dexter searched the Bureau files and, with obvious relief, confirmed Deira's identity. Sol, however, posed a different problem.

'I thought he was one of yours,' Dexter said to Ferrelli. 'Haven't you got anything in your records?'

Ferrelli searched her system and from the look on her face it was clear she'd come up with a big fat zero. She eyed Sol with suspicion.

'Well cowboy, there's fucking nothing on you. Any idea why that'd be?'

For once, Sol was at a loss for words, and Deira decided it was time for her to make a contribution.

'Agent Smith's currently seconded to the Bureau and his details are tagged top secret – level ten security clearance or above required to access. I'm only level eight, so I can't help you, but since you've validated my identity, that'll have to be enough for you.'

Ferelli glared. 'I guess you ought to know what's going on in your own Bureau, Agent...' she leaned across the desk as far as she could given the size of the thing, '... but as far as I'm concerned something fucking smells round here – and I'm not talking about his BO!'

Looking like there really was a bad smell in the room she stood abruptly and went to the door. The young admin guy was still standing in the corridor where she'd left him and Ferrelli snapped at him in what appeared to be her normal conversational tone.

'Show Agent MacMahon and Agent Smith to some spare rooms and give them a pass for the Base refectory.' She turned back to Deira. "I don't expect any trouble from either of you during your stay. Use the refectory whenever you like but don't wander round the Base outside the habitat modules. Is that clear?'

'Completely.' Deira wanted to knock the woman's pock-faced head off. 'I'd like to...' she stopped as she found herself talking to a closed door. She glanced at the young man standing next to her. 'Is she always like that?'

'Pretty much. Don't take it personally. I'm Jake, by the way. Come on, I'll show you your rooms and give you a quick tour of the habitat modules.'

It turned out that the design of the Base was almost identical to Euro-Base, both having been modelled on the highly successful Mars Base. Jake transferred a schematic to Deira's wrist console for future reference and they set off down the featureless corridors. Deira just wished someone had shown a bit more imagination with the décor, which was either battleship grey or mint green.

At the end of the tour, Jake showed them to their rooms, checked the time, and hastily took his leave, scurrying off in the direction of Ferrelli's office. Deira and Sol headed to the refectory and got stuck into huge hamburgers, fries, and all the trimmings, Sol treating himself to a large beer for good measure. When they'd finished, Sol leaned back in his seat, stretched, and gave a low groan of pleasure.

'Shit, that was good. I'd forgotten what a good Yankee hamburger tastes like!'

Deira felt like she'd never have to eat again. 'You've couldn't have been that hungry. You've been on Euro-Base for three days.'

'Depends what you're used to. Food was a bit fancy for my liking, and the helpings a bit small.'

'I suppose you do have a big mouth to fill!'

'Well that's a bit below the belt, Special Agent! You're not one of those ball-breakers we get in the Agency sometimes are you?' He grinned. 'I've got to tell you I'm a sucker for an Irish accent. Some ancestors of mine were from the Old Country and there's quite a community of them where I come from in Boston.' He stopped abruptly and his grin got wider. 'Well how about that! More memories! Things are definitely looking up.'

Deira smiled at his obvious pleasure in being able to retrieve a memory. When she'd begun her pursuit of Sol she'd never dreamed she'd end up having a very enjoyable meal with him. It all seemed a bit surreal. She screwed up her napkin and tossed it on her plate. 'I think it's time we put our cards on the table.'

'Could get complicated.'

'Okay. In that case we need some privacy. Your room or mine?'

'Thought you'd never ask.'

'In your dreams! We'll use my room and contact Amadi over at Euro-Base.'

They made use of the Base schematic and negotiated the series of corridors back to Deira's room. It wasn't particularly large, which was to be expected on an off-world Base where every cubic metre cost a small fortune to maintain, but it was considerably larger than Deira had expected – about six metres by five. It could have been an expensive hotel room back on Earth.

Sol gazed round the room and, after an initial look of surprise and a degree of subvocalizing, informed Deira that it was cheaper to live on Titan than other planets or moons because there was no need to pressurise the Bases. This might account for the relative generosity of the space.

'And you know this – how? Do I detect a little of that PWC communication again?' Deira sat on the sofa and looked expectantly at Sol. 'How about I share in the conversation?'

Sol wasn't sure about that. After all, the bonding sessions he'd undergone with Chard hadn't been short or easy and he'd always considered his dealings with the AI to be confidential. Chard appeared to have no such hang-ups and his deep masculine voice emerged from the region of Sol's belt holster.

'Good morning Agent MacMahon. It's a pleasure to make your acquaintance.'

Deira was taken aback. She hadn't known what to expect but it certainly wasn't this film-star voice.

'Okay. Who am I speaking to?'

Sol took the PWC out of its holster and put it on the table. He didn't look at all happy, but Chard seemed keen to talk.

'My name's Chard and I'm Sol's Personal Weaponised Companion, or PWC. I'm glad to be able to talk to you directly because there's more going on here than any of us understand. Perhaps comparing notes will bring us closer to a solution.'

Deira looked quizzically at Sol. 'Your PWC is male? And why "Chard"? I thought that was a vegetable.'

Sol shrugged and went to sit on the sofa next to her. She glared at him and he got the message, hurriedly moving to the table and sitting on one of the work chairs instead.

'The semisents all have gender-specific personalities,' he said. 'They choose their own names – I've never asked on what basis.'

'Semisents?'

'Sorry. It's short for semi-sentients. Chard's a level ten semisent – the highest level. He has fully autonomous reasoning capabilities and there's an ongoing debate about whether this level should be classed as fully sentient, with all the rights that go with that designation.' Sol looked bemused for a moment and then grinned. 'Hey, that's another pre-mission memory. It came from nowhere and seems to be out of some manual – for sure, I couldn't string words together like that. You may be good for me, Agent.'

Deira focused on Sol's staff again. 'Chard, I'm completely out of my depth here. Perhaps you'd give me a rundown on the events of the last few days?'

'Certainly, Agent...'

'Call me Deira.'

'Thank you, Deira.'

Sol felt now was as good a time as any to go for it. 'Can I call you Deira, too?'

'Maybe – when I've heard from your electronic friend and decided whether I can trust you or not. Please continue, Chard.'

For the next ten minutes, Chard gave a comprehensive summary of everything that had occurred in the last few days. He explained that the time before they'd arrived on Titan was blank due to dual memory failure, though Sol had regained one or two isolated memories such as that relating to his origin in Boston. When he'd finished, Deira looked thoughtful.

'So you don't remember me on Mars?'

'I'm pretty sure I'd have remembered that,' Sol said.

Chard had no recollection of Mars either.

'Don't you remember me giving you that bruise?' Deira pointed to the blue-green mess on Sol's cheek.

Sol's hand went up to it instinctively. 'You did that?' He looked impressed.

Deira proceeded to give her half of the story, including the investigation on Mars, Sol's presence, their subsequent fight, and the eventual transfer from Mars to Titan, when it appeared that Sol had PHASEd out straight after her. When she finished there was silence for a moment before Chard spoke up.

'This is all very interesting but it's impossible to reconcile our two stories without further data. Are you sure Sol actually followed you through the PHASE cubicle on Mars?'

Deira nodded. 'We've already confirmed that with the PHASE technician on Mars. She saw him leave. We also know that Amadi received a point of origin signal from Mars. What we don't know is what happened to Sol *after* he PHASED since he'd apparently been on Titan for three days by then.'

'I seem to be The Man from Nowhere.' Sol looked distinctly uneasy.

Chapter 15

Deira put in a call to the PHASE terminal on Euro-Base and caught Amadi in the middle of eating a sandwich. He hastily put it down when he saw her, making her feel guilty all over again at her previous treatment of him.

'Agent MacMahon!' He grinned broadly. 'Everyone's been going crazy worrying about you! A storm blew up just after you left and we lost sight of you. We thought you might have fallen into a tar pit.' He glanced down at his instruments and frowned. 'Are you on the American Base?'

'Yes Amadi, we're sheltering from the storm. Agent Smith helped me get here and…'

Sol pulled a face at the use of his surname and was about to protest but Amadi was on a roll.

'He's there too? So you caught him then. But you said he helped you…?'

'Amadi, please calm down and listen to me. Agent Smith and I…'

'Aw, give me a break.' Sol had had enough of being called "Agent Smith".

Deira smiled at him and continued.

'… Agent Smith and I have been trying to work out what's been happening over the past week but nothing seems to make sense. Did you and Amelie come up with anything?'

Amadi was almost bubbling over with excitement. 'Yes we have. It's something really unexpected – the only likely scenario – even if it's not that likely.'

Sol wondered what a likely, but unlikely, scenario was and peered over Deira's shoulder at the screen. She hated this – people looking over her shoulder – but managed to keep quiet as Sol engaged Amadi.

'Hi, Ammy old buddy. How are you doing?'

'Hello Sol. I'm fine thanks. Are you on our side now?'

Sol looked to Deira for her take on that and when she reluctantly nodded he continued. 'Yeah, Ammy, it'd seem so. Now then, what have you and your lovely-sounding lady on Mars found out while we've been house-calling over here?'

Amadi paused and consulted his wrist console. 'It's quite complicated so I'll take it slowly. Sol, you were first sighted on Mars fourteen days ago, round about the same time Amelie noticed a strange reading on her instruments that nobody could interpret. Although we still don't understand that reading, to make sense of later events we've had to assume it represented activation of the PHASE terminal. There was no point of origin recorded, but the quantal signature was identical to the one I found when you transmitted to Titan. We had to think laterally to make any sense of it at all.'

Sol was interested now. It sounded like the techies might have come up with something.

'And what does your sideways thinking make of it?' he asked.

'I'll get to that in a second.' Amadi switched his attention to Deira, becoming more confident as he got deeper into his specialist area. 'We know that Sol transmitted off Mars immediately after you left, Agent MacMahon. He used a kind of neural dampener on Amelie but it had a very short-lived effect and Amelie clearly saw him transmit out.'

Deira glanced at Sol. 'Do you have that sort of facility in your PWC?' Sol nodded, and looked uncomfortable. 'Okay Amadi, please continue.'

'Well, that pretty much deals with the Mars side of the equation. Sol transmitted in from an unknown point of origin about fourteen days ago and transmitted out straight after you, Agent MacMahon.'

'But disappeared straight after transmitting,' said Deira. 'What happened and where did he go if he didn't come to Titan?'

'That will be clear in a moment. So, if we look at the Titan side of the equation now, Sol transmitted in three days ago as an obvious emergency PHASE from an unknown source locus. Amelie and I are now pretty confident that his point of origin was Mars.'

'So we're back to him being in two places at once.' Deira said.

Amadi grinned triumphantly. 'That's where the lateral thinking comes in – helped by our in-depth analysis of the PHASE records and a further look at Sol's unusual quantum signature, which suggests he doesn't belong in our space-time at all. We discovered that Sol had a high level of tachyon contamination, and that this was very much higher at the Mars end than the Titan end of the transmission.'

Deira looked blank and Sol scratched his head.

'You're getting a bit technical there Amadi,' he said. 'What the shit is a tachyon?'

'Tachyons are fundamental particles very similar to photons. The major difference is that, while photons travel at the speed of light, tachyons travel faster than light. Amelie and I think that you first PHASEd to Mars as a stream of highly compressed, information-rich tachyons instead of photons. How our equipment managed to reintegrate you is beyond me but I'm sure Professor Chayka will be able to figure it out when he arrives.'

Deira had a substantial body of knowledge in electronics and computing but was struggling to see where Amadi was going with this. Sol was floundering badly.

'Amadi, I'm lost,' he said. 'If these tachyons travel faster than photons then surely I'd just get from one place to another quicker. I still don't see how I could be in two places at the same time.'

Amadi was grinning broadly, clearly enjoying the effect he was having.

'Ah, but tachyons aren't *just* very fast photons. You'll remember that, according to relativity theory, nothing can travel faster than the speed of light?'

Sol frowned. 'But you just said that tachyons *can* travel faster than light.'

'No, what I said was that tachyons *always* exceed the speed of light – but they can't do it in the normal space-time framework.'

'Aw, there you go again with space-time frameworks. Did anyone ever suggest you should see a therapist?'

Deira nudged him hard in the ribs and encouraged Amadi to continue.

'Well,' he said, 'the only way that tachyons can travel faster than light is by travelling backwards in time. That means that PHASEing using tachyons is a means of achieving time travel – only into the past, of course.'

'What?' Deira couldn't help herself. 'You're suggesting that...'

'Sol's from the future!' Amadi was clearly pleased at the effect of his revelation. 'That accounts for his quantal signature – he actually *does* belong in a different space-time. We think Sol originally PHASEd from Earth sometime in the future to Mars in our time. When he later followed you into the chamber on Mars he still had a residual tachyon contamination. The chamber was set up for Titan so he was transmitted to Titan, except that the residual tachyons resulted in him arriving three days in the past – three days before he set out. Do you see now? That would mean he'd arrive on Titan while he was still on Mars. He would be in two places at the same time.'

Deira was stunned and unable to think of anything to say. Sol was sub-vocalising again.

'Oh, for Christ's sake let's all hear it!' Deira snapped. 'Chard, what do you make of this?'

Chard's voice emerged from Sol's PWC.

'Amadi's analysis is correct. It's only by invoking the time vector that all the observations make sense. While this doesn't answer all our questions it at least explains some of the more awkward ones. Thank you, Amadi.'

Amadi was looking round for the source of the voice.

'You're welcome. Who is that?'

'Long story,' Deira said. "We'll brief you when we get back to Euro-Base.' She looked across at Sol. 'I'm still having difficulty processing this but it would seem to answer my questions about Chard. It always seemed unlikely that you Yanks were so far ahead of us tech-wise.'

'Yeah. It fits my feelings about your tech being antique too.'

In fact, things clicked into place relatively easily in Sol's mind. Although travelling backwards in time should have seemed absurd, it didn't – it felt right. There was only one question that sprang to mind.

'So what year is this?' he asked.

'2066,' Deira said. 'I don't suppose you know when you're from?'

Sol shook his head. 'Not a clue. That's gone with all the rest. I guess...

'2143,' Chard said, making both Deira and Sol start. 'Although the saboteur wiped many of my memories, he couldn't remove the original date stamp on my main processor without rendering me completely useless. We originate in 2143 – seventy-seven years in your future.'

'Okay, so that's different.' Deira gazed at Sol. 'Sol Smith, Agent from the Future! That wasn't on my radar at all!'

Deira had loads of questions she wanted to explore with Sol and Chard so she thanked Amadi for his help and discontinued the comm link. She began to have doubts about the wisdom of talking about their tech almost immediately.

'Should we be discussing technology from the future? Isn't there a risk of contaminating the timeline or something?'

Sol shook his head. 'I've already done plenty of contaminating. I'd guess my time doesn't exist anymore.'

'So you've lost everything.'

'It'd seem so. I wonder if that's why I've lost my memories too. Perhaps if the future changes memories of that future get wiped.'

'That's getting too deep for me.' Deira couldn't imagine what Sol was going through. First he'd lost his memories of family and friends – memories he'd hoped to recover one day. Now, he'd discovered those people probably no longer existed, or at least didn't exist as he knew them. And the reason they were gone was directly due to his actions in this time.

Chard cut in again. 'There is another possibility. It's been suggested that time may inherently resist any attempted changes – so-called "temporal inertia". That would mean the future is fixed and cannot be changed. Our time may still be there.'

'I don't think so.' Sol looked remarkably calm. 'I can't help feeling I've had this discussion before. I think the whole reason for sending me back in time was to change the timeline or it would've been pointless. I'm pretty sure I was briefed on the consequences.' He looked down. 'It still hurts though.'

There was an awkward silence while Deira tried to work out what to say. How do you comfort someone when their entire future has just disappeared? Perhaps you couldn't.

'You seem to have made the case for a discussion of your tech, anyway,' she said. 'Are you up to answering a few questions?'

'Whatever. Chard can probably answer most of them better than me but I'll chip in when necessary.'

First and foremost, Deira wanted to explore the concept of the PWC itself. Her staff had a substantial amount of inbuilt electronics, both to facilitate its various combat modes and to enable the uploading of memories prior to PHASEing. It wasn't unreasonable to expect future developments to concentrate on making the relationship between man and machine more synergistic.

Chard was able to furnish an account of the technological systems that enabled him to communicate with Sol and influence his neurochemistry and muscle power. He described the neural node in Sol's brain that acted as the hub of the system, and the nannites that had been deposited in muscles and endocrine glands. That led to an explanation of "New Combat Mode", an enhancement and partial override of the agent's normal reflexes and muscle power so that an opponent's actions could be countered almost as soon as they were initiated. Deira had already had first-hand experience of this on Mars and could testify to the incredible augmentation of speed and reflexes that could be generated. The fact that Sol had been augmented at the time explained her own apparent inadequacy and made her feel considerably better about herself.

The A.I. itself was of the highest order that was available in Sol's time and, as he'd said, was possibly soon to be designated as fully sentient. It communicated with Sol by direct input to his temporal cortex and usually received input by means of "structured thinking"–a euphemism for talking inside one's own head. It was a method of structuring brainwaves so that the AI could interpret them – and Sol had never mastered it. This was the reason for his reliance on sub-vocalisation.

In addition to the controlling AI, the PWC also contained a huge database and had sophisticated networking abilities that enabled it to download data from almost any electronic device within a few hundred metres. If that happened to be another networked device, so much the better because that extended its abilities even further .If the device was linked to international or interplanetary networks then the sky was truly the limit.

Deira could only dream of what it might be like to have a staff with these capabilities and she gazed wistfully at Chard with a twinge of envy.

After some time picking apart the technology, they decided that enough was enough for one day and Sol departed gloomily for his room. Deira watched him go. Her view of him had changed a lot in a very short time. Even before the revelation that he'd come from the future, she'd begun to think of him as an ally instead of a possible murderer. However, the issue of Fournier's death hadn't gone away and there was always a chance it was something to do with Sol's mission. So, they needed to find out what that mission was – and they wouldn't get very far unless Sol could retrieve his lost memories. What were they going to do about that? There could only really be one answer. She placed a call to Professor Chayka on the Q-ship. She didn't have to wait long before his long, thin face appeared on the screen.

'Yes? Who are you?' The long thin face that appeared on the screen was so famous that she immediately had some misgivings, and the fact that the ship's operator hadn't passed on her ID didn't help. It was difficult talking directly with a living legend.

'Hello, Professor Chayka. I'm Special Agent Deira MacMahon of the European Bureau.' She paused for a moment to give Chayka a chance to say hello, but since nothing was forthcoming, thought she'd better move on. 'I'm trying to piece together some outstanding aspects of Dr Fournier's murder.'

Chayka sat impassively for a few moments then apparently realised it was his turn to participate in the conversation.

'Agent MacMahon, you can't begin to understand how distressing this whole business is. I started this journey with a team of five – and now one team member is dead and two more are suspects in his murder. The team dynamics are completely destroyed and I'm of the opinion our transfer to Titan is wasted effort. If you have anything new to tell me please do so now. If not, please leave me alone.'

'Actually Professor, that's my main reason for contacting you. I've just discovered something that's of great interest to me and might be of interest to you too.'

Deira went on to explain what Amadi had surmised about Sol and the subsequent confirmation that he was from the future by the date stamp on the AIs master board. That got Chayka's attention and he began stroking his beard absently. She then explained about Sol's memory loss.

'We need a break, Professor. We need Agent Smith to get his memories back. You're the acknowledged expert on photonic transmission so I'm guessing tachyonic transmission might be something you could relate to. Do you think there would be any way we could recover those memories?'

Chayka sat for some time, unmoving and unresponsive – so long, in fact, that Deira began to wonder whether he'd experienced a seizure of some kind. She was about to put out an emergency call to the Ship's medics when he suddenly seemed to re-boot.

'This is an absolutely fascinating problem, Agent MacMahon. Clearly, I can't answer your question immediately but I'll devote all my spare time to it between now and our arrival at Titan. I'm told we'll get there in two days but if I come up with anything before then I'll contact you straight away.'

'Thank you Professor.' Maybe this was going to work after all – at least he hadn't dismissed the problem out of hand. 'Obviously, this is highly sensitive. It's still possible that Dr Fournier's murderer is on board that ship and you could be personally at risk if he gets wind of what you're up to. Do you understand?'

Chayka nodded. 'Rest assured that I'll pursue this completely privately in my own time. It's a project worthy of my skills and the answer to your question will certainly result in a considerable enhancement of transmission technology. I'll report any findings directly to you on Titan Base.'

Deira offered silent thanks to whatever deities there might be out there. 'In case I'm not on the Base when you try contacting me, please don't leave a message under any circumstances. I'm at the American Base on Titan at the moment and there's a storm raging outside so I may be delayed getting back to Euro-Base. This must be eyes-only, Professor, either electronically or in person.'

Chayka nodded again. 'I've said I understand. I look forward to making your acquaintance Agent MacMahon. You seem like someone I can do business with.' He cut the connection.

Deira looked at the blank screen in surprise. She knew the professor wasn't exactly known for his social skills – but that sounded like a compliment.

She switched off the terminal and suddenly felt bone tired. It had been a hell of a day. She used the bathroom and hit the sack. Sleep came almost immediately.

She was still deeply asleep when there was a loud and persistent hammering on the door. Groggily she struggled out of bed, stumbled across the floor rubbing her eyes, and opened the door. Sol was standing there, fresh as a daisy, fully dressed and ready to go. He seemed to have shrugged off the gloom from the previous evening and had obviously planned some quip because he started to speak before the door was fully open – then he stared at her and abruptly shut up. He was completely lost for words and even felt himself blushing – again!

'Whoops!' he said, 'Seem to have caught you at a disadvantage.'

Deira was bleary-eyed and in her underclothes. She looked vacantly at Sol – then down at herself.

'Oh crap!' She shut the door in his face.

She hurried to the bathroom, checking the time on the way. It was past 0800hrs, which meant she'd slept for over nine hours. Cursing and grumbling she spent the next twenty minutes making herself more presentable. When she was finally satisfied with the result and had checked herself for the third time in the mirror, she opened her door again. Sol still stood there, leaning casually against the wall.

'Have you been there all this time?'

'Good morning to you too!' His grin had reappeared. 'I wondered whether you'd like to join me for breakfast.'

'Seems like a plan.' She paused, the phrase eliciting an image of Adam smiling at her. She moved on rapidly. 'How'd you sleep?'

'Like a baby. The bed seemed a bit lumpy at first but I guess I must have been tired because I was out like a light. You?'

'Yeah – good. That's why I overslept this morning. Sorry for being tetchy.'

'No problem. You'd have got far worse if you'd caught me in a similar position.'

'I can vouch for that,' Chard chipped in. 'He sleeps naked.'

'Thanks buddy. I knew I could rely on you!'

'You're welcome!'

Deira couldn't help smiling at this interchange and any awkwardness between them had vanished by the time they sat down in the refectory.

'So what's the plan for today?' Sol shovelled bacon into his mouth like it was his last meal, chewed pensively, then ventured, 'By the way, can I call you "Deira" now that we've got to know each other better?'

Deira had wondered when this would come up again and had decided there was no reason to stay on formal terms. 'I guess so – when we're alone, anyway.' She smiled. 'Of course I still might have to clap you in irons, but until that time… yeah, okay.'

Sol's face slipped into what Deira had come to think of as his "pleased hound-dog expression" after the episode with Ferelli yesterday – and that was probably about the worst thing that could have happened. She immediately bristled.

'You can cut that out though' she snapped.

'What?' A look of vacuous innocence that suggested he didn't know what she was talking about. In fact, at that moment, he didn't.

'You know very well what! That body language crap you're always using. We learned about that in the Bureau, you know. If you want to be on first name terms, that's fine – but the crap stops here. Otherwise it's back to "Agent MacMahon".'

Sol lapsed into his "crestfallen look" and then realised what he was doing and pulled his features back into some semblance of normality.

'Sorry! It's partly me anyway, but significantly enhanced by Chard. It's meant to be a social lubricant.'

'Fine! I can just about tolerate the "you" part but I could do without the lubrication. Perhaps Chard could keep his electronic finger out when you're with me?'

'I'm very sorry, Deira,' Chard actually sounded sorry. 'We've been on alert for so long that I've neglected to let Sol relax. It won't happen again.'

'Apologies accepted all round. Now – about a plan for today. I suppose that depends on what the weather's like. Chard?'

'I'm afraid the storm's still raging. They can sometimes last for several days so we may be stranded here for some time.'

'Unless they've got a PHASE chamber,' Sol said.

'Unlikely, Deira said. 'The inter-planetary PHASE was developed in secret by Professor Chayka and his team and Adam and I were the first human test subjects. The Americans won't have it.'

'Never heard of industrial espionage?'

'Sure, but unlike the Yanks we don't have leaks and our security's top notch.'

'What about the space hook? I read there was quite a scandal round that particular breech.'

'That was different, it…'

'There's no evidence of a PHASE chamber on this Base,' Chard piped up, putting an end to the argument. 'I've conducted a review of the station layout and there is no such facility. A deep scan shows no evidence of sub-quantal activity except for the gravity generators.'

Deira frowned. 'Well in many ways I'm glad about that, but it would've been damned useful. Now we're stuck with walking back to Euro-Base – and with the weather as it is we won't be doing that any time soon.'

There wasn't much they could do at present and since they were restricted from exploring the Base they made their way back to Deira's room. By mutual understanding, this had become the "office" and, once they were private, Deira told Sol of her conversation with Chayka the previous evening.

'I'll take all the help I can get,' Sol said, 'but Chard reminded me last night that he'd lost memories too. Putting it all together, it doesn't seem likely that these losses could be due to a change in the timeline, and the form of the memory loss isn't consistent with transmission failure. We came back to our original thought – that we've been sabotaged.'

Deira hadn't expected that. 'Who would do that? Who *could* do that? And why?'

'No idea. We can't make any sense of it at all. But it does mean that those memories might still be retrievable'

'Damn!' said Deira, 'Just when you think you're beginning to see the wood for the trees someone comes along and plants a few more trees. Sol, you seem to be at the centre of all this. You're from the future – how can I bring myself to say that so matter-of-factly? – and you're unable to remember your mission brief. Now we find there's a possible third party involved who may have sabotaged your PHASE. Is there anything else you're holding back?'

'Not a thing. I know I'm from Boston in 2143 and it's obvious I was sent back to this time on a mission. I don't know what that mission was, but I think it has to be linked to Dr Fournier's death in some way. By the way, I can't explain it but I'm pretty sure it wasn't me that killed him.'

'I've come to that conclusion too – though I don't know why.'

'Well thanks for the vote of confidence. It's good to hear.'

'There's just too damn much going on here,' Deira said. 'Were taking two steps forward and one back. I just hope Professor Chayka can recover at least some of those memories of yours. That might be the break we're looking for.'

'Amen to that.'

Although frustrated, Deira was also fascinated by the complex scenario that was unfolding. Where it was leading she couldn't begin to guess but she had a very strong feeling that Sol would prove to be one of the good guys. He was an unusual man and most of the time she liked him. She thought it unusual that they could chat together so easily after such a short time, and she remained not a little disconcerted by the feelings of arousal she'd had ever since he first looked at her in the airlock. She glanced across at him and found his eyes firmly fixed on her. As they locked gazes, something passed between them that was far more than just nascent friendship, and as if by general agreement they simultaneously looked away, clearly embarrassed.

Chapter 16

Deira and Sol were lucky–by the afternoon of the following day the storm had abated. The wind died away and the towering thunderheads dissipated, leaving the persistent light breeze and what was for Titan a bright summer's day. With considerable relief, they offered their thanks to Ferrelli and lost no time suiting up and getting back outside.

This time there were no mishaps–visibility was good and Chard was on hand to provide directions. Deira insisted on taking a look at the evaporation zone on the way back. It was exactly as she'd imagined it–a black, sticky mess – and seeing it like that brought it home to her how much she owed Sol. She still found it amazing how two days could so completely change her view of him. He'd been her prime suspect at the beginning – no question – but having got to know him better she now found it very difficult to imagine him responsible in any way for Fournier's death. He just didn't seem the type. She knew this might simply be wishful-thinking brought on by her undoubted physical attraction to him but she had a hunch it was more than that – and what had Monroe said about her hunches?

The trek back to Euro-Base took just under two hours. Once back inside, they decided they'd better get properly logged in with Admin to avoid any future embarrassment and, to make life easy, they stuck with Deira's story about Sol being on loan to the Bureau from the American Agency. The process was pretty pain-free and they were soon on their way to their adjacent rooms in the habitat zone – rooms that were considerably better than either of them expected because of their status as special agents. Deira was still admiring her room when the doorbell rang and Sol breezed in. He gazed round at the almost palatial surroundings.

'So how about this?' he said. 'Mine's the same. Come up in the world a bit, haven't we?'

'Actually, I was always at this level – it's you that's come up.'

Sol ignored the barb. 'Now me, I never concern myself about social status, and as for digs, well – any place with a bed, a john, and some running water will do. I can even do without the john if need be, I simply…'

'Yes, I'm sure, but I could do without the intimate details if you don't mind.' Deira glared at him. 'I get the message – you're a real man's man and you can doss down anywhere and still come up smelling of roses'

Sol kicked himself for his stupidity. 'Sorry! Can we start again?'

Deira immediately felt sorry for her outburst and put her hand gently on his arm. 'I'm sorry too. I'm not sure what that was about. There's just something about you that seems to get under my skin sometimes. Is Chard still doing that social lubrication stuff?'

'Not me, Deira,' Chard said, 'What you see is all Sol.'

'I think some of your shit must have rubbed off on me buddy,' Sol grumbled. He looked at Deira and she could have sworn he blushed. 'Actually, I think I'm over-reacting to you. The fact is, I like you and…' He found he couldn't go on. He simply couldn't conjure up the right words. He turned to the door. 'I'm going to see Ammy. He may have come up with something useful since we last talked to him. Smart little bastard, you know!'

Deira smiled. She was in two minds about helping him out with his little difficulty by admitting that she felt something for him too. However, when it came right down to it she discovered she was as tongue-tied as he was when it came to admissions of that sort.

"Good idea,' she said, 'I'll come too. That's if you don't mind. I wouldn't want to come between a man and his buddy.'

Sol gave a long sigh. He could see he was going to have to work hard at this relationship if he wanted to make a success of it – and he most assuredly did!

'I'd welcome the company and I'm sure Amadi would be pleased to see you too.'

'I wouldn't bet on that – I put him through a fair bit of grief when I first met him.'

They set off for the PHASE terminal, Sol berating himself for not having got off to a very good start with Deira and vowing to be less irritating in the future.

Deira was thinking that, irritation or not, she liked the big oaf.

Amadi was nowhere to be found when they sauntered into the PHASE terminal but he appeared after a couple of minutes with a mug of coffee. He looked surprised to see them.

'Agent MacMahon! And Sol! Good to see you both again.'

He glanced guiltily at Deira and hastily deposited the coffee on his work desk.

'You too, buddy,' Sol said, 'Sorry to disturb your coffee break. We thought we'd call in and see if you'd made any more discoveries since we last talked. You were really pretty impressive you know.'

'It was a bit unexpected, wasn't it? Unfortunately, nothing else has turned up. I've been looking at historical reports of post-PHASE memory loss and I'm afraid the outlook's uniformly poor. As you know, the staff was developed to preserve memory in case of transmission loss. Upload loss is extremely uncommon – there're only two reports in the literature. You seem to have suffered a unique combination of both transmission and upload loss. It would make a very nice paper if you'd give your permission for me to use it.'

'Use it by all means if it'll help you,' Sol said, 'but you'll have to keep it on ice until we've found out what's going on. I guess I'm not really surprised to hear I'm unlikely to get the memories back. I'll just have to pin my hopes on the professor and...' He stopped suddenly as he remembered the Prof's work was supposed to be secret. 'That is... aw shit, Deira, we should just tell him.'

At the mention of the professor, Amadi looked excitedly from one agent to the other.

'Professor Chayka? You've asked Professor Chayka?'

'Told you he was a smart little bastard,' Sol said, looking apologetically at Deira. 'Sorry for the slip but he's going to find out soon anyway – and I trust him.'

On reflection, Deira agreed. Amadi was an integral part of this, his contribution already being highly significant. He deserved to have their trust.

'Yes Amadi, the professor's doing some work for us,' she said. 'He'll report directly to me if he finds anything.' She suddenly had a thought. 'I suppose that Q-ship can't be far away by now can it?'

'It's due in tomorrow morning,' said Amadi. 'We'll have a much better chance of sorting out Sol's memory problems when Professor Chayka arrives. I look forward to it.'

'Tomorrow morning? That's great! Let's hope he's come up with something.' Deira looked doubtfully at Amadi, 'I don't think you know the professor very well, do you? If I were you, Amadi, I'd keep your head down and just do what you're told. He comes with quite a reputation.'

'I know – I've worked with him before. In fact, he arranged for me to get this posting because much of the work he's going to be doing is PHASE-related and he wants a techie he respects.' He looked embarrassed. 'Those are his words, not mine.'

Deira hadn't thought about this possibility but it certainly made sense. Amadi was proving to be more of a surprise than she'd anticipated. Sol was obviously impressed too.

'I repeat – he's a smart little bastard,' he said. 'I think the next few days could be very interesting indeed.'

Deira nodded, thinking of the challenge that Chayka posed and trying to equate that with the word "interesting".

The next morning was something of a red letter day for Sol. His memory problems had lasted for days now and he was finding it difficult to imagine getting any of them back. Chayka might be the key, but they'd heard nothing from him since Deira's first contact so he might not have been able to find a solution. Sol wasn't usually prone to anxiety but today was the exception that proved the rule. His stomach was fluttering like a flock of birds.

The Q-ship entered Titan orbit at almost exactly 08.00 and the transfer of passengers down to the surface was scheduled to commence at 09.00. Amadi thought the professor would probably stop off in his room first to drop off his bags but would almost certainly want to check out the PHASE facilities as soon as possible, so Deira and Sol were ready and waiting in the PHASE terminal at 09.15.

Amadi bustled about ensuring his tech was up to scratch – he knew Chayka of old and didn't want any criticism for running a slack operation. Deira paced – from the PHASE chamber to the exit and back again, over and over again, while Sol, lounging in a chair in the waiting area, wondered idly whether it was possible to create a channel in the floor by simple friction. A sudden bleep from the network terminal signalled an incoming transmission and Amadi scurried round his bank of apparatus to take the call. It was Chayka wanting to speak to Deira and she hurried round to the screen. Strangely, he still seemed to be in his cabin on board the ship.

'Morning, Professor,' she said, 'Is there a problem? We were expecting you here about now.'

'Good morning Agent MacMahon. Yes, we're told there's a minor delay so I propose using the time to get the PHASE terminals modified. The problem you gave me was fascinating – it provided endless hours of pleasure during the last few days of this very trying voyage.' He leaned forward slightly and, just for a moment, looked like he might smile. 'I believe I may have the solution.'

Sol felt the birds in his stomach take flight. This was what he'd been hoping for and dreading at the same time. Deira managed to keep her excitement in check.

'That's great news. I've got Sol and Amadi with me and they're both up to speed on our little secret, so you can speak freely. I'll put you on conference call.' She shunted the terminal into virtual screen mode and the professor's image appeared in the air. For once he appeared quite animated.

'I'm most gratified to see Mr Okafor because I'll need his help to make the required changes. May I speak with him please?'

'Of course,' Deira turned to Amadi, who was almost bouncing with anticipation behind her. 'Amadi, the professor would like to talk to you. Would you mind…?'

She didn't even get the question out before Amadi was speaking.

'Hello Professor. It's truly wonderful to see you again.'

Sol nudged Deira and winked in Amadi's direction. She nodded and smiled. Amadi went on,

'I know all about the tachyonic transfer, Professor – in fact it was me that developed the hypothesis. I hope it meets with your approval.'

Chayka actually smiled! Neither Sol nor Deira could believe it, and even Amadi seemed briefly disconcerted.

'Mr Okafor,' he said, with obvious pleasure, 'It's very good to see you again. I was extremely impressed with your work and feel it will get you a very prestigious publication…' he glowered briefly at Deira, '… that is if our esteemed Bureau allows it, of course. Now, I need you to make a few small adaptations to your equipment that should be well within your capabilities. You will also need to contact your opposite number on Mars to ensure the same modifications are made to that terminal. We will need to…'

With that he was off into what was, to Deira and Sol, a string of scientific gobbledegook. Amadi concentrated on every word and made copious notes on his wrist console.

Finally, after about ten minutes of this and a few repeated instructions, Amadi turned to Deira.

'He wants to talk to you again Agent MacMahon.'

'Yes Professor?' Deira said.

Chayka appeared to have calmed down and now stared impassively from the screen. 'Ah, Agent MacMahon. I've instructed Mr Okafor in the amendments to the transmission chamber. Once these adaptations have been made, my equations suggest that Agent – Smith, is it? – yes, Smith, will have to pass back through the two terminals that he has used since his original transmission. That is, he will have to transfer to Mars and back. The reason is esoteric but relates to tachyonic contamination of both Agent Smith and the transmission terminals, which should be purged by the course of action I'm suggesting.'

'He'll get his memory back?'

"I can't say for certain. My work suggests that it probably wasn't the original tachyonic transfer that caused the memory problems. More likely it was the subsequent transmission from Mars when the still contaminated chamber interacted with the tachyons remaining on Agent Smith. The solution I'm proposing should correct any associated memory loss from this source. Clearly, however, it will be ineffective on memory loss not caused by the contaminated transfer. It should take Mr Okafor about two hours to make the required technical changes to the transmission apparatus and by that time I should be on the surface with you. The transmission itself should be straightforward and I see no reason why we can't have this completed by mid-afternoon at the latest. I'll take my leave for now. Goodbye.'

Deira was about to respond when she realised she was looking at a blank screen. Chayka had terminated the transmission.

She looked at Sol. 'Could do with a bit of your social lubrication. I don't suppose you could do anything about that Chard?'

'Unfortunately not Deira. I need to have…'

Deira laughed. 'It's okay. My sad attempt at a joke.' She checked the time and sighed. 'Looks like we're into the damned waiting game again. More coffee?'

'Why not? You know we're becoming regulars in the refectory?'

'How about going to my room instead then? We can make coffee there.'

Sol thought that was a good idea so they left Amadi to his work and adjourned to Deira's room. Sol lounged in an armchair trying to think of anything but his upcoming double PHASE.

'So how did you end up with this mission?' he said, watching Deira as she made the coffee.

'Almost accidentally, I think. My supervisor and I had just completed a mission to retrieve some Q-ship security details and we'd had some unexpected help from a strange agent.' She stopped and looked questioningly at Sol. 'That wouldn't have been you by any chance, Mr Time-Traveller? The guy was about your size, his force field was orange, just like yours, and he moved like you do when you're augmented.'

'I don't think so.' Sol frowned. 'I don't remember, but it doesn't feel right, somehow.'

'So are there any more like you at home? If not, how do you explain the similarities?'

Sol shrugged. 'I can't. I just don't think it was me, that's all.'

'Hmm. Anyway, we'd just completed this mission and it happened to coincide with your appearance on Mars. The Bureau Director wanted an immediate presence on Mars so decided to send my supervisor by PHASE as the first interplanetary transferee. I think I was a kind of optional extra.'

Sensing that Sol was seeking a distraction from his upcoming ordeal, Deira continued with the story of the Mars transfer and the subsequent fallout. Actually, being able to talk about it like this was strangely therapeutic. She enjoyed Sol's company and she trusted him. She also had other feelings that were demanding to be recognised but which she continued to push away.

Chapter 17

DEIRA CHECKED THE time again and sighed – four hours since Chayka's last contact. Because of a technical hitch with one of the Q-ship's shuttles, the "minor delay" in disembarkation had been extended until all the flyers had been thoroughly checked over. The two agents had wandered from Deira's room to the refectory then back to the PHASE terminal, and they were now in the last throes of terminal boredom. It came as a bit of a shock, therefore, when the door to the terminal slid open to reveal Professor Chayka.

Deira and Sol stood to greet him but he completely ignored them and marched straight over to the PHASE chamber to interrogate Amadi about the technical adaptations. Deira was left standing with her hand extended, feeling stupid and awkward – and that made her angry. Sol could read the signs – she was about to say something she might regret later. He gently put a hand on her shoulder.

'Don't let it get to you,' he said. 'He's obviously on a roll. If this works I can sure put up with a bit of eccentricity.'

Deira, face flushed and clearly mad as hell, took the hint.

'I know really. He's just so damned rude.'

The two agents waited silently and not-so-patiently until Chayka deemed it the appropriate time to talk to them. He was deep in conversation with Amadi, and there was much gesticulation and pointing as first one piece of apparatus and then another came under his inspection. After about ten minutes of this he seemed satisfied and turned his attention back to Deira and Sol. There was no attempt at any sort of greeting or apology and by now they'd have been surprised if there had been.

'Mr Okafor and the Mars technician have been extremely thorough', he said. 'They have carried out my adaptations to the letter and we're ready to go whenever you see fit.' Deira was about to suggest that immediately would be as good a time as any when Chayka continued. 'I just require an hour or two in my room to freshen up after the long delay in disembarkation.' Deira closed her mouth and looked deflated.

Sol grumbled under his breath, 'Aw, what the hell – we've already been waiting hours. What's a couple more between friends?'

Deira sighed and nodded. Like Sol, she'd have preferred to have got started there and then. However, given the potential risks to Sol, she wasn't going to put any pressure on Chayka. She wanted him in the best possible state, both physically and mentally, so she was prepared to cut him a little slack.

'We're at your disposal, Professor. We'll probably get some refreshments while we're waiting. Let us know when you want us back here again.'

Chayka gave a brief inclination of his head, turned, and walked out. The tension in the room left with him and it was as if everyone could suddenly breathe again. Amadi was a nervous wreck and sweating profusely. He flopped into his chair and put his head in his hands. Sol walked over and put his arm round his shoulder.

'Hey, Ammy buddy, you did good! The Prof thinks you're the best. Cheer up – you should be celebrating.'

Amadi looked up gratefully and smiled. 'Thank you, Sol. That was the most intense grilling I've ever had but you're right, he did seem satisfied with my work.'

'Satisfied? Aw man, he said you were "extremely thorough". I don't imagine many people have heard that from him for a long time. Well done buddy.'

Deira smiled at the way Sol handled Amadi. It seemed to her this whole "social lubrication" thing worked better with men than women. Perhaps that was because men were more gullible!

At that moment a call came through on Amadi's terminal – it was from Amelie on Mars and she was clearly quite agitated. Deira walked round to take the call.

'Hi Amelie – what's up?' she said.

'It's this double PHASE Professor Chayka wants to carry out. I've done all the alterations to the chamber here but I don't see how I can go along with it in the face of the ban that's in force.'

Deira had forgotten all about the ban and could appreciate Amelie's position. However, this might be Sol's only chance of getting his memories back – and that might provide the break they needed in the Fournier case. She looked at Sol for help but he just shrugged, knowing he had no say in this. It was all down to her.

'Amelie,' she said, 'my mission is to find out what happened to Fournier – specifically to discover whether the unknown man on Mars had anything to do with his death. The Director of Operations himself provided the mission brief. Now, I understand the medics have got some sort of ban imposed but this is our only chance of successfully completing the mission. That being the case, I'm over-riding the ban for this one transfer. My responsibility alone – to be documented as such.'

Amelie looked doubtful. 'I'm not sure...' she began.

'There's no real down-side,' Deira interrupted. 'Professor Chayka's convinced it'll prove therapeutic for our unknown American – who says sorry for stunning you, by the way. If he gets his memories back we might crack the case.' She looked pleadingly at Amelie. 'Please. Buy you a drink next time I see you.'

There was a long pause while Amelie struggled to make a decision.

'Okay,' she said at last. 'As a favour to you. But if I get into trouble I'll...'

'Don't worry, I'll make sure you don't. You're doing this under duress. The professor and I will take any flak. Thanks so much!'

'Fine. I'll get things fired up and placed on stand-by. See you.'

The call ended and Deira saw Sol watching her.

'What?'

'Oh, nothing. I was just wondering whether your old job at GCHQ is still available.'

Deira smiled, but the smile disguised a real worry that she'd overstepped the mark. She didn't have the authority to countermand a Bureau edict and she should really have reported the situation back to the Director for clarification on how to proceed. She just had a horrible feeling that the whole case would then get tied up in red tape as people tried to make sense of Sol being from the future. She might even have the mission taken away from her and somebody more experienced put in place. No way was she having that.

'Cross that bridge when we get to it,' she said, trying to sound confident. 'So – what about a bite to eat before we really get stuck into things?'

This was music to Sol's ears, and even Amadi approved of the idea so they all adjourned to the refectory to await Chayka's call to action. For some reason, time always went faster in the refectory than anywhere else on the Base, and they were still enjoying a coffee after their meal when a call came through in the form of a terse message from the Administrator's secretary telling them that Professor Chayka required them in the transmission terminal *now*. They gulped down the remains of their drinks and hurried back to the PHASE terminal – to find Chayka already busy with the equipment. Amadi scuttled off, looking horrified that anyone, even the professor, would interfere with what he clearly thought of as *his* equipment in *his* domain. The two scientists fussed and clucked while the agents sat and waited.

Deira took Sol's hand. 'How do you feel about this? I though a single PHASE from Mars to Titan was bad enough but this is something else again.'

Sol was leaning back in his chair, staring at the ceiling as if there were something fascinating up there. Now that the time had come to try to recover his lost memories he had mixed feelings. If he failed to get them back he'd never know who he truly was, where he came from, and what his past life contained. On the other hand, if he was successful in recovering them he might discover he was responsible for Fournier's death – and that would lead to a prison sentence. He glanced at Deira's hand in his and saw the worry etched on her face.

'Done it one way, so why worry about a return journey?'

He squeezed her hand and went back to examining the ceiling. Deira didn't push him. She could only imagine what must be going on in his head and couldn't think of anything to say or do that might help. An uneasy silence settled over them while Amadi and the professor continued their preparations.

Finally, after about twenty minutes and with Sol about to complain that there had been no reason for him to rush his coffee, Chayka turned and announced that all was ready.

'Everything's finely tuned. The transmission time will be approximately forty minutes, so a return journey, including the necessary inter-transmission cycle on Mars, will be about an hour-and-a-half. Are you ready, Agent Smith?'

'Ready as I'll ever be, Prof. Let's do it!' Sol walked briskly to the PHASE chamber and lay down on the couch, clasping Chard to his chest. He looked up expectantly.

'Ready to go.' he said in Amadi's direction. 'Fire at will!'

Chayka nodded his permission to begin and Amadi set about the usual preliminaries to a PHASE. Deira walked up to the outside of the chamber and peered in. She was surprised that Sol hadn't made some sort of parting quip before taking his place for transmission and felt a little hurt that he hadn't said goodbye. She suspected he was scared shitless.

As she gazed through the soundproofed plastic he shifted his head slightly so he could see her better and raised his hand in a farewell gesture. She placed her hand against the plastic and mouthed 'luck!' He produced that stupid grin of his and formed his thumb and first finger into a circle – the universal symbol for "piece of cake!" Then he froze as Amadi hit the transfer button. Deira backed away, not wanting to see the next bit of the process – and when she looked again, he'd gone.

'Transmission successful,' Amadi said from his position by the bank of instruments.

Deira checked the time – nothing to do now but wait. She wondered again why everything about this damned assignment involved waiting. It seemed that nothing – absolutely nothing – happened at a speed that satisfied her need for action.

She sat for a while and fidgeted, then paced aimlessly round the terminal, then sat again. When the forty minutes passed and there was still no sign that Sol had arrived she began to become seriously concerned. She needn't have worried, however, because, after forty-two minutes and eight seconds there was a "ping" from one of Amadi's monitors.

'Arrival confirmed on Mars,' Amadi said.

This was the first time Amadi had initiated an interplanetary PHASE and he was clearly on an adrenaline high. For Deira, the huge sense of relief she felt was tainted by the knowledge that this was only the halfway point. Having suffered over the past forty minutes, she now viewed the next forty with considerable trepidation.

Amadi turned from his instruments. 'While the chamber re-cycles Amelie will be doing a rapid check on Sol to ensure he's okay. If there are no problems he'll be PHASEd back in about five minutes.'

Another wait. Another "ping" but on a different monitor.

'Transmission initiated from Mars,' Amadi said 'Sol should be back with us in forty-two minutes.'

Deira was stretched out with nerves. This final wait was proving to be one too many and she felt she had to get out of the PHASE terminal for a while.

'I'm going to get something a bit stronger than coffee while I wait, Professor. You and Amadi are very welcome to join me.'

Chayka shook his head. 'I don't personally indulge in alcohol. I'd usually welcome a cup of coffee, but on this occasion I must remain with the equipment to ensure there are no problems. Mr Okofor will also have to remain – he has an incoming transmission in progress.'

'I understand. You both need to stay to monitor the transmission – but I can't stand it any longer. I'll see you in about half-an-hour.'

She turned on her heels and walked smartly out of the terminal, feeling good just to be moving purposefully again. When she reached the refectory she found there was some sort of Happy Hour going on, and found it liberating to do some introductions, get herself some hard liquor, and generally relax for a few minutes. She discovered that her reputation and the particulars surrounding her arrival were common knowledge among the Base personnel and for a brief moment she wondered how that could be – then a light came on. It had to have come from Amadi. She clearly needed to have a quiet word with him about the phrase "need to know" – but that could wait for now. She swiftly downed a tequila and got a refill. She'd reached number three by the time a message arrived on her wrist console.

'Oh crap!'

She glanced at the message, realising she'd lost track of time. She'd been gone thirty-seven minutes and Amadi wondered whether she'd like to be in the PHASE terminal when Sol arrived in five minutes time. Would she! She leaped up from her barstool, bid a hasty goodbye to her new-found drinking buddies and was off down the corridor like a greyhound. Two minutes later she ran into the terminal, panting slightly.

'Ah, Agent MacMahon – just in time!' Chayka gave her a sidelong glance while he busied himself at the console next to Amadi. 'Any second now we'll find out whether we've been successful in the retrieval of Agent Smith's memories.'

Deira found she couldn't care less about Sol's memories – all she wanted was to get him back intact. She would even sacrifice her ongoing investigation providing Sol was all right. The awareness shocked her – the realisation that, after a very short time indeed, she'd come to care for this man. She was still reflecting on her feelings for Sol when the door to the terminal slid open and a strange little man bustled in. She couldn't help but stare inanely – then blushed and turned away in embarrassment as she realised this was Dr Nicolau Dominguez, the eminent sub-quantal physicist. Nicolau went over to Chayka and tapped him on the back, something the professor wouldn't have tolerated from anybody else.

'Professor, sorry to disturb, but...' He was interrupted by another "ping" on Amadi's instruments and Sol re-materialised in the PHASE chamber. Deira craned her head to get a good look, eager to see that he was in one piece. He certainly seemed to be, and she experienced a huge sense of relief.

Sol's sudden re-materialisation had a very different effect on Nicolau. Whatever he was about to say to Chayka was forgotten in an instant and his face went deathly white. With an unpleasant grimace, and keeping a wary eye on the cubicle, he began backing slowly towards the terminal exit. Deira watched him with confusion. What had caused this sudden change?

Sol opened his eyes. He must have felt fine because he sat up immediately and swung his legs off the couch. When he saw Deira he gave a huge smile and thumbs-up – then his gaze wondered and he saw Nicolau.

'You!!'

Deira saw the word form on his lips even though she couldn't hear it through the soundproofed chamber. She also saw his face contort into a look of pure hatred – a look she'd never witnessed before and never wanted to see again. Sol leaped off the couch and hurtled through the chamber door. At the same time, Nicolau turned and ran across the terminal at a speed that Deira couldn't believe was possible from his stunted legs. He barrelled through the exit and shot off down the corridor with Sol in hot pursuit.

Deira shook off her momentary paralysis and ran after them but lost sight of them when they rounded a corner. She ran on, not completely sure where she was – then she arrived at the airlock and found Sol standing outside fuming.

Nicolau was inside pulling on an exosuit, the intellifabric moulding itself to his tiny body. He glared at them through the airlock door with an almost feral look then the outer door opened and he was out and onto the surface. The airlock automatically closed the outer doors and began cycling back to stand-by.

Deira stood with her hands on her hips, breathing heavily.

'What the hell was that about? Did you get your memories back?'

Sol furiously grabbed an exosuit and began pulling it on. Deira looked at him in alarm. Was he going outside again? If so, he wasn't going on his own. She began to pull on her own exosuit. Sol grumbled and cursed.

'Fucking little turd! Yeah, I got the mission-specific memories at least – and I remember that little rat-faced shit-head stringing Phillipe Fournier's body up on that rock face. He's the guy who murdered him.' He paused for a moment while he concentrated on fitting his oxygen tanks, then turned back to Deira. 'And there's more. He's not even human!'

Deira was already having trouble imagining Nicolau heaving Fournier's body up the steep rock on Mars, but she felt Sol had gone a little far with his last comment.

'That's hardly fair. He's an achondroplastic dwarf. He has a genetic condition – and he's achieved so much in spite of it.'

'Fuck – you still don't get it do you? He does *not* have a genetic condition – except in the sense that none of his genetic material is human. When I say he's not human I mean exactly that.'

'You mean…'

'I mean he's not of Earth! He's a fucking alien – and he definitely doesn't have mankind's best interests at heart!'

Chapter 18

DEIRA HAD BECOME quite adept at putting on an exosuit by now – just as well given that her mind was elsewhere. Sol's last comment had left her normally pragmatic world view in tatters. Aliens just weren't part of her personal universe and if she gave them any thought at all it was in connection with B-rated tri-vids where the aliens were of the scary-monster type. She had real difficulty linking the concept to what appeared to be a human dwarf.

'An alien?' She pulled on her helmet and checked the oxygen supply. 'A real off-world alien?'

Sol ignored the question and spent a few minutes ensuring his holster, containing Chard, was securely fixed on the outside of the exosuit for ease of access. After all, if he managed to get within spitting distance of the dwarf he wanted to make it count – preferably by slicing the little shit's head off. He was furious. He didn't think he'd ever felt so angry – angry that the dwarf had killed Fournier on his watch, angry that he'd lost him on Mars, and angry that he'd evaded him again here on Titan. *So far*, he told himself. He turned and looked back at Deira who was just pulling tight the last few straps of her own exosuit. He didn't know why he felt the way he did about her but he couldn't bear to see her put in harm's way – and Dominguez was definitely a force to be reckoned with.

The airlock finally cycled and the inner door opened. He stepped inside and pressed the "close door" button.

'No need for you to come,' he said. 'You wouldn't be able to do anything even if we did catch him – and that's very problematic at this stage.'

Deira looked up, aghast, as the door began to close and instinctively put her foot squarely in its way. She couldn't believe Sol would try to exclude her from this.

'If you think I've got you back from a double interplanetary PHASE just to let you go again you obviously don't know me very well. Don't patronise me – I'm a Bureau agent and I'll make my own decisions about what I will and won't do. Now shift your bulk from the entrance and let me in.'

Sol could see from the body language and the flashing green eyes that he didn't stand a chance. With a wry smile he moved to one side to let her in and the two of them waited silently and slightly awkwardly for the airlock to do its thing. Finally the outer door opened and they stepped out into another summer's day on Titan – just the ever-present orange-brown gloom and a light breeze. There were no clouds to be seen anywhere and Chard confirmed that no storms were expected.

Sol scanned the terrain in vain for the fleeing Nicolau and let out another choice expletive. Thankfully, Chard could detect emissions other than visible light and a moving heat signature to the northwest identified the position of the dwarf. They set off in pursuit at a fast lope, Sol leading and Chard providing regular updates.

'How did he get so far away?' Deira said. 'And where's he going? He's got nowhere *to* go! If he goes to one of the other Bases, even the Chinese, he'll be extradited – and he can't stay out here longer than two hours because of his limited oxygen supply.' She paused for a second to get her breath. 'An alien?'

'A real live alien. I know it's hard to believe. I thought it was a crock of shit too when Fournier told me. I soon got to believing it when I ended up fighting him on Mars. For a while I thought I'd end up on a slab.'

'But he's been working with Professor Chayka for – I don't know – forever! He helped develop sub-quantal physics and the QUAVERS. You must be wrong, surely?'

'I'm not wrong. First of all, the little shit's fast – really fast! I don't know how he does it on those little legs of his but he can easily outrun either one of us. Second, he's fucking strong. Again, it's not what you'd expect – and that's how he's been overlooked so far during your murder investigation. I wouldn't like to take bets on how long he could make his oxygen supply last.'

Deira remained doubtful. She'd been brought up on stories of the brilliant Professor Chayka and his right-hand man, Dr Dominguez. They were almost folk heroes for their work on QUAVERS and it was incredibly difficult to imagine Dominguez as a bad guy.

'Are you absolutely certain about all this? Is there any chance – even a slight one – that you've got him wrong?'

'Fuck! How many times do I have to say it?' Sol stopped and glared at Deira. 'I've seen this piece of garbage up close and personal and I was lucky to survive the encounter. What more do you want me to say?'

'Sorry. It's just so difficult…'

'I know. The whole thing's difficult – in fact it's a bloody fiasco. Fournier's dead and I still can't get to grips with Dominguez. They sure chose the wrong guy to send back in time. I'm a complete fuck-up!'

He started off in the direction of the dwarf again – Deira

running alongside and wondering how long she'd be able to keep this pace up.

'So what did you do after you lost Dominguez on Mars?'

"I looked for him for quite some time before I learned he'd left on the Q-ship. Then I heard about you, and how you'd persuaded Monroe to open a murder investigation. I thought we might work together until I discovered you'd got me down as one of the main suspects. Then we had our little fight and I became really confused. To begin with, I thought you were just pulling your punches – sparring if you like.'

'Because I had no Chard to augment my reflexes.'

'Yeah. I thought you were just testing me – but you didn't up your game, and it soon became clear that you couldn't. That was all you had. So what was I supposed to do? I disarmed you and would have skedaddled out of there if your partner hadn't suddenly appeared on the scene.'

Deira blushed behind her helmet as she reflected on her behaviour at that moment. 'And I accused you of killing him,' she whispered.

'Yeah, that was pretty harsh. Still, you were sort of out of it at that point – not rational. So I beat it.'

'What did you do then?' Deira was becoming short of breath trying to keep up. She felt the sharp pain of stitch down one side and wondered how much longer she could carry on like this. She'd always kept physically fit but Sol was being enhanced by Chard and she realised she was soon going to delay his progress.

'Well there wasn't much I could do until I found you about to PHASE to Titan. That was exactly where Dominguez was going so....'

'So you followed me through the PHASE chamber.' Deira was puffing considerably now, making it difficult to carry on with the conversation. 'I never understood that... but I was so caught up in events... I didn't pursue it. You went through after me... but now we know that because of the tachyon contamination... you arrived three days earlier.'

'Minus my memories. That really did screw things up.'

'Well at least... you've got some of them back. We now know... who killed Philippe Fournier... and how he did it. What we don't know... is why?'

It was no good. Her breathing was coming in jagged gasps and she was beginning to fall behind Sol. She pulled up, hands on her hips, panting.

'Can we stop for a second?'

Sol stopped in his tracks and looked back, concern etched on his face.

'Sure, take a minute.'

'That won't be enough.' She paused a few moments to take some big breaths before continuing. 'You were right in the airlock – I'm not going to be any use to you. In fact I'll just slow you down. You'd better carry on alone and try to catch Dominguez. I'll go back to the Base and see how our new Security Chief's getting on.'

Sol was secretly pleased at this turn of events because Deira would be back in the safety of the Base, but he made a half-hearted attempt at getting her to change her mind. Deira was having none of it. She'd made her decision. Though she desperately wanted to go with him, she had to acknowledge her limitations. With him augmented, she had absolutely no hope of keeping up.

'Just go!' she said. 'Every second you wait, he's getting

farther away. I can still see the Base so I'll be fine getting back. Go – now!'

Without giving Sol any more opportunity to argue, she turned and began to lope steadily back towards the Base. After a few metres, she stopped and glanced back. Sol was still watching her.

'By the way, exactly what was your mission?'

'It's complicated. I'll explain when I get back. Okay?'

'I guess it'll have to be. Go on – you've got a fugitive to catch.' Deira turned back towards the Base again and trotted off.

Sol turned towards the fleeing dwarf and gave it all he'd got, taking risks he'd never have considered had Deira been with him. What was it about that woman that had got under his skin so much? He tried to focus on his previous life in the hope that something would present itself. He'd been truthful with Deira when he'd said that his mission-specific memories had returned. Unfortunately, all those predating his original PHASE were still gone, leaving him with nothing but an occasional flash of something. Would they return? He ought to assume they wouldn't and move on but somehow he couldn't give up completely.

He focused again on the fleeing dwarf and concentrated on maximising his speed without tripping over one of the many rocks. He bounced across the surface, taking bigger and bigger jumps, and was astonished at how long he could stay in the air after each one.

'Atmospheric density,' Chard said, answering the unasked question, 'Remember the unique characteristics of this world – low gravity and relatively high atmospheric density. It's been suggested that a man could probably fly under his own power if he had wings.'

'That'd be good. Shame we haven't got any.'

'We could institute a partial solution if you think that would be helpful.'

'What? How?'

'We couldn't make wings, of course, but we could still get up in the air and improve our speed.'

'Huh?' Sol was making good progress with his leaps and bounds but still falling behind Dominguez. 'I'm not sure what you're talking about buddy but we're sure as hell not going to catch this guy without a serious change of strategy – so just tell me what to do.'

'It's really relatively simple. You need to reposition my holster inside the exosuit and place it horizontally across your hip. That's it.'

'That's it? That's what? What've I accomplished except for making you less accessible – and what about exposure to the atmosphere when I open my suit?'

'It would be better if I demonstrate the result of the manoeuvre rather than trying to explain it. It should take you no longer than thirty seconds to accomplish – twenty after augmentation. Exposure to the atmosphere should not be a problem. Your suit is designed to continue functioning in the event of damage to the exterior fabric and will automatically augment your oxygen supply to ensure an adequate inhaled concentration. You will, of course, be exposed to small amounts of hydrocarbons for the duration, as well as to the low external temperature, but I'm confident that neither will cause any real problem.' Chard paused. 'Have I ever let you down or knowingly put you at risk?'

'You sure haven't, buddy. Okay, if you say this is the way to go, let's do it!'

Sol stopped and undid the belt and thigh strap that secured his holster. He paused for a moment, psyching himself up for the main part of the manoeuvre, then did a mental ten second countdown. On "zero" he rapidly unfastened the exosuit and secured the belt round his waist, placing the holster horizontally across his pelvis. Then he closed the suit again. It was as simple as Chard said it would be. There was a faint smell of hydrocarbons, which faded rapidly, and the low temperature didn't seem to be an issue at all.

'Well that wasn't so bad, I guess. What now?'

'Simply this!' Chard extended the length of the PWC slowly to its full length of two metres. Not only did the intellifabric of the suit stretch with it, but this stretching fooled the internal algorithms of the material into assuming that the occupant was a good deal larger than Sol. Consequently, the suit further expanded over the chest, abdomen and arms.

'Erm, this feels a little weird, buddy.

'Extend your arms!'

Sol did as he was told and was astounded to see the result – a fabric membrane stretching between his arms and the extended PWC.

'Now try jumping again.'

Sol found it a little difficult moving in his new expanded suit but, after a few minutes experimentation, got the hang of running again and gave a test jump. The result was spectacular. He stayed in the air... and stayed in the air... and stayed... for a good three minutes. He felt like a giant flying squirrel.

'Fuck me! You'll believe a man can fly!'

'You need to gain more altitude if you are to remain in the air. Can I suggest emulating the take-off characteristics of large birds? Run as fast as you can and take some large jumps – but this time, flap your arms.'

'Copy that.'

Sol did as Chard suggested, leaping and bounding as he had before, but this time flapping his arms as soon as he was airborne. It seemed to have the desired effect, generating lift and enabling him to gain altitude. Before he knew it, he was a good thirty metres up and making good progress over the ground. He grinned. This was more like it. Now he had a real chance of catching that little shit.

There was just one problem. With Chard now inside his suit, he had to work out how to tackle him when he did.

Chapter 19

Sol's anger evaporated once he was up in the air, his previous dark mood replaced by sheer exhilaration. He felt great. This was some kind of story to tell his kids – assuming he got out of this alive and actually had any kids. He was flying through the amber murk of Titan's atmosphere chasing an alien dwarf bent on the destruction of mankind. Hell, it was better than most of the tri-vids he'd seen. Perhaps they'd even make a tri-vid about him.

With Chard's help, he experimented with various flapping motions to maintain altitude, and they finally found an intermittent slow arm movement that seemed to work best. With a means of staying aloft in the absence of rising warm air thermals he could convince himself that he was really flying and as he settled into a rhythm he found he had time to take in the surface features of the landscape in more detail. The surface was mostly flat rock with scattered boulders but there were occasional large rocky extrusions and even areas that reminded him of magma flows on Earth.

'Cryovolcanism.' Chard had accessed Sol's optic input and anticipated the question before it was asked. 'The early fly-pasts of Titan suggested volcanic activity and the Cassini-Huygens probe in the early part of this century pretty much confirmed it.'

'What about the giant mushrooms over there?'

'They resemble Earth stromatolites – layered rock with micro-organisms. However, water and photosynthesising bacteria are theoretically necessary for such features to form and they're not available here because of the low surface temperature. It's a fascinating find and requires further investigation.'

'Okay, but it won't be us doing the investigating because we're coming up fast on the dwarf. Your directions were perfect!' Dominguez was below and a little ahead of them.

'I suggest a full dive to bring him down,' Chard said. 'Bring your arms to your sides and keep your feet together to minimise lift. Tilt your head and shoulders down and I'll guide your angle of descent by direct muscular control.'

With Chard's help, Sol powered straight down on top of the unsuspecting Dominguez. Titan gravity may only have been a seventh of Earth's but Sol's mass, combined with his velocity, ensured that the dwarf was comprehensively flattened.

Unfortunately, the force of the landing sent Sol tumbling helplessly head over heels for some distance. He was dazed when he finally came to a halt and by the time he'd regained his feet and things had stopped spinning round him Dominguez was already some distance away and running fast. Sol silently cursed, wondering how he was going to catch up with this guy, let alone capture him. Sighing, he ran forward, flapped, jumped, and lifted off again, ready to repeat the whole process.

Chard was unhappy. 'Dominguez has changed direction. He's now very close to the evaporation zone – clearly a deliberate ploy on his behalf. If you dive-bomb him again you run a significant risk of overshooting and becoming mired in the tar.'

"Copy that. Any alternatives?"

"I can't think of any. We can't catch him on the ground.'

'Then we go with what we've got. Keep feeding me the best parameters for a dive and keep your electronic fingers crossed.'

Sol didn't have time to gain much altitude this time round so his new approach would be shallower and more technically demanding than the first one. With Chard's help he once more executed the dive perfectly, coming down directly onto the dwarf – but Dominguez wasn't about to be caught by the same trick twice. He waited until the last possible moment then ducked, and dodged to the left. Sol flapped hard, struggling to regain some altitude, and he did manage a few metres. It was far too little and far too late – he was committed to his dive. He couldn't turn and, despite more frantic flapping, he ended up executing a slow fall – straight into the sea about thirty metres from the shoreline.

Chard reacted instantaneously, activating the uniform's heating element and force field. It was a good try. The force field extended fifteen centimetres from Sol's uniform, thereby encompassing the entire exosuit, and Chard's intention had been to use it to exclude ethane from the fabric of the exosuit in the same way that it had previously excluded the methane raindrops during the storm. However, the field had been designed to prevent the passage of objects with a high kinetic energy and, while the methane rain possessed sufficient kinetic energy to be excluded, the liquid ethane molecules in the sea didn't.

The result was predictable – the force field leaked. Sol immediately noticed the smell as liquid ethane began to soak into the outer layers of the exosuit. Then, in spite of his uniform heater, he felt the change in temperature.

'Shit! We're screwed.'

Because of its trapped nitrogen, the exosuit provided some degree of buoyancy, and for a few minutes Sol bobbed round on the surface of the sea. However, as the nitrogen became displaced by liquid ethane, he began to sink, a process that would continue until he was completely submerged. He knew once the suit's insulating capacity had gone his uniform's heater would be insufficient to prevent him becoming hypothermic. He also knew that liquid ethane would ultimately flood the exosuit. So how would he die – from drowning or hypothermia? Try as he might, he couldn't see a way out of this.

Luckily for him, Chard could. The AIs voice sounded confident in his head.

'We know from basic physics that the kinetic energy of liquid molecules increases with pressure. My calculations suggest that at a depth of five metres the liquid ethane molecules will possess sufficient kinetic energy to be excluded by the force field. Although it is counterintuitive, to save yourself you need to sink as rapidly as possible.'

'Copy that. It's already getting cold.'

Sol did what he could to reduce his buoyancy, crossing his arms and keeping his legs and feet together. Chard had already retracted the staff to its normal length to assist the process by allowing the intellifabric to return to its normal size. As liquid ethane continued to displace nitrogen in the suit, Sol sank rapidly, and he'd soon slipped completely beneath the surface. He shivered, partly from the cold and partly from his innate anxiety about being under the sea. He'd never been much of a diver, he now recalled, and had an instinctive dislike of having a height of liquid – any liquid – above his head. Now he had to do what was completely against his nature and go deeper if he were to stand a chance of surviving.

Chard kept up the encouragement with a business-like voice that suggested he was in complete control.

'Three metres... four... five. Leakage appears to have stopped but the outer layers of your suit are completely saturated. We need to purge them of ethane and dry them out.'

'That'd be nice. How do we do it?'

'Now that the suit's no longer absorbing ethane, your own body heat plus the uniform heater will cause the ethane already in the suit fabric to evaporate. It'll then be vented through the device that allows carbon dioxide clearance in normal use. It'll take a few minutes and will be unpleasant and possibly dangerous to breathe until all the ethane has been eliminated. Can I suggest you hold your breath?'

Sol mentally shrugged, inhaled deeply and held it. Holding his breath, like diving, had never been part of his skill set, but this time he excelled himself and it was a full one-and-a-half minutes before he had to breathe again. It smelled like an oil refinery and his head swam from the effects of the vapour. He hoped there wouldn't be any long-term toxicity. Luckily, the fumes were eliminated rapidly through the exosuit vent and, by the time he'd taken a further half dozen breaths, the smell was minimal. To his great relief he was also beginning to feel warmer.

'Hydrocarbons expelled,' Chard said. 'Now, the combination of uniform heater and energy shield, together with the natural insulation of the exosuit, will protect you from the chill. The atmospheric filtration capability of the suit will not function in liquid so you will have to breathe a pure oxygen atmosphere. Expired carbon dioxide will be eliminated in the usual way so the main problems are solved. However, oxygen reserves will be an issue. I suggest making a strenuous attempt to get back to the Base quickly.

'No kidding? You suggesting I swim?'

'Not at all. However, you might try walking.'

'Huh? I may be three times blessed, buddy, but I still can't walk on wat... er... ethane.'

'No, but you *can* walk along the seafloor. At this distance from the shore, it's about seven metres down. You simply walk back up to the surface. Clearly, the suit will leak again once you get above the five metre mark, and it'll be a challenge to wade through the tar pit, but I'm confident you'll be able to handle it.'

'Copy that! What would I do without you, buddy?'

'No comment. I'll monitor the situation carefully and keep you going in the right direction. I'm now switching on the exosuit's exterior light.'

The floodlight attached to the suit's helmet flared on and lit up the surrounding gloom. Chard's plan re-energised Sol exactly the way it was intended. Now that the uniform/exosuit combination was working well he felt out of immediate danger. He forced himself to relax and, despite his dislike of diving, was soon taking an interest in his surroundings.

Off to his right he saw a stream of bubbles rising towards the surface. He angled his descent so he could get a better look and found that the bubbles were coming from a large conical structure situated next to what looked like a crack in the seafloor. Something was obviously coming out of the crack because the ethane round it roiled and churned.

'Fascinating,' Chard said, 'Active cryovolcanism – and the mound is a live stromatolite.'

'What about the water and photosynthetic organisms you said had to be present?'

'Oh good, you were listening! Yes, on Earth those factors are critical. Here, however, we have a situation similar to the deep thermal vents on Earth. The organisms that form the stromatolite are relative thermophiles and chemoautotrophs. Some probably obtain their energy needs directly from heat radiated by the cryovolcanic fissure. Others undoubtedly combine oxygen with hydrogen sulphide to form useful sugars.'

'I didn't think there was any oxygen on Titan.'

'There is none in the atmosphere but the bacteria would be able to extract it from surrounding water.'

'I didn't think there was any water, either.'

'Orbital scans suggest there may be large underground lakes, or even seas, and it may surprise you to learn that its liquid water you can see welling up from that crack. We're currently walking through a layer of liquid water-ammonia, made possible by the warmer environment round the crack. Sol, we may be the first to observe indigenous life on Titan.'

'I'm overwhelmed – though I don't think we're going to be doing much first contact stuff with a bunch of microbes.'

'To have simply seen this microscopic form of life is significant enough. Our scientific colleagues at the Base will be thrilled.'

'Well I'm sure thrilled they're going to be thrilled! I'd have thought having a piece of alien macroscopic life in the form of a shit-head dwarf would be far more entertaining for them – but who am I to say? Now can we concentrate on getting out of here? Please?'

'I've not forgotten our primary aim, but being down here is a unique opportunity to make observations that may not be forthcoming again.' Chard paused for a moment before continuing. 'Sol, we have a problem.'

Sol groaned and wondered what could be a bigger problem than being stuck on the seafloor of an ethane sea.

'Okay – what now?

'Your oxygen tanks are almost depleted.'

'What? Shit! I thought you were monitoring things.'

'I am, but this has happened catastrophically and quite suddenly. There's a leak at the junction of your oxygen tank and breathing tubing. It wasn't there when you left the Base so I suspect the damage occurred when you hit the sea. It didn't become obvious until a few minutes ago – and you now have only twenty minutes of oxygen left.'

Sol cursed and began walking as fast as he could along the sea bed. Chard did his best to help.

'Turn ninety degrees to your left. The ground will start to rise towards the shore quite soon. Try speeding up. Eighteen minutes of oxygen left'.

Sol grunted. Walking against the resistance of the liquid was exhausting. The ground did, indeed, begin to slope upwards, but it was an extremely shallow gradient and Sol didn't think he stood a cat's chance on Titan of getting his head back above water before his oxygen ran out. Then he realised that even that wouldn't help because there was no oxygen in the atmosphere. He was screwed.

'Fourteen minutes.' Even Chard was beginning to sound worried now. 'Please try harder, Sol. You can still make it if you give one last push.'

'Unnh,' was all he got in return as Sol pushed his way

desperately through the troublesome liquid. It seemed like he'd been doing this forever – like some kind of unending penance that a malevolent god had laid on him. He began to mentally count off the seconds.

Suddenly there was a voice in his head – and it wasn't Chard!

'Sol Smith.'

Sol stopped and looked round, his first thought being that his oxygen must be almost gone and he was beginning to suffer from hypoxia. The voice continued.

'I know this contact will come as a shock to you, but I think you already know you're going to run out of oxygen well before you can get back to your Base. If you wish to live you must follow my instructions.'

The voice sounded so real – but there was no evidence of anyone nearby. There was another of those stromatolite things a few metres away, but Sol didn't think he was somehow communicating with a colony of microbes.

Twelve minutes said his internal clock. That made him think. If he had twelve minutes of oxygen left he shouldn't be having audio-hallucinations yet.

'Chard buddy,' he said, 'what's going on? We seem to have got ourselves a party line or something.'

There was no answer.

Sol was nowhere near as calm as he sounded. Here he was at the bottom of an ethane sea on a strange world, about to die from oxygen failure, and suddenly there was a strange voice in his head. The usual voice that belonged to his friend and confidant was silent – like Chard no longer existed. The new voice spoke again.

'Sol Smith, your electronic companion has been taken

off line temporarily because I need to utilise your node to communicate with you. He won't be harmed. I'll explain who I am later, but right now your oxygen reserve is almost gone and you won't survive unless you do exactly what I say. Can you do that?'

'Fuck!' Sol grunted. He looked up. There was still a considerable height of liquid above him and he knew perfectly well there was no way he could get back to the Base in time. He didn't know whether he was already in the early stages of oxygen deprivation or not but at that precise moment it didn't seem to matter that much. He'd got nothing to lose.

'Okay. I don't know if I'm talking to myself but tell me what to do and I'll do it.'

Ten minutes.

'Good! Turn a hundred-and-twenty degrees to your right and walk for ten paces.'

Sol complied, and after the ten steps the voice came again,

'Now turn forty-five degrees to your right and walk for six paces.'

Sol struggled on, wondering whether this had been a good idea or not.

'Finally, turn forty-five degrees to your left and walk for five paces. You will reach a rock face with an opening in front of you, to your left and at ground level. Go through this opening.'

Five minutes

Sol came up to the rock face and looked for the opening. It was right where the voice said it would be but it looked too small for him to get through. The voice had obviously anticipated his reaction because it spoke again.

'It's only the opening that's small and you should be able to manoeuvre yourself through. It opens up inside and will allow you to crawl easily.'

Sol decided he'd come this far so he may as well comply. He was starting to gasp now as his oxygen atmosphere ran thin so he applied himself to the task in hand. He struggled down onto his belly and pushed himself towards the opening, his wriggling disturbing mud from the seafloor and turning the surrounding liquid murky brown.

Two minutes.

He pushed his head through and looked round. It was lucky he did because there was a sharp piece of rock jutting out near his right ear that would have probably lacerated his suit if he'd continued. The equivalent of an alarm sounded in his head.

Time's up. Oxygen's out.

Chapter 20

Sol lay with his head in the hole thinking this was one hell of a bad way for everything to end. He felt light-headed but his body felt heavy as if it were sinking into the ocean floor. A wave of warmth passed over him, starting at his feet and ending at the top of his head. He felt weird. Then he realised why – he'd stopped breathing, his chest frozen in a position halfway between inspiration and expiration. He supposed that made a sort of sense given that he'd no oxygen to breathe – but if that was the case why was he still conscious and able to move? It all seemed like madness.

Madness or not, it was happening – he really could think and move in the complete absence of any oxygen. He had no idea what was going on but he strongly suspected it wouldn't continue forever and he needed to shift himself if he were to stand any chance of survival.

He pulled his head out of the hole and glared at the rock face. What to do? He took out his knife, reached through the hole, and gave the offending rock a sharp stab with the handle. It seemed to move slightly so he hit it again – then again. After several attempts the jagged shard broke off and he thought the hole was probably safe. This time, he decided on a different approach. He rolled onto his back, flexed his knees, dug in his heels and pushed, getting his head back through the hole.

Cursing to himself he managed to squeeze first one shoulder and then the other through the gap. He paused for a moment to take a rest and realised he was sweating inside his suit. That seemed kind of ironic given the environment he was in, and he allowed himself a small smile.

As the voice had said, the opening was the worst part and, having got his shoulders through, the rest of him followed relatively easily with just a little pushing and wriggling. Sol then found himself in a much larger passage and was able to get to all fours. He crawled on hands and knees for what must have been about fifty metres, going down all the time – and then came up against a wall of solid rock. He stared at it in horror. There was no way he could turn round and there didn't seem to be any way forward.

'Look up!'

Sol looked up and saw with relief that the tunnel didn't end in front of him but went directly upwards. Indeed, it appeared to terminate just above his head. He pushed himself to his feet and his head cleared the liquid ethane, leaving him standing in a pool that came up to his chest. He lost no time scrambling out onto a lip of solid rock that surrounded the pool and found he was in a small cave. Its walls sparkled and shone under the suit's floodlight, reminding him of stories of the Arabian Knights from his childhood. More memories! He smiled ruefully as he remembered the stories. In his current predicament he could sure do with that genie.

'Okay, job done,' was what he tried to say before realising he had no air to form the words and his chest was still immobile.

He keeled over and blacked out.

Sometime later, he struggled back to consciousness and opened his eyes. Everything was black, so either he was in complete darkness or he'd gone blind – or he was dead.

He got to all fours and began feeling round, soon reaching the edge of the pool he'd recently emerged from. That was comforting because it confirmed his last memories of the place and confirmed he wasn't dead.

Then it all came back to him.

'Fuck!' he said. Then, realising he was breathing again and actually able to talk, he said it again for good measure. 'Fuck!' It felt so good. Obviously he was getting air from somewhere so things were looking up.

'I'm pleased you are awake, Sol Smith.' The strange voice was in his head again.

'So you *are* real! What the hell happened to me? I had no oxygen. I wasn't breathing. I should be dead. Did you do something to me?'

'No, you did it to yourself – switched to anaerobic metabolism in a most efficient manner. We have little time, so the answer to how you managed that switch will have to wait. For now, allow me to introduce myself. I am the Speaker of the Eich – you may call me Speaker.'

With his metabolism returning to normal and his breathing more regular, Sol's confidence returned.

'I'll call you Speaker if you stop calling me Sol Smith. Sol will do just fine. Now, who the fuck are the Eich and what's happened to my oxygen reserves?'

'I'll take your second question first, Sol. While you were unconscious we repaired the defect in your suit and refilled your oxygen tanks. The rock around you contains water ice which can be used to produce oxygen.'

'Well it'd be rude not to say thank you, but call me suspicious – why would you do this? What do you want from me?'

'We simply want you to survive, Sol. The reason will become plain in time. To answer your first question now, we are the Eich. We did not originate on this worldlet you call Titan. We came from a planet fifty-seven light years away and several millions of your years ago.'

'You're aliens! What is this, Alien Central? I don't suppose a certain shit-faced dwarf is one of yours?'

'Indeed not.' The Speaker sounded almost offended by the suggestion. 'We'll get round to him later.'

'You seem to want to leave an awful lot until later. What's wrong with clearing the air now? And why are you hiding in the dark? If you're looking to build up a certain trust it doesn't help to keep yourselves concealed.'

'All your questions will be answered in time. For the moment, I can categorically deny that we are hiding in the dark. We reside much deeper in this world's crust, where the greater warmth allows the formation of a liquid water ocean. Like you, we require water and a warmer environment to survive. The surface of Titan is too cold for us. We were able to carry out the necessary repairs on your suit by certain means at our disposal that do not require us to leave our habitat.' There was a pause. It seemed the Speaker was either pondering something or conferring with somebody else. 'We could show you our physical forms but prefer not to at this time. Your racial archetypes would make it a most unpleasant experience for you. Later perhaps.'

'Well at least that's honest. Okay, I'll go with that for now. Next question: how and why are you subverting my technology?'

'A long time ago we had technology like yours, and we still retain the capacity to make use of it when the occasion demands. However, over many millennia we have chosen instead to study and employ the science of the mind. We can't usually enter into direct dialogue with other beings but the presence of your node makes you unique in this time period. I am communicating with you via the same channel in your node that Chard uses. Unfortunately, that has resulted in him being excluded from this conversation.'

'So why are you concerned with me? You said earlier that my survival was important to you.' He suddenly had a thought. 'If you're into mental science are you the ones responsible for my memory loss?'

There was a brief but telling pause.

'As you have discovered, your memory loss is multifactorial. That due to the tachyonic contamination has been recovered. We are unclear how your other memories were affected but we are aware of another... group... that may have been responsible.'

Sol wasn't sure about that response at all—it seemed a little vague, and he was very aware of the preceding pause, as if the Eich weren't expecting that particular question and took a few seconds to formulate a satisfactory answer. He filed this away for future reference.

'This "other group" you refer to—would that be the dwarf's bunch or somebody else again? Are there any others you've not told me about?'

'The other group is also alien to you but is not of the same race as Dominguez. There are almost certainly millions of races scattered throughout the universe. There are also a significant number in this galactic spiral arm, but it's unlikely you'll meet them for reasons that will be made clear to you. For now, you only need to know some basic facts.

'We've been monitoring the rise of your civilization for a long time – ever since mankind first walked on two legs, in fact. During the last two hundred years things have begun to get… complicated… and events have now reached a critical point. Professor Chayka's actions over the next few days will determine whether your civilization survives beyond the next century – and he's already made the wrong decision once! We're hoping your presence here will change the dynamic.'

'Whoa! Steady there! You're getting way beyond me. Did you say the professor's already made the wrong decision once? That implies you're able to see into the future and…' He stopped, his mind racing.

'Yes Sol, we can see something of the future, but only in a very limited sense and not how you would imagine it – and of course you are, or were, part of that future. The important thing is that the future is not fixed. The timeline can be changed. Indeed, a change in the timeline is precisely what your mission was intended to accomplish.'

Sol took a moment to contemplate that. It was exactly what he'd felt himself – and what he'd said in the American Base. Somehow he knew the Eich were correct – his mission was all about changing the timeline.

'So…'

The Speaker interrupted.

'I suggest the remainder of this conversation is carried out in more comfortable surroundings. Your oxygen reserves are completely full and it's time for you to return to your Base. I'll contact you again very soon and explain more at that time.'

Sol got up and checked his tanks. 'You're just going to leave me with a partial explanation? That seems a bit churlish under the circumstances. Surely you can tell me something more?'

'There's certainly a lot more to tell, but we'd prefer to involve Deira MacMahon as well. Whatever we tell you here will be doubted when you get back to your Base, so we suggest leaving the details until later. It's enough for now that you know of our existence.'

Sol knew he'd been dismissed. 'Okay, but I expect another contact in the near future. You seem to know things about me that I don't know myself, and that's kind of irritating. Now, if you'd let me have access to Chard again it'd sure as hell improve my chance of getting out of here in one piece.'

'Chard will be back with you when you exit the tunnel and begin your climb to the surface. Farewell for now, Sol. We'll be in touch again soon.'

There was silence, and Sol was left alone with his thoughts. He needed to put the Eich to one side and concentrate on getting out of here. He climbed into the pool and started back down the tunnel. He knew where he was going now and it didn't seem long before he reached the narrow exit. Once again, he squirmed and wriggled his way through, and he'd no sooner got out than Chard came back on line. At least the Eich were true to their word over that. Perhaps he could trust them after all. He grinned behind his mask.

'Chard old buddy! Great to have you back! I've missed you.'

'I'm sure. What happened? There's a disparity between my internal clock and my memory, suggesting I've been off line for a while.'

'Long story, I'll brief you later. Right now I need your help to get out of here in one piece.'

Chard sensed the urgency in Sol's voice. 'I see we're

still under the sea but your oxygen reserves are now full. I presume that's part of your long story too? Alright, let's start the process of extricating ourselves from this mess. Turn left ninety degrees and walk a hundred paces.' Sol did as instructed. 'Turn left forty-five degrees and walk fifty paces. Good! You're doing fine.'

'May feel fine to you, buddy, but its damned hard work!'

Sol was sweating again with the effort of walking against the resistance of the liquid, his feet skidding occasionally on the sand-like surface of the seafloor. He'd have liked to have turned his suit heater off but knew that would be a very bad idea under the circumstances. He'd simply have to put up with the relatively minor discomfort. He knew there was worse to come.

'Turn left twenty degrees and then keep walking straight ahead,' Chard said. You're performing admirably.'

'Thanks for the moral support!'

After fifteen minutes or so the seafloor began to shelve steeply up towards the shore and Sol realised that the real test of his endurance was imminent. He struggled on, and the sand-like surface began to change and take on a distinctly sticky feel even with his force field on. A few more steps and he smelled ethane again. He'd reached the five metre mark and the suit was leaking again. Now was the time he really had to go for it.

He pushed on, each footstep harder than the last, the force field now being the only thing keeping him going by reducing the friction between his feet and the viscous layer of hydrocarbons underfoot. His head hurt like hell from the ethane fumes, and the temperature plummeted as the suit's insulation became compromised.

'Shit!' he groaned, between chattering teeth 'I'm not sure I can do this.'

'I'm confident you can,' Chard said.

Even in his dire situation Sol was amused. All he needed was this – an AI who thought he was a motivation coach!

'Well I'm glad one of us is.'

Sol checked his suit thermometer and wasn't surprised to find the temperature was down to minus ten Celsius even with the heater on maximum. He concentrated on putting one foot in front of the other, trying to ignore the cold and the smell. Suddenly his head cleared the surface and he could see the shore line no more than five metres away. A few metres from safety yet he felt he was freezing to death in a gasoline factory.

He couldn't feel his feet, fingers, or nose any more, his head hurt like crazy, and his eyes were swimming from the effects of the ethane fumes. His sense of direction had completely gone and it was only Chard who kept him walking in a straight line. After what seemed an eternity, he finally left the liquid behind and entered the tar pit. This should have been easier to negotiate since he no longer had the resistance of the liquid to impede him, but he was exhausted. Every step was a monumental effort and the only thing keeping him going was the thought that he'd soon be on solid rock and could rest awhile.

He continued to make slow progress and could see the edge of the tar pit about thirty metres away. He focused on that and the thought of being on firm ground once more. As he doggedly placed one foot in front of the other and saw the boundary coming closer he started to feel more confident. He was doing this. If he could just hang-on in there and let Chard guide he could get back to safety.

He plodded on one step at a time, effectively on autopilot. He forced himself to stay awake by sheer willpower and relinquished control of his muscles to Chard. The tactic seemed to be working. Then disaster struck. Ever since he'd left the sea behind, the combination of his rising body heat and the suit heater had been slowly evaporating the ethane from the material of his exosuit. As the suit's material gradually increased its insulation capacity the temperature in the suit rose. This resulted in more ethane evaporation, which brought the temperature up even more. This continued until a critical point was reached and the suit temperature was sufficient to cause a sudden and exponential rise in ethane concentration. Last time this had happened he'd held his breath while the vapour was purged through the exhalation valve. This time he was at the edge of his endurance and his breathing came in great ragged gasps. Holding his breath just wasn't an option.

He gritted his teeth and tried to go on but his head seemed to explode with pain and his sight began to fade. Pushing himself to the absolute limit he made one last effort to get out of the tar – and it proved too much. His vision contracted to a black tunnel and he felt suddenly nauseous. As he tried to stop himself vomiting inside his mask his balance failed and he stumbled and fell into the gloop. He desperately tried to keep his eyes open and get up again and, with a herculean effort, he got as far as his knees before his strength gave out completely. With a last despairing sigh, he collapsed unconscious, face down in the tar.

He'd given everything he had – and it hadn't been enough.

Chapter 21

Deira left Sol to continue his pursuit of the dwarf and walked disconsolately back to the Base. She'd always been highly competitive and it was depressing to find she couldn't keep up with Sol and would always be second-best no matter what she did. Perhaps there was a chance of retro-engineering Sol's tech – the AI and associated components – so she could have a PWC too. It was probably a big ask but worth exploring.

Back inside the Base, she found the new security module already in place and atmosphere-tight. The security team was busying about getting it up to full operational capability and she recognised Chief Cabello from the pictures she'd seen on the Mars security camera. He had a master plan projecting on his virtual screen in conference mode and he constantly referred to it as he directed the various operations. He stopped what he was doing when he saw Deira's Bureau uniform and wondered over.

'Agent MacMahon I presume.' He shook her hand somewhat tentatively as if he was afraid he'd damage her in some way. 'I'm Julio Cabello, Chief of Security.'

'Good to meet you Chief. Hector Monroe said you did a fantastic job on the ship.'

'Thanks for that, but I think Hector's being altogether too complimentary. Our investigation was pretty unhelpful. On the other hand, I've just heard you've apprehended the fugitive American. Well done! I should soon have a holding cell available.'

'Ah yes. That's a little complicated actually.' She checked

the time. Sol had been gone for forty minutes. She knew he wouldn't return until he'd either apprehended Dominguez or his oxygen reserves ran out so that gave her an hour and twenty minutes to play with.

'Is there somewhere we can talk privately, Chief?'

Cabello raised an eyebrow but said nothing. He showed her into one of the interview rooms in the new module and firmly closed the door.

'So what's going on?'

Deira updated him on her pursuit of Sol, the recovery of his memories by Professor Chayka, and his claim that Dominguez was Fournier's murderer.

'Dominguez? The dwarf? That seems highly... improbable, to say the least. You believe this guy?

'He's an agent, Chief, and yes, I do believe him. Unfortunately, that's the least of it.'

She went on to describe what they'd learned about Sol's origins and his assertions that Dominguez was an alien. Cabello laughed.

'So we have a time-travelling agent chasing an alien dwarf? I don't think so.'

'I know it's hard to take in, but the time travel bit's pretty solid. The fact that Sol got his memories back...'

'*Says* he got them back. He might never have lost them.'

'That's possible I suppose – though I don't think it's true. Professor Chayka's convinced by the theory of tachyonic time-travelling and it's supported by the date stamp on the AIs motherboard. I accept that Dominguez being an alien's a bit of a stretch, but you haven't seen how he can move. I don't think an ordinary dwarf could outpace us, both in the Base and on the surface.'

Cabello gazed at her, remembering his conversations with Hector Monroe. Monroe respected Deira – and Cabello respected Monroe. He nodded briefly and smiled.

'If anyone else had come up with this story I'd have thought they were mentally unbalanced. In your case, I'll give you the benefit of the doubt. It would help if I could talk to the American, though. Where exactly is he?'

'He's gone after Dominguez.' She described the dwarf's flight upon seeing Sol and Sol's subsequent pursuit. 'He's been gone for – she checked the time again – seventy-five minutes, so we probably won't see him back for another forty-five.'

'That's if he comes back. If I were him I'd make for the American Base again.'

'Point taken. I was probably stupid to let him go – but I believe the guy and I'm convinced he'll come back.'

Cabello got up and opened the door. 'Ah well, time will tell.' He paused as he had another thought. 'Incidentally, I'm told you have a background in IT and cryptology.'

Deira nodded. 'I don't think it's any secret I worked at GCHQ before joining the Bureau. Why? Oh – you want me to take a look at that pad your man contacted me about?'

'I think maybe you should. My IT guy can't get past the first page because of heavy encryption but he's confirmed it belonged to Fournier's father. Might be important.'

'Okay, give it to me and I'll see what I can do.'

Cabello retrieved the pad and Deira examined it with interest. During all her time at GCHQ, she'd never encountered one of these little things. They'd been briefly popular in the early part of the century but had been superseded by wearable tech, particularly the now common wrist consoles with virtual screens.

She turned it on and input the password Baxter had discovered. This took her to a second screen that was fascinating. The level of encryption was formidable – military level at least. Now why would that be required on an old machine like this?

Cabello watched her reaction with interest. 'Think you could do something with it?'

'Yeah, I think I can crack this, but it'll take some time.'

She settled down and got stuck in, leaving Cabello to return to the main security office. It seemed no time before he was shaking her by the shoulder. She emerged from her analysis with a start.

'Thought you might want to know your American friend's been gone an hour-and-three-quarters. Would you like me to organise a search and rescue team?'

Deira was mortified she'd so lost track of time. Unfortunately, it was an issue when she became engrossed in a technical challenge. She readily agreed to Cabello's suggestion, and a three man team, consisting of two security guys and a medic, were soon on their way. The medic carried a full emergency med kit and the other two took a hover-stretcher and extra oxygen. By the time they'd finally made it to the surface, two hours had passed, and there was still no sign of Sol. Deira paced up and down and watched the three men move away from the Base. This was no good – she had to get outside and help.

She suited up, pushing the pad into a pocket in the exosuit before processing through the airlock. She stood for a moment, gazing at the now-familiar surface and wondering what direction to take? She'd left Sol heading north, which would have taken him towards the sea. Since the tar pit was the single greatest risk she knew of, this seemed a good place to start, so she began to lope towards the rippling mass of ethane in the distance. She noted the rescue team had gone northeast towards the American Base – again not unreasonable. She hadn't gone far when a familiar voice came through her helmet comm.

'Agent MacMahon, this is Chard. Can you read me Deira?'

'Chard? It's Deira here. What's going on? Are you in trouble?'

'Deira, I'm relieved to hear you. We have a problem. Sol is lying unconscious in the tar pit. His oxygen reserves are fine but his breathing's slow and shallow and his heart rate is irregular, suggesting ethane toxicity. I require assistance to get him back to the Base.'

'What's your current location in relation to the Base?'

'Almost due north. I'll emit a beacon you can home in on.'

'Copy that.'

Deira immediately heard a low pitched beep through her comm. Chard said he'd modulate the beacon's tone to reflect distance, and she found it becoming distinctly higher as she went north. She informed the rescue team of the beacon and watched as they changed direction. Soon they were all converging on the same spot and, as Deira squinted through the gloom, she could just make out Sol lying face down in the tar. He looked to be in a bad way.

She turned on her force field and waded out to him through the gloop. She crouched down and could see that, beneath his helmet, his face was very pale with a sickly blue-green tinge. She tried to get her arms under his shoulders to drag him out but soon realised the futility of this. Titan might only have one-seventh Earth gravity but Sol's mass remained the same and there was the added problem of the viscosity of the tar. She realised if she wasn't careful she'd get plastered in this crap. So what to do?

She caught a movement out of the corner of her eye and, looking up, saw the rescue team had arrived at the edge of the tar pit. They paused, and one of the security men tentatively put a foot in the gloop before removing it hastily. This was a problem because, without a force field, there was no way they could go any further without becoming stuck themselves. Deira had a sudden idea and walked back to them.

'Give me the hover-stretcher. If I can just get him onto it I can push him out.'

She waded back into the gloop, the stretcher skimming along in front of her. She positioned herself on Sol's right, and the stretcher on his left, ensuring the gravitational brake was securely on. Then she heaved him up onto his side and pushed him straight onto the stretcher. The stretcher gave a judder and moved slightly at the sudden application of Sol's weight. This meant he wasn't completely centred and his one arm dangled off one side of the stretcher. Deira thought it would do. He was probably secure enough even now but once she'd pulled the safety straps round him and snapped them shut he definitely wasn't going anywhere. Okay – job done. Letting off the brake, she pushed the stretcher ahead of her and waded back to the waiting rescue team where she handed Sol over to the medic.

'Probably acute ethane toxicity,' she said, relaying Sol's vital signs from Chard. 'We need to get him back to the infirmary fast.'

Nobody argued with this, though the medic was clearly wondering where she got her information from, and they made haste to get back into the Base. This meant going through the airlock as two groups because the lock took a maximum of three people – or two if one of them was on a stretcher. The medic took Sol first, the stretcher folding to a vertical position for entry, and Sol secured by straps in the groins and armpits. Deira waited with Landau and Fingal, who were the designated security operatives on the team. Nothing was said, but she could see that the two men were giving her appraising looks. She hoped they were looks of respect.

Having divested herself of the exosuit and retrieved the pad from its pocket, Deira went straight to the infirmary. A whole gang of medics was working on Sol, but things looked a bit grim. He was hooked up to a monitor and connected to a ventilator by a tube down his windpipe. There was a bag of fluid connected to an I.V. in his left arm and, while she watched, one of the medics began inserting another line under Sol's collar bone. She used her Bureau privileges and asked to speak to the doctor-in-charge. A portly middle-aged man separated from the team and came over.

'Agent MacMahon.' he said, extending a hand. 'Roger Samuels. I gather you suspected ethane toxicity here?'

'It seemed like a good bet given the environment he'd been in.'

'I agree. We could smell residual fumes when we took him out of the exosuit. Now, the bad news is that he's obviously been exposed to high levels of ethane, which can cause severe central nervous system depression. That's why he's in a coma and his heartbeat is abnormal. We've put him on a ventilator to augment his oxygen supply because ethane can impair oxygen use by the body. He's also severely hypothermic with borderline frostbite of his feet'

'Is there any good news?'

'I think so. He was probably exposed for a relatively short period of time. According to the suit log it had virtually cleared of hydrocarbons by the time you found him. Such a short exposure time ought to result in a good prognosis.'

'You mean he's going to be alright?'

'He *should* be alright. I expect him to be awake sometime tomorrow, but you can never second-guess these things.'

'I'll take his personal effects if that's okay.' Deira had seen Chard propped up on a nearby chair and Sol's uniform slung casually over the arm.

'Sure – no problem. Help yourself. Now if you'll excuse me?'

He took his leave and hurried back to supervise the team looking after Sol. Deira gave them one last look, picked up Chard and the uniform, and headed for her room. She hated seeing Sol like this and was far more worried about him than she felt she had any right to be. Unfortunately, she couldn't *do* anything and she hated that more than anything. She needed something to take her mind off things.

She noticed that Sol's uniform still reeked of ethane so she took it to the laundry for cleaning. That must have taken at least five minutes. So now what was she to do? Back in her room, she fixed herself a coffee and was about to take another look at the pad when she realised she'd got Chard with her.

'Chard, can you communicate with me without Sol being here?'

'Of course Deira, I am a fully autonomous AI. My limitations are in respect of my weaponry, which can only be activated when I'm in contact with Sol.'

'Understood. What happened out there?'

Chard gave a detailed account of Sol's recent pursuit of Dominguez, including the period he'd spent off line. Sol had clearly performed above and beyond – but it didn't change the fact that the dwarf had escaped.

'You've no idea what happened to Dominguez?'

'None whatsoever I'm afraid. Logically, he should be in the Base but there are no records of the airlocks being used either side of our return from the chase.'

'Do you think he could still be alive? His oxygen would have run out hours ago.'

'I have every expectation Dominguez would have found some means of surviving. Whether he still poses a risk to us remains to be seen, but I wouldn't take anything for granted.'

'Hmm. And you have no idea what happened while you were off line?'

'No idea at all. We'll have to wait until Sol regains consciousness to find out. It may be that his experience, whatever it was, will provide us with further help with our mission.'

'I agree. Hopefully he'll be up and about again tomorrow.' 'I'm going to have another crack at Fournier's pad for a while, I think.'

She sat down with the pad and was soon deeply immersed again. A couple of hours later she still hadn't cracked it and she knew she wouldn't get any further today. She was just too damned tired. With all the excitement and the subsequent cryptographic analysis she'd quite forgotten to eat anything recently so she had a light meal, immediately feeling better as her blood sugar rose. She chilled out with a tri-vid for a while but found she couldn't concentrate on the story so she gave up on it and prepared for bed. She might as well have an early night tonight because she'd need to be fresh tomorrow for another crack at Fournier's pad.

Unfortunately, she found her anticipated sleep hard to achieve. She tossed and turned, worrying about Sol and hoping he hadn't suffered any lasting effects from the ethane exposure. She couldn't work out why she felt like she did about him but the word that kept coming to her was "familiarity". Sol seemed like someone she'd known and cared for all her life. It didn't make any sort of sense. She certainly found him attractive in a rough-and-ready sort of way, and he was easy to be round if you could put aside one or two of his little idiosyncrasies. Perhaps she shouldn't ask so many questions and just go with the flow. With these thoughts swirling round in her brain she eventually drifted off to sleep.

Chapter 22

DEIRA WAS UP early the next day. Having taken a long time to get to sleep she'd subsequently had a very good night and felt eager to get going. Her first thought was of Sol and she made haste to get to the infirmary. There she found his room clean, tidy – and empty. The bed was freshly made and there was the unmistakable odour of disinfectant. There was no sign of Sol.

She looked round, imagining the worst and wondering why nobody had contacted her. Her heart was pounding and she was beginning to hyperventilate when, luckily, a nurse appeared. The nurse immediately recognised Deira's uniform and, more importantly, the look of panic on her face. She tried to reassure her.

'You must be Agent MacMahon. Don't worry – it's not how it looks. Agent Smith woke up this morning – rather too quickly unfortunately. Before any of us could get to him he'd ripped off his monitoring leads and iv and was about to take out his endotracheal tube. He's a strong guy and he could have done himself harm so we had to take steps to restrain him. It took a number of us to hold him down and we elected to re-sedate him so we could get things done in a more measured way. We had to make sure all his vitals were okay before taking him off the ventilator and…'

'Yeah, I get the drift.'

Deira was both relieved that Sol was alright and irritated because her face had clearly betrayed how concerned she'd been. She didn't want to be the subject of Base-wide gossip.

The resolution of her anxiety, together with the irritation at betraying her feelings, resulted in her being sharper than she would have chosen to be with the nurse.

'Where is he now?'

'He's through there. First door on the right. You can go right in if you want...'

Deira certainly did want. She threw open the door ready for anything – except what she found. Sol was sitting up in bed looking the picture of health and holding court with a number of young nurses, who were laughing and giggling round his bed. She just stood and stared. The moment Sol saw her he grinned and shouted a welcome.

'Deira!'

'Agent MacMahon to you!'

Deira watched the grin fade, the hangdog look that replaced it appearing genuine for once. Perhaps she shouldn't have snapped but... well, what did he expect? She scowled at him.

'I can see you're none the worse for your little jaunt. If you're up to it, and your harem can spare you, I'd quite like a debrief on your attempt to catch Dominguez.'

Sol was clearly distressed and encouraged the nurses to leave.

'Doc says I'm good to go. I can be up and dressed in no time.' He got out of bed and began to fumble round. 'That's if I can find my uniform.'

Deira quickly turned away, her irritation turning to amusement He was stark naked, and his frantic fumbling under the bed had provided her with a view she could have done without.

'I've had your uniform cleaned. It should be ready if

someone could go and get it.' She chuckled to herself. 'I suggest that someone isn't you until you're a little more decent.'

Sol got up from his grovelling on the floor and stared at her, uncomprehending. Then he realised his state of undress and made a grab for a sheet to cover his embarrassment. Deira left him to it.

'By the way,' she called over her shoulder, 'I've got Chard in my room. Stop by when you're dressed.'

Sol was in her room within fifteen minutes, a picture of contrition. He saw Chard lying on the table and rapidly holstered him before sitting at the table and looking expectantly at Deira.

'Are we still on first name terms?'

'After that little scene in the infirmary?' she looked fiercely at him and his face fell. Then she looked pensive. 'I guess that could have been due to the residual effects of ethane toxicity.' Sol nodded his agreement and looked more hopeful. She smiled. 'Yeah, we're good.' She hugged him – much to Sol's obvious delight. He hugged her back, feeling her curves pressing against him in all the right places.

'They tell me you saved my life out there.'

'Payback time. Now we're quits.'

Sol guessed that was as much as he was going to get for now so he released her and sat in one of her armchairs.

'So you want a debrief?'

'Yeah. Chard's already told me most of it, but there was a period of time when he was off line. We'd both like to know what happened during that time.'

'I don't think you're gonna like it.'

'Try me and see.'

Sol proceeded to tell her about the Eich, watching her face for a reaction. He didn't think she'd come to terms with Dominguez being an alien yet, and now he was dropping all this extra shit on her.

Deira did her usual pacing thing while she listened to the story. What the hell was it with this guy that he seemed to keep meeting aliens? She'd had enough trouble with the concept of Dominguez being an alien but that seemed almost inconsequential when confronted by this new tale of aliens beneath the sea. As he went through the story she tried her best to find logical inconsistencies. There weren't any. When he'd done he looked doubtfully at her, as if he had no expectation she'd believe him. He didn't try to add anything – just remained silent and waited for her verdict. She stopped pacing and sat next to him.

'I'm tempted to think that the ethane exposure's addled your brain.' Sol nodded and looked miserable, expecting the worst. 'However, your oxygen reserves were filled up by someone or something so clearly something weird happened out there.' He began to look more hopeful. 'I guess I've really no choice but to believe you. To paraphrase Chief Cabello, we've already got a time-travelling agent and an alien dwarf. So what's to stop us adding in a couple of extra ETs into the mix?'

Sol punched the air. 'Yes!'

Deira grinned. 'What's this anaerobic metabolism stuff?'

'No idea. That's what the Eich called it. All I know is my oxygen ran out and I stopped breathing – but somehow kept moving and thinking until I reached the cave. It shouldn't have been possible.'

'Hmm. I've had a few strange things happen to me recently but nothing like that. I wonder if you've been affected by the interplanetary PHASE too – in addition to the memory loss I mean.'

'Could have been, I guess. I haven't checked out the DNA tests Amadi did when I arrived. Perhaps I should.'

'I think you definitely should. If this metabolic switch was cause by the PHASE it's very different to the things that happened to Adam and me.'

'Maybe they're just different sides of the same underlying change – except for Adam of course. He seems to have been plain unlucky.'

'Hmmm. Okay, we'll get back to Amadi asap and see what he's got. Our problem at the moment is lack of corroborative evidence for your story. It'll be difficult to get Cabello on board without it. He's very much the pragmatist. Just like me – but more so.'

She suddenly realised there were more revelations to be shared.

'By the way–what about those memories you retrieved? You were going to update me on those too.'

'It's complicated.'

'I'd expect nothing less from you–but I still need to hear it.'

Sol took a while to get going. First, he insisted he needed a coffee and, when he'd drunk that, he said he'd missed breakfast and felt hungry. Sometime later, when he'd been sufficiently fed and watered, Deira sat him down again.

'Enough of the deflection activity. Can we get on with this?'

'Fine.'

He wriggled in his chair and would have got up again but Deira wasn't having any of it.

'Spill it! Now!'

'Alright, alright.'

He paused again, wondering how to begin.

'It all starts in my time – your future,' he said. 'That future has a big problem. You know that the average human life span has been increasing since the middle of the twentieth century? Well that trend continued right up to my time. The average life expectancy then is 130 for men and 135 for women, with many living longer than that. Unfortunately, from the middle of the twenty-first century, the birth rate began to decline, and by my time it was very low and continuing to fall. Imagine a society made up predominantly of old people, many of whom require some form of special care, and the burden that places on the few youngsters available. It was unsustainable – the whole fabric of society was collapsing.'

'That's horribly fascinating but I don't see what it has to do with your mission.'

'Give me a chance. I'll get there.' Sol grabbed a bottle of whiskey and poured himself a shot before continuing.

'Okay, so we've got this collapsing society. Well, the boffins finally worked out that it was more than just society that was collapsing, it was the human genome itself – and the cause of this genetic collapse was the widespread adoption of mass PHASEing some years before. They tried all sorts of things to halt the process but were eventually forced to recognise that it was irreversible. The species was heading towards extinction.

'Everyone was busy wringing their hands and wondering what to do when Professor Chayka, the guy who'd triggered the whole process, came up with a potential solution.'

'Professor Chayka!' Deira interrupted. 'But he must have been ancient. I mean…'

'He was 135 years old, in a wheelchair but still working. He came at things from a completely different angle. It was known that mass PHASEing had caused the problem, and it was also known that simply halting mass PHASEing wouldn't save the species. He suggested it might be possible to send a man back in time to prevent mass PHASEing from ever happening. He proposed to do this by employing tachyonic transmission, something he'd been working on for some time.

'Clearly, there was nothing to lose. A new tachyon transmitter was constructed and I was the chosen transferee. I was to take with me a set of equations that demonstrated the genetic dangers of mass PHASEing. My mission was to get these to Chayka's team, preferably to Fournier because they related to his specialty, sub-quantal genetics.'

'Just a minute.' Deira looked confused.

'What?'

'Why you?'

'Excuse me?'

'Why you? Why not a scientist who'd be better able to explain the equations?'

'It's simple really. For photonic transmission you need the gamma mutation. For tachyonic transmission you need an additional double mutation, the rho-lambda mutation. Can you guess at the chances of having that particular triple mutation?'

'Hmmm. Not really.'

'Well it's almost impossible to calculate. I was told there were only eleven of us in the world, and most were over eighty years old. I was one of only three who were in the right age group, and physically fit enough. The clincher was I was also an agent.'

Deira was still unconvinced. 'I follow what you're saying, and I know I've a suspicious nature, but don't you find it just a little bit coincidental that of all the people in the world who could participate in this new form of PHASE you happened to be an agent? You talk about calculating odds – well try calculating the odds of that.'

'Are you suggesting a conspiracy.'

"I'm simply saying I don't believe in coincidences. Think about it. Just when they needed to send someone back in time by means of a new technology that only a very limited number could use, there you were, fully trained and ready to go. Come on Sol – surely you can see it?'

Unfortunately, Sol could see it, and in seeing it an awful lot made sense.

'My whole life! I must have been groomed for this my whole life – including being accepted into the Agency. Everyone has their genome checked at birth, sometimes before birth. They must have thought their luck was in when they saw my mutations. I guess it was probably them who sabotaged my memories too – so I wouldn't put it all together.'

Deira put her arm round his shoulder. He seemed somehow diminished and she gently prodded him to tell her more.

'What happened on Mars?'

With a great effort, Sol dragged his thoughts away from the odious thought that he'd been manipulated throughout his life and turned back to subsequent events.

'Well, they didn't get the timing quite right and I found myself on Mars several days before Chayka's team arrived. I stayed holed up whenever possible but I had to venture out now and then. I also needed ongoing intel about when the ship might arrive and I thought the local bar was a good place to get it. I made friends with the regular barkeep and had a few good evenings while I waited.

'When the passengers from the Q-ship disembarked, I went to find Fournier. He was leaving his room when I came up the corridor, and I was about to stop and talk to him when Dominguez followed him out. Fournier looked kind of wrung out but the dwarf was smiling – if you can call that particular contortion of his poxy shit-face a smile. I didn't know what had been going on but I obviously couldn't talk to Fournier then so I kept walking and hoped he'd gravitate to the bar that evening. I was lucky – the whole bunch of scientists, including Fournier, arrived at about 20.00.

'I watched them for a while and it was clear Fournier wasn't a happy bunny. When I got an opportunity I introduced myself to him – told him I was an agent and I needed to talk to him. I was a bit surprised when he jumped at the chance, but he was reluctant to talk there and then because, as I found out later, he was scared witless of Dominguez. We agreed to meet up outside the bar.

'We found ourselves a little spot on the Mall and he soon told me everything. He'd been secretly carrying out DNA tests on Chayka's team because the professor was going to embark on unauthorised research into – guess what – mass PHASEing. Of course, Fournier had the surprise of his life when he got the results of Dominguez's DNA because it obviously wasn't human.

'Fournier told me he'd tried to tell Chayka about his results but he'd caught him at the wrong time and the Prof and given him a flea in his ear. It seems that somehow Dominguez got wind of what Fournier had done and realised his cover was blown. He spun a yarn that he'd been stranded on Earth many years before and had been working ever since to help get sub-quantal technology up and running so he could get himself home. Fournier wasn't entirely convinced so Dominguez made him an offer he couldn't resist – a complete set of equations describing mass PHASEing if he stayed quiet about what he'd found.

'Fournier admitted he hadn't been able to resist this and he'd even flaunted the equations at Simon Chandler, who was a professional rival of his. It was only later on Mars that he started having second thoughts, but Dominguez visited his room there and apparently suggested he might have more to offer if Fournier stayed quiet. Again, greed got the better of him and he agreed not to say anything.'

Sol paused as he saw the sceptical look on Deira's face.

'So you're saying Fournier got evidence that Dominguez was an alien and didn't seem to think that might be a bit strange? We're talking about a real-life alien here, not exactly a routine event. He must surely have had some suspicions.'

'I'm sure he did, but the lure of professional advancement was too much. You have to get into the skin of these scientific types to understand how they function. They're all obsessed with publications and professional fame. Anyway, he later relented and decided to confess to Chayka, but before he could do that he met me – and I seemed to be the answer to his prayers.

'This was all music to my ears because I thought Fournier would almost certainly buy into my story and agree to prevent mass PHASEing ever coming about. Mission accomplished. I told him where I was from and what the result of implementation of the equations would be – and to remove any doubts he might have I gave him the equations I'd been sent back with so he could examine them at his leisure. We agreed to meet up again the next morning so he could let me know what he'd decided. That was a mistake because I think Dominguez had somehow eavesdropped on our conversation.'

'That'd make sense,' Deira said. 'He left the drinking contest just after you and Fournier went out and he was away for about forty minutes. I remember thinking it was a long time but I didn't connect things – probably because he wasn't on my radar as a suspect.'

Sol continued. 'Once Dominguez knew that Fournier was going to tell Chayka about him, and that he had my equations, he had no option but to get rid of him before he presented them to Chayka. In other words, I'm largely responsible for Fournier's death. Even if I didn't actually do the deed, I set the guy up. I'm culpable.'

Sol really did blame himself for Fournier's death but if he was hoping for some words of comfort from Deira he was to be unlucky. She'd already assimilated what he'd said and moved on–her empathy mode taking a holiday and analysis mode kicking in. She got up from the table and started her usual pacing routine.

'You said before that you actually saw Dominguez with Fournier's body. What exactly happened?'

Sol got himself back into gear again and carried on.

'Yeah. After I'd given Fournier the file with the equations I went to lie down for a while in my shelter in Hydroponics. Unfortunately, I was too wired to sleep so I went for a wander round the Skydome. I guess it'd be about five in the morning by that time.

'I'd just come up to a rock formation when I saw Dominguez on top of it hauling something heavy on the end of a rope. I was intrigued and watched him fasten the rope to a rock spur and ease whatever it was off the cliff so it was swinging from the end of it. It was only then I realised it was Fournier – and he'd obviously been dead for some time. I yelled something at Dominguez – I can't remember what – probably rude, knowing me. He was pretty startled to see me but recovered quickly and shimmied down the rock face as if it was a walk in the park. Then he grinned at me and pulled a knife. I tell you, I've never seen anybody move so fast in my life. It was a good thing Chard was monitoring the situation. When the dwarf came at me, he just flipped me into combat mode.

'We must have fought for about five minutes, though at the time it seemed a hell of a lot longer. You'd think that with my extra height, weight and built-in tech I'd easily take him – you've seen how fast I am in combat mode – but I just couldn't get an advantage. At one point I thought he might actually get me – and he definitely would have if it hadn't been for my electronic buddy. In the end, he seemed to realise that we were pretty evenly matched and that wasn't to his taste at all, so he turned tail and skedaddled. I tried to follow but lost him at the exit to the Skydome. I knew there'd be a fuss when the body was discovered later that morning and I didn't want to be connected so I went back to Hydroponics and hid again. And that was that!'

Deira said nothing. She'd stopped pacing while he'd been talking but began again now, frowning while she went over his story in her mind. The minutes dragged by, and Sol was watching her back recede across the room yet again when she returned to the table and sat down again facing him.

'Everything you've said fits together. I believe you. That means the murder investigation's over. In fact, my entire mission's over.' She thought that over for a moment. She should really report back to the Bureau. It was just… there were more important things to deal with now.

'I suppose the most important thing now is to get your equations to Chayka – safeguard the future and all that. God that sounds portentous!' She saw the look on Sol's face and a sinking feeling of impending doom came over her.

'You've still got them haven't you?'

'It was kind of – a mistake.' Sol saw a disaster in the making.

'A mistake? You mean you don't have the file anymore? What happened?'

'We obviously *had* the file,' Sol said bitterly, 'but we lost it during the fight – because of that fucking little shit of a dwarf!'

Chard cut in. 'Dominguez uploaded a virus into my core which attacked a number of my major functions simultaneously. It was unsuccessful, as Dominguez knew it would be, because of my high level anti-virus protection. Unfortunately, during the short time I was… distracted… a second virus, which was piggy-backed on the first, attacked and destroyed the file. It was a highly sophisticated attack. More to the point, it was clearly directed against me despite Dominguez having no direct evidence of my existence. He managed to deduce my presence and take steps to nullify my usefulness all in the space of a few minutes. He's a truly awesome adversary.'

Deira couldn't believe her ears. How could one dwarf, alien though he might be, outmanoeuvre a trained agent with Sol's amount of extra tech? Then she remembered how Dominguez had eluded them in the Base and on the surface.

'It's possible the file still exists somewhere,' Chard said.

'It's probably one of those deleted from Fournier's wrist console,' Deira said. 'We've been trying to find a data wafer copy of those files for the past few days. Nothing so far. If we can't find them soon we'll have to assume our only means of convincing Chayka to abandon mass PHASEing has gone for good!' She grimaced. 'You two don't seem to have accomplished much during your stay in our time, do you? Is there anything you can think of that might help us out here?'

There was silence from both Sol and Chard.

'I didn't think so.' Deira stood again and resumed pacing. 'Okay – think! If you were Fournier and you'd just been given some highly sensitive data what would you do?'

There was silence for a moment and then Sol suddenly brightened up.

'I'd have copied it! Fournier was scared for his life, but he'd seen my equations so he'd have been scared for the future of humanity too. I'm damned sure he'd have made some backups somewhere – an insurance policy in the event of his death.'

'So where would such a copy be? Chief Cabello's team has searched the ship extensively and came up with nothing. What's left?' Suddenly her eyes went wide.

'What?'

'The pad! Fournier's father's pad. It's protected by high level encryption, and everyone's been wondering why. Now it seems pretty obvious doesn't it?'

'A backup? But I thought it'd been found on board the Q-ship? How could Fournier have copied my file while he was on Mars and leave it on an old-fashioned pad that was still on board the ship?'

'Crap! He couldn't – the pad has no datasphere connection. So whatever the pad has on it isn't your file – and it's your file we desperately need. Damn!'

'I think I've found at least part of what we're looking for.'

Deira had forgotten about Chard and started slightly when his voice emerged from Sol's PWC.

'Anything you can do to help would be greatly appreciated Chard.'

'It occurred to me that the shuttle that brought the scientists down to Mars would have remained there for the length of their stay. That being the case, one could theoretically place a file in the shuttle's memory for upload to the ship's core when the two subsequently synchronise.'

'Of course!' Deira said. 'We just need to look…'

'Excuse me interrupting but I have already taken the liberty of accessing the ship's core and I have discovered the following.'

Deira's virtual screen flared into life and a long string of equations were displayed.

'That's not my file,' Sol said. 'I assume that's the mass PHASEing file Dominguez gave Fournier.'

'Yes,' Chard said. 'This is the file we do *not* want to be released so I have removed it from the core. I suggest it might be worth making a data wafer copy and keeping it in the security office safe as evidence.'

'Will do,' Deira said. 'Unfortunately though, we're no further forward in finding Sol's file – if it still exists.'

'Perhaps we ought to ask Chief Cabello for some help,' Sol said. 'I don't know about you but I'm out of ideas and could do with a bit of fresh thinking.'

'Works for me.'

'Unfortunately, we have another problem,' Chard piped up. 'We have been pre-empted. Dr Chandler has just placed the file for mass PHASEing on his Base terminal. Dominguez must have given it to him before reaching Titan and now it's out in the scientific community.'

'Oh shit!' Sol said. 'If we can't persuade Chayka not to use it the mission's dead – and so is humanity.'

Chapter 23

T HEY FOUND CABELLO finishing off his afternoon briefing. He dismissed his men and came over.

'Agent Smith I presume. Public enemy number one turned Captain America! How're you feeling after your recent bit of excitement?'

Sol grinned. 'Better than I've any right to feel – and due in no small part to the efforts of your men.'

Deira wasn't sure how much of what Sol had shared with her he wanted to make public, but she didn't think she could create a plausible scenario for Cabello without telling him everything. She pulled Sol to one side.

'How much can I tell him?'

Sol seemed surprised she'd bothered to ask.

'Everything. We're all on the same side here.'

They turned back to Cabello, who was standing with his arms folded, looking expectant.

'Something else you'd like to share with me?' he said.

'Yeah – how'd you guess?' Deira said.

'Do I really need to answer that?'

'I guess not – and if you thought the last stuff was outrageous, you're going to love this'

'I knew it could only get worse before it was over. Do we tell the men too?'

'I think so. We all need to be on the same page if we're going to work together effectively.'

'Fair enough, but before you start I should warn you I only have a level five security clearance – and the men have none at all. Are you sure you still want to go ahead on that basis?'

'Yeah, I'm not worried about security clearance. The Bureau doesn't know a damned thing about this yet and I'm in no particular hurry to tell them. They probably wouldn't believe me anyway.'

'Fine – it's your call. I'll get the men together.'

Cabello assembled his team and everyone took seats round the new conference table. The two agents were introduced to those men they hadn't already met and Cabello opened the briefing.

'Agent MacMahon briefed me earlier today about a break in the Fournier case. I hope you'll appreciate why I haven't shared it with you when you hear the details. I'm now told there are more revelations to come that I haven't been party to as yet, so you'll hear those too. Agent Smith will conduct the briefing.'

Sol launched into his backstory then moved on to his recent experience on the surface – his struggle to catch the dwarf, his gliding experience, and his fall into the sea. There were looks of deep respect round the table. Regardless of his tech, which made much of what he'd achieved possible, the men were clearly impressed and looked at him with a degree of awe. That helped when he moved on to his meeting with the Eich – but there was still a stunned silence when he finished. Even Cabello was quiet.

Deira thought she'd better get in first and try to allay the obvious doubts.

'You're all being very diplomatic,' she said, 'but it's all too obvious what you're thinking. What hard evidence do we have? Well, the date stamp on the AIs mother board supports Agent Smith's claim to come from the future. Then there's the alleged episode in that undersea cave. Something strange must have happened out there because Sol's oxygen bottles had been inexplicably filled up when we found him. I realise that doesn't prove the story about aliens but it's damned hard to find another explanation.'

There were silent nods round the table, though it was still difficult to see how much the men had been convinced. Deira carried on.

'We don't have much else. We've been able to find a copy of the files for mass PHASEing that Sol says Dominguez gave Fournier. The cynics among you would probably say we only have his word for that,' she glanced at Cabello, 'but I believe Sol. What we've lost is the critical file that Sol says he brought with him from the future. Finding that file would pretty much confirm Sol's story. More importantly, it's also the only way we're likely to persuade Professor Chayka not to instigate that field of research. So we badly need to find it. Anybody got any ideas?' A hand went up. 'Yes Mr…'

'Baxter.'

'Yes, Mr Baxter. Apologies for not remembering your name – there were quite a few in a short time.'

'That's all right. I was going to ask about the pad Dr Altmeyer found. It was heavily encrypted and…'

'I'll stop you there if you don't mind,' Deira interrupted. 'We wondered about the pad – but it was on the ship the whole time Fournier was on Mars and it has no means of networking available to it. I think it probably does contain some very important information – just not what we're looking for.'

'Point taken. So what about the shuttle that went down to Mars? Has that been properly searched? As far as I remember the search we conducted on the ship didn't take in the shuttles.'

'You're right, Mr Baxter,' Cabello said. He looked at the two agents. "I suggest instituting a search of the shuttles immediately we finish this meeting. Furthermore, given the importance of the file we're looking for I think we should search the ship again as well.'

'Sounds good to me.' Deira said. 'You'll have to be quick, though, because the ship's due to leave tomorrow.'

"Get the crew to help out,' Sol said. 'They'll be keen to get home, so tell them the sooner the search gets finished the sooner they'll be able to leave. They might have had a bit of R&R on the Base over the last few days but it's hardly Seamus O'Malley's Pub on a Saturday night!'

'Seamus O'Malley?' Deira said. 'Another memory flash?'

Sol looked bemused. 'I guess it was – I don't remember much except for the name and the association with a really good time. I think it was in Boston, though, not Ireland.'

Deira laughed. 'I'm not sure there are many genuine Seamus O'Malleys left in Ireland. But Boston? Yeah, I can go with that.'

There was an awkward pause for a moment while each wondered what to say next. They were saved by another hand going up. Cabello jumped in. 'Yes Mr Petrelli?'

'What about copies in other computers?' Petrelli said.

'We've searched all the computers likely to be available to Fournier,' Deira said. 'Found nothing. Any other suggestions?'

Petrelli consulted his wrist console for a moment. 'Well, it'd seem from the Chief's interviews that Dr Blumstein was one of the last people to see Dr Fournier alive. He went to her room round 02.40 on the morning of his death and left about an hour later. He'd probably have had time to place a file or files on her computer.'

'Of course,' Cabello said. 'That's why Fournier went to see Blumstein that night. It didn't make sense given how she'd treated him in the bar, but it makes perfect sense if his motive was to leave a copy of the file somewhere safe. Her console will need searching.' He gazed round. 'Good suggestions so far. Anything else?'

Nobody could think of anything so Cabello swiftly organised some details.

'Petrelli, Dr Blumstein was your idea so you get to check out her wrist console. Hunstan, get Monroe's team on the comm and ask them to check the terminal in the room where Dr Blumstein stayed on Mars just in case Fournier used that instead of her wrist console. Fingal and Landau, I need you to search the shuttles and Q-ship. Feel free to enlist help from the ship's crew if it's likely to take too long. Baxter, I'm afraid you're on general duties.'

'Mr Baxter,' Deira said, producing Fournier's pad. 'I'm going to take a look at this again. Would you be prepared to get stuck into any analysis if I can get past the encryption?'

'No problem.' Baxter was looking for any excuse to get out of general duties.

Sol turned aside and sub-vocalised Chard. 'Couldn't you decrypt this thing a damned site faster than Deira?'

'I could if I could access it but, if you recall, it's had its networking capability removed.'

Deira settled down with the pad and got to work. Baxter tried to look over her shoulder.

'Not now, Mr Baxter. I'll call you when I need you.' Deira looked across at Cabello. 'Do you want Mr Baxter here to continue with general duties?'

Cabello confirmed that Baxter should continue his original task and he shambled off, clearly disappointed. An hour passed. Deira was so completely focused on decrypting the pad that she was oblivious to the comings and goings round her. Hunstan returned from his task with nothing to show for it. The team on Mars had examined the terminal in the room Tirzah had used during her stay only to find it hadn't been used at all during her occupancy. Cabello re-assigned him to help Fingal and Landau with the ship-wide search. Sol just mooched about feeling kind of useless, and embarrassed that this exercise was only happening because he'd lost his file.

All was quiet until Petrelli ran in clutching a wrist console.

'Sorry I've been so long,' he said. 'Dr Blumstein was damned hard to track down and when I did finally find her she insisted on having a shower before she'd talk to me.' Sol smiled. Dr Blumstein sounded like his sort of person. 'She didn't want to let me near her console to begin with,' Petrelli continued, 'but I told her I'd lock her up if she didn't comply. Sol's smile turned to a grin as he saw the look on Cabello's face. He didn't look pleased, that was for sure, and Sol thought Petrelli would probably be for the high jump later on. 'Anyway,' Petrelli went on, 'here it is – her wrist console.' He placed it on the table.

'Is there anything on it?' Cabello asked.

'No idea. I'm not into that sort of thing.'

Cabello looked irritated and picked up the wrist console. 'Baxter, get over here and do your stuff with this thing.'

'Our file's there,' Chard said to Sol. 'I've uploaded it for safe-keeping.'

Sol was delighted. However, he'd deliberately kept back some of Chard's abilities when he'd briefed the security guys so he now had to pretend to be ignorant of the console's contents. Baxter hurried over, happily ditched his general duties, and in less than ten minutes had found what they were looking for – a hidden file that had a date stamp of the evening before Fournier's murder. There was a general hush as he prepared to open the file. Cabello turned to Deira.

'Do you want to see this Agent MacMahon,' He got no reply and realised he wasn't going to get her attention until she'd solved the encryption puzzle. He shrugged. 'Okay, let's do it Baxter.'

They all held their breath and Baxter opened the file. There was a brief moment of panic when it seemed the file had been corrupted but then, there they were – rows and rows of equations running down the page. Sol pretended to examine them carefully before confirming they were the equations he'd lost. Baxter transferred the file to Sol's wrist console – something he'd been given by Deira to help him blend in – and made a data wafer copy to be kept in the safe with the other set of equations. Finally, he deleted the file from Dr Blumstein's console and Petrelli was detailed to return it to her. Job done.

Now that the files were safe they could all relax and engage in some mutual congratulations. Sol joined in – it would have looked odd if he hadn't – but beneath his jovial exterior was a huge sense of relief. This had been a close-run thing. His inability to look after the file had almost resulted in disaster and the fact that Dominguez was a particularly powerful adversary wasn't a good enough excuse. He was supposed to be an agent, for God's sake – an agent entrusted with the future of mankind – and he'd failed at the first hurdle. Hopefully, with Dominguez apparently out of the picture and the equations safe he'd now be able to progress his prime mission objective of persuading Chayka to abandon mass PHASEing.

He smiled grimly and vowed to himself that this was going to be successful – if for no other reason than it had to be. He would up his game to whatever extent necessary to ensure that success. He'd just sub-vocalised Chard for a consultation on the matter when Fingal, Landau and Hunstan suddenly reappeared, flushed and excited from their search of the shuttles.

'We've found it,' shouted Landau, holding out a data wafer. 'It was stuck under one of the seats in the shuttle Fournier travelled down to Mars on.' He looked round at the celebrations. 'What's going on?'

Cabello took the wafer and looked questioningly at Sol. 'Duplicate file, do you think, or something else?'

'No idea. Let's just stick it in the terminal and see what we've got.'

What they had was a very complex file detailing the results of the investigations Fournier had carried out prior to his death. Unfortunately, they were couched in scientific terms so abstruse that nobody had a clue what they were about. They were just so much gibberish.

'DNA samples on the scientific team,' Chard said silently to Sol. 'I've uploaded the file into my memory for safe-keeping. The results are fascinating – Dominguez has thirty-two pairs of chromosomes instead of the human twenty-six. This is hard proof that Dominguez is an alien.'

Guided by Chard, Sol described the tests to the security team and pointed out the difference between human DNA and the dwarf's. This was the signal for another round of congratulations. Thinking of Dominguez as an alien had been a big problem for all the security guys, including Cabello, but now they had proof. They also had proof that Sol's equations were real. The two pieces of hard evidence backed up Sol's story.

'I never doubted you really, you know,' Cabello said, clapping Sol on the back and grinning broadly.

'Of course you didn't. I could always see you were a convert!'

The two men laughed and Sol put the wafer in the security office safe with the others they'd collected.

'Well, that's three out of three,' Sol said. 'Original mass PHASEing equations, my equations, and now the DNA file. We've had a pretty good day so far. I wonder what Deira will find on the pad.'

Almost on cue, Deira emerged from her efforts and triumphantly displayed the contents of the pad. There were masses of data – interviews, magazine articles, excerpts from books, pictures, and much, much more. What it all meant she couldn't begin to guess. She was about to turn it over to Baxter for analysis when a small file caught her eye. It was different from the rest – a string of numbers that immediately piqued her cryptographic interest. It also had a date stamp two days before Fournier's murder so had presumably been inserted by Philippe. She guessed the rest of the stuff was his father's. She uploaded the short number file onto her wrist console and called Baxter over.

'All yours Mr Baxter. There's enough in here to keep you out of mischief for quite a while. I think you ought to make a few copies and put at least one in the safe.'

'Much obliged,' Baxter grinned broadly. General duties were clearly not going to be any part of his workload for the foreseeable future. He glanced at Cabello and, having received a nod of approval, sat at the desk and immersed himself in the data.

Sol quickly updated Deira on their success in finding the various files. She was already fired up from cracking the encryption on the pad and this was the icing on the cake.

'Yes! So we're finally good to go and see the professor.'

'Exactly so,' Sol said. 'We may be about to successfully complete the mission.'

'Shouldn't be too difficult now we've got your equations, should it?'

'I think the proverbial pigs might be flying soon.' Sol looked unconvinced.

'Unfortunately, I think you may be right,' Cabello said. His experiences of Chayka hadn't left him with any confidence of being able to deflect the man when he'd set his heart on something. He thought they would almost certainly need to resort to force.

Deira frowned. She'd firmly believed that Sol's equations would be enough to persuade Chayka not to proceed with the research into mass PHASEing. After all, that was why Sol had been sent back in time – by Chayka himself, for God's sake. Sol and Cabello obviously thought otherwise, so perhaps it wouldn't be that easy.

Easy or not, they were going to have to give it a go –

and they also needed to sort out the issue of Dominguez once and for all. She turned to Cabello.

'So what do you think we ought to do about Dominguez?'

Cabello looked surprised she'd asked.

'I'm afraid I assumed Dr Dominguez was dead,' he said. 'We know there was no airlock activity, except for our own, from the time he left the Base until now because I checked – and I don't see how he could have survived outside the Base without access to extra oxygen.'

'I agree he *should* be dead, but we know he's extremely resilient and resourceful – and we don't know enough about his alien physiology to make assessments of what he might be capable of. I think we should assume he's still alive until we find a body.'

'Okay, point taken. I'll set up a silent alarm on the airlocks for the next week or so. If anybody comes in we'll get a warning in Security. I don't know what else we can do. I'm afraid we don't have the manpower to conduct a search outside.'

'I'm sure that'll do just fine,' Deira said, relieved to have something in place. 'Okay Sol, we can't put this off forever. It's time to pay a visit to Professor Chayka.'

Chapter 24

D<small>EIRA TRIED CONTACTING</small> Chayka on the comm but all she got was an automated response informing her that the person required wasn't connected to the system.

'Darned scientists!' she fumed. 'The security team got themselves hooked up to the Base comm as soon as they arrived but Chayka's lot couldn't care less whether they can be contacted or not.'

'Too mundane,' Sol said. 'Not cerebral enough. They probably see being contacted as a distraction in any case. I'm sure they'll get a little nudge from Admin in due course.'

Deira nodded, wishing she could be as laid back about it as Sol. 'Yeah – just different priorities, I guess. Damned irritating though.'

They tried Chayka's room but there was nobody there. Next stop was the PHASE terminal. No good – it was in darkness.

'So where could he be?' Deira stood with her hands on her hips, frowning.

'I believe the new science module has recently been unloaded,' Chard said. 'Professor Chayka is most likely supervising its installation.'

'Hell, yes – that's where he'll be. Any idea where it might be, Chard?'

For once, Sol was one step ahead. He pulled up a schematic of the Base and its projected future extensions on his wrist console and pointed down a corridor to their right.

'That way – about four hundred metres. The science lab service corridor should be off to the left.'

Sure enough, after a bit of a hike they came upon a work detail installing Chayka's lab. It was already atmosphere-tight and, even as they watched, the final link was made to the Base computer network. Chayka was good to go.

The man himself was supervising the attachment of a large console at the far end of the lab. He failed to notice the two agents so they waited patiently a few metres away while he fussed about some particular detail with the men who were installing his apparatus. They finally managed to catch his eye when he glanced up briefly and the look that came over his face suggested he wasn't particularly pleased to see them. He made a few parting comments to the installers and wondered over.

'Agent MacMahon and…Agent Smith, isn't it. We didn't get very well acquainted the first time we met, Agent Smith. You chased my colleague out of the Base and I haven't seen him since.'

'Yeah, sorry about that Prof.' Sol looked anything but sorry. 'That's partly what we wanted to talk with you about.'

'So can I assume we were successful in returning your memories to you?'

'Oh… yeah… I meant to thank you for that but events kind of took over. I got a shed-load of memories back and they clarified quite a few things.

'Including something about Dr Dominguez? He looked scared to death of you when he ran off.'

'Yeah. Look, I know you're almost fully briefed you on the matters at hand but there are a few other issues now and I think Agent MacMahon is the best placed to update you.'

Chayka switched his gaze to Deira. 'So, Agent MacMahon, how is it that I am "almost" fully briefed and what are these other issues?'

'Perhaps we could go somewhere more private?' Deira said.

Chayka looked around at the ongoing activity in the lab. 'We'll use the new briefing room,' he said. 'But I insist that my team is involved too. They've all been adversely affected by ongoing events and I may require their input if you wish me to render any further assistance.'

'Fair enough.'

Deira realised Chayka had a point. Each of his remaining team members had special knowledge and skills and any one of them might prove crucial to the success of the mission. In any event, Chandler was heavily involved with the mass PHASEing file so it was only really Drs Blumstein and Altmeyer who were still in the dark. They deserved to know the situation.

Everybody filed into Chayka's new briefing room and Deira ensured the door was firmly closed and there were no open comm channels, before summarising everything they knew so far, including Chayka's role in the recovery of Sol's memories. The mention of mass PHASEing equations elicited no response from Chayka but Chandler looked decidedly uncomfortable. Everything seemed to go well until the mention of Dominguez being an alien – then there were looks of complete disbelief and Dr Tirzah muttered something to Walther. Chayka was more forthright.

'This is nonsense. I've worked with Dr Dominguez for more than twenty years. He often talked of his parents, his early life in Portugal, and the discrimination he faced because of his condition. Is this the best you can do to explain your treatment of him.'

'Suppose we provide you with hard evidence?' Deira said.

Chayka raised an eyebrow. 'And what evidence would that be?'

'Some very convincing DNA data, actually. I think you know Dr Fournier was analysing DNA samples from your team prior to his death. What do you think his reaction would have been when he saw that Dominguez had thirty-two pairs of chromosomes made up of three different sets of base pairs.'

There was a sharp intake of breath from Tirzah.

'Let me see them,' she said.

'You can all see them,' Sol said. 'I've just transferred the file to your wrist consoles.'

There was a flurry of activity as they accessed the file and Tirzah gasped when she saw the analysis, flicking through the results enthusiastically. The others looked to her for confirmation and she nodded vigorously.

'This is amazing,' she said. 'It'll open up a whole new area of science – exogenetics!' She rapidly became immersed in the detail of the alien DNA.

Deira glanced at Sol, wondering whether they should go on, and he nodded encouragement.

'So Professor,' she said. 'We know Dr Fournier obtained the DNA samples because he knew you'd need them to pursue your research into mass PHASEing. However, we also know that there's no longer any need to carry out that research because Dr Chandler already has a complete set of equations describing mass PHASEing. He got them from Dominguez.'

To his credit, Chayka lived up to his reputation and managed to maintain his expression completely neutral.

Not so Chandler, who went white and began to sweat. He looked hopefully across at Chayka but it was evident he wasn't going to get any help there. The two agents waited silently, having no intention of letting him off the hook. Finally, after a few moments of uncomfortable silence, he admitted he'd been given the equations by Dominguez.

'But he only gave me an outline,' he protested. 'I've spent many hours since then developing the theory so I think I'm entitled to claim it as my work.'

Deira was fascinated and disgusted at the same time. All he was interested in was getting his name on a paper. He didn't seem to get the wider connotations.

'We know that's not true,' she said. 'Dominguez gave you a complete set of equations – the same set he gave to Dr Fournier in an attempt to bribe him not to release his DNA data. What did he want from you?'

'He didn't want anything.' Chandler was shaking uncontrollably. 'We'd just had a bit of an argument and he said he was trying to make peace between us again – and I believed him. But he really did only give me an outline, not the full set.'

'Surely you must have wondered where he obtained this "outline" – or didn't you care?'

Chandler spluttered indignantly. 'Nicolau said he'd got the equations from Phillipe. I already knew Phillipe had them because he pushed my nose in them before we got to Mars. So I believed Nicolau. Why shouldn't I?'

Chayka had been following this exchange closely. Deira found it hard to interpret his relatively impassive face but she got the distinct impression he hadn't known Chandler possessed the equations. She thought she'd detected a brief look of annoyance when she'd made the revelation and felt he'd been deliberately allowing Chandler a few minutes of intense discomfort. Now, however, he clearly felt he ought to speak up for his beleaguered colleague.

'I'm surprised and disappointed, Agent MacMahon,' he said. 'From our earlier discussions I had high hopes of a fruitful collaboration with you but it's clearly not to be – you're no different from the rest of your Bureau colleagues. Now please desist from bullying my staff when they're simply trying their best to do what they were trained for.'

Deira was stunned. Neither Chayka nor Chandler got it. They were completely hung up on attributability and intellectual property rights and didn't appear to care where the equations might have originally come from. They were so wrapped up in their own little world that they were just not capable of seeing the bigger picture.

She glowered at Chayka, preparing to let rip, and was only prevented by Sol gently touching her arm and signalling she should calm down. With a huge effort, and seething within, she managed to control herself. When she did speak it was with a voice you could have used an ice-pick on.

'I don't have to justify my actions to you, Professor, and I resent being called a bully. All I'm trying to do is get some sense out of a group of socially retarded scientists. I'm tempted to lock you all up on a charge of obstruction to an ongoing investigation.' She paused for a moment to let that sink in before going on. 'Okay, we'll park the issue of the mass PHASEing equations because I hope what I'm going to show you next will make them redundant.'

She nodded to Sol and he downloaded his equations

into the scientists' wrist consoles. She gazed round the group, meeting stares in return ranging from amazement, through hostility to continued impassivity. She continued.

'Agent Smith has just downloaded a set of equations he brought back with him from the future. I need you to examine them – and I hope they'll convince you that mass PHASEing will be a disaster if it's ever implemented.'

Another round of rapid activity followed while the scientists opened the file and scrolled down the equations. It was Chayka who spoke first, still maintaining a level voice in the face of quite severe provocation and giving nothing away as to his true feelings.

'These are very interesting but it's difficult for Dr Chandler and I to interpret them because we have no context. Since Dr Fournier's area of expertise was biochemistry I can only surmise that these relate to that discipline. Perhaps Dr Blumstein could take a look at them.'

Hearing her name, Tirzah jerked her attention away from the DNA samples and back to the discussion. She examined the new equations with interest.

'I'm pretty sure they relate to sub-quantal genetics. It was Philippe's specialty.' She squinted at the screen and slowly scrolled from top to bottom, concentrating intently. 'Yes, this work relates to the effects of mass PHASEing on the human genome – and there appears to be an explicit warning at this stage.' She pointed to an equation about two-thirds of the way down. 'I'm afraid I'll need more time to analyse them properly, and I'll need some assistance from Simon and yourself Professor.' She looked at Deira. 'At first glance they do appear to give a clear warning of future disaster.'

Deira allowed herself a small sigh of relief. At least they'd managed to get one member of the team to acknowledge the dangers posed by the original equations. Perhaps now was the time to butt out, let emotions settle, and give them all a chance to dig a bit deeper. After all, there would have been no point in sending Sol back in time unless the equations could stand up to such an analysis. She just had to hope they'd back off from the project when they saw the likely consequences.

'I think it's time for us to leave you to it for a while.' Deira said. 'I need you to understand the gravity of this business with mass PHASEing and I hope the equations we've given you will help with that. I must emphasise that there can be no more secrets. This is far too important for hidden agendas.'

They all nodded and turned their attention to their virtual screens and it wasn't long before they were completely oblivious to everything except the equations. Deira was initially amazed by this but then she thought back to her own efforts in cryptology and how she tended to "zone out" until she'd reached a conclusion. Perhaps the phrase "people in glass houses" was particularly apt on this occasion. She left the lab quietly with Sol, keeping her fingers crossed for a positive outcome.

'I guess that could've been worse,' she said, once the lab door had closed. 'He did get to me that one time but luckily you were there to stop me completely losing it. Thanks for that.'

'My pleasure. The guy's a complete prick. Incidentally, I thought your put-down was just great. Socially retarded scientists! Priceless!' He grinned.

'It might have been far worse.' She smiled. 'So what do you think – will he play ball with us over the equations?'

'I truly don't know. I'd like to think he would but you know what they say about information – you can't unlearn it.

Now they know about the equations they're going to want to publish. They'll be scared that if they don't, someone else will. I think it's fifty-fifty or less – and I don't trust Chandler one bit.'

'Hmm,' Deira said. They'd just reached the habitat zone and she was determined she was going to crack that number file she'd extracted from Fournier's pad. 'I hope you're wrong because I don't know how we'll deal with it if you're not. By now I expect they've got copies stashed away all over the place.'

'I hadn't thought of that. It'd be almost impossible to find them all.'

Deira stopped at the door to her room. 'I'm going to have a go at that number code of Fournier's and I'm going to need some peace and quiet to do it. Catch up later?'

Sol nodded. Having seen Deira in code-breaking mode he understood what she meant.

'Sure. I'll pass the time somehow. See you later.'

He moved on to his room and checked out the local tri-vid. There was nothing of interest so he made himself a coffee and had a companionable chat with Chard for a while. He'd barely finished his drink when a call came from Deira over the comm.

'Do you want to come round? I've cracked that code.'

'Already?' Sol knew she was good at this but – he checked the time – twenty-three minutes was pretty awesome. 'Yeah, sure. See you in a minute.'

When he reached Deira's room, he found her looking energised.

'So what have you got? It couldn't have been much of a cipher if you solved it so quickly.'

'It was very easy, actually. I think Fournier probably put it together in a bit of a rush. The numbers break down into four sets of fourteen. The first six of a set then represent a date while the second eight represent geographical coordinates. What we end up with is: June 28th 1914 (Sarajevo); 31st March 1920 (Berlin); 27th October 1962 (the sea off Cuba); 2nd November 1933 (Moscow).'

'And that tells us – what precisely?'

'No idea. I did a quick search of the datasphere for notable events connected with those times and places. June 28th 1914 was easy – it was the date that Archduke Franz Ferdinand and his wife were assassinated in Sarajevo, setting off the First World War. I couldn't find anything of note for the Berlin date or the Moscow date, but October 27th 1962 seemed to be in the middle of the Cuban missile crisis. Apparently nuclear war was very narrowly averted on that day when a junior Russian officer on board a submarine managed to persuade his colleagues not to launch their nuclear missiles even though most were convinced that World War Three had already started.'

'So we've got one date at the start of a major conflict and another when a conflict's just been avoided. Can't be a coincidence. Makes you think the other two must also be related to wars or disasters.'

'I couldn't find any. Even if they are, how does that help us? What does it all mean?'

'God knows.' Sol was tired of Fournier and his apparently endless mind games. 'Perhaps Baxter will be able to tell us when he's sorted out all that stuff on the pad.' He got up and wondered aimlessly round the room. 'What say we give it a rest for now and chill out a little? I could happily down a drink or two and it won't be long until dinner. We might get a better perspective on this if we come at it fresh.'

He watched Deira. She was thinking intently, fired up about this pad thing and not wanting to let go. To Sol, this new-found enthusiasm gave her a kind or radiance that made her even more attractive. His mind started to wander, and he imagined her doing things with him that almost made him blush.

Deira suddenly made up her mind to give it a rest for a while. A drink sounded like a good plan.

'You're right. I could do with a stiff one too.'

Sol almost choked at this *double entendre*, coming as it did on top of his already elaborate fantasising. She got up and started to move to the door at the same time Sol was heading in the opposite direction and they almost collided – ending up chest to chest and looking into each other's eyes. For a split second, something passed between them that made Sol wonder if his dreams were about to come true – then the moment passed and Deira turned away.

'Come on,' she said, as if nothing had happened. 'I'm buying.'

Sol heaved a huge sigh, reflecting on opportunities missed, and they walked together to the refectory. It was a pleasant evening and when they finally got back to their rooms they were relaxed and happy. They stopped outside Deira's room to say goodnight. Sol hadn't given up, and was hoping for some suggestion that the evening wasn't over yet, but he didn't want to push it.

'That was a great evening,' he said

'Sure was.' Deira looked up at him. 'I feel much better. Thanks for being you.' She opened her door and was about to go inside when she changed her mind and turned back. 'Good night,' she said, and planted a kiss on his cheek. Before he could react, she'd gone in and closed the door, leaving him in an agony of indecision.

Was this an invitation? Should he knock on the door? Was she waiting for him to do exactly that? But what if he'd read it completely wrong? He was stymied. He waited a moment and listened at the door. No sound from the other side. Eventually he bottled out.

'Damn!' He turned away.

Inside her room, Deira stood with her back to the door wondering why she'd not gone the extra mile. Although she felt herself growing close to Sol, she still baulked at intimate contact. What was the matter with her? Was she frigid? She was about to open the door again when she heard a quiet "Damn," followed by footsteps moving away.

Too late, she realised, with a mixture of sadness and relief.

Chapter 25

S OL WAS OUT of bed early the next morning having had a pretty crappy night's sleep. His brain had been too active, and he'd veered between worrying about the ongoing mission and fantasising about Deira. He stopped at her room on the way to the refectory hoping she might fancy breakfast, but she wasn't in and a call on the comm established she was already ensconced in Security with Baxter, going through his findings. It was clear she'd got the bit between her teeth and wouldn't stop until she'd solved this latest puzzle.

Sol dawdled over breakfast, wondering what to do with himself. He thought he should really check on how his equations had gone down with the scientists. After all, Chayka was vital to their plans even if he was a complete prat and seemed to have a bad effect on Deira. Sol smiled. She was kind of volatile, and it was usually quite entertaining when she erupted, it just wasn't always very helpful. Perhaps he could take some of the load.

He set off for Chayka's lab and had just reached the end of the access corridor when Tirzah Blumstein came hurtling through the door and ran straight into him. She grunted what sounded like an apology and pulled away, sniffing.

'Hey, what's up?' Sol said. 'Are those tears?' Tirzah kept her head down and began to walk away.

'Talk to me. It might make you feel better.'

'Leave me alone!' she sobbed. 'You can't help anyway.'

Sol was a sucker for a woman in tears. He followed her down the corridor.

'You never know. I'm a man of many talents and I can be *very* helpful when the occasion demands it.'

Tirzah paused and turned back, sniffing and wiping her tear-reddened eyes. Sol noticed that some of her eye make-up had run. Hell, he hadn't even noticed she wore make-up the first time he'd seen her. She was certainly a stunner even though she didn't get his hormones going like Deira.

'I know now what Philippe wouldn't tell me on Mars,' she said. 'I knew he'd been stealing DNA data but I didn't know about Dominguez and the mass PHASEing equations. I think he was trying to protect me – and I treated him terribly.' She sniffed a couple of times and blew her nose.'

'You weren't to know.'

'No, but I should have given him the benefit of the doubt. He was a lovely guy.'

'I'm sorry – but I think you need to move on now. What about the equations? Have you all had a chance to examine them yet?'

'Huh!' Tirzah looked exasperated. 'They've caused nothing but trouble. Simon's still insisting the mass PHASEing equations belong to him and that's really upset the professor, who was expecting to get at least half the credit when they were published. As to your equations, everyone agrees they predict a genetic disaster for the species – and I think that should be enough to put a moratorium on further research.'

'But?'

'But the others are all fired up and want to publish anyway. The predicted disaster won't happen for many years and they're convinced they'll find a way round the problem. I don't think there is a way round it – and that's what the guys in your time are trying to tell us. Professor Chayka's mad at me for being so negative and says he wants me out and he'll find a replacement for me.'

She began to cry again and Sol gently put his arms round her. She hugged him back and laid her head on his chest – just as Simon Chandler came out of the lab. He glared at Sol and turned back the way he'd come. Tirzah hadn't noticed him but Sol had and he could read the signs. Too bad, the guy would just have to sort it out with Tirzah later.

He looked down at the woman pressed against him and gently eased her away. He hadn't been sure what the team's reaction would be to the equations – could have gone either way – but now his worst fears were confirmed. He'd been hoping for a soft landing but it looked like they were in for a crash. He and Deira would have to stop Chayka and the team before they passed the point of no return.

'Dr Blumstein.'

'Just Tirzah please!'

'Okay – Tirzah. The guys in my time took a big risk sending me back to stop research into mass PHASEing. I've tried being Mr Nice Guy – tried to get Chayka to abort the research himself – but if that's not worked I'm quite prepared to be Mr Nasty. I promise you, there's not a hope in hell I'm going to let that research continue, Chayka or no Chayka.'

'You don't know the professor! He'll find a way. He always does.'

'And you don't know me – or Agent MacMahon. Leave it to us, Tirzah. This isn't going to happen.'

'I hope not. Thanks for the support in any case.' She rubbed her eyes, then looked with horror at the make-up she'd just spread over her fingers. 'Oh hell! I must look

awful! Excuse me, Sol is it? I've got to find a bathroom.'
She hurried off down the corridor.

Sol watched her go, feeling sorry for her. She was the
only team member with an ounce of common sense yet she
was apparently being victimised and threatened. He sighed
and began to turn back towards the lab. Time to confront
Chayka.

Suddenly, what felt like a sledgehammer crashed across
the back of his head. He fell flat on his face, momentarily
stunned, and would have still been there when the next
crashing blow arrived had it not been for Chard instantly
turning on combat mode and forcing him to roll to the right.
He heard the sound of something hard hitting the floor where
he'd just been lying and leaped to his feet – simultaneously
drawing his PWC and activating the laser. Simon Chandler
was facing him, panting slightly, a thick metal rod of some
kind in his hand and a look of pure hatred on his face. He
had the weapon raised for a third blow but he thought better
of it when he saw the laser.

'Stay away from Tirzah!' he growled. 'And stay away from
me. You're not wanted round here – and if you hadn't got
that thing…' he pointed at the PWC, '… I'd teach you not
to poke your nose in where it's not welcome.'

Sol's head throbbed. His first instinct had been to lash
out but he automatically risk-assessed his adversary as his
training took over. Chandler was an un-augmented civilian
and posed no threat now he was in plain sight. Sol turned
off the laser and holstered Chard, sub-vocalising an order
to terminate combat mode. He locked eyes with Chandler.

'You've got me all wrong, Dr Chandler. I wasn't making
a pass at your lady friend – she's very pretty but not my type.'

'I don't believe you. She's mine.'

'She's nobody's. You don't own her even if you're sleeping with her. Get a grip man.'

Chandler growled again and began advancing with his metal bar. Sol sighed. He'd tried, but the guy wasn't going to let this go without a fight.

'If you're sure that's what you want,' he said, 'I'm happy to oblige. Oh, and I promise not to use "that thing".'

That was all the incentive Chandler needed. He roared, and came at Sol like a maddened bull. On paper, the two men were physically well-matched – about the same height, weight and muscle bulk – but Chandler initially took Sol by surprise by the speed and rawness of his attack. He charged at Sol, aiming the bar wildly at his head. Sol sidestepped and flung his arm up, taking the blow on his shoulder. He then grabbed the arm wielding the weapon and brought it down smartly across his knee, hard enough to force Chandler to drop the bar but not hard enough to break a bone.

Chandler howled in agony and lurched forward trying to get Sol in a bear hug. That was enough for Sol. This had gone on long enough. His head and shoulder hurt and he'd run out of patience. Time to finish it. Using Chandler's weight against him Sol exercised a perfect judo throw that left the man sprawling at his feet.

'Stay down, Dr Chandler. I don't want to hurt you.'

Chandler roared again and tried to stand. Sol shrugged. 'Have it your way,' he grunted, slugging him hard on the side of the head. Chandler collapsed in a heap and didn't get up.

Sol called the infirmary. 'Medical attention required at Professor Chayka's lab,' he said. 'Probably only a mild concussion but needs checking over.'

He retrieved the metal bar Chandler had used and stayed with the man for the few minutes it took for a medical team to arrive. Then he contacted Deira on the comm.

'Hi Deira, it's me! Thought you ought to know about a little episode I've just been involved in outside Chayka's lab.'

He went on to describe his recent chat with Tirzah and his encounter with Chandler. Deira groaned when she heard about the fight.

'You actually knocked him out?'

'What was I supposed to do? The guy was off his head.'

'I guess so, but I was hoping to do some bridge-building with Chayka and you've effectively killed that off.'

'Sorry.'

'Not your fault. Listen, I'm just finishing up with Baxter. Suppose we meet up in an hour and confront Chayka together?'

'Okay. See you then.'

Now he really didn't have anything to do for an hour so he wandered along to the refectory to see if there was anybody available for a sociable drink. He knew the medics would say he shouldn't drink after a head injury but Chard confirmed there was no concussion so he had no qualms. When he got to the refectory he found his luck was in. There were three off-duty engineers indulging in a little R&R with a bottle of Bourbon – and they seemed perfectly happy for Sol to gate-crash their party. A few drinks and good company had the desired effect, and he soon began to feel his usual mellow self again. Unfortunately, he also completely lost track of time and it took a call from Deira to bring him back to reality.

'Where are you? I'm waiting outside Chayka's lab.'

'Shit! Is it that time already? Sorry! I'll be right there.'

He took his leave of his new friends and hurried to Chayka's lab where he found Deira pacing and frowning.

'Sorry again! Got kind of tied up with some engineers.'

Deira gave him a knowing look. 'Yeah, I can guess.' She sniffed. 'Is that whiskey I can smell? Isn't it a bit early in the day for that?'

Sol cupped his hand over his mouth, exhaled and sniffed. 'Yep, a particularly good Bourbon – and no, it's never too early. Right, shall we take our chances with the professor again?'

When they entered the lab they could see Chayka in his office. He was sitting in front of his terminal poring over something – probably one of the sets of equations. When he caught site of them he leaped to his feet and hurried out, his usual impassive features radiating hostility. He ignored Sol and glared at Deira.

'Agent MacMahon, how dare you bring that muscle-bound ape into my lab. Do you realise Dr Chandler's concussed and confined to the infirmary for the rest of the day?'

'Hey! Hold on there!' Sol protested. 'I wasn't the one that started that little fracas. If I hadn't sent Dr Chandler to the infirmary – with a pretty minor injury I'd have to say – I might be lying half-dead by now. Have you ever been hit over the head with one of these? It smarts.'

He produced the metal bar Chandler had used and indicated the large bruise over the left side of his head that was now competing for attention with the bruise Deira had previously given him. The blood on the bar told its own story and made Chayka pause. However, he made no attempt to apologise and stared at the two agents as if that, in itself, would make them go away. When it didn't, he sat back down at his terminal and turned away, declining to make eye contact.

'Well? What do you want?'

Deira tried to be diplomatic, though she could already feel her temper rising. 'We need to discuss the equations again, Professor. We gather you've had some thoughts about how to proceed.'

'Dr Blumstein, I presume?' Chayka spluttered, his face turning pink. He turned to face them at last. 'That woman has no idea about the importance of scientific progress. If it were left to the likes of her we'd still be in the stone age!'

Deira hadn't realised Chayka could get so worked up – after all, he hadn't become known as "the great stone-face" for nothing. She glanced at Sol, hoping he'd got her back in case she lost her temper again. He seemed to know what she was thinking because he smiled and nodded. Emboldened by this, she continued.

'I'm not here to discuss your team, Professor – that is if she's still a member of your team?'

Chayka must have realised his reputation was soon going to be lying in tatters because, with what must have been a great effort of will, he visibly brought himself under control. He glared at Deira but refused to be drawn on the status of Tirzah in the team.

'So what about Agent Smith's equations?' Deira tried to match the professor for self-control, keeping her voice carefully neutral.

'The equations he supposedly brought from the future? Well, as you say, they predict that the widespread adoption of mass PHASEing will result in a genetic catastrophe for the human race – possibly even an extinction event.'

Deira didn't like the way he said that in an almost throwaway manner. 'I'm glad that's been cleared up,' she said. 'So you…'

Chayka interrupted her. 'Dr Blumstein thinks we should destroy the mass PHASEing equations and stop research in this area of sub-quantal science. The rest of the team take a more measured approach.'

Deira glanced at Sol, who shrugged as if he wasn't surprised. She was actually staggered. The guy had just said that mass PHASEing could lead to an extinction event – yet he was still advocating carrying on with the work and taking a "more measured approach". What was his problem?

'How can you take a measured approach to the extinction of mankind? Surely, if anything were a reason to stop a particular avenue of research, this is it?'

'No, no! Not at all! There have been many lines of research in the past that contained significant dangers. For example, the genetic engineering of viruses and bacteria as weapons of war when it was clear that the release of such bio-weapons would destroy large sections of the world's population. Then there was the development of the atomic bomb, which went ahead in spite of the misgivings of many of the scientists involved in the Manhattan Project who feared the possible extinction of mankind.

'In both these cases the risks involved were considerable, but the worst-case scenarios failed to materialise – they were controlled – and both pieces of research produced many beneficial spin-offs. We'd contend that the same is true for our current projected research. The risks shown by your equations only apply if photonic transmission is taken up by greater than sixty percent of the world's population, and even then would take a few generations to come to fruition. This makes the situation manageable – in the same way that the atomic bomb was manageable.' He paused for a moment. 'I'd also have to say that once something is discovered, you can't un-discover it. Things have a habit of coming out.'

Sol had already made exactly that point earlier, and now had a look on his face that said "I told you so". Deira turned to him. 'Perhaps you should let the professor know what the Eich told you,' she said.

Chayka looked expectant but remained silent and Sol knew that whatever he said wouldn't make the slightest difference. He gazed at Chayka.

'They told me that your actions over the next few days will determine whether our civilization survives beyond the next century. They also said you'd already made the wrong decision once! When I pressed them on that they informed me that the future can be changed. They implied that your actions had resulted in a catastrophe in the future and that one of the reasons I'm here is, in their words, "to change the dynamic". Now, I don't know about you but, for me, this kind of resonates with what we're currently talking about.'

Chayka stared at Sol with obvious dislike. 'Agent Smith, while I have to acknowledge that you come from the future, I find it increasingly difficult to reconcile some of your more outlandish assertions. You have yet to prove to my satisfaction the existence of highly evolved entities on Titan who appear to wish to communicate with us – or, rather, with you. The fact you didn't mention this latest assertion earlier suggests to me that you're making things up as you go along to suit your own requirements.'

Sol had to admit to being impressed by Chayka's reasoning. The man was certainly rational. He was correct that risks had been managed successfully in the past. The problem was, Sol knew only too well that it wasn't possible to manage this particular risk. He could see that his earlier feelings were correct – he wasn't going to sway Chayka. But he had a promise to keep to Dr Blumstein, as well as to himself. Time to become Mr Nasty.

'Okay, I've heard enough,' he said. 'I can't let you continue with this. We were hoping you'd give up this line of work voluntarily when you saw the dangers involved but as you won't...' He opened his wrist console and pretended to carry out some operations on line while he sub-vocalised Chard to delete the files. 'All copies of the original mass PHASEing files have been deleted. I'm sorry.'

Chayka was left gazing speechless at a blank screen.

'You can't do this! You don't have the authority!'

'No he doesn't – but I do,' Deira said. 'You knew when you were sent on this trip that work on mass PHASEing had been forbidden by the Bureau – yet you elected to continue with it anyway. One of the unfortunate results of that decision was the untimely death of Dr Fournier. As the only representative of the Bureau on Titan, I'm authorised to terminate any non-sanctioned work – and that's exactly what Agent Smith's just done on my behalf.'

She turned towards the door and beckoned Sol to follow. Chayka sat at his terminal gazing into space, appearing virtually catatonic.

'Goodbye, Professor,' she said.

There was no reply. They walked the length of the service corridor in silence, stopping only when they were safely out of earshot. Deira took a big breath and let it out slowly.

'Well that's done it now,' she said. 'Thanks for the help, Sol. Chard, your contribution was invaluable too!'

'Well thank you, kind lady,' Chard said.

'Crap, he sounds more like you every day!'

Sol was pleased at the praise but doubtful about the effectiveness of what they'd just done.

'Like you said, they've almost certainly got copies on data wafers,' he said. 'There doesn't seem to be anything to stop them carrying on where they left off.'

'I've been thinking about that. They might have copies on wafers but to carry out any work on them they'll have to transfer them to a terminal. I'm sure Chard could effectively monitor the terminals to ensure that doesn't happen – couldn't you Chard?'

'It would be my pleasure Deira.'

'The only other thing we have to guard against is them somehow getting a data wafer onto the Q-ship to be taken back to Earth. Hopefully, their concern that someone else might steal their work will be enough to prevent them from doing that.'

Sol nodded, not entirely convinced. 'You're probably right,' he conceded, 'but I'm still worried about Chandler – he's a slimy bastard. We need to ensure access to the shuttles is secured.'

'Good point. I'll ask Cabello to arrange it. Incidentally, would you like to see Baxter's analysis of the data in the pad? He should have finished by now.'

'Sure would. Should be interesting.'

When they arrived at the security office, Baxter was

still putting the finishing touches to his report but he was very happy to put it to one side and handle Sol's briefing.

'There's a load of stuff in this little thing, Agent – I don't rightly know how it all fit in. Anyway, the pad belonged to Armand Fournier, Dr Fournier's father. There's quite a bit about him on the datasphere. He was a well-known conspiracy theorist in his time, but he also had a longstanding psychiatric condition and spent much of his life in a mental hospital in Paris.'

'Wait a minute,' Sol said. 'Wouldn't that have had an effect on his son's psychological tests for space travel?'

'We thought that too, but apparently not. It's a non-inheritable condition – and Philippe was known to be remarkably resilient. Now, Armand's main obsession was with a notion that Earth's history was being manipulated...'

'That's a tired old story,' Sol interrupted again. 'The Illuminati. Surely we're not giving that the time of day?'

'It was more outrageous than that. He believed history was being manipulated by an extra-terrestrial agency.'

'Aliens?' Sol began to take an interest.

'Aliens – and it struck Agent MacMahon and me that this was getting a bit close to home, so to speak.'

'Hmm,' Sol pondered on that. It did seem like a coincidence, that was for sure, but if Dominguez had been influencing Earth's history he'd have to be one long-lived and busy dwarf. It just didn't sound plausible. Deira took over the story.

'Fournier Senior had accumulated a fair body of data in support of his theory – and at least some of it fits with the dates in Phillipe's number file I decoded. For instance, there was a mass of stuff on the First World War and the episode during the Cuban missile crisis. Unfortunately, the rest, while coherent, doesn't make much sense. Some of it relates to the Second World War and some to Professor Chayka himself. The key must be the other two dates of the number file, but I'm struggling to see how they fit.'

'I think I may be able to help with that,' Chard said.

Baxter visibly started. He'd heard about the AI, of course, but most of the time Chard had elected to stay silent unless Deira and Sol were somewhere private, so he'd never heard his voice. Sol took the PWC and placed it on the table in front of them.

'The floor's all yours buddy.'

'I've been analysing the dates and places in the number file,' Chard said, 'and I've found something quite interesting. Deira said that 31st March 1920 isn't associated with any major world event. That's true. However, it *was* the date Adolf Hitler was discharged from the army and became a full time worker for the National Socialist German Workers Party in Berlin. In a way, this was the start of his rise to power in Germany and hence the indirect start of the Second World War.'

'Bingo!' Sol said. 'So now we've got three dates connected with world wars or close-run things. But what about the last date in 1933?'

'I believe that may be an error,' Chard said.

'Huh?' Deira said, 'It fits with the numbers.'

'Indeed it does. But it doesn't fit with any world events. You need to review your conclusions.'

Deira looked mystified. 'The date was written quite clearly in the six-figure format – 021133 or 2nd November 1933.'

She frowned in concentration then blushed deep crimson.

'Oh my God! I can't believe I missed that. Some sort of cryptologist I am!'

'Well would one of you super-intelligent guys please explain it to Baxter and me?' Sol said.

'If you represent a date by six figures,' Deira said, 'the year is shown as the last two numbers only – 20 means 1920, and so on.'

'Yeah, I get that. So what?'

'So, Chard's very diplomatically drawn my attention to the fact that, in the original number sequence, 021133 appeared in the last group of fourteen. It was me that moved this group to third place, after 1920.'

Suddenly, it dawned on both Sol and Baxter simultaneously.

'You mean the date wasn't meant to be 1933,' Sol said.

'No, it must be 2nd November 2033.'

'But what's special about that date? I don't remember any world wars or anything.'

'Neither do I. Back to you Chard. What happened on that date?'

'It was the date Professor Chayka published his seminal paper on sub-quantal physics,' Chard said.

There was a stunned silence. Baxter immediately went back to his report and said that the fit between that date and the information in the pad was perfect.

'I don't know why we didn't see it before,' he said. 'It's so obvious.'

'I guess it always is when somebody points it out to you,' Deira said. 'Thank you Chard.'

'You're most welcome.'

'So how does it help?' Sol said. 'We've got three wars or

near-wars linked to the dates – and then the discovery of sub-quantal physics. Is this just another way of saying that PHASEing will be a disaster for mankind? If that were the case then surely the date in your number file should correspond to that when the equations for mass PHASEing are published. I don't get it.'

'Neither do I,' Deira said. 'If we go back to Armand Fournier's belief that human history's being manipulated by aliens it becomes even more confusing now we have the Chayka connection. I don't see how the dates work. Would aliens help to instigate two world wars and then prevent a third one? What's their motivation? Each answer we find seems to generate more questions.'

Sol and Baxter remained silent because neither could think of anything that might move things on. Even Chard was silent. Deira looked at the other two in exasperation.

'We're obviously still missing some data and I don't see how we can make progress with this unless something else pops up. Perhaps we should focus on the professor for now. We've upset his pride – and I suspect that's a big thing for him. If we can just get him to see the big picture he might calm down.'

Sol grinned. 'He ought to. He's the one who gave me the equations seventy-seven years from now.'

Chapter 26

'Sol Smith.' The voice of the Eich woke Sol from a deep sleep.

'You choose your times!' he groaned, sitting up and rubbing his eyes. 'Shit – its 2.00 am. What's wrong with daylight hours?'

'I apologise for waking you, but the absence of interference from other waking minds assists communication. It is important that Deira MacMahon takes part in this discussion. Please summon her.'

'Summon her? I don't think that'll go well.'

With great reservations, Sol placed a call to Deira. She was obviously deeply asleep too because it took a moment for her to answer.

'What? It's two in the morning, for God's sake!'

'They're here – the Eich. And they want you to be involved too! You need to get over here.'

'What? Oh! Right, I'm on my way.'

She pulled on a pair of jogging pants and a t-shirt, ran her hands quickly through her hair, rubbed her eyes, and hurried out of her room. Sol was waiting for her, sitting up in bed bare-chested with Chard propped up on the nearby table. He gestured for her to come in, unconsciously staring at the outline of her breasts under her t-shirt. Deira noticed his gaze and, for her part, was fascinated by his muscled torso, imagining what lay beneath the duvet.

No sooner had she sat down than a voice came from Chard's external speaker.

'Welcome Deira MacMahon, I speak for the Eich. We need to confer with you. Specifically, it is now essential that you and Sol Smith understand the background to the situation you find yourselves in.'

Deira looked at Sol, who shrugged his shoulders and winked. 'Okay,' she said hesitantly, 'I'm listening. Let's hear what you have to say.'

'We will begin with a species called the Cthon. They are a very old race, able to trace their post-industrial history back more than fifteen million of your years. When they first achieved interstellar travel they found the galaxy swarming with sentient species and they had hopes of forging cultural alliances to the benefit of all. Unfortunately, that was not to be.

'The Cthon discovered that most species are inherently irrational, making them untrustworthy and dangerous. Furthermore, they found that technological proficiency almost always outstrips psychosocial development – in other words, science outpaces wisdom. The result is increasingly sophisticated warfare – which drives further technological progress – which leads to even more deadly warfare.

'There is a critical point beyond which this cycle is irreversible, the period following this being characterised by increasing aggression and, ultimately, societal collapse. The Cthon called this period of violence "the technocline" – and it is during the technocline that most species develop space travel. The result is usually space warfare, either between different groups of the same species or between equally aggressive stellar neighbours, and the resulting carnage frequently spreads to non-involved bystanders – something I think you would call "collateral damage".'

Deira had begun to pace again, much to Sol's amusement.

'I hope this is all going somewhere,' she said, irritably. 'You've disturbed my sleep for what seems to be a science fiction story–I should warn you that patience isn't my strong point.'

'Indeed, it of the utmost relevance,' the Speaker said. 'I urge you to hear me out.'

'Okay. So carry on, then. Just don't drag it out too much – I need to get back to bed.'

Sol grinned. He always found it amusing when Deira's patience snapped – as long as it wasn't with him–but he suspected the Eich weren't used to being berated because there was a short pause before the Speaker began again.

'The Cthon witnessed this sequence of events many times over the centuries. They had not been involved in any of the conflicts so far, but realised that, by the law of averages, this would not continue indefinitely. Therefore, for their own protection, they decided to abandoned space travel altogether, opting instead to develop mentalics, the science of the mind. This was a turning point for them. By placing their psychological development ahead of their technology they were able to develop and maintain a planet-wide society at peace with itself. It appeared to be the perfect solution – and would have been if not for the Phthask.

'The Phthask originated on a planet just three light years from the Cthon and emerged into space at virtually the same time as another race in the same stellar neighbourhood. A savage war raged between these two species for over a hundred years, bringing death and destruction to many non-aligned species – this time including the Cthon. As ever, both warring species eventually collapsed to pre-industrial civilizations, but for the Cthon this was a defining moment. It took many years to repair the damage to their planet and they determined that such destruction should never happen again.

'Their solution was species containment. Using their mentalic science, they were able to monitor the development of all sentient species in a volume of space extending two hundred light years from the Cthon home world. They then mentalically intervened in any society that had reached the technocline – to ensure it self-destructed prior to developing space travel. The ethics of this were simple. The society was doomed to implode regardless of external intervention. The Cthon were simply ensuring the implosion remained on the planet and did not get translated into space.

'The interventions they employed to achieve this end were usually subtle. During the course of social development there are always control points – points in time when the direction of travel of a civilization can be affected by the actions of a single individual or small group of individuals. The Cthon were able to identify these control points and target their interventions accordingly. The policy proved to be highly successful. Although it resulted in the premature collapse of numerous societies over many centuries, the Cthon remained safe.'

'Sorry, but I'm getting kind of tired of this too,' Sol said, giving a mighty yawn. 'I'm sure sorry for all these aliens but I don't see how it relates to what we're up against.'

'Actually, I'm beginning to see a little light at the end of the tunnel,' Deira said. 'This intervention in species' development is essentially what Fournier senior was concerned about. Am I right?'

'You are correct, Deira MacMahon. However, you have, as you would say, jumped the gun somewhat. You will understand better if you have the entire background.'

'Copy that. I'm all ears.'

Sol could have sworn he heard a small sigh from Chard's speaker, then the Speaker resumed again.

'Although the Cthon policy appeared to have been successful, the Phthask proved more of a problem. They were a highly adaptable species, not dissimilar to your own and, over a period of several centuries, they rebuilt their civilization. On this occasion, however, they developed a form of neurobiological technology – not mentalics as such, but with enough similarities that it revealed to them the presence of the Cthon. Predictably, they searched for, and found, a defence against Cthon intervention – a personal mentalic dampening field – and with their advanced biological science they proceeded to engineer this dampening field into their DNA.

'The Cthon soon discovered they had lost control of the Phthask. They realised they had two options, either they could leave the Phthask to their own devices, with the inherent risk that a conflict might involve the Cthon world again, or they could implement a more permanent solution. In this case, because of the rapid adaptability of the Phthask, the only permanent solution appeared to be physical annihilation of the species.

'The debate on whether and how to proceed raged for many years with emotions high on both sides. Eventually, a large majority of Cthon agreed that the protection of their own world should come before the survival of the Phthask. However, they also felt that the species shouldn't be completely destroyed – a small number should be kept as breeding stock. Paradoxically, this group was to be specifically bred to enhance their dampening fields. They were to be living weapons that could be used if the Cthon were ever attacked by beings with mentalic powers similar to their own.

'The relatively small number of Cthon who disagreed with this policy were appalled. Genocide on this scale would never have been countenanced in previous ages and they saw it as evidence that the Cthon had finally succumbed to the irrationality they'd observed in so many other species. This group of Cthon went further than simply opposing the proposed genocide, they also argued that the policy of species containment itself was unethical and should be halted. They were shouted down by the majority and labelled as traitors.

'The destruction of the Phthask went ahead as proposed, but the dissident Cthon became what you would term activists, interfering in a number of ongoing containment projects and sabotaging key interventions. Because of their actions, a number of species went on to develop space travel and the usual widespread interstellar warfare resulted. Although the Cthon home world escaped the worst ravages of war on these occasions, there was planet-wide anger at the dissidents and demands that something be done about them. Consequently, they were rounded up, placed on a small planetoid that orbited the Cthon home world, and ejected from Cthon space. They were exiled.

'For many years the Cthon had been able, on a personal level, to fold space by means of mentalics. Now, by a huge effort involving virtually the entire planetary population, they used the same technique to transport the planetoid fifty-seven light years to a system with no intelligent lifeforms. This wasn't entirely without incident because the Cthon didn't have the necessary skill to place the planetoid appropriately. They successfully placed it in orbit round a gas giant, but couldn't control the fallout resulting from an object of this mass suddenly appearing round a planet which already had a family of moons. The gravitational surges that were generated caused two moons to collide, the resulting debris being swept up by the gas giant to create...'

'Rings.' Deira had finally tuned into the story and put two and two together. 'The gas giant was Saturn and the planetoid that was moved was Titan. You are the dissidents!'

'Indeed, Deira MacMahon. The name "Eich" in our language means "exiles"–for that is how we see ourselves.'

'The "other aliens" you mentioned to Sol were the Cthon and, as I thought, Fournier's father found evidence that they'd been taking an interest in Earth. But that means...'

'Yes, from the beginning of your twentieth century the Cthon identified humanity as being on the technocline and initiated the usual mentalic interventions.'

'And yet we're still here and have successfully developed space travel. What went wrong?'

'We went wrong, Deira MacMahon. If I may continue?'

'Sorry! Sure – go ahead.'

'The first Cthon intervention was...'

'June 28th 1914,' Deira interrupted again. 'The assassination of Archduke Ferdinand leading to the First World War. I suddenly get it. This is what the number file's all about – the dates are the dates of Cthon interventions.'

'Yes. The first intervention was on the date you mention. The planned assassination by Gavrilo Princip, a member of the Serb Black Hand, would have failed had the route travelled by the Archduke not been changed at the last minute. Gavrilo had given up on the attempt, and was sitting in a café, when he was amazed to see the Archduke's entourage pass by. He stood and fired, and the rest is history. What history does not record is the reason the route was changed was because of Cthon intervention with one individual on the Archduke's staff. The war was a Cthon attempt to "reset" human history. It was one of their rare failures because humanity rebounded rapidly. However, they soon tried again.'

'31st March 1920,' Deira said. 'Adolf Hitler begins his rise to power.'

'Yes. In this case, it was Hitler himself who was a tool for the Cthon. They interfered with his decision-making on a number of occasions in an attempt to cause worldwide devastation.'

'But if I remember correctly, part of the reason for Hitler's eventual downfall was that he made some extremely bad strategic decisions. How's that possible if the Cthon were guiding him?'

'Adolf Hitler was what you might call "conflicted" because he was influenced by us as well as the Cthon. We have monitored humans from the very beginning of their evolution and have developed a – proprietorial interest – in them. After all, mankind exists as part of what we now consider to be "our" solar system. We detected what the Cthon were up to with Hitler because we'd been expecting it for some time. Unfortunately, we missed the first critical point because it was extremely subtle and involved a split-second decision by one individual. We were careful not to miss any more. While we could not affect directions forced on Hitler by the Cthon we could impose our own changes – and we did. Had we not, the Cthon would have achieved their goal of worldwide ruin.'

'I'm getting the measure of this,' Deira said. 'The next date, the 27th October 1962, was in the middle of the Cuban missile crisis. I presume your intervention prevented a catastrophe?'

'Correct. On the day mentioned, Soviet nuclear armed submarines were present when the American naval blockade of Cuba looked like it might be breached. They were out of touch with their command and had no idea what was going on. The Cthon influenced no less than four of the officers on the bridge of a submarine that day. All were convinced that war had already begun and they should launch their missiles. Had they done so, it would have been the start of a nuclear war that would have rapidly spiralled out of control. Much of humanity would have perished, both in the war and the immediate aftermath. Most of the rest would have died as a result of nuclear winter. The Cthon would have achieved their objective. We had limited resources to combat this most potent threat, but we were able to influence one young officer on the bridge, a certain Vasili Alexandrovich Arkhipon, and he, in turn, was able to talk his comrades down from the brink. It was an extremely dangerous moment for your species. Unfortunately, on this occasion, our intervention drew attention to us.

'The failure of their previous attempts had surprised the Cthon. It was not unknown for their containment policy to require more than one intervention, but they had previously never required more than two. After the failure over Cuba they became convinced that someone was acting against them – and they began looking for that someone. It was not long before they detected our presence and tracked us down to Titan. You must remember that many millions of years have passed by since our exile and the Cthon had forgotten about us. That changed when they discovered us on Titan and identified us as a potent threat to their continuing safety.

'You have discovered that the last date of importance is 2nd November 2033, when Professor Chayka announced his discovery of sub-quantal physics. That event is different to all the others. Once they knew of our presence in this system, the Cthon realised that any further attempts at mentalic intervention would be futile. Instead, they decided on a different approach – the use of a physical mediator to achieve their goal. That mediator was Nicolau Dominguez. Dominguez is a Phthask – and he is in physical contact with the Cthon at all times by means of a neural node similar to Sol's own.'

This time it was Sol who interrupted. 'But that would've required a long-term strategy because Dominguez has been working with Chayka for years.'

'That's true. Chayka had been identified by the Cthon as a "critical individual" because of his early work on quantum field theory. Brilliant he undoubtedly is, but it is unlikely he would have come up with sub-quantal physics on his own. Dominguez was placed in the Moscow Academy specifically to befriend Chayka and subtly channel information to him from the Cthon. The fact he is a Phthask meant that his dampening field prevented us getting anywhere near Chayka, and sub-quantal physics, with all its applications, was duly discovered. Dominguez proved to be exactly the mentalic weapon the Cthon envisaged so many years ago. He is also more than just a mentalic weapon – he is a physical weapon. He is a trained assassin.'

'I can certainly confirm that,' Sol said. 'He was successful at eliminating Fournier and he had a damned good go at me.'

'But killing Fournier was not part of his original plan. We, the Eich, are his primary target.'

'What?' Deira had followed everything until now but found this a bit hard to swallow. 'So are we to believe Dominguez is still alive in spite of everything? And could he actually succeed in his mission?'

'He is well able to carry out his mission,' the Speaker said. 'It was Dominguez who engineered the explosion in the laboratory on Earth that resulted in the transfer of the whole team to Titan. He knew he needed to get here to get to us. As to how he could do it, well, Dominguez was not only educated into the higher reaches of sub-quantal theory and practice, he was also provided with a piece of technology that he could use to annihilate us – a nuclear bomb.'

'That's not possible,' Deira said. 'Everyone was screened for explosives and other weapons when they embarked on the Q-ship. Routine practice.'

'But in this case Dominguez himself is the weapon. The explosive device is technologically very advanced. It is biologically integrated with his body and carefully concealed within his chest cavity. It is undetectable by your technology.' There was a brief pause. 'As to his physical status at this time

– we know he is still alive because his mentalic dampening field is still operational.'

Sol looked thoughtful. 'In my time, Titan was off limits because of radiation contamination following a nuclear explosion. Could that have been Dominguez?'

'We fear so,' the Speaker said. 'In your timeline it is virtually certain that Dominguez succeeded in his mission and eliminated us. The only reason he has not already detonated the bomb is because a surface blast will not reach us – we are well protected underground. However, that could easily change. It is fortunate that Professor Chayka suggested sending someone back in time to prevent the species genomic failure. Your presence here, Sol, changes the parameters and gives us a chance of survival.'

'So assume, in the original timeline, the bomb blew up underground and you were all killed,' Sol said. 'Our experience from underground explosions on Earth is that they don't contaminate the surface – so how would you explain the significant surface contamination present in my time? And if there was a significant surface effect, how could Chayka have survived so that he could later send me back in time? It doesn't seem to hang together.'

'There are specific physical factors operational here,' the Speaker said. 'If Dominguez finds his way to us it will be via a cave system. Our modelling suggests that the blast from a detonation would be directed by the cave system itself, both down to us and up to the surface. It would emerge from the cave entrance as a huge spume travelling high into the atmosphere, and would eventually contaminate the entire surface. Because of the protection against charged particles provided by the gravity generators, the inhabitants of the various Bases would be safe until they could be evacuated. However Titan would be useless to your species for generations to come.'

Sol was still unconvinced but had to accept this as a possibility. Deira was more interested in the practicalities of the here-and-now.

'So the dwarf's still alive! But if he's blanketing the Base with his dampening field how are you communicating with us now?'

'The time of night is helpful because most of the Base personnel are asleep, reducing background interference from their conscious thoughts. However, our main means of communication is through Sol's node, which provides us with a non-mentalic channel that cannot be blocked by Dominguez. It is another reason why you are here, Sol. You are our only means of getting to Chayka and thereby preventing the further development of sub-quantal physics.'

'I think we've put the mass PHASEing issue on hold for now,' said Sol. 'We've confiscated all the equations from Chayka. Even if he has a copy somewhere he can't use it with us monitoring all the terminals. So that just leaves the dwarf. We've obviously got to get to him before he gets to you.'

'There is one more issue.'

Sol and Deira exchanged weary glances.

'Why am I not surprised?' Deira said. 'Does this relate to the apparent dangers of sub-quantal physics itself, as suggested by the fourth date in the pad?'

'Indeed it does, Deira MacMahon. As well as the dangers posed by mass PHASEing, the primary danger of sub-quantal physics is the QUAVER. The quantum vacuum reactors that are now so widespread on your planet, function by extracting energy from the vacuum itself – apparently representing free energy. Unfortunately, nothing in the universe is free, and there is a natural limit to how much energy can be extracted in this way before the vacuum in local space becomes unstable.'

'What'd happen then?' Sol asked, thinking he probably didn't want to know the answer.

'A large implosion would occur. The timing and size of the effect would depend upon the density of the reactors, which is currently greatest on Earth itself. However, as your expansion into space continues, these reactors will increasingly appear throughout the solar system. This means that the centre of the implosion, when it occurs, will be Earth, but it will affect the entire system. It will also destabilise the sun, causing it to rapidly expand to red giant status and resulting in the destruction of all the inner planets, including Mars. The Cthon have been very clever about this intervention because it generates two separate threats. It is clear that they have decided upon species genocide once more.'

'Fuck!' Sol exploded. 'It's one thing stopping the dwarf and preventing further use of Fournier's equations but it's another goddamned thing again to roll back the established use of QUAVERS. Even if we could persuade the powers-that-be to go along with it we'd push the world into an energy crisis. Seems to me the Cthon have won whatever we do. Humanity's doomed and it's just a question of whether we take half the solar system with us. This definitely wasn't in my mission brief!'

'No it wasn't,' the Speaker said. 'The scientists in your time failed to deduce the effect of continued vacuum energy extraction on local space because they were focused on the effects of mass PHASEing on the genome. Professor Chayka developed the equations which showed that the reason for genetic collapse was his own discoveries in sub-quantal physics. He would have realised that it was too late to save the species unless he could reach back in time and change his past behaviour. To that end he developed tachyonic transmission, which included the ability to reintegrate the transmitted individual using standard the photonic equipment of this time.

'What he didn't appreciate was that residual tachyonic contamination would lead to severe memory loss following subsequent photonic transmission. He has recently deduced this, which is how you were able to regain some of your memories. Regardless of what you may think of him, Professor Chayka is a genius of the highest order.

'With regard to finding a way out of this situation, we would not have recruited your help if we felt there was no hope for your species. We will talk with you again about how humanity can be saved when you catch Dominguez. If you cannot catch him, he will undoubtedly detonate his bomb, destroying both us and the future of mankind. Stopping Dominguez is critical for us all.'

There was silence.

'Hello?' said Sol. There was still no answer so he had to assume that was the end of the briefing for now. He just wished the Eich would cotton on to some basic courtesies – like saying goodbye, for instance. He looked across at Deira, staggered by the immensity of the task they faced, and could see she was shocked too.

'Crap!' she said. 'They seem to be saying they'll help us – but only if we get rid of Dominguez.'

'Fair negotiating tactic, I guess.' Sol said. 'I think we should get Cabello and his team involved and see what we can do about developing a strategy.'

'Yeah – that'd make sense.' Deira yawned and checked the time. 'Shit, I need some rest if I'm to function tomorrow – though I don't know how I'm going to get any sleep after that!'

She started towards the door.

Sol gazed at her retreating back. 'You don't have to go.'

Deira stopped. 'What?'

'You don't have to go – if you don't want to. Stay with me.'

Deira turned and stared at him. 'Is the rest of you as naked as your top half?'

'Why don't you come over here and find out.'

She paused in an agony of indecision, wanting Sol but scared of the consequences. Finally, she gave in to her hormones. She stripped off her joggers, t-shirt, and underclothes and climbed in next to him. They lay, simply touching each other for a few minutes and then came together in a gentle mingling of limbs.

Afterwards, they slept, still wrapped in each other's arms.

Chapter 27

NEXT MORNING, DEIRA woke to the sound of gentle snoring and it took a moment for her to realise where she was – and who she was with. A small smile played across her lips as she recalled the previous night, and she lay quietly for a while, savouring the warmth of Sol's body next to hers and watching the small facial movements he made while he slept. Finally, she slid out from under the duvet and slipped on her clothes. She tiptoed across the room and quietly let herself out before returning to her own room.

Half-an-hour later, on her way to the refectory for breakfast, she stopped off at Sol's room to see if he was awake. He was not only awake but dressed and hungry. He looked at her expectantly and was about to say something – then decided not to. She just smiled and chatted about the "visitation" by the Eich the previous night.

'I suggest we ask Cabello if he'd get the security team searching for Dominguez,' she said. 'They're quite capable of mounting a search round the Base, and we know the dampening field only stretches for about 500 metres so they've got a manageable search radius. I don't think we need to pull any punches now. He's not likely to detonate the bomb unless he's deep enough underground to get the Eich in the blast – they're his primary target after all.'

'So, shoot to kill?'

'Given your previous experiences of him, I'd say definitely yes.'

'And are we taking part in this search too? We haven't got much else to do and we've been on the surface a few times. Talking of which, I've been thinking about my gliding experience. Chard says that if we had a good set of wings we could probably fly, so why not get some? What do you think Chard, buddy? You're the one that got me thinking about this.'

'I agree that flying would be a very efficient mode of travel,' Chard said. 'I can readily provide plans for strap-on wings which should suit your requirements. Do you have any means of getting them manufactured?'

'I think so. I was having a drink with some engineers the other day and they were complaining about not having enough to do. I think they'd be quite happy to make us eight pairs of wings.'

'Eight?' Deira said 'That's a bit of overkill isn't it?'

'Not really. Differences in height and weight make it easier to have customised sets – two for us and six for the security guys.'

Deira smiled at his obvious enthusiasm and touched his hand affectionately. 'So how was last night?'

'For me, it was great! I thought you might be regretting it.'

'No – no regrets.'

'So how about sharing beds on a more regular basis?'

'Works for me – but perhaps we ought to put that on hold for now and think about how we're going to stop that dwarf.'

'Okay, my libido's on hold – until tonight anyway!'

They finished their breakfast and lost no time getting over to the new security office where Cabello was holding court with his men. He stopped when they walked in and Deira could tell he'd read her face perfectly. She'd always known she'd make a lousy poker player.

'Do I detect that look again, Agent MacMahon? More revelations?'

'You read me too well, Chief.'

Amidst much muttering, Deira told them the story presented by the Eich the previous evening. This time, the men were less convinced, but the bit about Dominguez being a walking nuclear bomb got them going. Why hadn't he already detonated it?

'A surface blast won't reach the Eich,' Deira explained. 'He needs to get deep underground.' She looked at Cabello. 'The main issue is he's still at large. He's effectively blocking the Eich's access to Chayka's team, so that means he's within five-hundred metres of the Base. We wondered whether you'd help us conduct a search?'

'No problem if we've got a limited search radius. I was wondering what we were going to do if things stayed quiet. My concern now is how to contain the guy if we do find him. I'm minded to authorise lethal force on this one. What do you two think?'

'I thought the same thing,' Deira said, 'If Sol can't stop him, even in full combat mode, we have no chance individually. The only way is to overwhelm him with numbers – and shoot to kill.'

'I completely agree,' Sol said. 'Don't give the little shit any quarter and always work with a partner.'

'That's agreed then,' Cabello said. 'I'll have a quick chat with the men to get the details sorted and then we'll be good to go.'

He took his men off into the briefing room and shut the door. Sol turned to Deira.

'While Cabello's busy I'll check out the engineers and see how the guys feel about making us some wings.'

He took himself off and found his erstwhile drinking buddies still bored out of their brains. Sol's project to assemble Chard's wing designs was just what they needed and was greeted with considerable enthusiasm. If they proved to be successful, the wings would be truly unique in the solar system – a real Titan first. With much laughing and joking the engineers scrambled to get to their workspaces to see who could produce a pair first. Sol was assured that the designs weren't complicated and they'd have all eight sets ready by the next day at the latest, so he left them to it and hurried back to Security.

Deira looked up when he came in.

'Just in time!' she said. 'The Chief's got everything nicely organised.'

'So what's the plan?'

Cabello took out an old-fashioned paper notebook and described the details.

'We'll work in pairs. One of my team will stay behind to mind the shop and Baxter will also stay to continue his work with the pad. That means two teams of two security personnel and you two agents as a third team. I've arranged for each team to have heat-seeking equipment because Dominguez should stick out like a sore thumb on Titan, even with the exosuit.'

'Good thinking,' Sol said, 'but Chard and I used that trick before and I don't think he'll be caught the same way again. How are we dividing the search area up?'

'Simple 120 degree segments, Base as centre, search radius 500 metres. There's very little cover out there so if Dominguez is within five-hundred metres we should find him pretty easily.'

'I wish I had your confidence.' Sol looked at the men, who were lined up waiting. 'Okay – are we ready to go?'

Cabello nodded. 'Let's do it!'

They trouped out of the security office, leaving Baxter hard at work on the pad and Landau looking rather forlorn in his role as house sitter.

Once on the surface, Cabello distributed the heat-seeking equipment and they took up position in their respective segments. By now, Sol and Deira were completely familiar with the surface features, and Landau had previously been out with the team that rescued Sol, but it took the other three a few minutes to get their "walking legs". When everyone was ready, Cabello gave a signal and they turned on the heat-seekers. Sol took one look at his screen and cursed.

'Fucking bastard dwarf – I knew he'd pull something like this!'

There were at least twenty heat signatures visible within the 500 metre radius – and they were all moving! Any one of them, or none of them, could be Dominguez. Sol growled again,

'Come on lads – don't just stand there. Let's go get the little shit!'

With that he was off at a fast lope, Deira struggling to keep up.

'We've got seven suspects in our segment,' she said, puffing along behind Sol, 'but there doesn't seem to be anywhere to hide.'

'I know. Chard's got them all fixed. He says they're all identical and they differ from his original record of Dominguez. My guess is they're all red herrings and Dominguez has found a way to shield himself from our sensors. That's what I'd do if I had the tech. So, I vote we ignore them and just do a sweep.'

'Sounds good to me.'

Deira pocketed her heat sensor and peered through the orange gloom at the flat landscape. There really didn't seem to be anywhere to hide except behind one of the three large boulders she could see. Interestingly, Sol wasn't heading towards any of those.

'What about checking out the boulders?'

'We will as part of the sweep but I get the feeling he's not in our segment. Chard's monitoring sound and movement as well as heat sources and he's picking up nothing except our own men in the other segments.' He stopped, and Deira almost walked into him.

'What the...' she started.

'Hell and damnation!' Sol slapped a hand to his head in frustration. 'Of course! He'll be in the ground.'

'What?' Deira said again.

'I just realised what you just said was true. There's almost nowhere to hide on the surface – and we should have realised that from the off. So he's got to have found a way of digging into the ground. That would minimise his heat signature and still allow him to blanket the Base with his dampening field. Chard – any suggestions on how to find him?'

'Ground-penetrating radar seems the obvious solution if it's available on the Base. If it's not, we'd have to request

EXILES OF TITAN – THE MARTIAN PHASE

a direct quantal transmission of a unit from the Bureau – and that would invite some questions.'

'Hmm. Okay. We'll need to return to Base and see what we can find.' He looked at Deira. 'Should we let the others know what we're thinking or let them complete their sweeps?'

'We should at least tell the Chief,' Deira said. 'It's his operation.'

Sol nodded and contacted Cabello. He explained what they'd been discussing.

'We wondered how you'd like to play it.'

He could see Cabello in his segment stop and gaze round while he thought it over.

'We'll complete our sweeps,' he said. 'It won't take long and it might blindside the dwarf. If we suddenly break off, he'll guess something's up and will probably change his position and tactics.'

'Fine – it's your call.'

The teams completed their searches uneventfully, exactly as Sol had predicted, and retired back to the security office to debrief and plan their next move.

'At least we've confirmed Dominguez is still alive,' Cabello said. 'I must admit I was very sceptical about that. What concerns me now is his apparent access to technology. Those rogue heat sources were tiny and highly sophisticated.'

'And he's got to have a way of making oxygen,' Sol said. 'The Eich said they could make it from water ice in the rocks so maybe he can too.'

'I'm still amazed by his adaptability,' Deira said. 'He was caught completely by surprise when Sol materialised in the PHASE chamber but he still managed to get away – and he's got all this tech. He's going to take some catching.'

'So what's next?' Cabello was keen to move on. 'If he's dug himself in we'll need some extra tech to find him.'

'Agreed,' Deira said. 'We were thinking of ground-penetrating radar but we don't know if there's a unit on the Base.'

'Hmm,' Cabello murmured. 'You're right – that should work. Geology would be the place to ask.'

He activated his comm and put in a call to the Geology Department. The geologists had been having a field day since arriving on Titan. They had a large expedition planned for a few days' time to a massive cave complex that had been discovered from orbit, and they were very excited. A ground-penetrating radar seemed to be an easy problem to resolve.

'They've got one – a brand new unit too.' Cabello confirmed. 'They didn't even ask what we wanted it for – just told me to help myself.'

'Good to know someone's happy,' Deira said.

Cabello took himself off to Geology to pick up the GPR. He'd already decided he was going to be the one to deploy this tech and he wanted to get a quick guide to its use. He wasn't away long and soon returned with what looked like an old-fashioned metal-detector. It certainly looked remarkably easy to use and Cabello confirmed this to be the case.

'You just turn it on and pass it over the ground,' he said, grinning broadly. 'If the dwarf's there he'll show up on this screen. Piece of cake.' He looked at Sol. 'Do you really believe he's in the ground?'

'Where else could he be?'

'I can't begin to imagine. On the other hand, I can't imagine him being able to bury himself for this length of time either, tech or no tech.'

'Good point,' Sol said, feeling less confident now. 'I guess we should just get outside and try it out.'

'I agree,' Deira said. 'Let's go test it.' She turned to Baxter. 'How're you doing Mr Baxter?'

Baxter turned from the screen. He looked tired and his eyes were bloodshot. 'I'm getting there, but it's going to be a while yet. The way this stuff's organised – or not – is a real doozy.'

'Great – Catch up later.'

As they were leaving she whispered in Sol's ear. 'Doozy?' Sol shrugged and looked blank.

Leaving Baxter working on the pad and "young Josh", as everyone called Hunstan, as housekeeper, they set off down to the airlock and were soon once again out on the surface.

'So what's the plan Chief?' Deira asked.

Cabello turned on the GPR and passed it gently over the frozen ground.

'Simple. Start from here and work outwards on a spiral path to radius 500 metres. If he's there we'll find him.'

They worked methodically outwards, the tension building with the anticipation of the dwarf leaping from his hiding place at any moment. It was a complete anti-climax when they came to the end of the search spiral. There was nothing. All was still. Sol was left feeling pretty stupid – again. This had, after all, been his idea. But he was also confused. Where the hell was Dominguez? He had to be within 500 metres of the Base to project an effective dampening field.

Then he got it.

'I know where he is' he said. 'This time I'm absolutely certain. It's so damned obvious it hurts. I don't know how I could be so stupid as not to see it.'

Everyone stared at him and Deira looked exasperated.

'Well if you're so stupid what does that say about me?' she said. 'I can't think where he might be, so come on – share your dazzling insight with the rest of us.'

'It's staring us in the face. We've all been taken in by Dominguez's adaptability and apparent access to technology. We know his oxygen would have run out hours ago and we've assumed he's got some wonderful tech to make oxygen out of water ice. We also know he has to be within a 500 metre radius to be effective – but we can't find him. What does all that tell you?'

Deira was still puzzled and shook her head.

'Beats me! We've been through all this before. There doesn't seem to be anywhere else he can… oh!'

She suddenly got it. The security team continued to look baffled.

'Yeah! You've got it now!' Sol said. He turned to Cabello. 'It's obvious! He's inside the Base!'

Chapter 28

THEY ALL HUSTLED back inside. While she stood waiting for the inner door of the airlock to open, Deira's temper finally got the better of her.

'Crap!' she exploded. 'We've been monitoring the airlocks. How could he have got back in?'

'No idea – but I'm sure that's where he is.'

Sol was both angry and frustrated – angry that he'd missed the obvious again, and frustrated at his apparent inability to second-guess the dwarf. He was also concerned because he knew Dominguez was highly manipulative. They'd all just spent a considerable amount of time on the surface, leaving the dwarf the run of the Base. Could that have been planned all along? If so, what for? He felt a sudden urge to get back to the security office as quickly as possible.

The airlock finally opened and they rushed to take off their exosuits. Sol almost tripped himself up in his haste but finally got himself sorted out, and they hurried to the security office.

Deira was the first to go in. 'How're you getting on Mr Baxter?' she called, opening the door. She stopped dead.

'What's up?' Sol asked. He pushed past her and was about to make a wise crack when his mouth suddenly went dry. He clammed up, and gawped at the scene in front of him.

One-by-one the security guys pushed in, wondering what the problem was – and one-by-one they stopped and stared, silently struggling to make sense of what they were seeing. Most of them had seen pretty bad sights before, but nothing in their previous experience came anywhere near this.

'Oh, fuck!!' Sol swore loudly.

'Crap!' came from Deira.

The security team continued to stand and stare – shock and incomprehension evident on their faces.

The room was a charnel house.

Blood and body parts were everywhere and the place had the sweet, sickly smell of an abattoir. Young Josh lay splayed out on the floor, a large hole in his chest and his heart rammed into his mouth. His abdomen had been slit open and completely emptied, the organs distributed around the room. His small intestine – all twenty-six feet of it – was draped like a Christmas decoration round the perimeter of the room. His eyes stared blindly from the top of a locker, and his tongue lay on the front desk.

Baxter sat where they'd left him at the network terminal – neatly skewered though the chest with a long piece of metal. His right eye and hand were missing.

The security team finally moved. They walked slowly into the room as if in a daze, avoiding the worst of the blood pools and trying not to vomit.

Cabello hissed and crossed himself. 'This is the work of the Devil,' he spat.

'Or as close to as makes no difference,' Sol said.

Cabello swallowed hard and tears welled form his eyes. 'I've known Josh for many years. I got him this job. I said it would be a boring posting but would look good on his CV. Just the sort of thing he needed at his age. What do I tell his parents now?'

Deira was completely lost for words but found her grief tempered by a hard sense of renewed purpose. She gazed grimly round. The dwarf never did anything unless he had a purpose – so what was the purpose of this abomination? Sol was overtaken by emotion and put his arm round the Chief's shoulder.

'You tell them he was a fucking good security officer and he died a hero. There's nothing else you or anyone else can say.' He banged his fist on the wall so hard he made his knuckles bleed. 'It's my fault! I've underestimated Dominguez every step of the way – and first Fournier and now these two guys paid the price.'

Deira was still trying to work out why Dominguez would do this. There had to be something. Then it clicked. Baxter was missing a hand and an eye – hand print and retinal scan. She went to the office safe and pulled the door open.

'This is what he was after,' she said. 'The data wafers are gone.'

This was the final straw for Sol. He'd been angry out on the surface when he found he'd been outwitted by Dominguez. Now, he was steaming mad. Deira had only seen him this angry once before, when he'd first seen Dominguez in the PHASE terminal. She tried to calm him down but with no success.

'The mass PHASEing equations will be all over the fucking Base again,' he said. 'Chard, can you access the network and wipe them?'

'No! Wait!' Deira screamed, but Chard was too fast.

'Accessing. I have found the files. I am wiping nnn…'

There was silence.

Sol was bewildered. 'What's up buddy?' he said, glancing at Deira and wondering why she was looking so horrified.

'Is Chard there?' she shrieked. 'Is he responding?'

'Can't get anything…' Sol started to say. Then it registered with him. 'Oh no! Oh fuck! Fuck! He can't have!'

Deira couldn't imagine what Sol must be feeling at that moment.

'I suspect he has,' she said. 'We know Dominguez was aware of Chard's existence when you were on Mars. He rightly saw him as his biggest threat. He's almost certainly been planning to get rid of him ever since, and this was his coup de grace. He probably planted some sort of super-virus on the network that was triggered when Chard went after the equations. I'm so sorry Sol, but I think you've lost your electronic friend.'

Sol continued to subvocalize frantically but there was no response from Chard. Tears appeared in his eyes and for one awful moment Deira thought he might break down in front of her. However, with what was clearly a monumental effort, he held himself together. Then the suppressed sorrow and rage bust out.

'If that little mistake for a dog's turd thinks he's won then he's in for a fucking great surprise,' he growled. 'When I catch him, and I will catch him, he's not going to die quickly. I'm going to make him suffer, like he made the youngster suffer.'

Cabello, whose grief had also turned to incandescent anger, nodded. 'I want to be in on that. We'll make the little bastard wish he'd never seen Titan.'

The other men growled their agreement and within a few moments there was a general baying for blood.

Deira somehow remained calm amidst this growing fury. She would grieve for Josh, as she would for Baxter and Chard–but not now. She gazed round at the mob that Sol and the remains of the security team had become and recognised how subtle and multi-levelled this attack had been. First, it had rid the dwarf of two security men at a stroke. Second, it had resulted in the equations becoming freely available again. Third, it had neatly removed Chard, who the dwarf rightly saw as a major threat. Finally, there was a clever manipulation of human psychology, which Dominguez clearly understood well. The team was destabilised. The men were overwhelmed by a flood of testosterone and weren't thinking straight. Deira knew she had to do something.

'Okay, gentlemen!' she yelled above the shouts and curses. 'You've done your manly stuff – now it's time to SHUT THE FUCK UP AND GET A GRIP!'

To her amazement, everyone shut up. Five faces turned accusing stares on her. Sol opened his mouth to start again but she held up her hand.

'ENOUGH!' He stayed silent, glowering at her.

'That's better,' she said, dropping her voice. 'I don't suppose it's occurred to any of you alpha males that this display of righteous rage is just what Dominguez is counting on?' The stares became a little less accusatory and the colour in some of the faces began to fade. 'He wants you angry. He wants you irrational. Why else do you think he did this? He wants you to act with your emotions instead of your heads. And it's working!'

She watched while the men began to come down from their testosterone and adrenaline-fuelled highs. It was clearly a struggle and the hatred was still almost palpable. Perhaps not surprisingly, it was Cabello who was the first to regain some self-control. His emotional outburst had been out of character and brought on by the sight of young Josh. Now, he looked embarrassed and moved swiftly to take charge of his men again.

'Thank you Agent MacMahon,' he said. 'We needed that.' He turned to face his men. 'Now then, this is what's going to happen. First, we get a Med. Squad and clean-up unit down here to sort out this mess. Then we all adjourn to my room for a stiff drink – *one* stiff drink.' He paused. 'Then, we'll come up with a plan to catch this filthy little shit.'

There were nods and a few half-hearted cheers from the remaining security team. Most of them would have preferred to have got blind drunk at that moment but they respected Cabello. Calls were rapidly placed to the relevant teams to get a clean-up underway and Cabello led the way out. He called over his shoulder to Deira and Sol.

'You two as well! We're all in it together – and we've all lost someone. Come on.'

Deira couldn't help but be impressed. One minute Cabello had been baying for blood with the rest and the next he was calmly organising his team. He'd even taken charge of Sol and herself which, strictly speaking, he had no authority to do. In this case, she was pleased he had. Sometimes it was so much easier to be told what to do instead of forever being the one to make the decisions – and, she admitted to herself, she was finding the decision-making process increasingly onerous.

As for Sol, he continued to inwardly rage at his perceived deficiencies but was inordinately proud of Deira and the way she'd handled the men, including himself. Looking back at the security office, he wondered if the guys would ever feel able to work in it again. He wasn't sure he would. He looked down at Deira walking by his side and couldn't help himself. Taking her hand in his, he bent over and whispered in her ear.

'You were spectacular back there.'

Deira was taken aback by the sudden compliment. Sol looked like he truly meant it.

'I did what was necessary, that's all.'

'I know, but I should have been able to do it and couldn't. The dwarf really got to me. Chard was more than a friend. Losing him, on top of all the memories of who I once was, pushed me over the edge. I've got nothing left now.'

Deira pulled Sol to a halt, her hand still in his, and waited until the security team had disappeared round a corner.

'Come here,' she whispered. She put her arms round his neck and pulled his face down to hers. Then she kissed him – a long, lingering kiss that momentarily transported them both away from this place of sorrow and pain. They held each other for some time before Deira pulled slowly away, leaving Sol with a look on his face somewhere between yearning and loss. She knew exactly what to say.

'You have me.'

Three words – but their effect was electrifying. Sol's shoulders came up and his whole demeanour changed. His eyes cleared and the ghost of a smile played across his lips.

'Yeah! Yeah – I guess I do, don't I!'

Together, they walked hand in hand to Cabello's room

The team assembled round Cabello's table and a bottle of twelve year old malt was opened. Cabello made sure the "one stiff drink" was a very good sized stiff drink and they fell to talking about the recent disaster. Like Sol, many of the security team, especially Cabello, felt indirectly responsible for their colleagues' deaths in one way or another and it took Deira quite some time to talk this through and get them to realise they weren't at fault.

Even when talk turned to a plan to catch the dwarf, there was still an almost palpable undercurrent of guilt, and Deira realised it was going to take some time for this to play out. A psychological support team would be useful since PTSD had to be on the cards for at least some of the men, but that would have to wait until they'd sorted out the immediate crisis. Strangely, though she'd also been affected by the recent episode, she didn't feel unduly traumatised by it. This was obviously of concern because she knew it wasn't how she'd normally react. She wasn't a naturally cold person. Perhaps she was as badly affected as the others but just responding in a different way – or perhaps the ongoing changes in her brain were suppressing her emotions. Only time would tell.

She shifted her attention back to the discussion, which had focused on how they were going to find the dwarf.

'How hard can it be?' Fingal said. "We're in a closed environment. There can't be many places for him to hide.'

Sol shook his head. 'Think again. Sure, we could search the modules one-by-one – but there are miles and miles of crawl space behind the walls, and there's no way we could easily search that. Even if we could, I wouldn't want to meet up with the dwarf in such a confined space. I'd say we haven't got a snowball's chance in hell of finding him.'

Cabello slammed a hand on the table. 'So what *do* we do?'

'We do something he's not expecting,' Sol said. 'The little prick's been manipulating us. He's probably sitting somewhere right now congratulating himself and laughing at us. He'll expect us to go for a Base-wide search next – a search he knows he'll easily evade. So we do something else instead.'

'What do you have in mind?' Cabello said, beginning to look interested.

Sol thought rapidly. He actually hadn't anything in mind. He just knew that a Base-wide search would play into the dwarf's hands. He badly needed Chard to bounce his ideas off.

'Go back one step,' he said. 'What we've learned is that Dominguez is playing this like a game of chess – always thinking at least one step ahead. Up to now we've been reacting to his moves instead of questioning them, and the logical reaction to his latest move is to initiate a Base-wide search. Let's assume that's what he wants. Why? Why would he want it?'

Cabello looked frustrated and began to say something–then stopped as an idea came to him.

'He could be playing for time.'

Sol nodded. 'Could be. But why?'

'Obviously, he's waiting for something – but for what?' Cabello was getting into the game now.

Sol was on the edge of figuring it out but couldn't quite get there.

'We must assume he's still focused on his main mission,' he said. 'He needs to get underground to blow up the Eich. How would buying time help with that?'

There was silence while everyone pondered on this – then Deira suddenly saw it.

'The geologists! They've got that expedition planned to the cave complex soon, haven't they? Perhaps he's planning to hitch a ride.'

Sol slapped the table, making everyone start. 'Yes! Of course! If he gets to those caves he's got a real chance of achieving his objective. It's a high-risk strategy because once he's out of his hiding place and in the open he's vulnerable to a well-organised attack. We need to keep a close eye on that expedition.'

'Actually, we also need to carry out a search,' Deira put in.

But we've just agreed that's exactly what he wants,' Sol said.

'Which is exactly why we should do it,' Deira said. 'He's expecting it. If we don't do it and he thinks we're on to him he might abort his use of the cave expedition. Then we're back to square one.'

'Damn, but you're right. We should set up a diversionary search so as not to tip him off and then aim to catch him when he infiltrates the geology expedition.'

Cabello smiled and pounded Sol on the back. 'Now that, my friend, sounds like a plan!'

Having decided on a strategy, the planning could now move ahead. Cabello dispatched Landau to Geology to find out about the forthcoming expedition. He also prepared a Base search that would appear realistic. The mood lifted and a sense of optimism took hold. For perhaps the first time, they were one step ahead of Dominguez.

While the security team busied themselves with their various tasks, Sol took himself off to Engineering to collect the wings Chard had designed. It was a bitter-sweet moment. It was good to think that the AI would, even in his absence, contribute to their ultimate revenge on Dominguez. On the other hand, there were eight pairs of wings – two too many. Cabello took the two that had been designed for Baxter and young Josh and placed them almost reverently in a cupboard. Then everyone had a fitting session.

Initially, there was disappointment because the wings didn't fit. Only after a lot of heaving on straps and general cursing did Sol realise the obvious – they'd been intended to be used on the surface, so were designed to fit over an exosuit and oxygen tanks. Fingal was sent to the airlock to fetch a full outdoor set-up and, once he'd put them on, his wings fit perfectly, folding back when not in use to lie neatly over the oxygen containers. Sol gazed on them with a certain melancholy as he reflected on how well Chard had designed them. He forced himself to move on again.

They were all clustered round Fingal, checking his set-up, when Landau reappeared. His trip to Geology had proved extremely useful. The details of the forthcoming expedition to the cave complex had been widely publicised and were available on a data wafer. Cabello took the wafer from Landau and loaded it onto his wrist console. With the console in presentation mode, they all gathered round the virtual screen.

It was clear the expedition had been planned for a long time. The caverns had been picked up by orbital scanners some years back and it was known they extended some distance below ground. It was hoped they might give access to the underground water ocean that had previously been detected by the Cassini-Huygens probe. If that turned out to be the case, the combination of a warmer environment with access to liquid water could facilitate more permanent human settlements, and there was an outside chance it might be the home to indigenous Titan life forms. Sol didn't mention the existence of the undersea stromatolites he'd seen. They'd occurred at just that boundary of heat and water that was mentioned on the wafer. He also remembered the Eich talking about their need for heat and water and that gave him great cause for concern as he examined the schematics of the cave complex. Hell, there was a chance the geologists could take Dominguez to exactly where he wanted to be. By the worried look on Deira's face she was having similar thoughts.

'So where exactly are these caverns?' she asked.

They hunted round in the file and were able to pinpoint the surface location. Sol whistled.

'Shit!' he said, 'They're a good fifty kilometres away. How were the geology boys and girls planning to get that far with oxygen reserves of two hours?'

That prompted some more digging in the file and the answer was obvious. The oxygen tanks they'd used on the surface were only designed for short trips. Longer excursions would require the use of one of the six available Titan Rovers. These were four-man, all-terrain vehicles, similar to Mars Rovers. They were capable of a top speed of twenty kph. and came fully equipped with all the essential requirements for four people for four days.

'That's our transport sorted,' Sol said. 'How many rovers are the geologists taking?'

'Looks like two,' Cabello said, flicking through the inventory. 'but this doesn't state how many personnel will be in each.'

'Three or less would be convenient,' Sol said. 'Then we could simply include one of our own guys in each rover.'

'I'm not sure about that,' Deira said. This is a published plan and the dwarf's likely to get suspicious of any sudden changes.'

'But the published plan doesn't specify numbers of men,' Sol said. 'I'd say we're home dry as long as we don't need to increase the number of rovers.'

Cabello opened his comm. 'Let's find out how many men they're taking,' he said. 'If it's six or less in total, we're in luck.'

The call to the Head of Geology swiftly confirmed that only six men would be going – two teams of three – but this hadn't been specified in the published details because it was subject to change at short notice. Cabello smiled and closed the comm.

'That leaves room for one of us in each rover,' he said. 'Perfect. The dwarf will never know.'

'That's fine as far as it goes,' said Deira, 'but if Dominguez is on board somewhere, one guy on his own won't be able to stop him. Sol and I need to be there as well.'

Cabello was unable to come up with a way of including Sol and Deira as well as having a security presence on each rover. He felt it was important that at least some of his men were involved at the end, so he wasn't prepared to simply let Sol and Deira go on their own. He also admitted to wanting to go himself.

'Sounds like we need a third rover after all,' Sol said.

'But that'd really screw things up,' Deira said. 'The dwarf would be bound to find out.'

'Not if we take a rover after the expedition's started off and make sure we stay well back.'

Deira was unconvinced but failed to see any other solution. Cabello made their minds up for them.

'It's got to be a third rover,' he said. 'And it won't just be you two in it – it'll be me too.'

Cabello wasn't going to be budged on this, so Sol and Deira

acquiesced. There didn't seem to be any reason he shouldn't go and he was keen to avenge his colleagues. Having assured his place, he got down to details.

'We'll just have enough personnel if we have one man on each rover and me, with you two, in the following rover,' he said. 'Clearly, there'll have to be a man left behind to mind the shop.'

This provoked a lengthy period of argument among the security team about who should do what. None of the men wanted to be the one left behind, and Landau protested loudly that he'd already done house duty once so should automatically be assigned to one or other rover. Eventually, Cabello decided they should draw lots.

Luckily, Landau acquired one of the coveted places on a rover, with Petrelli bagging the other. Fingal drew the short straw. Someone was always going to be unhappy, and it was apparent that Fingal was very good at it. He grumbled and grumped and eventually Cabello took him to one side. Nobody ever knew what had been said, but when the two men returned to the table, it was a very different Fingal who presented himself. Sol wondered what the guy had been promised. He didn't really care providing he stayed onside.

They went back to the data file from Geology and examined the detail of the rovers with interest. With the sort of speed the vehicles were capable of, the journey to the caverns should take no more than four hours, and probably less. If they included a good safety margin and allowed twelve hours for the return journey, they'd still have three-and-a-half days on site. If they couldn't catch Dominguez in that time, it'd be game, set, and match to the dwarf.

Deira was more interested in the schematic showing the interior of the rover.

'Dominguez is going to have to stowaway aboard one of these rovers,' she said. 'Would anyone like to tell me where he could hide?'

They examined the schematic in more detail and nobody could see a suitable hiding place. The rovers were extraordinarily space-efficient and there were no obvious areas that weren't either stuffed with gear or wide open for all to see. The only possibility appeared to be the waste container for the toilet.

'That'd be very apt for the festering little shit,' Sol said, laughing. 'Seriously, I wouldn't be concerned. He's highly innovative and he'll come up with something – even if it is the waste for the john. We should make sure our own plans stack up and expect the unexpected.'

Cabello nodded. 'I agree. The geologists have done most of the work for us. If Dominguez is planning to use this trip to get to the Eich, he'll have something planned and won't let the opportunity pass. We need to concentrate now on the diversionary search.'

'When's the expedition scheduled to leave? Sol asked.

'Three days' time,' Cabello said. 'Two complete days to go. We've got to make those two days count – convince Dominguez we're really trying to find him. You never know, we might just get lucky.'

'Or unlucky!' Sol grunted.

Cabello decided to wind things up. 'Okay. Search of the Base to start at 08.00 tomorrow.'

The group broke up, heartened to feel they were finally fighting back. Sol and Deira wondered slowly back to their rooms, hands linked.

'Okay for tonight?' Deira said.

Sol gave a deep sigh and smiled happily.

Chapter 29

Sol and Deira were ready to go early the next day. Because of the mess in the security office, the team had been allocated temporary quarters in a room that was usually used to store stationary. Since it was still storing stationary it was agreed that Sol's room would be the makeshift security office. Sol then decamped to Deira's room – which suited him just fine.

Cabello carried out a swift briefing on how the search would be carried out then made a formal announcement over the comm. The security team were planning to work in pairs but Cabello had made no arrangements to include the two agents. Sol and Deira insisted they should be a part of the search too and suggested that each of them was paired with a security man. Cabello reluctantly agreed and, after some discussion, Sol got Fingal and Deira paired off with Petrelli.

By chance, Fingal had been allocated Chayka's lab. Far from feeling concerned about this, Sol found himself looking forward to the looming confrontation with relish. Deira recognised the belligerent look on his face and pulled him to one side.

'How's your diplomacy this morning?'

'Don't know. Why?'

'I thought it might be on holiday somewhere.' Sol just grinned at her. 'Seriously, I wondered if you'd have another go at Chayka – see if you could persuade him to voluntarily relinquish those equations…' Her voice tailed off as she realised the near impossibility of what she was asking.

'I share your optimism,' Sol said, 'but I'll give it a shot. A lot depends on him really.'

'Okay. Do your best. If you can't hack it just try not to antagonise him too much.'

Sol grinned and gave her a quick hug. 'Que sera sera. See you later.'

Sol closed the security doors to Chayka's lab and stationed Fingal in the access corridor while he went inside. His reception was cool to say the least. Tirzah had obviously made her peace with Chayka because she was hard at work on a large DNA-sequencer in the far right-hand corner of the lab. She looked up when Sol came in but quickly resumed her work and kept her head down. Simon Chandler gave Sol a look of pure venom and retreated to Chayka's office where he and the professor watched him through the office window. If he wanted to distance himself Sol certainly wasn't going to argue. Walther Altmeyer was bumbling along in his own inimitable but highly effective manner. He was working on a module on the left-hand side of the room and was again being assisted by Amadi, who was holding his tools and passing others on request. Nobody seemed interested in the search and neither did they want to talk to Sol.

Sol smiled to himself as he moved round the room opening hatches and compartments and trying to work out how small a space Dominguez could squeeze into. He worked methodically anticlockwise round the room and soon reached the corner where Tirzah was working. She cast an anxious glance in the direction of Chayka's office and turned to face in the opposite direction.

'You won't find him here,' she said. 'The professor didn't think he should stay.'

Sol wondered if he'd heard that right. 'Who? Dominguez? Has Dominguez been here?'

'Yesterday. I'd been talking to the professor over the comm just before I left for the day and forgot to turn it off. When I got back to my room I found I'd forgotten a data wafer I wanted so I went back to collect it. I didn't bother to turn the light on because the professor was in his office and I could see where I was going, so I went over to my work station. That's when I realised the comm from the Prof's office was still on – and I could clearly hear him talking to Nicolau.'

'They were actually talking?'

'Well, Nicolau was doing most of the talking. He insisted the mass PHASEing equations actually belonged to him and Philippe had stolen them. He also said the second set of equations were entirely fraudulent. Then he told Chayka that he owed him and should help him now.'

'Owed him? Chayka owes Dominguez? Owes him what?'

'The Nobel Prize from what I could make out.'

'You mean Chayka plagiarised his research?'

'Well, not exactly. It was more like Dominguez hadn't been properly recognised for his contribution. It'd be a scandal if it ever got out – the Prof could even be stripped of his Nobel Prize.'

Sol glanced across at Chayka's office and saw that his conversation with Tirzah hadn't gone unnoticed. Chayka and Chandler were watching with interest. There was also a good deal of debate going on, presumably about whether or not to intervene. Suddenly, the decision seemed to be made because Chayka got to his feet and hurried out of his office. Sol thought rapidly. He'd potentially put Tirzah in a difficult position again and needed to help her out – fast. He leaned over and whispered in her ear.

'The professor's on the warpath. Follow my lead and things should be alright.'

Chayka looked angry, his face flushed and frowning but Sol was in no mood to receive another tongue-lashing from someone he was rapidly losing respect for. Time to get in first.

'Morning, Professor!' he said in his best professional manner. 'I was just talking to Dr Blumstein about Fournier's equations. They're all over the network again and I wondered if she'd had anything to do with that.' Tirzah looked suitably upset and Sol went on. 'She says she doesn't know anything about it and I'm inclined to take her at her word for now – but I've warned her that if she's found to have leaked them she'll probably get a custodial sentence. I'm sure you don't want to lose another member of your team.'

'Professor, I didn't do it!' said Tirzah, playing her part to perfection. 'You know I wouldn't do it don't you?'

Chayka was obviously thrown by this unexpected development. Tirzah was doing a wonderful job of appearing upset, even to managing a few tears, and he was clearly taken in by the deception.

'I know you weren't to blame Dr Blumstein,' he said. 'Don't let these people bully you.' He glared at Sol. 'You appear to make a habit of threatening my team Agent Smith. For your information, the equations appeared back on the network quite suddenly. None of us had anything to do with it. We assumed that you and Agent MacMahon had released them. Are you telling me that wasn't the case?'

'No, it certainly wasn't. I suppose Dominguez might have done it after he raided the security office.'

'Dominguez raid the security office? I can't believe he'd be capable...'

'I think you do believe it, Professor, but if it's proof you want...'

Sol thrust his virtual screen in front of Chayka. On it was a montage of pictures from the security office the previous day – no detail held back. Sol took great delight in watching the effect on Chayka. The man blanched and appeared to become catatonic.

'You can keep those,' Sol said, transferring the pictures to the network terminal. 'I'm sure the rest of your team would be proud of what one of their own has accomplished.'

Chayka remained speechless but it was all Tirzah could do not to vomit on the spot. She clamped a hand over her mouth and rushed out of the room. For a moment Sol wondered if he'd gone too far. He didn't think so. He felt that a good dose of common sense and realism was in order and if this is what it took, so be it.

'We know Dominguez is inside the Base,' he continued to the stricken Chayka. 'If it wasn't your team that released the impounded files then it must have been him – and to get to the files he carved up two security personnel. So, Professor, tell me – do you know where he is.'

For Chayka, reeling as he was from the photographs of the security office, this sudden direct question threw him completely. He retreated into silence. Sol wasn't in the mood for this, recognising the silent routine as a particularly effective escape route that Chayka employed when he was out of his depth. Well, he wasn't getting away with it today.

'I'm waiting, Professor,' he said. 'I'm in no particular hurry but…' he checked the time, '…I'm due elsewhere in forty-five minutes. If you don't answer me by then I'll throw you in a cell for obstructing an investigation.'

Sol sat in Tirzah's work chair and checked the time again before gazing expectantly at Chayka. The minutes ticked by and both men remained silent, Sol determined he was going to get a response. Eventually, Chayka conceded defeat.

'If you say Dr Dominguez is in the Base then I must believe you,' he said, the words forced between clenched teeth, 'but I have no idea where he is at this moment.'

'Of course not – but do you know where he *might* be? I think you do.'

There was another long silence before Chayka managed to whisper an answer.

'You might consider the crawl space.'

Sol decided this was probably all he was likely to get out of the traumatised professor but he couldn't resist one last dig.

'Okay. Now a warning. If you, or any of your team, are found to have given aid to this entity, you'll be prosecuted to the fullest extent of the law. Do I make myself clear?'

Chayka was bone-white and shaking slightly. He was way out of his comfort zone and his reply, when it came, was virtually inaudible.

'Perfectly clear.'

'Thank you Professor. Now, if you'll excuse me, I have a search to complete.'

Sol stood and meticulously continued his search round the lab, smiling at Chayka's discomfort. At one point the man had looked just like Tirzah – like he was fighting a battle just to keep his breakfast down! He glanced back at the professor and saw that he'd been joined by Chandler, who was trying to stir him out of his semi-catatonia. Apparently, he couldn't get anything verbal out of him, but he did manage to access the pictures from Security. Like Tirzah, he went white and his hand flew to his mouth. Unlike Tirzah, he couldn't control his visceral reaction and he puked on the floor at Chayka's feet. Sol chuckled, chalking this up as another minor victory. He knew it was petty, but he didn't like Chandler one little bit.

Sol completed the rest of the search quickly – he knew damned well he wasn't going to find the dwarf there. Then he lingered awhile, watching the ongoing attempt by Chandler to get Chayka going again and enjoying the effect of his continued presence. He had a quick chat with Amadi about nothing in particular followed by a grinding dialogue with Walther about whatever it was he was engaged in. Finally, he thought enough was enough and he called Fingal to open the security doors. The first person through was a cleaner who hurried to sort out the mess Chandler had made.

'Good morning's work,' he said to Fingal. 'No dwarf, though. We'll check in with Security then move on to the next sector.'

When they reached the new security office they found Deira and Petrelli, fresh from completing their sector, in conversation with Cabello.

'Anything new?' he asked. 'No sign of the dwarf in Chayka's lab – but he's been there.'

He told them Tirzah's story about the meeting between Chayka and Dominguez and the professor's later suggestion about searching the crawl space.

'Interesting,' Deira said. 'The bribery bit kind of backs up what the Eich said, doesn't it? The comment about the crawl space does suggest the professor's trying to be a little more accommodating.'

'He was under a bit of pressure at the time.' Sol laughed, and told her of his threat to lock him up.

'You threatened Professor Chayka?' Deira frowned. Although she'd made a vague threat against the whole team, she couldn't imagine having a go at Chayka himself.

'You better believe it – and it worked!'

Cabello had been listening in and now laughed out loud. Having previously been subjected to Chayka's silent tactic he heartily approved of Sol's approach and agreed the professor should understand that this behaviour wouldn't be tolerated anymore.

'You know,' he said, 'it wouldn't surprise me if Dominguez knew Tirzah was there when he was speaking to Chayka. He might have been trying to distract us again.'

'Could be,' Sol said. 'We've just got to stay focused. We dictate the agenda, not him. Now, where are we going next?'

The search continued all day and into the early evening so that only a few sectors remained for the following day. These sectors were sealed ready for the next morning and Sol and Deira left Cabello to conduct the daily debrief with his men. Following dinner, there wasn't much of the evening left so the two agents returned to Deira's room for a quiet drink before bed.

Later that night, with Deira fast asleep beside him, Sol lay awake thinking about Tirzah's story of the meeting between Dominguez and Chayka. If that had happened once it could happen again. Certainly, if Chayka felt somehow indebted to Dominguez he might well feel the need to pass information to him, so there could be a further meeting – maybe even tonight. Worth trying to gate-crash? Possibly. Sol made up his mind and slid silently out of bed, taking care not to disturb Deira. He padded across the room, quickly dressed, and holstered his staff. A few minutes later he was outside Chayka's lab.

He paused outside the door listening for any sound of activity. Hearing nothing, he made a swift entry and hunkered down, listening again. The ambient light in the lab was pretty poor, what there was coming from the small number of indicator lamps on pieces of equipment. It was enough, and after a few minutes he could make out the outline of the room. He found a convenient gap between two large consoles and settled down to wait.

He wasn't sure how long he waited because time took on a whole different meaning during stakeouts like this. He knew it must have been at least a couple of hours because he was beginning to get stiff. He was about to abandon things for the night when there was a sudden noise outside the lab and the door opened to reveal Chayka. The professor made a beeline for his office. He hardly had time to turn on the light and settle in his chair when a piece of the ceiling fell in and a small body jumped down. It was Dominguez.

Sol strained to hear what was being said. Unlike Tirzah, he didn't have the luxury of an open comm – everything was muffled and he couldn't make out individual words. Not a problem. He wasn't here to listen to conversations. He intended to kill Dominguez. Save everyone a whole lot of hassle.

Slowly and cautiously, sometimes bent double, sometimes on his hands and knees, he crept towards the office. He reached the open door and drew his staff from its holster. He listened again. The soft chatter had ceased. There was only silence. He squatted on his haunches and balanced on the balls of his feet as he mentally prepared himself. He knew exactly what he was going to do – leap into the room, activate his laser, and cleave the little troll in half.

He gave himself a ten second countdown. On zero he uncoiled and sprang into the office, the laser flaring on. Unfortunately, that was as far as his plan got, and he pulled back in a hurry when he saw the tableau that presented itself. Chayka had been forced to his knees and the dwarf was standing behind him with a wicked-looking knife at his throat. There was no way Sol could get at him without injuring Chayka, who was white as a sheet and whimpering gently.

Dominguez gave an ugly grin. 'Agent Smith! How nice to see you! Did you really think I wouldn't hear you move that bulk of yours across the lab? The noise could have woken the dead. But then again, I think not–your two security men are clearly way beyond that.'

Sol growled and swore but knew it would get him precisely nowhere. The last thing he wanted was a dead Chayka – but neither did Dominguez, surely.

'Really?' he said. 'You want me to believe you'd hurt the professor? You still need him to get the mass PHASEing project going.'

Dominguez was unperturbed and continued that ghastly smile. He got a better grip on Chayka's head and lightly stroked the skin of the professor's neck with the razor-sharp knife. A thin trickle of blood appeared and Chayka made a strange mewling sound and flopped forward slightly. Dominguez roughly jerked him back up.

'I'm sure you know better than that. Dr Chandler would serve my purposes equally well as far as mass PHASEing's concerned, and the Eich must surely have told you about the QUAVER-generated implosion that's going to destroy your civilization regardless of what happens to mass PHASEing. I admit I've become somewhat fond of the dear professor over the past twenty years – but I've no compunction about killing him if I have to.'

Sol was stymied. What the dwarf said was true – he didn't need Chayka to complete his mission. On the other hand Chayka was most definitely needed if they were to have any hope at all of dealing with these threats. His bluff had been called. He'd been out-manoeuvred – again!

'Alright, you win this time.'

'I appear to win every time, don't I?'

With the lack of space available in the office and the presence of the professor between the dwarf and himself, Sol didn't feel that Dominguez could get at him before he could slice him to bits, combat mode or no combat mode. Nevertheless, he kept his staff on laser mode as he began to back slowly away.

'I'm going to back out and leave the lab,' he said. 'Let the professor go.'

He continued his slow retreat, all the time keeping a close eye on what Dominguez was doing. The dwarf cackled.

'Good idea. We don't really want Professor Chayka to come to harm do we? You still have hopes he'll be useful, and I simply enjoy playing with you. When you've left I'll let him go – but if you try anything, his blood will be on your hands.'

By now Sol was out of Chayka's office. He turned, holstered his staff, and left the lab, still cursing under his breath. He shouted back to Dominguez,

'We know you're here now. You must know we'll find you – and I personally will make sure you die slowly and very painfully!'

'Good luck with that!' shouted Dominguez. 'I don't think you'll find me with your rather pathetic search, and I certainly don't think you can kill me – not without your late electronic friend at any rate!'

As the door closed behind him, Sol ground his teeth in anger, frustration and humiliation.

Sol wandered angrily round the Base. It was 02.00 and everything was quiet except for the gentle, all pervading hum of the gravity generators and the small number of essential personnel on night duty. He went to the refectory and got a whiskey from the automat, then sat in the near darkness going over and over this last encounter with Dominguez. Every time he'd tackled the dwarf he'd come off second-best – even when he'd had Chard in support. If this was a recurring theme, how on Earth could he, Deira, and the security team stop the guy?

He came to the conclusion that they had little or no chance and one or more of them was likely to end up dead. They'd been talking big, like it was a simple matter of dispatching Dominguez when they caught up with him, but they'd never really agreed a means of achieving this aim. It was all supposed to just happen, almost organically. They actually had no strategy – yet they were preparing to go up against the most dangerous entity in the solar system

He finished his drink and got a coffee, far too wound up

to even consider sleep. Half-an-hour later his brain was still going round and round, covering the same turgid thoughts over and over again. He was no further forward. He stirred himself and began wandering aimlessly down the featureless corridors and, whether by accident or subconscious design, found himself at the door to the PHASE terminal. He let himself in, flicked on the lights and walked over to the PHASE cubicle, thinking that the place seemed less impressive in the stillness of the night when the usual lights and noises of the transmission equipment were absent.

He peered in through the clear plastic wall of the cubicle and imagined himself lying on the couch sometime in the future, waiting to be transmitted to a past that he was supposed to utterly transform. What had he accomplished except getting three good men killed? And a good AI, he reminded himself. Chayka was still hell bent on publishing the mass PHASEing equations, the QUAVER threat hadn't been affected one jot, and Dominguez was still on target to achieve his main objective – the destruction of the Eich. Perhaps the past couldn't be changed after all. Everything that had been would still be and the future would remain as it was. Humanity was doomed to extinction.

He dragged himself away and left the Terminal, retreating back to the refectory for another drink. The dark thoughts just wouldn't stop coming and he slammed his fists on the table in frustration. Three more drinks later he was becoming even more morose but, luckily, had the good sense to call it a day. He returned to Deira's room and climbed into bed as quietly as possible, eventually drifting off into a fitful sleep. Deira didn't stir.

Chapter 30

S OL WAS UNUSUALLY subdued the following morning and
it took Deira some time to get him to open up about
the events of the previous night. She didn't know whether
to be pleased or angry.

She took Sol's hand and squeezed it, then pulled his
head down and gave him a long kiss.

'You're a stupid big lunk – you know that?' He nodded,
clearly expecting a roasting. 'In fact, you've probably done
us a favour. Dominguez will be all the more convinced we're
going all out to find him – he'll think he's still in control.
Just don't do anything like that again…' Sol looked down
at his feet. '… without giving me a piece of the action too!'

Sol head shot up and he grinned. 'Sorry! I'd forgotten
how much you enjoy the rough stuff.'

They walked together down to Security and found Cabello
feeling pleased with himself. The plan was proceeding well.
Petrelli and Landau had been successfully inserted into the
Geology Department the previous day and the geologists had
gone out of their way to make them welcome, even arranging
some basic training so they wouldn't appear too much out
of place in the expedition. Departure was scheduled for the
following morning.

With two personnel tied up in Geology, the search of
the remaining sealed sectors took up most of the day, and
Cabello insisted on getting round a fair bit of the crawl
space to add authenticity. Unfortunately, there were probably
kilometres of it – behind the walls, under the floors and

above the ceilings, and Dominguez could be anywhere. He was probably having a good laugh at them from wherever he was holed up.

Finally, with the search complete, they gathered back in Security. Cabello dispatched Fingal to get pizza and pulled out the schematics and operating instructions for the rovers.

'We should familiarise ourselves with these,' he said. 'After all, we'll be driving one tomorrow.'

'We could always familiarise ourselves with an actual rover,' Deira said. 'That'd be a damned sight more useful than poring over schematics and Dominguez is unlikely to see us in the vehicle bay.'

Cabello shook his head. 'Too big a risk. We've probably only got this one chance to get the bastard and I don't want to lose it by getting slack at the last minute. I'm sick of doing security sweeps. I need some real action.'

Deira was only too happy to let Cabello take the lead. He was particularly good at the detail of operations – even revelled in it – while she and Sol found it time-consuming and boring. She smiled and nodded.

'You're probably right – and I couldn't agree more about the need for action.'

Sol was about to say something when the door opened and Fingal returned with the promised pizzas. Suddenly, whatever it was he'd been planning to say wasn't important anymore and he joined the others as they got stuck into supper. There was an attempt at light-hearted banter but most of the jokes fell flat. In truth, they were all having difficulty getting past the recent atrocity, and silence descended on the little group as they remembered their fallen comrades. Had any of them been asked how they intended to obtain justice for the murdered men they wouldn't have understood the question. They weren't after justice – they were after retribution.

§

Half-an-hour later, with the empty pizza boxes in the trash and the mood grim but determined, they settled down to study the details of the rover that they'd previously skimmed over. It seemed to have been specifically designed for use by relatively inexperienced personnel and was, in effect, a larger and more capable version of the ubiquitous Mars Rover that had proved its worth over many years in an environment that was possibly even more inimical than that of Titan.

This version had six huge globe-shaped wheels upon which was mounted a massive cabin. The cabin was divided into two sections. The forward section had two rows of two seats, with the front-right seat taken by the driver and the back-left seat containing attached tech for navigation. The rear section contained all the essentials for daily living.

There appeared to be plenty of oxygen. In addition to the tanks already attached to the exosuits there were a further twenty-four tank sets stored in a specially-designed underfloor area. This gave a total of fifty-six hours of oxygen for EVA. The oxygen for the cabin was stored separately in a large tank that protruded above the roof of the rover like some monstrous growth. Extra water bottles for the water dispenser, together with food packages sufficient for four days, were stored behind the seats. The whole thing provided a perfectly acceptable short-term living environment for four people.

Cabello carefully examined the details of the engine. Like the Mars Rover, the main power source was electricity. In this case, however, there was also a backup facility consisting of an old-fashioned internal combustion engine that ran on methane, ethane, or a combination of both. This had obviously been designed to take advantage of the free availability of those fuels round their present location. As Sol said, it was really just a matter of popping outside and scooping some up.

They spent some time noting details – of which there were considerable. By the time they all felt comfortable with rover operations, it was getting late and they decided to call it a day. They needed to be fresh for tomorrow.

According to the geologists' itinerary the expedition was due to set off at 08.00 the following morning, so they were all up and ready to go by 07.00. They were staggered when they checked in with Geology and found that the team had been so fired up with excitement it had left at 06.30! Sol let off a few choice expletives and Cabello started grumbling about a complete lack of professionalism, but they lost no time grabbing their kits and wings and running down to the vehicle bay. There were four remaining rovers lined up against the wall. Deira picked one at random and they piled in, throwing their stuff in the rear and taking their seats.

They'd previously agreed that Cabello would be the lead driver, Sol his backup, and Deira would handle navigation, so Cabello and Deira took the driver's and navigator's seats and Sol sat next to Cabello. According to the operating instructions, it was imperative to carry out a number of safety checks prior to using a rover and Cabello wouldn't be rushed on this. Sol sat impatiently during the process and would have happily by-passed what he considered to be unnecessary bureaucracy. Deira also wanted to get moving but recognised the importance of the checks and thought again how lucky they were to have someone like Cabello on their team. Finally, Cabello pronounced himself satisfied.

'Ready to go?'

'I've been sodding ready for the last fifteen minutes,' Sol said. 'For fuck's sake just get going!'

Cabello chuckled and fired up the engine, letting it run for a few minutes while he listened for any knocks or rattles. The manual had been very specific about this – any odd sounds at this stage should lead to the rover being rejected. Thankfully, everything seemed okay and Cabello pressed the button to open the inner door of the vehicle bay airlock.

He gently depressed the drive pedal and they lurched a little unsteadily into the huge airlock. Pushing the "airlock" button closed the inner door and opened the outer. The familiar flat, rock-strewn landscape stretched away into the amber gloom. Deira fed Cabello the coordinates from her console and he floored the throttle.

The rover sped out of the vehicle bay at full speed and slewed slightly sideways.

'Whoops!' Cabello eased off on the throttle a little then gradually built up speed again until the rover had settled into a steady trundle across the surface at twenty kph. He grinned as he manoeuvred round rocks and boulders. He'd got his bit of action at last and he was clearly enjoying it.

They'd been driving for twenty minutes when Sol tapped Cabello on the shoulder.

'I know we agreed you'd be the lead driver but I think it'd be sensible for Deira and me to get a feel for this beastie too. How about we both take twenty minutes at the controls and then you can have it back again?'

Cabello didn't object. He was secretly quite pleased to have a brief break from concentrating on the surface. He slid out of his seat to let first Sol then Deira have a go. Both were impressed with how easy the vehicle was – it was literally point and drive! The main problem was, as Cabello had found, avoiding the rocks.

Cabello had been back driving for about ten minutes when he spotted something on his scanner.

'Something at eleven o'clock,' he said. 'Probably the other two rovers but we need visual confirmation.'

Deira found some field glasses. 'Yep! Two rovers it is. Ease off on the speed a bit. We can't risk being seen.'

Cabello cut the speed to fifteen kph and the other rovers promptly disappeared over the horizon. Deira called up the mapping software on her terminal and watched the two dots representing the other rovers moving slowly across the screen. Then she zoomed out until the site of the caverns was displayed.

'They're following the most direct route, she said. 'We can't risk getting too close so I suggest angling our path slightly and making for this rocky outcrop.' She indicated a feature about five-hundred metres from their projected destination. 'We can set up camp there and watch for Dominguez. Chief – angle five degrees right. You can speed up again but we need to keep a close watch for the others and slow down again if we see them.'

For the next two hours they played hide and seek with the other two rovers. Occasionally, they'd appear on the horizon and Cabello would slow down to let them get ahead again. Then he'd open up the throttle and wait until Sol or Deira spotted them again, when the process was repeated. Deira was a little concerned.

'I hope they haven't accidentally spotted us,' she said. 'I know they're aware of what we're doing but I don't want any idle chatter. If someone mentions us, and Dominguez hears, the plan's dead in the water. We should have briefed them on the importance of keeping quiet.'

'We did,' said Cabello, looking up from his driving, 'At least, I did. I also took the liberty of telling Petrelli and Landau to listen out for any loose talk and stamp down on it hard. Actually, I know they're excited but I think our geologists are fully aware of the potential risks. I suggested they concentrate on their expedition and try to forget we're out here.'

Deira was impressed. Once again they were in debt to Cabello's organisational skills. She checked the time and scanned the surface again before pointing ahead.

'We're getting close to our destination – I think that rock up there's what we're aiming for.' She checked her map again. 'Yeah, that's it. Park us on the right side of it so we can't be seen.'

'Will do.'

Cabello neatly steered the rover round to the side of the rock that faced away from the geology expedition and pulled up in the lee of a large overhang. He turned the engine off and they all sat looking at each other in the sudden silence.

'Time to get going,' Deira said, and everyone jumped into action. They carefully fit their exosuits and, on Sol's suggestion, attached their wings.

'You never know,' he said, 'they might be useful and they're not much extra carriage.'

Once they'd checked that everyone's suit was sealed Cabello popped the hatch and they climbed out. They loped to the edge of the rock and peered round to where the other rovers were parked up a few hundred metres away.

'No movement yet,' Sol said, 'unless the dwarf's already got out and we missed him.'

'Not likely,' Deira said. 'He'll be inside somewhere. That means he'll have to wait until the others have left before he can get out.'

As if to deliberately contradict her there was a sudden movement on the lead rover.

'What was that?' Sol squinted through the gloom trying to see what was happening. 'It looked like something fell off.'

Cabello scanned the area closely using the magnification option on the exosuit mask.

'It's the drainage hatch for the toilet,' he said, chuckling, 'and here comes Dominguez squeezing out!'

Sol gaped in astonishment. 'He actually did it? Hid in the waste container for the john?'

Cabello grinned. 'I guess he banked on it not being used on the outward run – and he's not planning on making a return journey.'

Dominguez squeezed through the relatively small hatch and dropped to the ground. He looked furtively round then scuttled over to the nearby rock formation where he disappeared from sight. He'd clearly taken some time preparing for this expedition because he was fully kitted out in an exosuit and carried a pack on his back.

'If he's found an entry into that tunnel system we could lose him,' Deira said. 'We need to get over there now.'

The three of them moved off trying to keep close to the rock face for cover.

'Shit!' Sol said, 'I hope we haven't accidentally led him straight to the Eich. Look, he'll want to get well ahead of the geology teams so there's little chance of him hanging round watching out for us. I think we should move – fast.'

With that he gave up all attempts at concealment and took off at speed towards what was now becoming obvious as an opening in the rocks. Deira and Cabello took one look at each other and ran after him. By the time they caught up he'd already gone into the cave and carried out a swift recce.

'The immediate cave's clear,' he said. 'Dominguez must've found some other way out.'

They hunted round and soon found a tunnel entrance at ground level near the back of the cave. Sol glared at it.

'It's damned small! I think it'll be a pretty tight fit for you and me, Cabello.'

'I think you're right.' Cabello looked doubtfully at the hole.

'Well, I can get through,' Deira lay on her front and started to crawl commando-style into the tunnel. 'If you two feel able to join me later please do.'

'Whoa, whoa!' Sol shouted. 'You can't go off on your own against the dwarf.'

'Then get down here and follow me.' Deira's muffled voice came from within the tunnel. Only her feet were still showing but, in seconds, they too disappeared into the darkness.

'Oh sod it!'

Sol flopped down and began to crawl after her. He got as far as inserting his head and had begun to push his shoulders through when he jammed up against rock. He wriggled slightly and twisted sideways and somehow managed to squeeze past the obstruction. After that, things got a little easier – he just hoped he wouldn't be asked to back out.

'I hate tunnels!' he grumbled, remembering his experience under the sea. He continued to make headway by employing a push and twist motion. 'How're you doing, Cabello?'

'Right on your heels. That first bit tested me but I'm through now. I just hope this doesn't come up against a dead end.'

'You and me both. Deira, are you okay?'

'Fine. The tunnel widens a bit further along so you two big lunks should have a bit more elbow room. I don't... oh.'

'Deira? Deira?' Sol's stomach did a little lurch. 'Deira, respond. What's up? You okay?'

'Yeah, okay.' Sol breathed a sigh of relief. 'The tunnel just opened into what seems to be a cavern, but I think the opening's quite a height from the floor. I only just managed to stop myself falling.'

'Any sign of Dominguez?' Cabello grunted as his nose came into contact with Sol's boot.

'No, it's pretty damned black in here – even the night-vision on my uniform isn't much help. So what do I do now? If I try jumping down I might injure myself – I've no idea how far it is to the ground. On the other hand, if I use the floodlight on the suit it'll be a dead giveaway. One thing's for certain, if I'm going to confront Dominguez I'd rather do it standing up, not crammed into this tunnel.'

Sol had been continuing to crawl during this exchange and his head now came up against Deira's boots.

'I agree we need to get out of this tunnel to confront him,' he said. 'The light's bound to give us away while a bit of noise might be interpreted as rock fall. I suggest jumping for it and hoping the reduced gravity will prevent an injury. We'll be right behind you.'

'Copy that! It's going to be more of a controlled fall than a jump because I'm going to have to go head first. Okay, here I go.'

The boots in front of Sol's head suddenly scrabbled for purchase sending a little shower of stones into his face. He closed his eyes – and when he opened them again the boots had gone.

'Deira?' he called. 'Deira, are you there?'

There was a moment's silence before Deira responded. She sounded a little winded.

'Yeah. In one piece. That wasn't the most elegant of manoeuvres. You two next.'

One after the other, first Sol then Cabello pushed themselves out of the tunnel and fell in a tangled heap on the cavern floor about three metres below. As he'd hoped, the low gravity meant they didn't injure themselves but Sol wondered how they were going to get back up there on the return journey – assuming there was a return journey.

They stood and brushed themselves down then looked for Deira. They couldn't see a thing in the stygian blackness and there was no response when Sol softly called her. He spoke briefly to Cabello and they agreed they'd have to use the floodlights on the exosuits regardless of the risk. Sol flicked on his light and was gratified to see Deira standing a few metres away. She made no attempt to move or speak.

Sol began to walk towards her, but there was something very wrong with the way she was just standing there – something that set off his internal alarms and told him to stop. He put his hand back to Cabello and, as they both halted, Dominguez stepped from behind Deira. He was smiling and had the same knife he'd used on Chayka pressed against her side.

'Well, well! Agent Smith again! Does this little scenario look familiar?' He gave a cackle, 'Chief Cabello too – I remember you from the ship. How nice of you all to join me on this free ride to the Eich. Yes, lady and gentlemen, these tunnels will take me exactly where I wish to go. The Eich are as good as dead.'

He snickered malevolently.

'And, of course, when they're gone, your species is doomed. What price Chayka's life now, Agent? Don't you wish you'd tried to finish me off when you had the opportunity? Now, if you two gentlemen don't want me to skewer the nice lady here can I suggest you take off your weapons and kick them over here? Then kneel down and put your hands behind your heads.'

'Sorry!' Deira said.

Chapter 31

T HERE WAS NOTHING for it but to comply. The men slowly unstrapped their weapons, dropped them to the floor and kicked them away. Then they knelt and placed their hands on their heads.

'Very good!' Dominguez kept Deira in front of him, the knife firmly against her right kidney. He picked up Sol's staff and threw it into his backpack then retrieved Cabello's gun, swapped it for the knife, and turned back to his prisoners.

'Now Agent MacMahon, I'd like you to tie these two up.' He produced some lengths of electrical wire he'd obviously acquired on the Base. 'Don't try anything clever,' he flaunted the gun, 'because I can pull this trigger before any of you get anywhere near me.'

His point was well made and neither Sol nor Cabello harboured the slightest hope they could do anything useful from their current position. Sol watched Deira as she took the wire from Dominguez, worrying she might try something stupid.

'For fuck's sake don't try to be a heroine!' he whispered as she bent to tie his hands.

'Don't worry, I won't.' she whispered back. She bound their hands and was about to move away when Dominguez snapped at her.

'And their feet! Let's make a good job of this, shall we!' Deira tied their feet and stepped back. 'Very good! Now your turn – lie on your front with your hands behind you.'

Deira obeyed and the dwarf walked over and tied her up too. He stood back and surveyed his handiwork.

'You may be wondering why I don't just kill you all now.' He smiled a particularly nasty smile. 'Well, I confess to being arrogant enough to want to share the success of my mission with you – and to give you time to contemplate your failure.'

He walked over to Sol and stared down at him. 'As for you, Agent Smith, I've had my fill of you! This is – for all – the grief – you've given – me!'

Each pause was accompanied by a hefty kick, first to Sol's middle then, when he doubled up in agony, to his head. Cabello growled and tried the knots of his bindings but was unable to move. Dominguez glanced at him and laughed.

'Ahh, the upright Chief Cabello – the control freak. This must be so frustrating for you!'

Cabello said something unintelligible and thrashed about, but to no avail. Dominguez smirked and turned away, shouldering his backpack. He cast one last backward glance at his captives.

'You'll know the end's come when you hear the explosion,' he said. 'Checkmate.'

He snickered again then set off into the darkness of the cavern. He was soon lost to sight, the sound of his footsteps getting fainter and fainter until they finally disappeared.

Deira wriggled round and sat up to face the other two.

'Sol! Are you alright?'

Sol had been lying still in an attempt to prevent further abuse from Dominguez. He stirred and sat up.

'Fucking little bastard.' He growled through clenched teeth, 'I swear I'll get that gall-covered dog's turd.'

He gave a hint of a wry grin through swollen lips as he realised this was one promise he was very unlikely to be able to keep.

'Well that went well!' he said tightly, obviously in pain. 'I assume he was waiting for you when you fell out of the tunnel?'

'Yeah. I didn't have a chance.'

Deira wriggled round and managed to get her tied hands over her feet and up to the front. Then she fumbled round the outside of her left boot. The other two looked on, wondering what she was up to. Finally, she found what she was after – a small blade she'd had the foresight to hide in the top of her boot. She cut at her bindings with vigour and, within a few minutes, was free. She jumped up and did the same for Sol and Cabello.

'I'm impressed! Cabello sat up and massaged his wrists, trying to get some circulation back to his hands.

'Well that makes a nice change' Deira said. 'It's usually me being impressed by you.' She looked across at Sol. 'Are you up to carrying on?'

'Sure – but I don't know what we're going to do now the dwarf's got all our weapons. We'll just have to try force of numbers I guess, but it doesn't look good.'

Cabello got to his feet and the three of them moved off in pursuit of Dominguez.

This time, because of the impenetrable darkness, they had no option but to use the exosuit floodlights, and when they turned them on the cavern lit up in spectacular fashion. The walls glistened and flashed in a light show that under other circumstances would have been fascinating to watch. At that moment, however, they were in no mood for sightseeing

– they were completely focused on finding the exit from the cavern and stopping Dominguez. They fanned out and searched the walls for a tunnel or cleft. It was a full five minutes before Sol shouted out that he'd found something.

It was another tunnel. It angled sharply downwards and this time was big enough for all of them to crawl on hands and knees. Sol took the lead and they plunged in, crawling for what seemed like an eternity. At times the tunnel became very tight for the two men. They were forced again to wriggle and squeeze their way through and, on one occasion, Cabello became completely jammed. The other two could only wait and hope while he cursed and squirmed, squeezed and pushed. He was clearly beginning to panic when he finally freed himself and slipped through the restriction.

He lay panting from a combination of exertion and sheer terror. He'd really thought that he was going to be entombed in this rocky nightmare forever – or at least until his oxygen gave out – and it was a few minutes before he could continue. Unfortunately, speed was of the essence and Deira had to exhort him to move before he would have chosen to. He gulped and pronounced himself good to go. He was actually far from good but he wanted to get his hands on Dominguez and that spurred him on.

They continued crawling, on all fours for the most part. On one occasion, the roof of the tunnel dropped so low that they only had space to crawl on their bellies and Cabello felt a looming terror again. Luckily, they were never in any danger of becoming stuck and the constriction only lasted for about fifty metres before the roof went up again. With great relief they got back onto all fours again and crawled on.

On and on they went, deeper into the dark underbelly of Titan, becoming more aware of the height of rock above them with every minute that passed. Sol was starting to think this ordeal was never going to end. His body ached from Dominguez's kicks and protested at being forced though this oppressive darkness. He wondered how Deira was coping. In fact, she was coping far better than she had any right to expect given her mild claustrophobia. Even so, like Cabello, she was finding this particular tunnel hard to take.

Finally, after what felt like an eternity but was actually only half-an-hour, the tunnel suddenly widened out into another cave and they emerged, gasping with weariness. Grateful for the extra height, they stood and stretched, giving their cramped muscles a short break before moving on once more. All they wanted to do was rest, but they knew that Dominguez wasn't going to stop so they forced themselves to look for the way forward.

The cavern they were in proved to be much smaller than the one they'd recently left and it gradually narrowed until it became a simple cleft in the rock that took another dive downwards. This was the only exit they could find so they took the plunge, squeezing between the two vertical sides. Sol and Cabello again found the going tricky at times but they took comfort from the fact that they could do their squeezing in a vertical position for a welcome change.

'Its times like this I can see the benefits of being a dwarf!' Sol said between swollen lips while he negotiated yet another particularly tight patch.

'Or a woman,' Deira said, passing through quite comfortably.

'Yeah, I guess. I'm not sure how much longer I can keep my stomach held in. How are we doing for oxygen?'

'We've been going for fifty-two minutes,' Cabello said. 'Halfway point in eight minutes. If we don't find Dominguez and deal with him by then we won't be going home.'

'Then we'd better get a move on,' Sol said. 'Hold on, I can hear something up ahead.'

They stopped and listened to the sound coming from their external auditory sensors. It sounded like running water.

'It can't be water because it's far too cold,' Deira said, checking her suit thermometer, 'but according to my briefing on Earth, there are known to be hydrocarbon rivers that feed the surface seas. Perhaps this is one of them.'

'Could be,' Sol said. 'Let's take a look.'

He squeezed through the last tight spot and almost fell into a much larger space. It was another cavern – and this one was simply enormous. The roof was easily 400 metres above their heads and in spite of their floodlights the far side was hidden in darkness. About 200 metres away and running straight across their path was a river – and standing on the near side of that river, was Dominguez.

He turned when their lights illuminated the cavern and gave what appeared to be a grimace. Then, before any of them could react he yanked a package from his backpack. While they watched, he pulled a cord attached to the package and it rapidly self-inflated to reveal a small rubber dinghy. He lost no time launching the dinghy into the river and the swift current quickly pulled him into mid-stream. Then he withdrew a collapsible paddle from his pack and began to paddle furiously towards the far bank.

'Crap!' Deira began to run as fast as the exosuit would allow, Sol and Cabello following hot on her heals. By the time they reached the swiftly flowing stream, Dominguez had reached the far side and climbed onto the bank. He threw them a swift salute, turned, and was off at a run. It wasn't long before he disappeared into the darkness at the edge of their floodlight range.

They stood for a moment in dismay and despair then frantically searched for something that might get them across the river. Sol was cursing roundly and Cabello looked as if he might explode with frustration. Deira paced angrily along the river bank.

'He was fucking prepared!' she raged. 'He had a boat in his backpack! A boat, for Christ's sake! And what have we got? Nothing!'

She stopped pacing. That wasn't strictly true. They weren't without their own innovations.

'The wings!' she shouted. 'Get them unfurled and we'll fly across!'

This hadn't occurred to Sol and he was particularly pissed off by the fact. His wings, for God's sake, and he hadn't thought to use them when they were needed. He unfurled his wings and helped Cabello with his set.

'So how do we do this?' Deira said.

'Not sure – I had Chard to help me last time and that was with our improvised set-up. Best guess is back up as far as we can, run, flap and jump. Hopefully we'll be airborne before we run into the river.'

'We'd better be. Come on then! Let's do it!'

They backed up as far as they could and started loping down the slight gradient towards the river, flapping as they went like some large waterfowl. It was a close-run thing but they found their jumps getting higher as they went and managed to become airborne just a few short metres from the river. For Sol, there was a distinct feeling of déjà vu when he looked down at the river beneath him. For the other two, it was simply exhilarating and Deira might have been tempted to experiment had it not been for Cabello bringing her back to reality.

'Great way to travel, Sol. I suggest staying aloft and trying to take down the dwarf from here.'

Sol steadied himself and flapped a couple of times. 'He'll see us coming for sure because of the floodlights.'

'Yes, but I suspect he won't be able to get a bead on our actual position. He might even be partially blinded by our lights all coming at him at once – especially if, as I suspect, he's using some form of night-vision lenses. I think it's our best bet.'

'Copy that! I concur. Deira?'

'I agree too. I don't think he'll be blinded because he'll almost certainly have polarising filters on his night-vision but, without our weapons, our best chance is to dive-bomb him simultaneously. Let's do it!'

At the speed they were moving it didn't take long for them to spot Dominguez. He was making swift progress across the surface and it was obvious he knew they were coming because he repeatedly looked back over his shoulder trying to fix their location. Even if he had polarising filters he was clearly having a problem identifying their exact position. Their chief advantage was the wings. Clearly Dominguez didn't know about them because he wasn't looking up!

As they drew near Sol indicated that they should initiate a steep dive. He received a thumbs-up from the other two and they all plummeted down towards the dwarf. It would have been good if it had worked. Unfortunately, without Chard controlling his descent, Sol undershot and hit the ground just behind the running dwarf. Deira and Cabello also missed, and all three ended up in heaps on the surface. They leaped up quickly ready for combat and found that Dominguez had stopped.

'I see you're more resourceful than I gave you credit for,' he shouted. 'Well done! I applaud you. It will make my final victory that much more satisfying.' He took off his backpack and withdrew Sol's staff. 'I've always wanted to use one of these,' he murmured.

Sol grinned. The dwarf had just made his first mistake. He didn't realise the staff was DNA-locked and was frantically pushing buttons trying to get it to work.

'I don't think so you little shit,' he yelled, and launched himself at Dominguez.

Dominguez threw the staff disgustedly to one side and grabbed in his bag for the gun, but by that time Sol was on him. A large fist slammed into the side of the dwarf's head, sending him reeling backwards, and Sol triumphantly picked up his staff.

'This is how to use it!' he said, flicking the laser function on and advancing on Dominguez.

Deira was having trouble. She'd scrambled up after the crash-landing intending to join the action but found that, no matter how hard she tried, she couldn't move. It was like being in the tar pit again, her legs held fast in the gloop. Then, to make matters worse, she began to feel strange – similar to the fugue state she'd experienced on Mars. A purple haze descended over her vision and she seemed to be receding from events, watching them as if down the wrong end of a pair of field glasses. What the crap was happening to her now? Whatever it was, it was happening at the wrong time. She couldn't afford it. She needed to get out of it quickly and give the two men some help. Unfortunately, she was completely helpless and could do nothing.

Cabello had taken the opportunity afforded by Sol's charge to make a dash for Dominguez. When the dwarf took the force of Sol's fist, Cabello launched into a flying tackle and the pair of them rolled over on the rocky surface. By dint of his size and momentum, Cabello ended up on top and landed his own right hook on Dominguez. Unfortunately he reckoned without the dwarfs' strength, and his second punch was parried by a strong right forearm before a flat palm to his chin sent him crashing to the ground. He was stunned but still making a valiant attempt to get back up when a sledgehammer blow from Dominguez to the back of his neck flattened him into unconsciousness.

Deira's problem continued to evolve. First, her hearing became muted, as if she was underwater. Then, when she tried to speak, her vocal cords wouldn't perform. All that came out was a garbled mumble. Finally, her legs gave way and she sprawled untidily on the ground. She struggled to a sitting position, desperately trying to get back control of her body, and was almost immediately hit by a wave of nausea as if she'd just had a bad PHASE. She gagged, and just avoided vomiting into her face mask, then felt dizzy and had the dreadful feeling she was going to lose consciousness.

Cabello's charge pushed Dominguez away from Sol just as he was bringing up his staff for the coup de grace. He was forced to keep his distance while the Chief was engaged for fear of hurting him, but with Cabello down, he finally found an opening and made a sweep with the laser. Again, Dominguez was too fast. He somersaulted under the flashing laser and came up inside the staff's arc. His fist flew out and took Sol in the solar plexus, knocking the wind from him. Then he dived for his bag and produced the gun.

He grinned as he aimed at Sol's head and pulled the trigger but, at the same moment, Sol's force field flared on and the bullet ricocheted off. Sol pulled himself up and leaped at Dominguez, bringing the laser up against his throat.

'Now I'm going to make you suffer, you little bastard!' he said, relishing the prospect.

From a great distance, Deira watched everything with growing alarm. Although Sol seemed to have the dwarf pinned, she had a premonition that something bad was about to happen. She found herself sinking into a mood of calm acceptance.

'I don't think so!' said the dwarf, and before Sol could react he'd dodged away from the laser again and come up by his side. 'I think I may have more luck with this,' he cackled and whipped out his knife. Before Sol could react he'd pushed it slowly, with all his prodigious strength, through Sol's force field, onwards through the protection of his graphene impregnated uniform – and between his ribs.

Sol's eyes opened wide and a soft whooshing sound escaped from the wound in his chest. He looked baffled, and his staff fell from his nerveless hand as he collapsed to the ground. Dominguez was left standing triumphantly over him, bloody knife in hand. He turned his attention to Deira who was still sitting on the ground, staring blankly into space, as if in a state of shock.

'Agent MacMahon,' he said, 'a little bird told me that you and the clunky Agent Smith here...' he kicked Sol in the head and Sol groaned and curled into a ball. '... have a nice thing going. So before I kill you I'm going to let you watch me kill your lover.'

He reached down and yanked Sol's head up, placing the knife against his throat and leering at Deira.

Deira was completely stuck in her fugue state now – the purple haze, the long-distance vision, the paralysed legs – but she no longer felt panic or concern, only a great calm. As she gazed at the dwarf, time itself slowed – not her own subjective time but real objective time. She watched, fascinated, as the dwarf's knife appeared to inch its way towards Sol's carotid artery. There was no fear. This entity was *not* going to take Sol from her. She could stop him. She held up her hand towards Dominguez.

'No!' she said, firmly. She had no idea what she was doing but it somehow seemed right.

The space round Dominguez shimmered and what looked like a hole in the air opened up, red, coruscating light flickering round its edge. The hole surrounded Dominguez and then consumed him – only for another hole to spit him back out about five metres away. He lay on his back, clearly stunned.

Deira suddenly found she could move again, and move with a speed she'd never thought possible. It was almost as if she were augmented. Without pausing to think, she launched herself forward and grabbed her staff from the dwarf's backpack. Then she activated the laser and approached him where he lay. He was grinning and making no attempt to rise. He pointed to his chest where the Eich had said the bomb was implanted.

'I don't know what you just did but you're too late!' he cackled. 'I've just been notified by my patrons that I'm within the killing zone for the Eich. I would've liked to have got much closer, but this will do.'

He made a biting movement and a white spot appeared on his chest, growing rapidly.

'The explosion will occur in 60 seconds. Killing me now will make no difference. I win!'

'I don't think so.'

The look on Deira's face as she stared down at Dominguez was pure contempt and he looked unsure, detecting something new in her manner. She seemed somehow distant – cold.

'This is for Baxter.' She casually swept the laser down, severing the dwarf's right leg at the thigh and simultaneously cauterising the wound.

He howled in agony and looked up in horror. She appeared emotionless and he could tell this wasn't over yet.

'You can't do this!' he screamed. 'You're an agent.'

'This is for Josh.' Deira ignored the dwarf's entreaties.

The laser moved again, slicing off his other leg. The animal-like howling redoubled in intensity and Dominguez wriggled and squirmed. Deira didn't normally consider herself a vindictive person but, as she watched him writhing, she realised she had a dark side she'd never fully appreciated. Part of her recoiled at the knowledge – but the main part embraced it, seeking the retribution she craved. She used the laser again.

'This is for Cabello.'

The dwarf's right arm came away at the shoulder. This time there was no howl, just a pathetic whimper. He knew what was coming next.

'This is for Sol.'

The left arm followed the right onto the rapidly accumulating pile of limbs. Thirty seconds had passed and Deira's brain appeared to be multitasking. One part was continuing the remorseless countdown while another carefully monitored the developing white patch on Dominguez's chest. She looked down at what was left of him – just a head and torso, though still fully conscious.

'The Eich said you're in contact with the Cthon through your implanted node,' she said, 'so, in a few seconds, they'll know they've failed. They need to understand that they'll always fail. If they try anything again we'll be there to stop them – and if there *is* a next time we'll take the fight to them. The message is clear – if they want to remain safe, stay away from Earth'

She stared coldly at Dominguez. 'As for you,' she said in a voice as hard as tempered steel, 'I'm done with you!'

She casually swept the laser down a final time and neatly severed his head from his body. It rolled away a few paces and lay still, sightless eyes staring at the distant cavern roof. Fifty seconds had passed. Without conscious effort Deira re-entered her time-heightened state and watched with interest the onset of the explosion in the dwarf's chest. When she felt she could wait no longer she raised her hand again.

'Go!' she said. The air shimmered again, and for a split second she saw stars against the black backdrop of space – then the torso disappeared through the hole, leaving behind the pile of limbs and the head. The hole closed.

Almost immediately, time resumed its normal speed and Deira staggered and almost fell. She had no idea what had just happened but right now she had to help the two men.

She ran to Sol and held him in her arms as she contemplated what to do next.

There was no way she could extricate both Sol and Cabello through the series of tunnels that connected this cavern to the outside world. Even if she had Cabello's help they would probably do more damage to Sol by dragging him back. Also, they'd now been on the surface for – she checked the time – sixty-five minutes. It was probably already too late to get back before the oxygen ran out. There seemed to be no answer. Though the Eich were safe, the rest of them definitely weren't.

'Deira MacMahon!' The voice of the Speaker came from Sol's staff.

'I'm here.'

'Deira MacMahon, you have accomplished what we always hoped you would. It took a moment of extreme stress to free you from your rational shackles and let your innate abilities emerge. We will explain everything in due course but time is now of the essence for Sol Smith. What you did to Dominguez you can also do for yourself, Sol, and Chief Cabello.'

'But what *was* that?'

'You folded space and translated the bomb away from this place. The Eich are safe. Now you must ensure Sol and Cabello are safe too. You must fold space again and translate yourselves back to the Base.'

Deira felt completely helpless. 'But – I don't know how.'

'Negativity is the enemy. If you believe you can't do it, you won't do it. You must believe what I tell you – that you can do this. You don't need to understand it or how it's controlled. That will come later. What you must do now is to desire with every fibre of your being to be back on the Base with Sol and Cabello. Want it with everything you've got.'

Deira concentrated. She really did want what the Eich suggested. She wanted it so badly it hurt. Nothing happened. Sol's breathing was becoming ragged. He gave a little cough and a gobbet of blood appeared on the inside of his face-piece. His head lolled in her arms and his body went suddenly limp. She knew he was dying – here in her arms – and there was absolutely nothing she could do.

Sol felt the dwarf's knife slide into his chest with an agonising slowness, passing through muscle and membrane and finally penetrating lung tissue and blood vessels. He tried to scream but no breath would come. His body sank helplessly to the ground. He retained full awareness despite his injury and was acutely aware of Dominguez holding the knife against his throat, about to slice open his carotid artery. On the face of it there didn't seem to be anything else he could do now, just relax and let the inevitable happen.

He tried to concentrate on what was going on in the cavern and became abruptly aware that Dominguez was no longer threatening him. Then he heard Deira talking to the dwarf and the terrified, almost primordial screams as she lopped off his limbs one-by-one. He smiled to himself when he realised she was out of danger and the dwarf was being taken care of. He relaxed again, and felt a change come over him, as if he was slipping into another place. This must be what dying was like.

His vision rapidly faded to black and he waited for oblivion to take him. However, whatever he was expecting, it certainly wasn't the sudden explosion of his awareness into a sea of red. It was initially terrifying, his imagination conjuring up racial archetypes of hell. Then he realised what he was looking at. It was blood – his blood – welling out of a torn pulmonary vein where the dwarf had pushed the knife. His awareness had focused inside himself, and with that knowledge came the realisation that he wasn't totally helpless. He could even now do something to help himself survive – and he badly wanted to survive. He had many things to accomplish yet.

Sol had no formal medical training, just some basic talks on resuscitation techniques, so the only thing he knew for sure about his injury was that he was bleeding into his chest cavity – and the blood loss was considerable. Briefly, he allowed himself a glance at what Deira was up to, and was shocked to see her standing over the head and torso of the dwarf with a pile of limbs near her feet. While he watched he saw her finally sever Dominguez's head and teleport the torso away somewhere. So she had some strange abilities too! He silently applauded her.

He focused on his injury and could tell that, whatever Deira was able to do, assuming she could do anything, it would be too late for him. By the time he got back to the Base he'd have bled out, and he knew that resuscitation from that position would be virtually impossible. Somehow he had to keep his circulation at least partially filled with blood. There was only really one option, but even that might prove disastrous.

The only way he could stem the bleeding was to stop the blood flow – and the only way he could do that was to stop his heart. Then he'd have about three minutes before he suffered inevitable brain damage. He was unsure. He heard Deira's conversation with the Eich and felt there was a good chance she'd be able to extract him – but would she be able to get him back to the Base within three minutes? He had his doubts. If only he could slow his brain function down he could prolong the period of cardiac arrest.

Suddenly, he knew what he had to do – and with knowledge came action. He'd watched Deira as she'd formed the hole that had teleported Dominguez away and he somehow knew he could do that too. He concentrated – and was rewarded by the appearance of a small hole through which he removed some of the fastenings of his exosuit so that it gaped open. He was now exposed to the atmosphere of Titan – and to the sub-zero temperature. His body temperature immediately began to fall, the process aided by a tweak of his temperature regulation centre in his hypothalamus to stop him shivering. The effect of low temperature on the brain was to reduce its oxygen consumption and prolong the time it could survive without a blood supply. Sol flinched as he realised that another effect would be to render him incapable of further mentalic feats. He had to act now, or not at all.

He reached into himself one last time and stopped his heart. His consciousness faded rapidly, and all became darkness.

Deira both felt and saw the sudden change come over Sol as his heart stopped. She desperately tried again to fold space but nothing happened.

'Noooooooo,' she screamed, trying again to transport them all out of this place. Again, she was unsuccessful.

'Stay calm,' the Speaker said, though even his usually calm voice was starting to sound unsure.

'I can't do it!' Deira cried, feeling utterly powerless. She'd failed. Sol was dying.

In that moment of helplessness, salvation arrived from a most unexpected quarter. She would have liked to have called it another consciousness, but she knew it wasn't conscious. It was almost primeval in its simplicity – but its sudden appearance had the effect of producing an intense relaxation in her, similar to that she experienced during her fugue state. Looking down at Sol in her arms, she felt her confidence suddenly return.

'No!' she said. He wasn't going to die. Not on her watch.

Time slowed, space folded, and the cavern disappeared.

Next moment, light exploded round her and she realised they were all, Cabello included, back in the Base. In fact, they were in the infirmary. Nobody was there so she let Sol go briefly while she pushed the emergency call button. She pulled him back into her arms again just as the emergency medical team arrived and ran over to help.

'Please,' she gasped, pushing Sol into the arms of the nearest medic, 'he's been stabbed. He's lost a lot of blood and I think his heart's stopped'

She began to fall and was caught by a nurse who helped her to a waiting bed. The last thing she heard was frantic shouting and somebody calling for adrenaline and a defibrillator.

Then everything went black.

Chapter 32

D EIRA OPENED HER eyes to bright white light and her first thought was that she'd had a bad PHASE – then the light slowly resolved into the stark walls of the medical bay and the harsh lamps overhead. She slowly sat up, slid her legs out of bed and tried standing. There was a short spell of dizziness and she clung to the bed as her vision became blurred, then everything cleared and she was able to stand. She gazed round.

Cabello lay in a similar bed across the room and was just beginning to stir. Suddenly, memory flooded back and she remembered Sol. How much time had passed? She checked and saw that she'd only been out for about ten minutes. So where was everybody?

At that moment a nurse came in and tried unsuccessfully to get her to lie back down again.

'I'm fine!' said Deira. 'But where's Sol – the badly injured man I brought in? Is he okay?'

The nurse frowned. 'He had a nasty stab wound in his chest and was in cardiac arrest,' she said. 'Luckily, he hadn't bled out and we were able to resuscitate him and transfer him to the OR. That's where he is now – they're trying to stop the bleeding. Is he a friend of yours?'

'Yes, he is.' Deira couldn't bring herself to say that he was far more than just a friend. 'What about the man over there? He's Chief of Security.'

'I'm told he should be fine. He's got a nasty injury to his cervical spine that we initially thought was going to leave him quadriplegic, but that doesn't appear to be the case and we now think he'll make a full recovery. He'll have to wear a neck brace for a while, though, and won't be fit for work for some weeks.'

Deira nodded. She could only imagine the frustrations that lay in store for Cabello and hoped that the man would eventually get back to the job he was so good at. However, her main concern was Sol. It was clear he wasn't out of danger – yet she was relatively calm. She seemed to be acting on automatic pilot. Perhaps a residue of her recent fugue state? She thanked the nurse and asked to be updated as soon as there was any news. She was about to leave when the nurse indicated a pile of objects on a table.

'Those are his belongings,' she said. 'The man in the OR, I mean. There are a couple of baton-like things as well as clothing. Would you be able to look after them?'

'Thanks,' Deira said. 'Actually, one of those is mine, but I'll certainly keep an eye on Sol's as well.'

She picked up the two Staves and Sol's uniform and left the infirmary, shambling along to her room where she pulled the door shut behind her and flopped onto her bed. Now it was a question of waiting – and she was pretty fed up with constantly waiting. She tried watching a tri-vid but found the content boring and, quite frankly, juvenile. She brewed a coffee and sat down with an e-book. No good – she just couldn't concentrate. She sighed and checked the time and found only ten minutes had gone by. This was no good.

She ran over in her mind what they'd achieved so far. Dominguez was out of the picture permanently so the Eich were safe. However, there were still the issues of the mass PHASEing formulae and the projected destruction that would be wrought by the vacuum implosion at some unspecified time in the future. They appeared to have only tackled the tip of the iceberg.

'Deira MacMahon.' It was the Speaker of the Eich, once more speaking through Chard.

'I'm here,' Deira replied wearily. 'If you're working through Sol's node can you tell me how he is?'

'The surgeons have tied off the cut vein and he's stable. They are in the process of re-expanding his lung and then they will close his chest. He will survive – but he will require a considerable convalescent period.'

Deira wasn't concerned about long periods of convalescence – she was just concerned about Sol being okay. It was beginning to look like things might be alright after all.

'Deira MacMahon,' the Speaker continued, '"you have saved our race from the Cthonic weapon. Now we need to turn our attention to saving your race.'

'But what's happening to me?' Deira said. 'You said back in the caves that you'd explain later. How did I manage to get rid of Dominguez?'

'It began with your genetic inheritance. As well as the so-called gamma mutation, which was a precondition for your selection as an agent, you also had other unique combinations of genes. These were affected when you participated in the interplanetary PHASEing programme. The technician on Mars told you about the need to sample and compress in order to transmit over such large distances. The samples of "you" that are taken at the transmitting end are filled in by the assembling computer at the receiving end. There was always the risk that this filling in process would make you less than you were before but, in fact, it made you far more – by introducing further enhancements to your already enhanced genome of which you have now had first-hand experience.'

'You said I could fold space. Is that how I made Dominguez disappear and got us back to the Base? Something helped me during that last move – was that you?'

'You were certainly successful at folding space and getting Sol and Cabello back to the base – but we did not assist you and are unaware of any help coming from another source.' There was a pause for a moment as if the Speaker was contemplating this but he failed to elaborate on it. He continued. 'The process is similar, though not identical, to that employed by the Cthon so many years ago when they moved Titan into its present orbit. You also have other abilities not as yet revealed to you. They will become obvious over time and it would be wrong to force their development. The space-folding ability is sufficient to work with for now – it means you will never again have to rely on transmission technology. You need simply fold space to travel to wherever you wish to be.'

'What about Sol? Does he have any abilities?'

'He has a similar genetic makeup to you and was similarly exposed to interplanetary transmission. He has precisely the same abilities as you, though they are emerging in a different order. Of importance is the fact that your children will inherit all these abilities too – and probably many more.'

'Our children? You're making rather a large assumption there.'

'Not at all. It may not have registered with you yet but you are pregnant with Sol's child.'

'Whaaat?'

Deira was thunderstruck. This couldn't be happening. What about her career? And what of Sol? What would his response be? There were so many questions.

'We think your future with Sol Smith looks good, Deira MacMahon. We now need to ensure that your descendants also have a future to look forward to.'

Deira had been so thrown that she'd forgotten once again that they'd only achieved half their objectives. Next they had to somehow persuade humanity to abandon a good chunk of sub-quantal technology – a technology that had solved the immediate energy problems of Earth and was powering space ships to reach the rest of the solar system. She couldn't imagine how they were going to accomplish that. The Speaker continued.

'We should first clarify that sub-quantal technology, as such, is not dangerous – it is purely the QUAVERS, and of course mass PHASEing, that represent an existential threat to your species We are downloading some equations to your Base network. They are heavily encrypted and only you will have the key to their use. One set of equations demonstrate the inevitability of a massive implosion if energy continues to be withdrawn from the vacuum. A second set detail the theory of cold fusion. We hope the two sets together will persuade Professor Chayka to recommend the abandonment of QUAVERs and their replacement with cold fusion reactors.'

"You think Chayka might get behind this change of direction?'

'We think a second Nobel Prize is guaranteed if he first alerts the world to the problems with sub-quantal technology and then puts forward the solution. He'll become the most famous physicist in history, even eclipsing Einstein, and I don't think he's going to throw that opportunity away. Do you?'

Deira had to smile to herself. The Eich appeared to have got the measure of Professor Chayka. They were literally bribing him to assist the world in getting rid of QUAVERs by providing a much better alternative. It was win-win and she could see no reason why it shouldn't work. She opened up her network terminal and saw the icon denoting the recent download in the bottom right-hand corner.

'I'll get right on it,' she said.

The last few hours had completely shaken her world view in more ways than one and she wondered if there was anything else to come.

When she reached Chayka's lab she found him hard at work as usual.

'Ah, Agent MacMahon!' He seemed surprisingly upbeat. 'I was just thinking of you and your friend Agent Smith.'

'Really?'

'Indeed. I've been reviewing the evidence against mass sub-quantal transmission that was provided by Agent Smith and I find it quite compelling.'

'You do?'

Deira thought she could see the work of the Eich in this sudden enlightenment. Of course, now that Dominguez was gone, they had a clear field of influence on Chayka and his team.

'I do. It's quite clear that the genetic inheritance of the species cannot be put at risk by the development of this new technology, and I propose to place all of this in print as soon as possible.'

'Yes, well, I'm glad to hear that Professor. But I've something else to tell you – something I hope you'll find equally enlightening. By the way, I know you obtained your original sub-quantal equations from Dominguez.' She saw the sudden look of alarm on his face. 'Don't worry, I'm not about to tell anyone. Your reputation and Nobel Prize are safe. But here's the thing – how do you fancy a second Nobel Prize?'

The look on Chayka's face changed from alarm to crafty calculation in a split second while he tried to see where this was heading. Deira called up his network terminal and showed him the file containing the new Eich equations.

'This file,' she said, 'contains proof that continuing use of vacuum energy will destroy Earth and a good chunk of the solar system.' Before he could protest, she went on, 'It also contains a fully worked up theory of cold fusion together with an implementation plan for cold fusion reactors that could replace the QUAVERS now in operation.'

She watched the emotions play across his face. First there was obvious excitement, then a devious look as he calculated how he might benefit from this. That then faded to doubt, as if he really couldn't believe that such an offer would really come his way. Finally, he looked worried.

'But where did these equations originate? Am I not compounding the risks to myself of being charged with plagiarism?'

'Let's be honest, we both know your original equations came from an extra-terrestrial source that wanted to destroy our race. These new equations are also from an extra-terrestrial source – but one that holds nothing but goodwill towards mankind. They're the final part of the puzzle. If you can implement this solution you'll remove all the existing threats to humanity – and you'll have personal glory on a scale unequalled in history. Are you up to that? Are you up to being the saviour of mankind – again?'

Chayka nodded vigorously. 'If you give me access to these equations, Agent, and they are what you say they are, I give you my word I'll do everything in my power to ensure that the direction of technological travel on Earth moves away from quantum vacuum reactors and that mass photonic transmission is never developed. However, you must give me your word in return that you'll never breathe a word about where they were obtained.'

'Why would I? And do you really think anyone would believe me if I did?'

'Hmm. Probably not!'

Deira left the lab smiling. She had a good feeling about this.

Chapter 33

EIGHT WEEKS LATER Sol was finally able to leave the infirmary. In the intervening period Cabello had been discharged and taken by Q-ship back to Earth for rehabilitation. The old security office had been thoroughly cleansed and refurbished and was once more the headquarters of security services, with Petrelli Acting Chief of the much reduced contingent. Sol had his own room back but he much preferred staying with Deira and she did nothing to dissuade him.

Chayka had been as good as his word and had already published several papers demonstrating the dangers of existing vacuum energy extraction technology and suggesting the alternative of cold fusion. Even at this relatively early stage, his name was being suggested for another Nobel Prize and moves were already afoot to discontinue the QUAVERs when the alternative cold fusion reactors were brought on line. Everything was looking good.

Deira had updated Sol on these events while he'd been lying up in the infirmary getting increasingly cranky from enforced inactivity. He'd been quite upset he'd missed some of the excitement but was keen to talk about their new abilities, and updated Deira on what he'd been able to do back in the caverns. For a moment Deira thought this explained the help she'd been given at the last moment but Sol swore he'd been far too busy trying to save himself to be able to help her. It remained a mystery – and Deira didn't like mysteries.

Finally, Deira had plucked up the courage to tell him of

her pregnancy. She'd been unsure what his reaction might be but she needn't have worried – he'd been completely bowled over. Now, he lay on the bed he shared with Deira thinking that, shit he was sore, but life really couldn't get much better than this. He was still counting his blessings when the door opened and Deira came in.

'So how's the invalid?'

'Bloody sore actually. Apart from that, though, pretty damn good. I've been thinking.'

'Ooops! That's never good. What about this time?'

'The Eich. They promised to enlighten us about everything in due course yet they've never got round to it.'

'It seems to me they've told us most of what we need to know. What else do you want from them?'

'Don't know really. It's just – I don't know – there seem to be loose ends.'

Deira considered this. She knew what he meant. The feeling of things that needed to be said – of explanations for events for which there were currently none.

'Perhaps we should just ask them,' she suggested.

Sol sat up on the bed. 'My idea too! Okay Speaker…'

'Deira MacMahon and Sol Smith.' The voice came out of Sol's staff – he'd long since stopped calling it "Chard" or even his PWC.

'Aha!' Sol said. 'You were listening in, I think. Well if you were, you'll know what we were talking about.'

'You wish us to complete the details of the story. Where would you like us to start?'

'The beginning's always a good place,' Deira said. 'That strange agent with the orange force field in the warehouse incident – who was he?'

'Unfortunately, that is the one question for which we do not have the answer. We are, however, confident that all will become clear in time.'

'Huh!' said Deira. 'That's a good start! Perhaps you should just tell us what you *do* know.'

'We will begin with you, Deira. You may have already wondered why you, a relatively junior agent, were sent on the original mission to Mars.'

Deira was taken aback. 'Actually, I'd never given any thought to that. I've always assumed it made sense given my background in GCHQ and being Adam's partner. You're implying there was more to it?'

'Indeed. Adam's choice for the mission was logical but there was no requirement to send you. Whatever you may feel about your expertise in cryptography, Adam could have managed without it.'

'So you influenced the Director to include me?'

'Yes, we did. We always intended for an agent to reach Titan, but we needed somebody with your specific genome if our plan was to stand a chance of working – and I have to stress there was no guarantee that it would. At the time of your selection, Dominguez had already obtained the requisite equations for mass photonic transmission from the Cthon. It was intended that he should get them to Chayka but, unfortunately, Dr Fournier discovered his alien DNA.

'You have already put most of Fournier's story together, Sol. What you do not know is that Dominguez had already decided to dispose of Fournier before you met him. You were not to blame in any way for his death.'

'I suppose you gave me a nudge in the right direction to get the suicide verdict overturned?' Deira said.

'No, that was all your own insight. We did, however, influence the choice of Sol and his subsequent transmission to Mars – and before you ask, this was again based on genome.'

'Just a minute,' Sol said, frowning. 'That makes no sense. If you were destroyed by Dominguez the first time round how could you influence anything in my time?'

'A tachyonic transmission into the past was planned in your time because the world was dying from genetic collapse. The scientists in your time – led by Professor Chayka – decided to try one last gamble, to send a man backwards in time to try to change the course of history. You are aware of your specific genetic mutation that enabled you to be transmitted tachyonically. What you are unaware of is that this mutation was not as limited as I think was previously inferred. There would have been quite a number of possible candidates for the mission but we had previously planted a suggestion in the professor's brain that guided him towards a much more specific genome. He had been working with the Bureau on the project for many years and was actively watching out for what we wanted. When you were born, you fulfilled our specification perfectly and you were, therefore, groomed for the mission, including your recruitment to the Agency.'

'But how do you know all that?' Deira said. 'Specifically, how do you know you planted a suggestion in Chayka's brain? Can you see into the future?'

'Not at all. It's really quite simple – we have already taken such a precaution in this timeline in case you were unsuccessful back in the caverns. We can only assume that we would have done something similar in the original timeline.'

There was silence for a moment and Deira could see Sol frowning as he followed some line of reasoning. She also had a question.

'About the caverns,' she said. 'When I found I couldn't fold Sol and Cabello out, why didn't you help me? Since Dominguez was dead you could have used your own mentalic powers.'

'You are correct. We could have folded you all out. Indeed, we were preparing to do just that when you managed it yourself. We were attempting to get your mind used to the process of space-folding. You had already achieved it twice in relation to Dominguez but it had not yet become embedded in your neural architecture. It required one further fold to achieve that and we assumed that would be forthcoming because of Sol's predicament. I admit we were becoming a little alarmed when you seemed unable to produce the fold, and we would have helped if you had truly failed. Luckily, that proved unnecessary.'

'Hmmm. That's taking tough love a bit far. It was a pretty close-run thing.'

'I agree.' For once the Speaker sounded genuinely sorry. 'However, the correct result was achieved so the risk was worth it.'

'You seem to be very comfortable playing fast and loose with other people's lives,' Sol said, drawing a questioning look from Deira. 'What about my memory loss? Why should it have been so severe?'

Deira was interested in the way the Speaker was responding to these increasingly hostile questions. Usually, the Eich came over as emotionless but there was no doubt that some emotion was beginning to leak through as they went on. Now there was the distinct sound of uneasiness in the reply.

'If we exclude the tachyonic contamination that Professor Chayka has already dealt with we have to agree with your assessment that sabotage is very likely. However, we remain unclear about who could have been involved.'

Sol looked thoroughly unconvinced. 'A saboteur you aren't aware of? That seems highly unlikely.'

'Again, we are forced to agree.' The uneasiness was still leaking through. 'Unfortunately, whatever happened appears to be irreversible.'

Deira saw Sol's shoulders slump and moved to his side. 'We'll create our own memories,' she said gently, 'You, me and junior here.' She placed his hand on her belly.

Sol's face lightened and he placed a hand on hers. 'Yeah – you, me and Fred!'

Deira feigned horror. 'He will not be called Fred!'

Sol laughed and kissed her. 'No, not Fred. I was thinking of Josh if it's a boy – and I'll be damned if he'll be called Smith. We'll stick with your name.'

'Works for me! By the way, when I was on Mars I mentioned to Amelie about using a shortened version of my first name like my sister Bernie. When I was at school they used to call me Dee, and I was wondering…'

She tailed off as she saw Sol change again. He'd been gazing into her eyes, lost in feelings of love and contentment, but now the blood drained from his face and he was jolted into another time and another reality. He continued staring into Deira's eyes but he didn't see her any more. He saw someone else – an old lady with startling emerald green eyes!

'Dee!' he whispered. 'But that would mean…' he stopped, looking stricken.

Deira stared at him with concern. 'What? What's the matter? You look like you've seen a ghost.'

'The Ghost of Christmas Yet to Come. How could I have been so blind? Your eyes – you're Grammy Dee – my great-great-grandmother! And you Eich – what did you have to do with this? Tell me the truth because, whatever you say about never getting my memories back, I suddenly *do* have them back! I remember my name is Solomon MacMahon. I remember all my previous life – and it's all down to those eyes. Shit, I can't do this.'

He got off the bed and walked away before turning back and giving Deira a look somewhere between longing and revulsion. She got up too and tried to move closer to him but he pulled away as if he didn't want to touch her. For one of the few times in her life she felt completely helpless.

'Speaker! What's he talking about? What have I done?'

There was a long pause as if even the Eich were shocked by the turn of events. Then the voice came again – and this time it was definitely concerned.

'We are amazed at the return of your memories, Sol. This was not supposed to happen.'

'So you *did* have something to do with it. I got the feeling you were holding something back – and now I know what. I'm having a baby with my own great-great-grandmother!' His face contorted as he followed the logic. 'That must mean I'm my own great-great-grandfather. Shit – of course! I was named after a famous great-great-grandfather – me!'

His face was now suffused and his eyes bulged. He was clearly panic-stricken but was still able to put two and two together. He shouted at the ceiling as if the Eich were up there somewhere.

'You keep saying the genome had to be right. You said it to Deira earlier and you just said it to me. The genome had to be right. I thought there was something strange about that but I think I understand now. You wanted us to get together. You pushed us together.'

He stared round the room belligerently. Deira just kept hearing the same words over and over again – "I'm having a baby with my own great-great-grandmother". She felt horror welling up inside her, all the happiness of a few minutes ago flying away down an impossibly long dark tunnel.

'You have intuited well.' The Speaker was leaking emotion all over now and sounded profoundly weary. 'However your suggestion that you are your own great-great-grandfather is a logical impossibility if you consider it rationally. You have very different genetic material to your great-great-grandfather and, consequently, whoever Grammy Dee met in her past was not you. Similarly, your own great-great-grandson will have very different genetic material to you. You will only exist as an older version of yourself in the new future that has been brought into existence.

'We knew this would be your reaction if you ever found out the truth, and we tried our best to prevent that happening by interfering with some of your memories when you reached Titan. The abilities that Deira has developed as a result of the spatial PHASE would not, of themselves, have been passed on to her children. For that we needed to breed back – and for that we needed you, her great-great-grandson. Your own son, for the baby is a boy, will now inherit all your new abilities and probably more, and that will be important for the safety of mankind – because we are sure the Cthon will continue to attack your race. It was a calculated risk that you would discover the ruse.'

'So you've used us both!' shouted Sol. 'We're nothing more than breeding specimens – just like the Phthask. What is it about you Cthon – because that's what you are – and breeding programmes? It wouldn't surprise me if there weren't others.' There was a long pause, the Speaker remaining silent, and Sol jumped to the obvious conclusion. 'There are others aren't there? How many?'

Deira was already feeling physically sick at the turn of events when she suddenly felt cold. She shivered uncontrollably and put a hand on her belly, worried about the wellbeing of her baby – then she entered her now-familiar fugue state. Her vision narrowed and became distant while her consciousness dissociated from reality. It was all very similar to her experience in the caves – just far more intense – but this time she was able to let herself relax into the familiar feeling of deep calm, appreciating it as a welcome antidote to the stress of a few minutes ago. She wasn't afraid of this anymore. She knew that whatever was happening was probably for the best and would run its course no matter how hard she tried to control it. All she could do was to wait.

Unexpectedly, her narrowed vision suddenly exploded outwards and her perceived reality took on a flowing iridescence, like oil on water. Like her previous fugue states she seemed to be an external observer and she watched with interest while the scene round her dissolved into a kaleidoscope of form and colour, only to abruptly solidify again into the Titan PHASE terminal.

At first she thought she was physically present there but soon realised she was observing the scene from near the ceiling as a disembodied awareness. Nobody else was there. No, she corrected herself, there was somebody there – in the PHASE chamber itself. She peered inside – that was as close as she could come to describing how she perceived events – and saw Sol, immobile. What the hell! Her awareness took in the timer on Amadi's bank of instruments and she realised that this was the day Sol had PHASEd into Titan Base.

While she focused her awareness on Sol she became aware of another presence in the chamber. It was a peculiar sensation, knowing that other entities were present but that they were there in mind only. They possessed a unique mental identifier that she'd perceived before but not really internalised – the Eich. Strangely, perhaps because she was temporally dislocated, they didn't seem to be aware of her.

While she watched, the Eich entered Sol's mind and attempted to eradicate his family memories. They were unsuccessful because the deeply imprinted memory of Grammy Dee's emerald eyes, together with the word "Dee", acted together as an "enabler" of the other memories. The memory of Grammy Dee had to be removed first to allow the others to be destroyed, but it was imprinted so deeply that it would remain untouchable until it was accessed by Sol gazing into her eyes in the future and her use of the name Dee. Then of course, it would be too late. Deira pondered on all of this, wondering how she could perceive memories and understand something that was so far beyond her normal experiences. She had no answers but knew that her ability to do so was vitally important.

After a number of failed attempts at eradicating the critical memories, the Eich paused to confer, then decided upon an alternative strategy – that of containment. The offending memories were gathered together and placed in isolation in a portion of Sol's temporal lobe. Deira could see that the intention was that they should never become available to him. However, once again she understood what the Eich apparently did not – that as long as the memory of Grammy Dee was present, those memories were always at risk of being accessed.

The Eich withdrew and Deira moved in closer. She saw Chard grasped tightly in Sol's hand and realised the Eich had forgotten about the PWC. No matter how well Sol's memories were hidden, all would be for nothing if Chard had full access to them. Luckily, with her new abilities, this was relatively simple to resolve and she rapidly accessed the AI's core and excised all his previous memories of the future and his data on Titan.

She next considered what to do about the memories that would come flooding out when Sol looked into her eyes in the future. For everybody's peace of mind, including Sol's, they had to be properly destroyed – and that could only happen when the memory of Grammy Dee was accessed. Once again, the solution appeared obvious and she knew what had to be done. In knowing, her mind responded with little or no conscious effort. The scene faded out, to be replaced by one that had taken place only a few minutes before – and this time she genuinely was physically present.

Sol was sitting on the bed next to her, his hand on her tummy.

'No, not Fred. I was thinking of Josh if it's a boy–and I'll be damned if he'll be called Smith. We'll stick with your name.,' he said.

'Works for me! By the way, when I was on Mars I mentioned to Amelie about using a shortened version of my first name like my sister Bernie. When I was at school they used to call me Dee, and I was wondering…'

He stared into her eyes–those startling emerald green eyes – and Deira could "see" his previously constrained thoughts begin to emerge as he realised he'd seen them before.

For Deira, time slowed to a crawl like it had in the caverns. She was aware of his thoughts beginning to coalesce round the image of Grammy Dee and she knew exactly what had to be done. She had to access those other memories, including that of Grammy Dee, and destroy them. The irony of the situation hadn't escaped her. Sol and Chard had mentioned sabotage and the Eich had talked about the possibility of a third party being involved with Sol's memory loss. They'd always assumed this third party would prove to be alien or, as an outside chance, the people from Sol's time. Now it was all too obvious that the saboteur came from much closer to home–it was Deira herself – and it was time for her to complete her work.

She paused uncertainly in the clear knowledge that whatever she did now would be irrevocable. She'd listened and sympathised while Sol had agonised about the loss of these memories, of friends and family he'd never see again. They were part of what made him who he was. How would she feel if someone took her past away from her? She didn't know if she could do this. On the other hand, if she didn't she was condemning them all to a future she didn't want to contemplate. What should she sacrifice, the past or the future? It had seemed so clear just a short time ago but now, as the nanoseconds ticked away, it was anything but.

She was mired in an agony of indecision, the arguments for and against excision of the memories endlessly cycling through her brain and paralysing her into inaction. In this slow-time state, she continued to "watch" the memory of Grammy Dee as it began to solidify in Sol's mind – and she knew she wasn't going to be able to prevent it.

Suddenly, she became aware of the presence of another entity. From its unique mental identifier it was clearly the same one that had helped her in the caverns, but it was now subtly different, its previous primal nature replaced by low-level consciousness, relatively unformed but already powerful. She watched in awe as it acted without compunction, swooping in and snatching the memory of Grammy Dee before it could fully form – then destroying it. She didn't know how this could be happening and, as far as she could tell, she was only the conduit for this powerful entity, whatever it may be. What she did know was that everything was being made right – for herself, for Sol, and for their unborn son. Someone or something was doing what she had been unable to do.

Having destroyed the memory of Grammy Dee, the "other" now attended to Sol's memories of his previous life that the Eich had isolated. Again, it worked swiftly and methodically and in no time had obliterated them all. Throughout all this, Deira was completely helpless. She watched with a degree of horror while this new saboteur did its work though, in truth, it was what she had wanted to do herself. Abruptly, it was over and the other presence vanished as quickly as it had appeared. Deira pulled herself out of Sol's head and normal time resumed.

She gazed for a moment at Sol. 'I think Josh is a lovely name,' she said, and kissed him.

He smiled at her and she felt herself relaxing. She could come to terms with having been his great-great-grandmother in another lifetime because she knew she wasn't destined to be in this one. Their great-great-grandson would contain completely different genetic material to Sol – and who knew what he would be capable of. After all, the future was yet to be.

Deira was aware that Sol and the Eich were still talking but, unexpectedly, she found herself dissociating again – and this time the fugue experience was very different. Her consciousness appeared to float in an inky blackness stippled with a myriad of sparkling points, almost like stars in a nascent universe, and she was aware that time was now passing so slowly that it had effectively stopped altogether. As she floated, serene and unworried, one of the points of light began to expand, becoming bigger and brighter as if it was approaching from a great distance. From its mental signature, she recognised it as the same entity that had helped her in the caves and destroyed Sol's memories – and now, with a sense of wonder, she knew who it was.

It was her unborn son!

The saboteur was not one person but two – Deira and her son!

His proto-awareness touched her, and she immediately understood that his interventions had been simple reactions to perceived threats – to Sol dying and, subsequently, to the consequences of Sol retrieving his family memories. There was no prior intent and no real understanding of what he had done. He had detected her distress and acted to make things right – from her perspective. Now he wanted nothing more than her reassurance and approval.

She mentally comforted him, told him he'd done the right thing, and expressed her immense pride in him. He radiated contentment and gradually, with her continued support and praise, his light faded and he returned to his pre-natal sleep. Deira was awestruck at the glimpse she'd been given of the potential growing within her and smiled to herself. Did the Eich truly realise what they'd helped to produce?

She snapped back to reality to find Sol staring at her.

'What?' she said.

'The Eich want to ask us something but you seemed to have zoned out. Are you okay?'

'I'm fine! More than fine, actually. But before you say whatever it is you want to say, I need to know something. In the caverns, I defeated Dominguez by folding space – and yet he was still in possession of his dampening field. How was that possible?'

'Ah,' the Speaker said, showing no evidence he'd detected Deira's tweak of time. 'That's a good question. The answer is that Dominguez's dampening field was designed specifically to combat the mentalic powers of the Cthon and by extension ourselves. Your neurology is very different, and your powers spring from that neurology. Simply put, you are immune to the Phthask dampening field.'

Deira whistled. 'That'll give us a huge advantage in any future run-ins with the Cthon. Good news! Okay, what was it you wanted to say?'

'We have a proposition for you,' the Speaker said. 'The Earth is safe for now, but the Cthon will not give up and will be looking for their next chance to destroy mankind. We are still here to monitor the situation, but what this episode has demonstrated is that we need a mobile physical presence that is capable of being deployed in an instant and can move freely round the system. With your original talents plus your new skills you two are our clear choice as the founding members of a new cadre which will assume guardianship of Earth and the solar system.

'We would very much like you to be our agents, Sol and Deira. Are we worthy of a response?'

'Oh my ...'

Deira was fully aware from the previous timeline she'd "pinched off" that somewhere in the solar system were other agents being groomed for a similar job, and she suspected that the children of these others would play an important role in her own children's lives – but she didn't care.

Neither did she care that she'd been manipulated by the Eich or that she was now part of some sort of breeding programme. All she cared about was being with the man she'd come to love and seeing their children grow up. It wasn't exactly what she'd planned for her life but she contented herself with the knowledge that there'd be plenty of action still to come – as an Agent of Titan.

'Heavy doesn't cut it,' Sol grunted.

They exchanged looks and knew that it had to be the right thing to do.

'Yes!' they said together.

'That is excellent news! We thank you in anticipation of many years of cooperation. As a parting gift we have been able to do some work on an erstwhile colleague of yours. We hope you are pleased with the result.'

With that, the voice went silent. Deira and Sol looked blankly at each other.

'What did that mean?' Sol asked.

'Search me!'

A well-loved voice suddenly came out of Sol's staff – a voice they'd never expected to hear again.

'Sol and Deira. I apologise for being off line for so long but I was having internal motherboard problems. I believe they're now fixed. How is the investigation proceeding?'

'Chard!' they both screamed at once.

Epilogue

Josh MacMahon pushed himself hard over the last part of the testing ground that the Eich had devised for training purposes. The test was progressive, becoming steadily harder as the agent developed his or her skills, and it always presented a combination of physical and mentalic challenges. On this occasion, Josh had joined forces with Tao Chen in a team challenge against Victor Borrego and Kadir Bhakta

Josh liked Tao. She was a pretty dark-haired girl of nineteen from Shanghai and liked to boast that her family could trace their roots back centuries. She and Josh, along with their eight friends from all round the world, were the spearhead of Earth's defence against the Cthon. Their whole lives had been spent training for whatever destiny had in mind for them.

Josh paused for a moment to take in what was probably the last hurdle – get past this and they'd won. But getting past it looked to be something of a problem. "It" was a mechanical construction, armed to the teeth, almost certainly controlled by an AI – and absolutely colossal! Josh reckoned it had to be at least fifty metres high.

'Sixty-two point three to be exact.' That was Swift, the AI in Josh's PWC. 'It's far too large for a mentalic assault – even the two of you together wouldn't be able to fold it out of here – and I'm doubtful about the extent of your combined physical prowess when it comes to tackling something of this magnitude.'

'Well thanks for the vote of confidence pal,' thought Josh. Unlike his father, he was fully adept at structured thinking and it always amused him to see Sol's sub-vocalisation efforts with Chard. 'Have you actually got any suggestions or are you just saying there are no logical ways to defeat it?'

'I'm afraid I can think of none,' Swift said. 'On the other hand, your hunches can occasionally throw up some ideas that can be of use.'

'So you're saying I need an illogical way to solve this problem?'

'Exactly so. The solution must be an entirely human-generated one. It is a way of removing my logic from the equation.'

At that moment Tao caught up with Josh. The previous challenge had needed a considerable time to overcome and they'd agreed that Josh should carry on and check out the final challenge while Tao remained and finished the job. She looked suitably impressed with the mechanoid.

'What the hell do we do with that,' she asked in impeccable English. 'Jiao's telling me there's no solution.'

'Swift's just told me the same thing. He thinks we need some lateral thinking. Any ideas?'

Tao looked doubtful. 'Nothing springs to mind.'

The two young agents stared at the monster before them, making a threat-assessment. The mechanoid had multiple limbs of differing sizes, some equipped with lasers while others had particularly nasty-looking multi-blade combos. There was no evidence of a force field but its armour-plating was pretty impressive and Josh wasn't at all sure their lasers would penetrate it. He turned to Tao to see what she made of it. She didn't get a chance to answer because the thing suddenly began moving in their direction, targeting lasers active and blades rotating viciously.

'Oops! Thinking time's over,' Josh said. 'We've got to act. Combat mode on.'

'Copy that.' There was an orange flare as both force fields came on almost simultaneously. 'I guess we'll just have to keep the thing at bay until we think of something.'

The metallic beast rolled down on them and they moved effortlessly into combat mode. Lasers flashed without effect on either side – the agents were protected by their force fields and the mechanoid's armour-plating did appear to be impregnable. Stalemate. Unfortunately, stalemate didn't work for the agents because they would eventually get tired while the mechanoid could continue indefinitely. They had to think of a way out of this impasse.

'We've no option but to go for a space-folding,' Josh said over the comm. 'Swift says we're not strong enough to move something this big but I wonder whether it's time we were – and this is a way of making us.'

'Worth a try. Just say the word.'

'Okay. On three. One, two, three!'

Using a technique they'd learned as children, the agents simultaneously activated the space-folding parts of their brains. A faint pink glow appeared round the mechanoid, but it was otherwise unaffected and continued its violent attack. It seemed that Swift had been correct – they simply weren't strong enough to fold it away.

'Damn this,' Josh said, 'There's got to be a way.' He redoubled his concentration, trying with all his might to make the thing disappear. He was rewarded by a yellow flare at the edge of the pink glow. Still no suggestion of a fold.

He didn't think he'd ever concentrated so hard in his life. His head was beginning to hurt and he felt distinctly strange, almost like falling from a great height. The mechanoid slowed down and stopped and, for a second, Josh thought he'd done something to disable it. Then he realised that everything else had stopped too. Tao was frozen in place part-way through a spectacular leap – suspended in mid-air like a tri-vid on pause. He had a split second to wonder what the hell was going on, then his vision narrowed and everything went black. He wasn't sure whether he briefly lost consciousness but the next thing he knew he was opening his eyes and the mechanoid was gone – along with everything else. Tao was nowhere to be seen and he was clearly no longer in the training ground. His first thought was that he'd accidentally folded somewhere. He had to get back to the training scenario.

'I would suggest you look round you before doing anything sudden,' Swift said. 'There is clearly something going on in this place. Your subconscious may have brought you here deliberately.'

Josh realised immediately that Swift was right. They were in some sort of dark, gloomy enclosure, which contained a number of large wooden crates – and there was the sound of many people in combat on the other side of the crate he'd folded in behind. He peered round the crate and saw the reason for the noise – a pitched battle that clearly wasn't going well for the two agents at the centre of it.

All his life Josh had been told that you always went in to help other agents, even at risk to yourself, so he didn't hesitate now. He was still in combat mode, so he dashed out and waded into the fray, making short shrift of the bad guys. He was perplexed however. The other agents had been wallowing badly. Had their combat mode failed them? He was about to ask them when Swift stopped him.

'Do not initiate contact! Priority One Alert. Leave four opponents for them to finish off and get back to the protection of the crate!'

Josh didn't argue. He'd never heard Swift issue a Priority One Alert before but he'd been drilled in what to do – obey without question. Turning on his heels, he gave a last parting salute and ran back to the crate, where he watched the agents finish off the bad guys.

'What was that all about?' he thought at Swift.

'I am unable to tell you at the moment,' Swift said. 'Be aware that Priory One Alert continues until I terminate it.'

'Okay pal, I understand. I'll do exactly what you tell me.'

At that moment there was a dull thruump sound that Josh recognised as a grenade, followed by a few smaller explosions that sounded like pressurised canisters going off. Whatever had just blown must have contained something pretty nasty because, while he watched, he saw clouds of noxious-looking vapour roll across the open space and thick black smoke came from some boxes that were on fire. He was pretty well protected from all this crap, but when he peered through the murk he could see the two agents struggling badly again. The male seemed to be heading towards an opening some distance away that Swift confirmed was a door to the outside. The female, on the other hand, was heading in completely the wrong direction.

Josh dashed out again, not waiting for Swift to give him directions. He passed through the roiling clouds of vapour, smoke and flames to the female Agent and grabbed her hand.

'This way! Take my hand!' he said, and together they struggled towards the open door. When the female agent was safely out into the night air, Josh turned back and ran to his crate again.

'I presume that didn't go against your Priority One Alert?'

'No indeed. It was actually essential. We now need to extricate ourselves from this place. However, a straightfoward fold will not suffice on this occasion. You need to mentalically simulate your fight with the large mechanoid and duplicate the changes that occurred in your brain.'

'What the hell for?'

'Just do it. This is still Priority One.'

Josh did what he could, casting his mind back to the giant robot and re-creating his moves. This was an incredibly difficult exercise, and one that he'd probably not have been up to even a few short weeks ago, but after his recent bouts of training it seemed to happen almost automatically. He began to feel the same aura of strangeness and then his sight went again. He closed his eyes reflexively and felt the falling sensation. When he opened his eyes again he was on his back in the training ground with a concerned Tao gazing down at him. The mechanoid was standing inert some metres away.

'What just happened?' Tao said. 'Where did you go? One minute we were both engaged with the robot and the next minute you'd disappeared and the robot just sort of stopped working. Then you reappeared again. It didn't look like any sort of fold I've ever seen, so what happened?'

'I've absolutely no idea, but I've been on Priority One Alert for most of it, so perhaps Swift can enlighten us. By the way, pal, is Priority One still operational?'

'Priority One Alert terminated,' Swift said out loud. 'I can now tell you what happened. Tao is correct that you did not fold anywhere.'

'But I must have folded somewhere. I certainly wasn't here so…'

'You folded some*when*,' Swift said.

'What?' Josh and Tao gaped at each other. 'You mean I folded *time*?' Josh said.

'Indeed you did. Time is simply part of the space-time matrix so the ability to fold space automatically implies the ability to fold time. You just needed a nudge in the right direction. This particular challenge was designed to stimulate you – and it worked perfectly.'

'But why Priority One?' said Josh – then it all became clear. 'Oh – potential for temporal disruption. But how do you know I didn't accidentally change the timeline in any case?'

'Because there is a clear record of the event in which you just participated,' said Swift, 'and you played your part to perfection. Think about the stories your parents used to tell you and I'm sure you'll get it.'

Josh already had, and his face was a picture. 'The warehouse mission Mum and her partner took part in. They were saved by a mysterious agent appearing out of nowhere. It's never been explained – until now. But isn't this a temporal paradox?'

'It most certainly is,' Swift said. 'However, had you not gone back and done what you did, this entire timeline would have been put at risk. Equally, had you deviated from the "prescribed script" that could also have proved dangerous. Once you were there, you had to execute every move perfectly – and thankfully you did. However, I would countenance against any further incursions into time unless they are very carefully controlled. You could do immense damage.'

'Copy that, but I'm assuming the rest of the guys will also have to go through this little initiation as well. How are we going to protect the timeline from possible perturbations?'

A different voice emerged from Swift.

'You'll have to trust us on that Josh,' the Speaker said. 'It is a difficult path to tread but an essential one if you are all to fully develop your powers. However, as of now please accept our congratulations on your recent success.'

There was a significant pause.

'Now we can take the fight to the Cthon.'

THE END